Prologue

July 24, 2409 AD
Arlington Cemetery
Arlington, Virginia
Earth, the Sol System
Saturday, 6:30 A.M. Eastern Time

"You ready to go, boss?" The artificial intelligence implanted clone in a full shielded armor suit with the markings of a First Lieutenant Armored Environment-suit Marine stood behind her with his helmet in the off position stowed over his right shoulder. The insignia on his left chest identified him as a fighter mecha pilot. The patch on his shoulder displayed a black demon figure wielding a pitchfork or trident that was firing a blue beam that zigzagged from left to right. The clone was tall, dark, and handsome in a weird robotic and nonemotional way. When she looked into his eyes she didn't see any love or hate, just programmed loyalty, which was most certainly what her grandmother had intended when she had made him, most likely for her. He was a very young clone but

1

with a very smart AI loaded into it. For the moment, she ignored him.

The rain fell softly over her closely cropped dark hair and the drops ran down her face mixing with tears and dripping into a puddle beneath her. She briefly reflected on how the ripples in the puddle as the drops splashed into it looked surprisingly like a teleport gate's event horizon. She ran her tattooed fingers across her forehead and then through her hair slinging water from her face and pushing her long dark uneven bangs back.

Her mother had not been very happy with her when she had shaved the sides of her head in stripes and up the back leaving only about five-centimeters standing up on top with ten to twelve centimeter bangs. Her father had hated it when she started getting the tattoos, especially the ones on her face and up the front and back of her neck. He hated that she'd had her eyeballs implanted with quantum sensors so that they glowed a blaze red when those were activated. If he only knew where all the tats were he'd have really been frustrated. The Marines hadn't had haircut or tattoo regulations or requirements for centuries and as far as she was concerned, she didn't give a damn. She was her own grown woman who had been through the trials and tribulations of harrowing combat. She had loved and lost. For now, she was the embodiment of death in a space fighter. If she wanted a freaky haircut, fireball eyes, and glowing tattoos up her crotch it was her business.

It hadn't taken her but about a year and a half to go from "Ms. Clean The Marine Former First Child callsign Apple1" who hadn't fallen far from the tree of her father

BRINGERS OF HELL

TAU CETI AGENDA SERIES

✧ ✧ ✧

TRAVIS S. TAYLOR

BRINGERS OF HELL

Copyright © 2018 by Travis S. Taylor

A Baen Books Original

Baen Publishing Enterprises
P.O. Box 1403
Riverdale, NY 10471
www.baen.com

ISBN: 978-1-4814-8380-3

Cover art by Kurt Miller

First Baen paperback printing February 2019

Distributed by Simon & Schuster
1230 Avenue of the Americas
New York, NY 10020

Library of Congress Cataloging-in-Publication Data
Classification: LCC PS3620.A98 B75 2018 | DDC 813/.6--dc23 LC
record available at https://lccn.loc.gov/2017052467

Printed in the United States of America

10 9 8 7 6 5 4 3 2 1

BRINGERS OF HELL

TAU CETI AGENDA SERIES

Dedication

This book is dedicated to all of the Army, Navy, Air Force, and Marine soldiers and sailors active, inactive, reserve, and retired that have offered insight and knowledge on the various military aspects I've included in these books. For those who complained about the language you can blame them for putting the idea in my head and also my personal overzealous desire to honor them. When I first wrote *One Day On Mars* I read it to a room full of Marines at a convention. Most of them suggested that I hadn't used the F-word near enough. And then they laughed. I told them then and there that I would endeavor to do better, maybe even over the top. I did it for them though I must admit it has been a lot of fun. I've enjoyed writing these books about military heroes immensely.

Oh, and seriously, I spent weeks talking with a Navy carrier bridge crew officer to get some of the feel and idea about how things went on a supermega navy vessel. I most definitely appreciated all his input and advice. And to any other soldiers out there that offered help, advice, consultation, or just a beer this book is dedicated to you as well. Thank you for your help, advice, and most of all, for your service and sacrifice. I hope you've all liked the books and could see your influence on them.

GUNNING FOR HER

"Warning—enemy targeting radar lock is imminent," Dee's Bitchin' Betty chimed. "Warning—enemy targeting radar lock is imminent. Take evasive action . . ."

"What the hell?" Dee spun her mindview and Bree quickly overlaid sensor and energy data. An alien porcupine in what Dee would call bot-mode released several rounds in her and Azazel's general direction. It was clear that the thing was gunning for her as the rounds seemed to trace across to her.

"Look out, Major!" Azazel jumped into her, pushing both of them down into a roll. The plasma cannon rounds hit behind them, exploding into the alien ship bulkhead material. A gaping hole large enough to drive a hovertank through was blown out, the molten edges still glowing red hot. "Guns, guns, guns!"

"I got this!"

to "Major Moore Than You Wanna Fuck With callsign Phoenix." In fact, most of her former counterparts and squadron mates called her "Major Moore Than You Wanna Fuck With" in whispers behind her back. Dee wasn't certain if it was because she was isolating herself from her past and her emotions and most of her former friends and colleagues thought she was too much to deal with, or if it was because she was so singularly focused on killing the enemy aliens that her former colleagues were growing fearful of her and knew not to fuck with her. Either way, she didn't care.

The rest of the human fleet had started to talk about her behind her back too, of that she was sure. Her father had warned her that the talk could make her "unpromotable". They also talked about the alien drone beetle that crawled around on her body as her pet. The alien Mru of the Thgreeth had given it to her to, at the time, save her life, study for weaponization uses against the Chiata, and use to her designs in such endeavors. It had helped repair her body when human technology couldn't remove a piece of Chiata metal from her spine. Mru had told her that it could help her in her conflict with the attacking alien horde.

She wasn't certain about how one alien robot bug could help against an attack wave of hundreds of billions but she kept it with her just the same. All in all, the beetle did pretty much anything she asked of it and that scared the living hell out of most people. She hadn't really used it to harm anyone, yet. She wasn't quite sure it would actually harm a person even if she told it to. It might disable them to protect her, though. She wasn't sure of that either. She had done her best to start a couple of barroom brawls just to find out, but she was too proficient at fighting herself to need much help. A year and a half of sparring with her Navy SEAL lover had seen to that—and having been raised by Alexander and Sehera Moore hadn't hurt either.

As far as she knew the bug was harmless unless you were a Chiata, but Dee wasn't telling everyone that little bit of information. And, she had yet to have to tell it to attack anyone for her. The alien Chiata-eating robot beetle gave her power that people had to both fear and respect. Being "unpromotable" didn't really bother her either. Once upon a time she had lived the fairy tale that she would be the greatest U.S. Marine mecha pilot that history ever recorded and that Marines throughout time would sing the praises of Deana Moore, but she no longer believed in such fairy tales. Not since the love, the prince from her tale, had been killed by the alien monsters.

They could kick her out of the military if they wanted to and it would no longer bother her, as she had let go of her fairy tale ending even if her parents had not. Deanna was in a good bargaining position as humanity, at least the people briefed and in the know about the pending invasion, needed that bug and the bug was hers. In fact, the thing seemed to respond only to her. So, the military couldn't get rid of her if they really wanted to or tried. Besides, her father probably wouldn't let them and nobody crossed paths with her father. Nobody, not even her.

Even if they were to manage to kick her out, they still couldn't stop her from avenging the deaths of her loved ones, friends, and family. It still wouldn't stop her from killing Chiata. She would always find a way to kill the alien bastards until such time as there were no more of them left to kill. If she had to, she'd get her historically blood-drenched and bloodthirsty grandmother to fix her up with a ship and an army, which is almost what the present case was anyway much to her father's chagrin.

"Squidboy, you see this one." She pointed at her chest as she pulled her uniform top down almost below her breasts. The alien robot beetle scurried up to her left shoulder skittering atop the tugged at fabric. A green and red stripe with a fanged dragon twisted about it was tattooed there and glowing slightly like the hues from armor shields when hit by plasma fire. The tail of the dragon twisted down and encircled her breast. The soft green and red glowing tattoo was very visible in the gray dim cloudy day. The green and red phosphorescence lit the drops of rain up as they splashed into the puddles around her reminding her of the red and green blurs of death, the Chiata, which needed killing. That had been the entire point. All of her tattoos had a glowing red and green blur element to them just to remind her of the path of destruction she was taking to the aliens. The Hell she was bringing to them.

"Took out a megaship porcusnail with nothing but my mecha squad. We barrel-assed through a breach in the hull all the way to the power unit for the blue beams of death from Hell. I did a full throttle Fokker's Feint inside a thirty-meter-wide corridor as I ripped through deck plates and all. I was damned near spinning on my mecha's head, upside down and backwards, with a goddamned alien mecha tendril protruding through my left thigh and white hot shards of plasma spraying from every nook and cranny of the cockpit. It was some real shit, and you'd have loved it." Dee paused and wiped tears and rain from her eyes again.

"Just as they were firing I ripped the motherfucking power couplings loose and shoved a green blur up its ass. Skippy here skittered inside the computer systems and did something, I'm not sure exactly what but between the blue beam conduit sputtering and choking and backfiring and whatever he did it caused quite a fireworks show. The shields on the Chiata's suit created a feedback pulse into the conduit and the ship started blowing up all around us. Damn blurs were gone so fast they didn't know what hit 'em. Damned alien tendril in my thigh exploded. That hurt. Lost an eye in the process too. Oh and my mecha pretty much exploded around me. My new wingman over there dragged me out in what was left of his. Docs printed me a new leg with no problem. Had to wear a fucking patch for three days before my new eyeball adjusted to my retina. That shit hurt worse than the leg. That's why I got this blue one across my left eye here where the wound was. I wish I could show you the one I got down there at the top of my new leg." Deanna Moore laughed. "Squidboy, you probably wouldn't think I'm so pretty anymore, ha ha. Mom hated I cut my hair the way I did. Hell, I could fit in with the bangers and college kids at New Tharsis U. But, I dunno, Davy, I like it. It, well, uh, for now, this is me." Deanna wiped at the tears in her eyes again as she caught a glimpse of her reflection in a puddle beneath her. She certainly was unrecognizable from just a year and half prior before she had lost him. It seemed like years.

"I, uh, I miss you sooooo much, Davy. God—why did you have to go now?" Deanna cried. She ached from all that she was. Her very being, her soul, cried deeply. She had never loved anything or anyone so much, and then to have it torn away from her by the damned Chiata was more devastating than anybody should be forced to deal with. "So much," she whispered and leaned her head against his cross, full flow of tears pouring down across the tattoos on her face.

"Ma'am, we only have seven minutes," the clone reminded her in the monotone voice that was disturbingly typical of the clones. "The admiral is going to be pissed if we hold him up again."

"I'm not leaving until he does." Deanna threw a thumb over her shoulder just as a white flash of light glinted against the raindrops making them appear as if they had stopped briefly in midair. The common sizzle of bacon sound followed. "Oh, well, I guess that's our cue. And Azazel, if you're going to say someone is going to be pissed, you should at least attempt to put some inflection in your tone of voice. Otherwise, it just sounds creepy."

"Roger that," the clone responded with no more or less inflection. It still sounded creepy.

Deanna turned from him shaking her head and then dropped her head and closed her eyes with both hands against the cross at the head of Davy Rackman's resting place. She said a brief prayer and then kissed her right hand and then touched it to the cross where Rackman's name was etched. Dee allowed herself to cry for a few more seconds before making one last big sniffle.

"I think I will always miss you, Davy. And the hurt just doesn't seem to stop. It hurts so much. Wish you could be here for this. I promise you that I'll kill some more of them alien sonofabitches for you today. I absolutely fucking promise!" Deanna stood and blew one more kiss at the cross, doing her best to turn the sorrow to hatred and anger. She blinked the water from her red glowing eyes and nodded at her guardian clone and wingman. She walked about fifteen paces and patted another cross where the admiral had been kneeling only moments before. "Miss you too, sis. I'll take care of DeathRay for you. And I promise that I will kill some of the bastards for you as well."

Deana stood straight and took in a deep breath. Rain splashed against her face as she looked up at the sky. There was just no way to explain to anyone how broken she felt. There was no way to explain to anyone just how alone she felt. To her, that was all that mattered. The thing that had broken her inside was the same thing that fueled the fire burning there. The Chiata had taken her loved ones. The Chiata had broken her inside and out. The Chiata were going to fucking die.

"Okay, Azazel, let's go." Deanna tapped the control on her wristband and flashed out from the cemetery. She could see him doing the same as the inside of a starship materialized around them. She stepped onto the armor deployer beside her new experimental FM-14X and the new shielded armored flightsuit technology custom-built itself around her in less than a second. Deanna liked the new armor and how easy it was to get on and off. She admired the big red serpent-tongued demon with horns and hooves shooting blue beams from his fiery eyes and wielding a pitchfork-like trident throwing fire that was painted on the tailfins of her mech. In a circle around the artwork read "Bringers of Hell" in a jagged and flaming font. Dee smiled inwardly and sneered outwardly as she activated the shields and deployed her helmet. The glow of red and green from her tattoos increased about her face and the new quantum sensor-based contacts she had had implanted in her eyes glowed red like fire. If there ever was a demon that the Chiata should fear, she was its embodiment.

The callsign "Phoenix" was written across the forehead of her helmet and on the front of her fighter. Surrounding the callsign were forty-three red and green glowing Chiata skulls with a knife stuck through the top of each. There were thirteen on the other side.

The days of "Apple1" had died with Rackman. She was a demon from Hell reborn from her fiery ashes and a harbinger of death and destruction to the Chiata and anything else in her path. She was the commander of the Air Group, and as the CAG, she led the mecha jocks and set an example by being even more brazen and fearless than the clone pilots in her squadron.

Bree, got the ship warmed up? she thought to her artificial intelligence counterpart or AIC supercomputer mounted just behind her ear and in her brain. *I just promised some old friends that I'd kill some aliens for them.*

Roger that. Battle plans are loaded and the team is ready to deploy on Admiral Boland's order, Bree replied.

Good. I'm sure DeathRay will be ready for us soon.

Phoenix took one hop with her jump boots pushing

against the deckplates and she was tossed upward in an arc. She felt the free-fall briefly at the top of the arc and for a brief moment the memory of her father tossing her into the air as a child flashed through her mind and the feeling of being caught in his warm superhuman arms rushed over her. She had been so innocent and had felt so safe then. She spread her arms and held her legs tight looking like a floating flying armored cross above her fighter. But the universe had moved on, as did her trajectory. Gravity took hold and she straightened out and fell precisely in place in the seat of her mecha. That warm safe universe was long gone. Autoharnesses and hardpoints snapped to her and tugged her into her seat.

"Skippy, you better get in your box," she said as the little alien robot beetle responded and crawled across her armored suit and into a compartment on her right leg.

Cycle the canopy, she thought. Icons for all the members of her squadron flashed green in her mind as each of her clone pilots brought their mecha online. She opened a channel on the pilot's tac-net.

"Alright, remember the battle plan, keep your wingmen covered, and let's force these porcupines and blurs into a bowl on the surface of the megaship if we can. Once we take out the ship's autodestruct we start clearing the ship and giving support to the ground teams. But don't let the tankheads and AEMs have all the fun. Remember the goal is not just to kill Chiata, it is to show them that they picked the wrong goddamned fight. It is to show them that we are the demons of their existence. We are the demons from whatever darkness they fear that will wipe them from existence and swallow their souls. We wipe every last one of them from existence. No Chiata leaves this system alive. We show them to our last breath and then some that WE ARE THE BRINGERS OF HELL!"

Chapter 1

July 24, 2409 AD
Mission Star 74
Chiata Expanse
783 light-years from the Sol System
Saturday, 6:37 A.M. Eastern Time

Rear Admiral Lower Half Jack "DeathRay" Boland settled into the oversized captain's chair in full armored suit with his helmet on and visor up. DeathRay displayed across the forehead of the helmet and in his cold hard steel gaze it wasn't hard to believe that he could literally shoot death rays from his eyes. Clearly he couldn't, but the mythos around him and his exploits was almost as impressive as those of ancient gods. He had been the most deadly fighter pilot in space for nearly forty years, but the time had come where he needed to maximize the damage he could inflict and he wasn't going to do that from within a single mecha. So, he went to the general and volunteered for deep expanse raid missions. He had been promoted and told to pick himself a crew. His missions were simple. DeathRay liked simple. If he ever planned on changing his name he intended to make that his middle one.

"Holding position steady at two light-years out, sir. Engineering reports that the quantum membrane teleportation system is fully functional and ready, all structural integrity field generators and Buckley-Freeman shields at optimum, DEGs charged, missile tubes loaded with gluonium specials, the BBD shows fully charged, and the Buckley superweapon can trigger on your command, Admiral," the tall blonde armored Teena clone first officer robotically announced. "All of the Bringers of Hell have reported to duty and ready, sir. Major Moore is ready and waiting the order."

"Understood, Commander Seven," he replied. Jack had started a new tradition in using the last one or two numbers in a clone's series number as their last name. He couldn't handle not having names to call his crew and too many of them had the same first names. He had thought about doing what Deanna had done and just give them all nicknames, but he didn't want to have to give callsigns to nearly four thousand crew. Other than Dee, the entire ship's complement was clones. The two of them, the two humans, only had room for one emotion and that was hatred for the aliens that had killed the two people they cared most for. Living among emotionless artificial intelligence controlled human clones made life easier for them. They could be robotic themselves and not expected to have to "feel" sad or any of that other stuff that would just get in the way of what had to be done—killing Chiata.

Candis, open me a private channel with Dee, he thought to his AIC.

Done.

Dee, you ready? DeathRay thought to her. For the longest time she had been like a little sister to him. Now, he wasn't out there with her to watch her back and for the last eighteen months she had been putting herself in crazy situations almost as if she had a death wish. But Jack knew that wasn't the case. Dee had a fire burning within her and the only death she wished was on the enemy. She had so much hatred for the Chiata bastards that she would kill every last one of them by her own hands if she could. Jack was going to accommodate her wish to the best of his abilities. He didn't care much for the sonsabitches either. As far as he was concerned the only good Chiata was one with its innards ripped out and its fucking head blown off.

Roger that, Admiral, she thought to him in her mindvoice. Jack wasn't sure but he thought he could sense her rage in her mindvoice. He hoped she wasn't going over some mental or emotional point of no return, but at the same time, he was right there with her, ready to jump from the precipice into the dark chasm. He had a mental image of her all armored up, tattoos glowing, her eyes red like plasma fire, truly embodying a demon from the underworld. He almost wished he was right there beside her in his mecha, still her wingman. Jack had been so destroyed by the loss of his wife that he was just as enraged as Dee. He understood her bloodlust. Himself, he only had three things in life he wanted to do any more and that was to kill Chiata. Kill Chiata. And kill more fucking Chiata.

Great. Watch your six and make me proud. You know the drill. We stick to the plan, DeathRay thought to his old wingman. It was a long-running joke that was more serious than not. Anyone who'd ever fought with DeathRay knew what his plan always was.

Yes sir! We go in there and we kill those mother-fuckers! Dee thought. Jack could feel her anger and it began to boil with in him as well. He could imagine in his mind's eye the snarl on her face as she formed the thought to him. He had a similar one on his face, along with a slight smile. After all, he'd invented that plan and it always, almost worked. Sometimes.

Good plan. Bring 'em Hell. DeathRay out.

"Alright, Seven, bring the tuning forks online." Jack shifted his suit into a more comfortable position in the oversized chair. The auto-harness mechanism deployed and locked onto his suit at the hardpoints. "As soon as we materialize in the system I want targeting algorithms running. Pick us out a straggler and that's who we take. We kill the rest of them. All of them. No Chiata can leave the system. Understood?"

"Aye, sir. The bot ships are in formation and ready on your command." Seven nodded to him. "Same battle plan as before is loaded into the fleet controllers."

"Okay, helm, let's go steal us another one," Jack ordered. "QMT when ready."

"Yes, Admiral," the red-haired Mike clone at the helm replied. Jack kept his popup bridge crew chart in his direct-to-mind view so that he could remember their designations. He was Mr. Ninety-one, an ensign.

The giant megaship began to hum slightly from bow to stern and from the four supercarrier class ships attached to it, two in front and two in back, from port to starboard. The commandeered and reengineered ship looked like a cross between a porcupine, a snail, and an alligator with stubby legs all covered in thousands of mechanized structures. The *U.S.S. Nancy Penzington* was the third of thirteen Chiata ships humanity had taken and converted. Following the final "Battle of the Ruins" two years before, they had figured out how to not only take Chiata ships for their own, but how to turn the Buckley-Freeman shields into a superweapon when combined with the alien blue beams of death from Hell generators. Jack had since used the superweapon on nine different missions. He was about to make it ten.

"QMT initiated, Admiral," Ensign Ninety-one announced in his robotic deadpan tone.

"Time to start the plan," he muttered to himself and clenched his armored fists until the shields flickered and green luminescence flashed across the surface of his suit. The personal shield ionized air molecules, throwing blue flashes across its surface.

There was the sense of being in several places at once, and then the large megaship sprayed a white beam in front of them, creating the large portal through space and time in the realm of quantum membranes that tied the universe together. Jack watched as the smaller bot-controlled supercarriers vanished through in front of him and then he nodded at Seven and the *Penzington* lurched through the portal, being slung forward from their present location to one almost two light-years away. Jack felt his skin tingle and then the frying bacon sizzled in his ears and instantaneously they were staring at a large red star.

"CDC, I want a full sensor sweep and target analysis now!" Jack ordered.

"Moons of the gas giant eight astronomical units out, Admiral." Commander Seven pointed at the main screen in the center of the bridge. "Large concentration of artificial structures. Chiata signatures are mainly concentrated there, sir."

"Anywhere else?"

"Not much out past that, but inward to the star is typical Chiata strip mining. They must not have been in this system as long as others as there does not appear to be any mining in the system's Kuiper Belt or Oort Cloud," Seven replied.

"Probably no one lived here to fight back at them, then. Alright, weapons officer, I don't see the BBDs firing. Let's see if we can take most of them before the second wave of the fleet arrives." Jack looked at the female clone sitting at the gunner's console. She was a pretty young ensign. From her number she was a very new generation and probably only a decade or two old. Tamara Fourteen, he noted in his direct to mind display. "Helm, calculate a hyperspace jump to the gas giant and be ready."

"CO! CDC!"

"Go CDC." DeathRay listened calmly but ready to start bringing it to the enemy. He was the embodiment of "the calm before the storm". He just couldn't wait for the storm part to hurry up and, well, start.

"Targeting analysis is complete sir. Uploading target list now in priority status."

"Good work, CDC." Jack turned to Seven. "Alright, Commander Seven, let's bull-rush into the middle of that cluster about four hundred thousand kilometers off the gas giant's largest moon and start swinging."

"Yes sir." Commander Seven stood from her console and walked behind the helmsman's station. Her full armor suit clanked against the deckplates ringing against the eerie quietness in the bridge. The clones tended to converse DTM rather than verbally as humans typically preferred. Jack had told his bridge crew to start talking more but it was still too quiet. He had considered having battle music played through the ship's intercom during battle but was afraid it would be distracting. Commander Seven was doing her best to accommodate his spoken order.

"This grouping here. We will use a standard fractal positioning algorithm," Seven superfluously announced and highlighted multiple enemy ships in the bridge crew's DTM battlescape views.

The helmsman tapped at the three-dimensional virtual touchscreen and waved her hands in the air at some icons in her mindview and then the ship swirled through a hyperspace vortex for a second or so. As the megaship reappeared in reality space, DeathRay felt the ship hum again and then the blinding blue beams tore out from the spires and zigged and zagged through space until they hit one of the Chiata megaships on the starboard side. Almost as soon as the beams fired, the ship lurched through another hyperspace vortex, rematerialized in reality space, and the blue beams fired again. It took the Chiata more than seventeen seconds to target them after a hyperspace jaunt, so the jaunt drive was beefed up to withstand continuous short jumps without taxing the power conduits or the vortex projector. DeathRay wasn't a physicist, a chief warrant, a CHENG, or an STO, but he understood enough to know that the *Penzington* was a damned marvel of science, alien technology, and human ingenuity. She was one of a kind, just like her namesake had been. As with most captains, his ship had become the love of his life, or had at least taken the place of the lost one.

"That one there, Seven!" Jack pointed and highlighted an alien megaship in the bridge direct-to-mind battlescape view. "Let's take that one!"

"Understood, Admiral. Good call—the battle analysis suggests that is our best target by a large margin." The AI clone had calculated millions or maybe billions of calculations in an instant to tell Jack what years of combat flying had taught him. He knew a good target when he saw one. That's why they called him DeathRay.

"Get us in there. Keep firing the BBDs. And let's loose the Bringers of Hell," Jack ordered. "Start moving the bot carriers in position."

"Alright, Bringers, we've got the green ball." Deanna took a deep breath and dropped her visor in place. The DTM heads up display windows kicked in with multiple pages and icons floating about her head. She brought up the window for targeting and trajectories and pulled open an icon marked QMT attack mode Beta. "We deploy on my mark and go to QMT attack mode Beta. I want us dancing in and out of reality space with firing solutions. If a porcupine even gets close to you snap-back or sling-forward manually. Don't wait for the autotrigger. Everyone got that? Nothing different from the last nine system invasions."

"Roger that, Phoenix."

"Yes, ma'am."

"Affirmative."

The responses from the team, while all were in the appropriate pilot jargon and in English, sounded almost as if they were foreign, or worse, alien. The AI minds in the clone bodies simply had no use for emotional displays. Dee figured it was their way of showing humanity that it was a waste of time. The clones had perfect human bodies with the brilliance of the human brain combined with the computational power of quantum supercomputer intelligence. The process for combining the AIC implants with an empty human brain was a secret that Sienna Madira, her grandmother, and the alien slug, Copernicus, had yet to reveal. So, while nobody understood how they were built, there was no doubting that they bordered on superior to humans in many ways. Dee wondered if their lack of emotional reaction was because they didn't get emotional reaction altogether or didn't care. Dee did her best to be like that when the time called for it. But at the moment, she preferred anger over a lack thereof.

"Alright, here we go." Dee flipped channels quickly. "Air Boss, Air Boss, Bringers of Hell are ready to deploy."

"Roger that, Phoenix. You are cleared to deploy at your discretion. Good hunting."

"Roger that, Phoenix out." She flipped back to the Bringers' tac-net. "Alright, let us Bring some Hell in three, two, deploy, deploy, deploy."

Dee slapped the QMT control and slammed the throttle forward so that as soon as she rematerialized outside the ship in "the shit" that she'd be moving and not a sitting duck, but then again, everything was moving relative to everything else in space. Dee preferred her relative motion to be under her control as best she could manage. The light flashed in a ball about her new FM-14X and then she was in space. The new experimental quantum-bouncing mecha spent less time in reality space than it did in membrane space. The fighter was a phantom that the Chiata couldn't track. Or at least they hadn't figured out how to track them in the last nine raid missions. If they had, they hadn't lived to tell about it.

Blue flashes from the *Penzington's* BBD ripped through a porcusnail megaship's tuning fork spires to Dee's starboard, causing its shields to flicker in a wave of light across the surface of the ship starting from the BBD's beam impact point. As the shields flickered and failed, armored hull material vaporized and expelled orange plasmas into space. The megaships were tough, though, and it took a lot more than a single hit to take them down. Just as soon as the shields flickered, out of that ship poured a countless number of the fighter-class porcupines. For the most part they were all flying toward Dee and her squadron. That would have scared some pilots. It made Dee happy. Very happy.

Okay, Bree, start the dancing algorithm and get me something to shoot at, Dee thought to her AIC. *Won't hurt to kill a few as we push through to the objective. That is, if we happen to find targeting solutions along the way.*

QMT trajectory prediction running. Switching to trajectory energy optimization screen for targets, Bree replied. *Vectors are up now.*

Got it. Dee could see several yellow targeting Xs pop

up in her mindview. The DTM view was fully spherical in all directions as if her fighter wasn't even there and she was floating in space. She could see the Chiata megaships and the thousands of porcupine fighters starting to scatter about and fill the ball around where the *Penzington* had been seconds before, but then they seemed lost briefly until they reacquired the attacking human ship. The ship bouncing in and out of reality space kept the Chiata spread out and mixed up their formations.

Her fighter flashed out and reappeared several hundred meters ahead of where she'd been and then flashed again fifty meters to her port side. With the random key generated for position vectors that followed a general trajectory like the quantum cloud of an electron's orbit about an atom's nucleus, the new FM-14X mecha was damned near impossible to target and track according to the laws of physics known to humanity, and hopefully, aliens as well. Her squadron was the first to fly the birds and they had implemented them with amazing success for almost sixteen months with minimal casualties in flight. The casualties usually happened once they got onboard the Chiata ships and were fighting in close quarters mecha-to-mecha and hand-to-hand. In that situation, the QMTs were harder to accomplish because there was other matter in the way and it was difficult to project randomly into the cramped spaceship interior. Occasionally, one of the mecha jocks would attempt an interior ship jump without proper mapping and unfortunately, horrifically, and devastatingly rematerialize inside a bulkhead. The outcome was never pretty. Any attempt to place two pieces of matter in the exact same spot simultaneously usually ended creating a miniature star fission-fusion-fission explosion throughout the pilot's body and mecha. There was never anything left in those situations.

That didn't mean that bouncing inside ships was off the table, though. As long as they could target an open space they could bounce to it, but every now and again, somebody made a mistake. And, it was usually a horrible, horrific, and explosively grotesque mistake.

"Phoenix! CO *Penzington*." She heard the admiral's voice over the command-net. His avatar popped up in the corner of her mindview.

"Go, DeathRay," she grunted as she pushed through a reality space maneuver to line herself up with the uncertain location of her wingman. The quantum key generated by the algorithm kept them lined up with their jumps, but only loosely. They were like a pair of electrons sharing the same energy level orbit around an atom. While their orbit was known, their precise position was uncertain. And the faster they moved, the higher the position uncertainty grew. They were close but couldn't share the same location exactly. In fact, the Meghan clone that was the STO of her new home ship had explained it as actually having something to do with the Pauli Exclusion Principle governing bound state fermions but Dee's eyes glazed over about thirty seconds into that conversation. Listening to the clone STO was even harder than listening to Commander Buckley when he was trying to explain something. At least in those circumstances, she and Rondi could make fun of the CHENG's various tics and mannerisms, but not to his face of course. With the damned clones it was like hearing an autoreader explain the inner workings of a dishwasher. And there were never any tics to poke fun at.

There were some things that Dee missed about being on the *U.S.S. Sienna Madira* with her human friends she'd practically grown up with, but friends and family were too much of a distraction to her current agenda and why she'd had to beg her father for the transfer. He wouldn't hear of it, but DeathRay had somehow managed it for her.

"Megaship to your starboard and down seventy thousand kilometers," RDML Boland ordered her. "That's our target! DTMing coordinates now."

"Understood, Admiral!" Dee flashed out-and-in again and then toggled back her attention to the tac-net. "Azazel, you got my six? We're going full bore at the target coordinates I'm sending out to the squadron now. Punch a hole through the fighter wave and into the belly of the beast. Got that?"

"Understood Phoenix. Watch the porcupines to port—they have detected our general path and are doing their best to generate targeting locks," Azazel responded. "Too bad we do not have time to let them think they have us."

"We'll get plenty of chances, Azazel. Keep it frosty."

"Affirmative, Major."

"Alright, Bringers, you've got the target coordinates. Last one to the alien engineering section gets demoted to Navy cook. And I really mean it this time!" Dee jostled and pitched upward a bit as interdiction fire pitted against her nose shields. The mecha flickered blue and white but was unharmed. The structural integrity field generators were reading all in the green. She was good to go.

She flashed in and out again, this time appearing closer to the target megaship almost thirty meters from the vector of an alien fighter. Dee barrel rolled over and toggled her mecha to bot-mode. As she rolled upside down and above the alien fighter she aimed her cannon with her right arm as the targeting X turned red in her mindview. The g-loading on her abdominal muscles was crushing, but Dee grunted through the angular acceleration of the turn and squeezed her abs so tight that she felt as if her eyes would bulge out of the sockets. The organogel layer inside her suit surrounding her abdominals and her large leg muscle groups became taut and swelled rapidly, squeezing her stomach and legs to the point that it hurt. Much needed blood was forced into her brain as she took slow long breaths and grunted through the maneuver. She squinted her eyes against the sweat that beaded up only for a microsecond as the suit quickly adjusted the humidity level and sublimated it out of her face.

"Guns, guns, guns." Dee continued to track the fighter as the bright plasma balls first pounded against the alien's shields, throwing green luminescent flashes washing over its surface with each hit. She continued to fire until the shields finally failed and then armor plating started vaporizing. "Fox Three!"

A mecha-to-mecha QMT guided missile spiraled out from the launcher on the bot-mode fighter's shoulder. The propellantless propulsion pushed the missile forward on a violet dancing light until it closed the gap between Dee and the alien fighter craft. The missile burst through the alien hull plating in an orange and white ball that quickly dissipated. Dee toggled back to fighter-mode quickly. The abrupt pitch and then spin of the transformation left her stomach briefly doing somersaults, but she shook it off quickly and juked and jinked around the shrapnel blast wave right up until the point that she flashed out of reality space momentarily and then reappeared even closer to the megaship and another alien fighter. Her targeting X flashed between yellow and red.

Bree, can we close energy solutions on that one?

Perhaps, but it would lead us from our wingman. Her AIC quickly displayed several alternate energy curve traces of red and blue intersections DTM. None of them looked good enough for Dee to pull away from her present course.

Shit, thought so.

"You counting Azazel?" Dee swiveled her head about, watching for targets and lock ups and her wingman. His mecha popped into reality just a few tens of meters out in front of her in the middle of a pitch-over maneuver. Dee followed right up behind and over his nose. She could see the clone's helmet in her peripheral vision glancing up at her as she passed by. "That's one."

"Yes, ma'am. I have tallied your kill. Thank you for alerting me." The emotionless response came from her wingman as he bounced in and out of reality space about her energy curve.

"Watch it, First Lieutenant, that almost sounded like sarcasm and appropriately used," she said. "Would hate to think some of my more human traits were rubbing off on you."

"No, ma'am."

His mecha flickered in and out like a blur and reappeared several hundred meters to port. Several more of the yellow targeting Xs in Dee's mindview flickered red then yellow then red again and Dee hated that she couldn't flash over there and kill some of them, but she ignored them and kept to her mission. Suddenly, she caught a glimpse of a possible energy curve intersecting with her wingman from beneath and past his three-nine line. And it was coming fast!

"Azazel! You've got a Chiata Gomer doing its best to lock up your underbelly! Take evasive maneuvers into my energy curve!" Dee ordered him nervously. "You've gotta move it Marine!"

"I see it, Phoenix," her wingman replied as calm as ever. Dee slammed the HOTAS forward, burning full throttle in fighter-mode to help close the gap. The QMT bouncing algorithm flashed her out-and-in almost within two hundred meters of her wingman's vector.

"Azazel, pull back the HOTAS and feint just before your next out-and-in," Dee ordered him. "Let's see if we can't sell this bastard some ocean front property in Nevada."

"Roger that, Phoenix. Hitting the brakes in three, two, one."

Her wingman's mecha seemed to almost go backwards as he cut the relative velocity between the two of them. Dee closed the gap onto his energy vector almost instantly and so did the Chiata fighter. Just as it appeared the alien would get a sensor lock on Azazel, he feinted over, confusing targeting for a brief second longer and then he flashed out and back in more than three hundred meters above them. The Chiata must have been stunned because it reacted very slowly. Dee, on the other hand, wasn't stunned at all and knew exactly what was going on and had the red targeting X to prove it.

"Guns, guns, guns! Fox Three!" she growled. Again the cannons burst through the shields, softening up the alien fighter for the missile. The mecha-to-mecha missile finished the job throwing another orange fireball with green flickering plasma and shrapnel in every direction.

"That's two, Davy," Dee whispered to herself just as she did her own out-and-in.

"Thank you, Phoenix," Azazel said.

"You make good bait, wingman! That's two. The tat shop's gonna need a new jar of ink before the day's done. Now let's cut the goof-off time and do what we came for."

"Understood."

Another out-and-in. This time she was up close and personal with the Chiata target megaship. Playtime was over. It was time to go to work. Dee traced several energy lines in her DTM battlescape view and chose the most efficient one to target.

She was too close to the targeted megaship to worry about engaging more enemy fighters unless she wanted to create an upside down bowl on its surface and fight running and bouncing about from the low ground. Any good mech jock worth her weight in shit knew better than to take the low ground with no top cover. Besides, she needed to place her focus on breaching the hull of the megaship. While she wanted to kill a few more of the Chiata, her mission was the same as it had been for sixteen months. Breach the hull and stop the power grid from being set to self-destruct. She was certain that there would be plenty of opportunities to kill aliens once on board the megaship, but as it stood the mission was top priority—stop that self-destruct sequence. Doing that was a feat easier said than done.

They had learned the trick from Nancy Penzington's last efforts. She had discovered how to disrupt the megaship self-destruct algorithm by taking out the power conduits between engineering and the BBDs. There had been no other combat pilots available during the engagement that was turning south on them, so as captain of her ship, the *U.S.S. Roscoe H. Hillenkoetter,* she took it upon herself to board a mecha fighter and take matters into her own capable hands. As soon as she managed to take the energy conduits out, she had been overwhelmed by Chiata and was killed in action. But Captain Penzington had been on her own and in an older mecha.

USMC Major Deanna "Phoenix" Moore was *bringing it* with the new mecha that was more heavily armored and armed and equipped with quantum membrane teleportation uncertainty engines. Not to mention, the Buckley-Freeman shields and THE most bad-ass marine mecha pilot to ever a hump a Navy SEAL, an AI-driven clone, a full ruck, or anything else worth humping was working the hands-on-throttle-and-stick (HOTAS) flight controls.

Dee jockeyed the HOTAS while her AIC worked the uncertainty flashes in and out of reality space. The Chiata fighters had no idea how to track them or target them. At least they didn't yet. Dee hoped like Hell it stayed that way. As the Bringers of Hell closed on the bridge region just behind the BBD tuning fork, Dee could see in her DTM battlescape view the four supercarriers of the clone attack force beginning their ramming sequences on the targeted megaship. The bot-driven supercarriers punched into the hull of the alien vehicle firing all weapons, missiles, and directed energy guns. All the while, the *Penzington* was firing DEGs from the supercarrier legs and the Blue Beams of Death from Hell zigged and zagged about the engagement zone at targets of tactical priority, creating chaos amongst the Chiata. Random hyperspace jumps added to the chaos as well. It was clear to Dee that DeathRay was flying his megaship like it was a mecha fighter and there was none better, at least in the Navy.

One of the BBDs from the *Penzington* hit home on the target ship's wingman megaship. The beams blasted through the shield generators and continued into the hull, throwing vaporized metal and shrapnel in a wake of destruction behind it. DeathRay had gotten lucky and hit it just at the right place at the right time.

What a lucky hit! Dee thought.

Too bad we can't do that with every shot, Bree agreed.

That ship must've been in trouble at the precise second and position the BBD hit it. Otherwise the shields should've held.

Perhaps the Chiata megaships are more vulnerable than we know.

Who knows? But, holy shit!

The ship bulged at the center just behind the blue

beam guns and then it looked to Dee as if someone had inflated the ship with orange plasma that could no longer be contained. The ship burst at the seams, throwing orange and white plasmas from every rivet. Secondary explosions continued to run bow to stern of the ship until it finally gave up the ghost—assuming the Chiata had ghosts. The megaship exploded with the force of a gluonium bomb, throwing shrapnel in a spherical wavefront that pinged off the shields and armor of the larger ships and was no fun for the fighters either. The ball was filling up with debris that would become taxing on the shield generators after a long enough period of time.

The uncertainty of the trajectories of the Bringers' mecha drove the probability of hit by the spreading debris field to almost zero, but the possibility was still there. Dee kept her eyes peeled for anything in her path, but the radar, lidar, and QMT sensors fed into the state vectors for the flight trajectory algorithm and kept her clear of the shrapnel fields as fast as computationally possible—and that was pretty damned fast.

The Bringers of Hell hit the surface of the ship at more than two kilometers per second relative velocity. The mecha of the squadron flared and rolled and pitched and yawed against the almost nonexistent but still there atmosphere of ionized hull plating, smoke, propellant, lubricant, and fluid leaks that always followed a starship of that size to bleed off energy until they all metamorphosed to bot-mode skittering, bouncing, judo rolling, and strafing targets on the surface of the alien ship. The dozen bot-mode mecha bounced around looking like skittering fleas on the back of a much larger animal. But these pests had no intent of cohabitating with the host. They planned to kill it and keep the carcass for their own purposes.

"Bravo Team, take the bridge!" Dee shouted through her abdominal clenching and guttural growls against the heavy g-loading and extreme jerk of the maneuvers. "Alpha team is with me to engineering. We have to stop that self-destruct sequence."

"Fox!" First Lieutenant Azazel, her wingman, fired a heavy warhead armor buster into a seam near an airlock. The missile exploded just ahead of Dee who went to guns to help push through the bulkhead.

"Guns, guns, guns," she shouted. The volleyball-sized green plasma cannon rounds finished opening up the rest of the hole the missile had started and the FM-14Xs began bursting through the gaping jagged hole that was still glowing red-hot. "We're in. Stay with me team."

Chapter 2

July 24, 2409 AD
U.S.S. Sienna Madira III
Thgreeth Abandoned Outpost
Planet Deep in Expanse
700 light-years from the Sol System
Saturday, 6:37 A.M. Eastern Time

"I know, dear, but it seems to me that she only has focus and a taste for vengeance, violence, and if my sources are correct, sex with clones." General Alexander Moore was frustrated and in fear for his daughter. Since the loss of the one man she'd loved in the battle for Thgreeth she had turned dark, very dark. Deanna was no longer his straitlaced princess, or even a hard-as-nails-by-the-book U.S. Marine. No, she was in a much darker place. She had cut herself off from almost all humans except for DeathRay, whom Alexander was also concerned for.

The only intimate contact she appeared to be having was with the emotionless AI-driven clones. The only thing she truly cared for any longer seemed to be killing the aliens. She was doing everything she could to make herself, at least in appearance, become a demon of alien death. Alexander didn't like it. He couldn't even look into his little girl's eyes any longer since now they glowed red, like the fire from the implants she had gotten. She had become almost disturbing to look at. He knew that was the point she was trying to make. She had every intent to become the devil incarnate to the Chiata, but by damn, she was still his little princess he'd swung from his arms and protected and had taken to Disney World all those years ago. Hell, he doubted they'd let her in looking the way she did these days.

"Alexander, there is no need in you to spy on her love life. It's probably against some law, since she is an adult," his wife scolded him. "Besides, I seem to recall a certain U.S. Marine major going through some very dark times at a similar point in his life."

"I never kept tally of my kills with tattoos and clone sex conquests!" Alexander harrumphed. "It isn't her. Not my princess. Hell, not even my Marine!"

"All we can do is be there for her when she needs us, Alexander. She'll come back to us someday and we need to be there for her when she does," Sehera Moore said and looked her husband in the eyes, and Alexander could tell that she was worried and sad for her daughter's current state of being.

"I know. I know." Alexander hugged her to him. "It just . . . it breaks my heart."

"Mine too," Sehera whispered softly. "Tattoos can be removed. And someday she'll find love again. But now, we just need to make certain she stays with us."

"In this war," Alexander frowned, "there are just no certainties to anything. I just wish we could convince her to retire and move home. We can do *this* out here."

"That will never happen," Sehera said through a thin smile. "There's just too much of her father in her."

"Hmmph. And her mother, I think."

"General Moore, XO here." The intercom in their private quarters came to life, startling them both. Alexander raised an eyebrow to his wife and then smirked.

"Never a dull moment," Sehera added.

"Go ahead, XO. Moore here," he said.

"General, Admiral Walker just returned from her mission. Sir, we've got another megaship in our fleet." The XO sounded excited.

"Great news Firestorm. Tell Admiral Walker I want a debriefing as soon as she gets her team in order. I want to know about that system."

"Yes sir. She has already QMTed over. She is waiting in your ready room."

"Understood, XO. Tell her I'll be there in a few minutes. In the meantime, make her comfortable."

"Absolutely, General." Firestorm almost chuckled. "But I can't say that I've ever seen the admiral 'comfortable,' sir."

"Do your best, Sally." Alexander laughed and closed the channel. "I think she's right. Fullback hasn't looked comfortable since we played football against each other a million years ago. I'd better go."

"Don't worry about me. I'm going on an expedition with Dr. Hughes and some of the warrant officers into the ruins today. There's plenty down there to keep me busy and out of trouble," Sehera told him.

"Well, do that. Stay out of trouble." He kissed her on the forehead and looked into her eyes. He could see the concern there too. He knew she was just as worried about Dee as he was. "She'll be all right. That's the only way I can see it. But I don't have to like what she's doing to get there."

"She'll be alright." Sehera nodded in agreement. "Only way I see it too."

"I have to say sir, the new FM-14Xs would have made this mission easier," Admiral Walker grunted. "Why do we keep waiting for them?"

"You'll wait no longer, Sharon. I got word from Madira while you were away that the new fleet of fighters is complete and ready for delivery to all of the super ships. When DeathRay gets back, we'll have the Bringers of Hell give lessons to all the mecha jocks before our next wave of raids."

"That's great news, Alexander." Fullback paused uncomfortably. "How is the *Penzington's* new captain holding up?"

"DeathRay is singularly focused, as is his crew." He thought of his daughter again.

"Yes. Tales of their exploits and derring-dos are starting to permeate the fleet. Even the clones are starting to talk about them," Admiral Walker noted. Alexander wasn't sure if by "them" she meant DeathRay and Phoenix or Boland's entire attack group. "They are becoming almost iconic. If I thought the aliens cared for spying on us I'd be concerned about the *Penzington's* crew."

"We've gotten no indication of singular targeting of

specific personnel or assets. Although, it would be nice if there were a boogeyman that spooked the aliens." Moore thought about that for a second. Maybe that is what Dee was shooting for. "But, we've made it a point not to let any aliens escape our raids, so they should have zero knowledge of whom and how. Assuming we were successful in hunting them all down. Who knows? There are always so damned many of them in each of the systems we raid, I'm not so sure we can get all of them."

"You can never kill all the fire ants in a hill. Somehow, they pop up a few meters away later on."

"Yeah, and these damned Chiata are infesting the galaxy out here far worse than any fire ants," Moore agreed.

"Perhaps we should let a few escape?" Walker replied with a raised eyebrow. "With pictures and intel."

"Perhaps. Let's think on that." Moore sat down in his chair and spun to look out the big window in the ready room. The view from there was almost as good as the view from his personal quarters or even the big bubble dome of the bridge. "Those aliens that built the ruins, the Thgreeth, they had all that technology and still ran from the Chiata. Dee's report said they were afraid of the numbers game. You'd think they could have wiped out the blur bastards, but they ran instead. We only have a double handful of super ships with the BBDs and the Buckley weapon. I doubt we'd put fear into them."

"Alexander, from what I've gathered from listening to Madira and that alien friend of hers, Copernicus, no Chiata system has ever been retaken. We've taken over a dozen now in just over two years. The Chiata have lost communications with them. That has to have percolated to the top of their 'what the fuck' list."

"I guess it would mine too. What do you suggest, Sharon?" Alexander turned and looked her in the eye. To do so he had to look up at her. The woman was a big beautiful ebony amazon of a woman that was more muscle than anything else. She had a body that would have made any fullback in the NFL jealous and most forwards in the NBA dread having to post up on. "You don't think it's too early to leak our secret raids somehow? I mean, we still only have a dozen super ships and only one of them presently equipped with the new fighters."

"I'd bet they are already leaked whether any survivors escaped or not," Sharon replied. "Think about it. If we suddenly lost contact with several outposts, we'd get suspicious. We'd send forward recon. We'd send probes. Hell, you'd go yourself."

"Yes, true. But, the Chiata must have hundreds of thousands or more outposts. This might just be a grain of sand on the beach to them or a flea bite on a camel's ass."

"That makes it even more significant. Out of hundreds of thousands, they've never lost one. Now all of a sudden they've lost several. Now there is a demon out there in the dark that they know nothing about. There's a demon out there for the Chiata to fear in the night that keeps sneaking deep in their territory at random systems and killing all of the inhabitants. And, from recent images from the *Penzington*, I can think of a perfect personification of that demon. Recall how spooked we were the first time we saw the Chiata? Well just maybe it's their turn to be scared shitless of us." She paused and looked him in the eyes. Alexander was sure she was making sure he saw the magnitude of her statement. He did. It wasn't lost on him who Fullback was implying to be the demon that would drive fear into the hearts of the Chiata at night. But at the same time, he liked being able to zip in and take a system and all the while keeping the Chiata guessing about what had happened.

"I get it, Sharon. And, you're right. They probably are getting worked up. We would be. They might even be thinking of response strategies, but that seems almost arrogant to think that, to my mind. They outgun us by sheer numbers alone to the point that we couldn't stop a full-on advancing attack wave of them." He exhaled and looked up at the ceiling as if for inspiration. He wasn't sure what he thought about his little girl becoming a demon, but there might not be anything he could do to stop it. In fact, he was probably too late on that one. "Alright, I hadn't thought of this. I should have. Were it me in their shoes, I'd up the timetable for invasion. I'd want to press the advantage of numbers that I knew I still had."

"That is exactly what I'd do," Sharon agreed. "I suspect a shit storm is coming. And soon. We've got to speed up our preparations."

"Shit."

Chapter 3

July 24, 2409 AD
61 Ursae Majoris C
31 light-years from the Sol System
Saturday, 8:30 A.M. Sol System Eastern Time
(11:30 A.M. 61 Ursae Majoris C Capitol
Standard Time)

"You're starting to get the hang of it, Copernicus." Sienna Madira rolled over onto her back and pulled the blanket up over her naked breasts. Her chest was still heaving as she panted for breath. Sweat rolled off her body sending further chills up her spine. "At least it was intense."

"Isn't intense a good thing, Sienna?" the alien-controlled clone body replied. Sienna Madira almost laughed at the response as she continued to gasp for air. She didn't really care if she hurt the crazy alien's feelings. She wasn't even sure he had them any more than the AI-driven clones did. So far, he was a better bed partner than any of her clones had been. She wasn't sure why that was. Perhaps because he had been her partner in crime for so long.

"Intense can be good. Personally, I like intense." She smiled at him. Since her last rejuvenation she had decided to take on a much younger image than she had used for the past several decades. She looked and felt much more like her agile and athletic self of her first time through the twenty-something decade. Sienna wiped sweat from her brow with the blanket and then managed to slow her breathing as she exhaled. "Yeah. Intense is good enough for now and, uh, maybe again later if you're up for it."

"Always. I appreciate these, uh, interactions, Sienna. It helps me understand humanity on many levels previously unavailable to me. The assimilation into this body is much different than the symbioses with our evolutionary hosts. Very different. It has taken me some time to understand and control it. Certainly, reproduction is different. It was never an activity that was meant for anything but procreation to my species. We had no desires to do it for other purposes." Copernicus looked at Sienna with an odd look on his face. Madira just chalked it up as the alien having difficulty understanding facial expressions. She smiled inwardly, thinking he hadn't learned to control it yet still after all these years.

"I suspect that my species likes it so much as an evolutionary necessity," Sienna said matter-of-factly, but then sort of chuckled as she thought about it. "If it was hard work, we'd have died off long ago. Humans will spend days thinking up ways to get out of a task that will only take minutes to do just because they don't want to do it. With sex, well, everybody wants to do it, so, we end up with billions of babies. Makes sense to me. It was a good plan within a plan. You should appreciate that."

"Yes. It is . . . enjoyable. Just different." Copernicus searched for the right words. Sienna thought he was almost cute, but only briefly. "Seems to be logical for human evolution . . ."

"I sense there is as 'but' in there somewhere?" she asked. "You trailed off. Logical for human evolution . . . but?"

"A but?" Copernicus hesitated briefly. "Ah, yes, I see. No, not a but. More like a, well, okay, it is a but."

"But?"

"But, I believe my people could thrive this way, without the procreation part. That shouldn't be necessary. We could permanently download into these clones and leave our storage facility altogether. I believe only then should we attempt to procreate and carry on as humans," Copernicus explained. "It is sad to think of leaving our evolutionary developed bodies completely to extinction, but there is really no other choice. I'm not sure the clone bodies would accept the parasitic control from our previous forms."

"I'm not so certain about the whole 'your people thriving' bit. Sometimes I think we need to incentivize the clones to start naturally procreating. But I wonder, even with your people, would you create a new whatever you are or just another human baby. I suspect a human baby. So your people would eventually go extinct just like the AI-driven clones if we don't keep making AIs to go in the bodies."

"I see your point." Copernicus made another strange expression, as if he were checking on something in his DTM mindview. "We would first have to start cloning our other forms as well as modifying these clones to become hosts. I'm not so certain that human bodies could host our symbiont forms. No, I think simply transferring to the clones is a better plan."

"At what clone production rate are we talking about?"

"There are over nine billion of my people that survived and are stored away. Your species is the first host body that has performed suitably for the quantum consciousness transfer. At the rate you have produced clones we could start the download process now and have a majority of my people freed in a few weeks," Copernicus explained. "That is assuming the assimilation process can be performed at such a high rate of exchange. But that is what the Oort Cloud facility was originally designed to do."

"Weeks? There are only about one billion unclaimed clones stored and production rate is only about one billion per year." Sienna looked up at the ceiling fan through the glass and out at the clouds passing over her penthouse in Capitol City, thinking more about the afterglow of sex than of the woes of her job and the plight of Copernicus' people. "Your math doesn't add up."

"Oh, but you have over sixty billion clones in this system already. I was thinking we could repurpose enough of them to support freeing my people." Copernicus replied nonchalantly, which instantly killed the afterglow and snapped Sienna into leader and defender of her people mode.

"Wait, you think I'm going to let you, in essence, kill eight billion of my citizens for you?" Sienna was immediately on the defensive. She had been waiting for the other shoe to drop with Copernicus for almost two hundred years. This was likely it. "Not going to happen."

"You wouldn't be killing them, Sienna. Don't be so dramatic. You could download and store the existing clones and then reinstall them as new bodies come online. You have plenty of clones and citizens. My people have been trapped in storage for thousands of years."

"This was your plan all along, wasn't it?" Sienna raised up, flung the covers back, and stood beside the bed pointing a finger at him. Daggers could have shot from her eyes. "If you knew that, then you should have said something beforehand. You should have told me this is what you needed before I brought billions of AI clones to life. They may be clones and they may be AI, but the I in AI stands for intelligence and as far as any Turing test can tell that intelligence is sentient and alive. Maybe with a plan from the beginning, we could have waited on loading the AIs into the bodies, but, now, NO WAY IN HELL!"

"Calm down, Sienna." Copernicus held up a hand as if he were calming a child. Sienna didn't like the bastard's arrogance. She was beginning to wish she hadn't had sex with him many times. "I had no idea you would react this way. You are so hard to calculate. Even after all these years I still do not understand you humans."

"You had better understand this." Sienna said still standing naked with one hand on her hip and the other pointing belligerently at the alien. "I've killed my own people before in order to get us to this point, where we can survive what is coming. I hated doing it , but there was no other way. I had no choice but to become a bloodthirsty killer. That part of the plan is over. That part of my life is over! You hear me? I'm through manipulating my people. I'm tired of the plans within plans within plans and the constant calculations of life and death on such grand scales. All the calculations and plans made death so impersonal. But death IS personal every single time. It was extremely personal when I had to kill Scotty. I'm sick to the core of these twisted plans with multiple hidden agendas and acceptable losses of life. The plan is straightforward now. I plan to stand with my people, humanity and AI clones alike, and see this thing through to the end. I plan to fight the thrice-damned Chiata with all the bloodlust I can muster. I will offer whatever I can to help humanity recover from the aftermath of the war that is coming. And then, well, and then I plan to burn in Hell for eternity, which in my mind just won't be long enough or punishment enough for all that I've had to do. Unless you could asssure me that giving your race those bodies will enable us to defeat the Chiata Horde's expansion wave, then forget it. You can absolutely fucking forget it!"

"Don't be unreasonable, Sienna," the alien stammered, looking shocked at her reaction. "You had to have guessed or 'calculated' as you say what the end goal was for me here."

"Can you guarantee that your people being placed into my clones will help us defeat the Chiata or not?"

"Of course not. They defeated many more times that of my people and that was with our symbiont bodies and our much more physically capable hosts." Copernicus almost seemed hurt. The expression on his face and his body language was almost right for the situation. Almost. Sienna didn't give a shit. The people of the Alpha Lyncis system were her people. She had built a peaceful, efficient, and happy world with billions of inhabitants that had families of sorts with daily lives that didn't need disrupting so abruptly. Sure, she could ask them this favor and as logically driven as the AI clones were she was certain they'd oblige. But she just couldn't bring herself to accept such a request as humane or even, well, sane. She wasn't about to force eight billion of her people to download themselves into some server somewhere only to wait no telling how long before they could be reinserted into a new body. At the current production rate of clone bodies some of them might be stored away for as much as eight or nine years when all things in the process were truly considered. She wouldn't do it. Not now and not ever.

"So, you can't guarantee it?" She asked rhetorically this time as she had already convinced herself of the answer he would give.

"Well, uh, no. I cannot."

"You damned right you can't. The answer is no. No way. You can take the empty billion clones now if you like. And you can live here with us or you can go somewhere else to one of my backdoor systems. Or you could go off and find yourself a new star system to live on. No, scratch that last. You'll have to pay your dues. We could use the soldiers. Either fight with us or support us."

"Pay our dues?"

"You heard me."

"I might remind you, Sienna. Who gave you the technologies that are making your stand against the Chiata even possible?" This time his question was rhetorical.

"Me, that is who! Were it not for me your people would have been overrun by the Chiata while you were still living in thatch huts and still developing the written language. My people have paid enough dues for humanity's sake."

"While I appreciate that, Copernicus, I truly do, if you aren't going to fight, you will simply have to support the effort in manufacturing or some other means. These bodies are meant to help humanity survive. It's a numbers game now and you know that we are way outnumbered. I can't just turn over such an important resource." She turned toward the bathroom as she grabbed her robe from the bedpost and slipped it over her shoulders and then stood firmly facing Copernicus as she cinched it tight at the waist. "Think on it. I have a meeting with my son-in-law I need to prepare for. And don't be spoutin' off such stuff around him or he's likely to kill you on the spot just to be cautious. If I didn't think you were so, um, useful, I'd probably do the same. And I'm rethinking that situation and might still decide to kill you soon or hand you over to him."

"You certainly know how to woo a man, Sienna."

"Was that a joke?" Sienna turned back toward the alien.

"It was an attempt to follow yours."

"The problem there, Copernicus, is that I wasn't joking."

Sienna stared out the window of her ready room just to the starboard side of the control dome, looking across the city below. Her builder-bot reengineered Chiata megaship hovered motionless only a few tens of kilometers above Capitol City. Her ship was the only megaship Moore had given her. It was her mission to figure out how to reverse-engineer it and build them from scratch. She hadn't got that far yet as the science behind the blue beams of death from Hell was still unclear, even to her and her team of AI clone scientists. Copernicus hadn't been much help in that regard either. But she had rebuilt it inside and out and repaired the supercarrier legs and beefed up their shield projectors. The megaship truly was *her* flagship.

She had christened it the *U.S.S. Scotty P. Mueller* in honor of Sehera's father, whom she had murdered when Deanna had been just a little girl. Sienna regretted that Dee never got to meet her grandfather, because he was a great man of history. She had loved Scotty dearly, but he would no longer allow her to continue with her and Copernicus' plans. They had become so bloody and on the verge of evil that Scotty had told her she had to stop on several occasions. The straw that had broken Scotty's back was when he had helped Nancy Penzington escape from her clutches and thwarted one of her plans. It was then that Copernicus had realized and insisted that Scotty had to be removed from the equations. So, Sienna took it upon herself to do the deed. She shot him point-blank in the head at the dinner table in her penthouse.

Seeing the cityscape below of the capital city of her star system that housed tens of millions of people, clones or not, made her take pause and think on what she had gone through to create her civilization and what she would do to keep it alive through what was coming with the Chiata. She wasn't sure she'd liked the conversation with Copernicus earlier either. He was always up to something.

It was the alien that had shown her the plans-within-plans-within-plans subterfuge that had shaped the last two centuries or so of human history. It was the plans that the alien had inspired her with that led to her causing the bloodiest civil war in human history.

It was those plans that led her to creating the dark tortuous times of the Martian Desert Campaigns where she experimented on soldiers, torturing and killing many of them as she investigated the alien's idea of cloning. In the process she had tortured one U.S. Marine who had escaped and become a brilliant shining light of defiance for humanity. That Marine had captured the hearts and minds of humanity along with that of her daughter. The alien's plans within plans within plans had to continuously be modified by the anomaly that was her son in-law. But nevertheless, Copernicus made whatever modifications were necessary and continued to do so, all the while expecting her to carry them out. She had carried out the plans diligently and with loyalty to the plans. It had been those plans that had led her to killing her daughter's father and the love of her life. The plans had required it so she did it.

The alien's plans, while having a positive end in mind, stopping the Chiata invasion of the Sol System, never seemed to have much empathy for the bloody pathways and human suffering required in their implementation of those plans. And Sienna Madira had been party to it from the beginning. Willingly and enthusiastically at times, she had been party to them all the while. But for Copernicus, she had always felt there was more to the plan. He was too driven to be purely motivated by vengeance. He was too calculating and cold to want to free his people from their storage place and then run and hide. It just didn't fit his personality. He hadn't shown all his cards yet, but Sienna knew it was time to count the cards and check his sleeves for aces. There was definitely something up his sleeves and she needed to figure it out before it was too late for everyone involved.

Somehow, and she had suspected it from the beginning, the alien's final plan was for there to be enough hosts available for his species to download into or to take over in some form. He was an invasion of sorts himself when she thought about it. She had at least optimistically hoped that his plans were benign where humanity was concerned, and that he just needed a little help in saving his people. He needed quid pro quo but to what extent was only now becoming clear. She just had never been completely certain if clones had been his original target host, or when the final implementation of the symbiont-host takeover would actually be implemented, if ever. He never told her all of his plans. As she thought about it, she wasn't certain she knew how to stop him from hacking the clones and inserting his people. She'd never really thought it all the way through. That was unlike her.

The other aspect that kept tugging away at her mind was that he had mentioned that the humans were the first species compatible for them since they had lost their evolutionary hosts to the Chiata. That was clearly why Copernicus had fought for humanity in the galactic legal system for thousands of years. It was part of his plans within plans within plans. But the concern that Sienna had always fretted over was to what end were those plans.

"Ma'am, the fleet is ready for quantum membrane teleportation when you are." Her new aide and bodyguard, a Malcolm clone she called Scotty because he reminded her of Sehera's father, interrupted her train of thought. He reminded her so much of the man she had loved so dearly that it haunted her a bit. She wished she hadn't had to kill him all those years ago. That was another reason she wanted to burn in Hell for eternity. And to top it off she had intentions of "training" Scotty in the same way she had been "training" Copernicus. There was something sick about that. Sienna knew it deep in her soul, but she had given up on her soul when she had started down the path she had been on for so long.

"Good. Let's push out to a higher orbit and start the sequence then." She nodded to him, putting the thoughts of "training" him in the back of her mind for the time being. She looked out the window and the city below was already dropping away beneath them as they formed up on a fleet of her latest set of battleships. The newest hope for fighting the Chiata were even larger and more heavily armored battering-ram nosed supercarriers with beefed-up structural integrity field generation systems, full up Buckley-Freeman switches and shields, larger directed-energy gun batteries, and mecha bays equipped with the new FM-14X mecha with the quantum membrane teleportation uncertainty engines. Each of the battleships had been upgraded in such a way to facilitate being appendaged to the Chiata Porcusnail megaships more easily. They would make the conversion to superweapon class ships more quickly and with less modification requirements by the builder bots. Up until now all the raids on Chiata systems had only enabled the capture of one Porcusnail megaship. Madira had a plan to change that. She hoped her son-in-law could execute that plan. If anyone could, it would be him.

"I've notified the captain. She is initiating the QMT now," Scotty replied. "She says we'll be at the Thgreeth ruins system momentarily."

"Thank you, Scotty." Sienna sat calmly awaiting the buzz and sizzle of the teleportation, but her mind couldn't help but wonder just what Copernicus was up to. It was time for her to dig a little deeper into whatever it was he was planning.

Chapter 4

July 24, 2409 AD
Ruins
Thgreeth Abandoned Outpost
Planet Deep in Expanse
700 light-years from the Sol System
Saturday, 10:14 A.M. Eastern Time

"All I know is that my daughter says the alien, Mru, I believe is how it was pronounced, told her that we would have access to their teleportation network," Sehera explained to the team of specialists, warrant officers, linguists, mathematicians, cosmologists, and anthropologists again, even though she knew they had all been briefed a million times on the subject. It was more of a rhetorical statement meant to reinforce the fact that none of them had a damned clue how Dee was able to open gates in the ruins that would QMT her to places mapped out on the glyphs all over the ruin walls. Somehow, during the battle for the ruins, Deanna had stumbled across a doorway that led her to be teleported to the alien, or perhaps the alien came to her. In that process, the alien gave her the ability to use the ancient quantum membrane teleportation system to her advantage. It also enabled her to perform QMT sling-forward and snap-back transportations that changed the tide of the battle in the human fleet's favor.

Deanna had fought hand-to-hand against countless Chiata to the point of her being paralyzed from the waist down, but she had still kept going. It was her perseverance that had pushed her and enabled her to make it inside the ruins and to decipher how to use them. Sehera couldn't help but think that the Thgreeth saw something in her, which they extrapolated to humanity perhaps, that triggered them helping her. In the end, the Thgreeth likely saved Deanna's life as well as all of humanity.

"Yes, ma'am. We get that," one of the team members, a linguist, replied. Johan Seely was his name, according to the DTM view from her suit. She pulled up his profile while he continued to speak. "There must be more to it. Perhaps her pet has something to do with it."

"She has assured me that her 'pet' isn't the reason. And it isn't a pet so much as a weapon, like a handgun. It's just one that can move about on its own. She calls it a robot that is designed to kill Chiata," Sehera replied. "Dee says that her connection to the ruins, well, it is more of a software patch that her AIC was given by the alien. Although, when her AIC, Bree, tried to find the patch as a transferable driver, she couldn't, in her words, 'encompass the file in such a way as to copy it'. It, again, in her words, 'was like the physical description of the code was too uncertain to fully comprehend'. Sounds like some form of quantum vacuum encoding to me, but I'm no expert."

"Well, Mrs. Moore," one of the scientists joined in, Dr. Cinnamon Hughes, again according to the DTM mindview in Sehera's suit. "That is why I'm here. Quantum vacuum computation in cosmology is my field of study and I believe your daughter's AIC might be on to something. Although I wish we could keep her here for a considerable amount of time, her last visit enabled us to open this particular set of glyphs and I believe this is a central control system."

Sehera looked at the activated wall. Before Deanna had turned it on it had looked like a stone wall covered in ancient glyphs and graphics. There was a myriad of circles and ellipses that crossed and intersected each other and they all seemed to be connected through what appeared to be Julia Set fractals of various dimension. The Julia Set fractals looked a lot like beetles with lightning-bolt-shaped appendages scattering about them in random directions. All of the fractal patterns intertwined and overlapped one another creating a multidimensionally and holistically connected map. Sehera figured that there was enough in the patterns alone to keep a room full of Ph.D. topologists busy and happy for the rest of their lives.

And then there was the cosmological aspect to them. It appeared as though all the patterns connected through other patterns to each other and to points that, as far as the team of experts, and Sehera, could tell, were star systems that on the surface of things seemed randomly spread throughout the galaxy. But upon a deeper investigation there appeared to be a sort of 'connectedness' between them that wasn't tangible as far as they could tell. Sehera had an idea about that connectedness, but needed more time to talk to the STO, or Commander Buckley, or even her mother, about it.

Once the glyphs had been activated, several of the ellipses lit up with a bluish-white glow and they were likewise illuminating pathways through the complex fractal drawings showing brighter spots stretched out across the galaxy. There were pathways of reds and greens of various hues also that were identical in spectrum in every way to the Chiata red-green blurs and the light they emitted through bioluminescence. Sehera and the rest of the team believed the ruins to be a map of the ancient war that took place between the Thgreeth and the Chiata. But at the same time it appeared to be updating itself. Each time the fleet took a system the red and green light changed spectrally to blue-white.

"Mrs. Moore, look at this one here," the linguist called to her and motioned for her attention.

"What is it, Mr. Seely?" Sehera said as she turned to the portion of the wall the man was standing before. "Something changing?"

"Yes, ma'am." Seely traced a red and green line across the surface to an ellipse that was deep within a sea of red and green systems. The one solar system was fading between the red and green to the bluish white light. "Something is happening here."

Pamela, where is Dee? Sehera thought to her AIC. For years she'd been afraid to have the super AI implanted in her brain like everyone else, and had carried her as a watch, necklace, datapad, and as other jewelry. She had thought for decades that Copernicus was her mother's AIC and that it had driven her mad. It had turned out that Copernicus was a living alien entity that was communicating to her mother through an AIC implant and the perceived insanity had been a ruse and part of a deeper, more twisted complex plan of plans. Sehera still wasn't certain what the end result of the plan was supposed to be, and she had yet to forgive her mother for many things, including the death of her father.

But she had put those feelings aside for now because the Chiata were a bigger threat, and like it or not, her mother was turning out to be very useful in the fight against that threat. Realizing that the AIC hadn't been what had driven her mother over the edge, Sehera had finally gotten over her phobias and had the AIC implanted behind her ear and she was still getting used to the direct to mind interactions without having to tap controls or speak out loud.

That is the system that the Penzington is attacking. Deanna is there, Pamela replied DTM.

"We should pay close attention to that," Sehera said. "We are currently attacking that system. It would be handy if we could zoom in, wouldn't it?"

"Zoom in?" Dr. Hughes asked as she approached. "Now that is an interesting idea . . . hmmm."

The physicist stepped between Sehera and the actively changing figure and studied the lines, dots, and curves around it. She opened her faceplate on her helmet and moved closer as if to remove the added graphics of her suit's HUD from the view. Sehera overheard the scientist's suit warn her that the carbon dioxide content of the atmosphere was too high to breathe for more than a few minutes.

"Perhaps there are view controls," she said. "Johan, work with me here for a moment."

"What do you have in mind, Cinnamon?" Seely asked.

"Well, this ellipse here is clearly the heliopause of this star system. The dots here and here and throughout on various ellipses are planetary objects or gravity wells and orbits. But look here at this set of symbols. I have no understanding what they might be. And, they are not connected to the rest of the drawings," the physicist explained as she traced the various lines and symbols with her armored fingers.

"No perspective? How do you mean?" Seely again asked. A few of the other technicians and warrant officers were looking up from their equipment and analysis of other sections of the ruin with piqued interest in the conversation. Interests were piqued, yes, but nobody had any brilliant ideas yet.

"I get it," Sehera interrupted. "If this were a map of spacetime and objects within it, what are these other symbols? A legend? A pull-down menu? Instructions?"

"Precisely," Hughes agreed. "So, Johan, you see why I ask? Are these symbols recurring elsewhere on these maps? They are clearly not objects or cosmological constructs that I understand."

"I see." The linguist nodded and looked as if he were in a brief conversation DTM with his AIC. "Look at this one here. Yes! This is a recurring symbol throughout the ruins, but not as frequent as the others. I've seen it one time in each of the ruin locations visited. And according to records from all data on the ruins about the planet it appears at least once in each."

"That's very interesting." Cinnamon smiled triumphantly as if she understood something the others didn't.

"Interesting how, Dr. Hughes?" Sehera wasn't sure where she was going, but understood that it might be key to understanding the ruins.

"Well, when Major Moore activated this wall for us, she didn't touch it. We all assumed she connected to it wirelessly through the quantum entanglement she somehow gained from the alien contact she had. But if you play back the sequence in your DTM you will note, as I just did, that this symbol was first to light up. What is the first symbol on any system to light up?"

"The power button," Sehera replied. "Okay, this is the on switch. But touching it doesn't seem to do anything." Sehera tapped at it several times with her armored hand.

"Maybe." Cinnamon's glove retracted, leaving her hand bare. She swiped across the symbol with her forefinger. Nothing happened. She did it again. Still no result. "Darn, I thought that was going to work."

"Wait, wait." Seely held up his hand. "These two symbols here and then these four here fit together with these others here. There are two sets of six. Major Moore's suit imagery video data showed that her alien had six fingers on each hand. This is a touchpad control. We need a key code perhaps. Maybe if we DTM replay the system coming on they will light up in a specific order."

The three of them watched a replay of Deanna starting up the wall and indeed there was a sequence in which the symbols lit up as the wall started. Sehera could see the sequence clearly from her vantage point and had her AIC memorize it for her.

"I have it," Dr. Hughes said as she started touching the symbols.

"Aren't you afraid you'll turn it off?" Sehera asked.

"I'm hoping it will ask us what we want to do next," she replied. "Perhaps, the system is running idle awaiting us to enter our username and password."

The three of them held their breath as the physicist tapped the symbol sequence, but again nothing happened. Sehera didn't think it would be that simple. The Chiata had been in that system for no telling how many hundreds of years and had not figured out how to activate the system. A simple key code sequence couldn't be the answer.

"The aliens must've had some sort of identification encoding, maybe even down at the quantum level." Sehera thought about it a bit longer. She actually wished her mother were there. This was her mother's specialty. She had created all sorts of information algorithms that hacked through security systems of humanity over the centuries. Sehera hoped she had learned a thing or two from watching her and fighting against her over her lifetime to present.

Pamela, what would mother do here, she thought.

While I'm not certain about that, I can say that historically and to my knowledge she always used hidden back-door approaches that had been left behind by system architects. She seldom used full frontal brute force firewall attacks and dictionary searches. Your mother is always more elegant and prepared than that, the AIC replied.

"Hmm, back-door approach," Sehera muttered to herself unconsciously. "Too bad Dee can't just come and play around with this stuff more. I need to talk to Alexander about that." She continued to mutter to herself oblivious of the linguist and the physicist on either side of her. Both of them were staring at her and paying close attention to her every movement. She focused her mind on how it was that Dee had been able to address the walls and why Bree had not been able to transfer the capability to others. There was something special about Dee perhaps.

"Wait a minute. I want us to play back Dee's meeting with the alien and pay closer attention to what was said there and then. There's something nagging me about this." Sehera nodded to Seely and Hughes as though she were ordering them. While Sehera had no rank and certainly was only "along for the ride as an advisor" she was still Sehera Moore.

Pamela, play it back for us DTM.

Yes, ma'am.

The three of them watched and listened to Deanna's first contact with Mru of Thgreeth. They occasionally paused and replayed sequences. There was nothing that was particularly illuminating until the alien began to explain why Dee was allowed to access the system. Sehera was getting perplexed by the conundrum.

"Yes. As the scourge covered the galaxy from the outer arms inward my people moved ahead of them and placed these safe havens and escape passages through space," the alien explained to Dee. "Our hopes were to enable multiple attack fronts unavailable to the enemy in the oncoming war. You have found how to access one of them. This is important in that no other species as of yet has been judged by the automated guardians as trustworthy enough to allow through. Perhaps they allowed it or perhaps you manipulated it. Either way, you are here now."

"Automated guardians, you mean the beetle bugs? That thing didn't like the way I tasted," Dee replied. Cinnamon chuckled at Dee's comment. Sehera shushed her. The video replay continued.

"Yes, I see this. That is exciting and intriguing for me. In seventy thousand years, no other species has triggered the tunnel system. But through testing your blood and reading the history stored in your artificial counterpart we could see that we should at least have a conversation with you," Mru explained. "That does not mean you are trustworthy."

"There!" Sehera stopped the playback. "That's it. Why'd we not see that before?"

"It is quite obvious isn't it," Johan agreed. "Her blood was key. While we assumed the alien configured the handshaking protocols for humanity, it might simply have been for Deanna Moore."

"Or perhaps, a Moore's DNA?" Cinnamon asked. "You should have quite similar markers, Mrs. Moore."

"Perhaps," Sehera said as she retracted her glove.

Pamela, reproduce as much of the handshaking protocols as Dee's AIC was able to transfer as best you can, she thought.

I am running the sequence now.

Sehera touched the symbols in the sequence that they had turned on in Dee's initial startup. At first it didn't appear that anything would happen, but then the symbols shifted and rotated into the wall and out of the wall and side to side. Finally, the room filled with translucent images that were more complex and more three dimensional than those that were on the wall. The room became the display, not just the wall.

"Everybody is seeing this, right?" Sehera asked unsure if it was only meant for her or if it was a general system display.

"Yes, we are," Johan said excitedly. "It's a real-time holographic map of the galaxy, I think."

"I'm pretty sure that's what it is. How do the alien ruins gather and transmit this information, I wonder? Look here." Dr. Hughes pointed at the system that was fading in and out from red and green to bluish white and back. "This system is still in flux."

"Yes, it is." Sehera hoped not for long and she reached up to touch the translucent image in front of her. When she did, it expanded before them and the sudden shift of view threw her momentarily off balance. "Whoah."

"Mrs. Moore, you have control of the map," Johan said, just as surprised by the sudden image perspective change as everyone else. "Please do that slowly or warn me next time. That made me nauseous."

"It would appear that I do have control. And, sorry about the sudden jump. I didn't like it too much myself," Sehera replied gulping back the lump that had risen in her throat. She carefully reached up with both hands and spread out a region in the system that was the epicenter of the color fading sphere.

The room suddenly filled with a section of the solar

system near a large gas giant planet about eight astronomical units' distance from the star. There were Chiata porcusnail megaships and blue beams zigging and zagging about. In the middle nearest one of the planet's moons was a large porcusnail-looking alligator-like megaship firing its own blue beams of death from Hell along with other directed energy beams and missiles. There were several supercarriers there and four of them had rammed one of the Chiata megaships in an attempt to seize another alligator porcusnail Fleet ship superweapon. Sehera's heart skipped a couple of beats as she realized she was watching the battle her daughter was fighting in real-time. She knew that Dee was on board that alien ship. She could feel it. She had to know.

Sehera, the system is, I don't know how to describe it, but it is scanning me, her AIC told her DTM.

What do you mean? Is it malicious? Are you safe?

Yes, I, yes, I . . . There was a brief pause and almost a loss of communications with her AIC. *I, I, uh . . . No. Not malicious. I don't think so, but I cannot stop it even if it is.*

What is it doing, then? Pamela?

I am not, wait, I understand now. It is not malicious at all. Yes, I understand. Watch the images ma'am. The AIC sounded less frightened as if it understood what was going on all of a sudden. Then the imagery in the room altered itself a bit.

"What are those blue dots?" one of the technicians watching chimed in.

"Well if you ask me, I'd say it's the Blue Force Tracking System?" a senior warrant officer added.

"Mrs. Moore? What is happening?" Dr. Hughes asked.

"The ruins are handshaking with my AIC. I think the alien system has incorporated our fleet troop trackers." Sehera thought for a second. "I wonder . . ."

Pamela, use standard command protocols and pull up names for the blue dots. Show me Dee, she thought.

Yes, ma'am. I am certain that will work.

Then all of the thousands of blue dots in the system had a nametag and vital sign icon attached and inside the Chiata ship, deep inside the ship, USMC Major Deanna "Phoenix" Moore's icon appeared. Sehera took a deep breath not sure what to do next. Seeing Dee in the midst of such a situation both paralyzed her and made her want to spring into action, but she wasn't sure how she could do anything to help.

"Look there." The same warrant officer bounced in closer. Sehera looked at her DTM to get a name for the man. He was Chief Warrant Officer Three Thomson Dover, an electromagnetic spectrum expert. "There is a field distortion taking place on the periphery of the combat zone. Zoom out a bit, ma'am, if you don't mind."

"Okay," Sehera said. She reached up and waved her hands together squeezing the resolution of the image. Again their perspective changed a bit and more of the system came into view.

"There!" the warrant officer exclaimed. "Look, a spherical distortion out about five or six AUs from the combat zone, completely encompassing the fleet. And look just beyond that at the gas giant there. Those red dots. They are hiding in the planet's atmosphere by the thousands. This is full up Red Force Tracker as well and there is a big chunk of the Red Force right there."

"What does that mean, Chief?" Sehera asked although she thought she knew the answer. There was no need to ponder the data longer as instantly hyperspace vortex tubes opened up inside the sphere of distortion and hundreds of Chiata megaships popped into reality space. Red dots from the gas giant vanished and reappeared just outside the combat zone a few tens of seconds later. It was clear what was taking place to all of them. None of them could believe it.

"Holy . . ."

"Oh my god, it's an ambush!"

"And I'll bet you that distortion is a one-way door," one of the others said. "It's a kill box."

"Mrs. Moore, I think that is a QMT damping field. They are trapped and don't realize it!" Dr. Hughes added.

"But the Chiata don't have those," one of the techs grunted.

"They do now," CW3 Dover replied. "Jesus Christ, this is awful."

"Sehera to Alexander. Emergency! Drop what you are doing now and flash to me! Now! Now! Now!"

Chapter 5

"Admiral, CDC."

"Sonofabitch! Go, CDC!" DeathRay replied through gritted teeth. Blue beams of death from Hell pounded into the Buckley-Freeman shields, causing the ship to jerk so hard that had the crew not been wearing armored suits and their helmets, as was standard combat protocol these days, they'd all have gotten broken necks. Even though the crew were all in their suits, casualty reports were still beginning to come in from all decks. A crack formed across one of the viewports on the starboard side of the bridge and builder bots appeared out of nowhere and immediately began skittering about the deck plates and bulkhead repairing the transparent super-alloys. For a brief second, DeathRay thought the bots crawling around on the equipment and

71

screens looked a little like Dee's pet that the Thgreeth aliens from the ruins had given her. The bridge dome material seemed to be holding strong. As far as Jack knew the engineers and scientists had yet to figure out what the dome material actually was made of. As long as the big-assed dome held up against the enemy fire he didn't care.

"The reality space signatures continue to grow, sir," the young clone from the Combat Direction Center said with very little if any detectable inflection in his voice—inflection no, urgency yes. Clones driven by AI computers or not, DeathRay was pretty sure that even they didn't care much for dying. "It looks like at least two hundred megaships, sir. And possibly more still coming through."

"Shields at seventy-one percent, sir," the STO announced. Jack double checked the shield status in his own mindview. While it wasn't grim yet, they had taken a good bit of damage. "That's the third direct hit. I recommend against more of those, Admiral."

"No shit, Two," DeathRay muttered. He did his best to grasp the entire combat ball around him in his DTM battlescape view. The attack plan had been going exactly as planned until all of a sudden the number of enemy megaships increased by over a hundred times. The bastards were crawling out of the woodwork, so to speak. DeathRay knew an ambush when he saw one. He didn't like it either. But the Chiata didn't have QMT technology and what he couldn't figure out was how they managed to get there so quickly unless they had been waiting for them. He didn't have time to figure that out at the moment, because at the present fucking moment his entire fleet was in a serious knife fight.

DeathRay was torn on what exactly to do. He debated his options which were: one, just chalk the objective up as lost and order a snap-back to safety, or two, pressing the advantage. He honestly had no idea but didn't like not being able to simply react. Being a mecha jock was so much easier. And DeathRay's first instinct from years as a fighter pilot was to do what he always did when outnumbered, and that was to press the attack. In a mecha, that was usually enough of an unexpected tactic that the enemy were caught off guard, giving him the upper hand. But with the Chiata, it was difficult to tell. And extrapolating flying mecha to megaships was a little less exact a science. He did it anyway.

"What do we do, Admiral?" The XO turned to him. DeathRay was pretty sure that the clone had just simulated a million battleplans and the majority of them likely appeared unwinnable. "We are too far down on the numbers game, sir."

"XO, I want you to rethink those numbers if we have two Buckley weapons active," he replied.

Candis, get me Dee, he thought. *I have to know how long it will be until we have a second megaship on our side.*

Roger that, his AIC replied in his mind. *You have a DTM channel to Major Moore open now.*

It's thick as shit in here, DeathRay. Dee's mindvoice was agitated and clearly preoccupied with the overwhelming physical, mental, and emotional task of combat. *It's thicker than ever before as if they knew we were coming. I think this could be a trap.*

I think you're right. Can you take the ship, Dee? I

need to know now. We've got hundreds more Chiata porcusnails in system all of a sudden. Without that other BBD, I don't think we can take this system. I need to know, Dee. No bullshit.

Understood, DeathRay! Dee's mindvoice almost shouted. *Give me a minute!*

One minute, Dee. That's all you've got. Clock is ticking down now.

"Helm, QMT us right in the middle of that largest formation of porcusnails. We fire the BBD twice then jump randomly again. We pick one ship and target that one ship until it is done. All DEGs, all missiles, everything. Do it!" DeathRay ordered just as the next jump initiated. "We need to buy the Bringers some time by distracting the enemy fleet. Consider ourselves bait. At least it doesn't look like the Chiata know what we're doing with the target ship."

59 seconds, Dee. Her AIC started a clock counting down in her DTM mindview.

"Shit, on your three-nine, Azazel!" Dee grunted against the crushing pressure of the rapid g-forces from her whirling mad spin. One of the Chiata porcupines was in the analog of bot-mode and had her wrapped up with its black tendrils and was slinging her about like an octopus slinging a rag doll. Fortunately, the Chiata tendrils had only wrapped her up and not torn through her vehicle, or her. And fortunately, her mecha was anything but a rag doll. She'd been there and done that and had promised herself to avoid doing it again if there was any way she could prevent it.

Bree, jump us! she thought. *We've gotta break free of the alien bastard's grip!*

We are very close to interior structures, Dee, it isn't advisable, her AIC replied.

Then lock this coordinate, bounce us outside in the clear, then bounce us right back in!

That is *a good idea,* Bree agreed. *Done!*

Instantly Dee could see open space spinning around her and the battle going on outside. There were porcusnail megaships and blue beams zigzagging across the attack bowl. The *Penzington* and the rest of the attack fleet were way outnumbered. The target Chiata megaship had all four supercarriers jutting out of it where the clone captains had rammed it as part of the attack plan. The amalgamation of the five vehicles looked like a cross between a porcupine, a snail, and an alligator and several other wild mechanized concepts thrown in just for fun. There were Chiata porcupine fighters and mecha from the clone supercarriers duking it out in the engagement ball about the megaship. Dee could see that while she had been inside fighting toward the engine room, the fight on the outside of the ship had become a serious furball. The numbers game was getting out of hand and overwhelming and she was even more certain that they had fallen into a trap. And then tracers pinged into her forward shields as the red and green blur of an alien porcupine fighter locked in on her.

"Shit!" Dee yanked at the HOTAS but her mad spinning from her entanglement inside the ship was overwhelming the reaction control system. She was in a mad and uncontrolled pukin' deathblossom and there was an alien bastard lining her up in its crosshairs. "Shit, shit, shit! Bree, get us out of here!"

Reality space flashed. Just as quickly as she had been in open space Dee was back inside the targeted Chiata megaship near the engine room and exactly where she had been a brief second before. To her advantage, the previous twirling motion of her porcusnail attacker and the sudden loss of counterbalance mass, Dee's mecha, had carried it a few meters forward and off balance by the time she had bounced back inside the ship. Her spinning slowed almost instantly as she hit the atmosphere of the cabin and it became more manageable as she *banged* and *clanked* into the bulkheads bleeding off energy with each spin. But with each bang and clank her body was thrown hard against the restraints.

"Damn, that's gonna leave a mark," she grunted.

The tactic had worked well, placing her bot-mode mecha directly behind the amorphous red and green blur Chiata mecha that was now spinning out of control with more angular momentum than it could bleed off rapidly enough to keep Dee from targeting—she hoped. The problem was, Dee was spinning just as fast and needed to bleed off the angular velocity herself. And she was still a bit dizzy from her mad spin in free space.

But her years of training, fighting, and flying with DeathRay paid off. Like spinning out of a puking deathblossom maneuver Deanna used the momentum of her wild spin to carry herself over the alien mecha as the thing reached out with several tendrils. The tendrils groped at her and made metal-to-metal screeching sounds but they couldn't latch hold completely due to their mad relative whirling motions. The friction from the Chiata porcupine's tendrils, the bulkheads, atmosphere, and Dee's reaction control propulsion system slowed her just enough to enable a judo roll. Her mecha went careening, making a screeching sound like giant alien fingernails on a chalkboard, into the alien ship's bulkheads and deck plating, throwing white sparks and orange glowing metal cinders in every direction. She continued her roll until she almost had full control of it, bringing her to her feet with her cannon at the ready. Marine mecha jocks were known for eating their own puke for breakfast and going back for seconds at lunch. The spins the Chiata had induced on her were first-year cadet shit, nothing compared to the infamous pukin' deathblossom.

"I got this shit!" she growled through her TMJ bite block as stims and oxygen blasted her face and she choked back bile. As she righted her mecha and released her abdominal muscles long enough to take a deep breath, the targeting X in her mindview turned red and she hit the guns. The alien mecha was still changing shape with tendrils swinging about trying to get itself balanced and under control. But it was too late for it.

"Guns, guns, guns!" The first volleyball-sized green plasma balls zipped from the cannon overpowering the thing's personal shield system at such close range throwing a quick flicker of red and green energy across it. Dee didn't stop firing and the cannon rounds continued tearing through the amorphous armor of the alien fighter throwing plasma and shrapnel from secondary explosions in every direction. It ruptured at what might have been the seams, revealing the Chiata pilot inside. Dee leapt in a forward moving front flip, pulling her huge mecha feet up to her torso, then over, and then landing feet first as she stomped through the writhing alien creature's body crushing what remained of life from it. It made a dying screech as viscous red and green luminescent liquids splattered about her feet and the alien ship's deck plating. The creature's tendrils went limp and collapsed to the floor.

"There's you one Davy. Nice and messy the way you used to like it," she whispered as she toggled her bot to eagle-mode enabling her more speed. The mecha rolled forward and altered itself to look like a space fighter with talons of an eagle and mechanical arms. One of the arms held the cannon at the ready. Deanna slammed the HOTAS full forward and to the right toward her wingman.

Dee, Azazel is in trouble.

I see him, she thought. *Show me the energy curves.*

Roger that.

"Azazel, cut right!" He was being locked up. "Fox Three!"

The mecha-to-mecha missile ripped across the corridor into the back of the armored Chiata that was trying to get the drop on Azazel. The violet plasma from the propellantless engine glowed against the smoke from the battle damage and then burst into an orange and white explosion that ripped one of the tendrils clear of the alien mecha throwing burning viscous glowing fluids in every direction. Apparently, the alien blood was quite flammable as the glowing spray ignited with dazzling bursts of blue green flames.

Dee had gotten the creature's attention long enough for her wingman to QMT bounce out-and-in to a completely different position a few meters to the right of where he'd been. That truly caught the alien bastard off guard and unaware.

"Guns, guns, guns," Azazel shouted. The Chiata mecha was so taken by surprise that its response was much like that of a deer frozen in headlights of an oncoming vehicle—it got splattered. The plasma rounds overwhelmed the alien's armor and it was blasted to Hell and gone.

41 seconds, Dee.

Highlight the power conduits we have to hit. How far are we?

Here, here, and here, Bree replied as schematics of the ship appeared in her head. *One deck down and over. We are almost there. At our current pace and projected resistance there are still many timely attack solutions but there is no time to spare.*

Any reason to believe this ship is different from any of the others?

No.

Then get schematics from megaships we've got and overlay them on the battlescape.

"Warning—enemy targeting radar lock is imminent," her Bitchin' Betty chimed. "Warning—enemy targeting radar lock is imminent. Take evasive action . . ."

"What the fuck?" Dee spun her mindview and Bree quickly overlaid sensor and energy data and an alien porcupine in, again what Dee would call bot-mode, released several rounds in her and Azazel's general direction. It was clear that the thing was gunning for her as the rounds seemed to trace across to her.

"Look out, Major!" Azazel jumped into her, pushing both of them down into a roll. The plasma cannon rounds hit behind them, exploding into the alien ship bulkhead material. A gaping hole large enough to drive a hovertank through was blown out, the molten edges still glowing red hot. "Guns, guns, guns!"

"I got this shit!" Dee bounced up from the deck into a maximum speed run the FM-14X could do in bot-mode. She closed the forty-meter distance across to the alien continuously firing from the hip with her cannon. The alien did the same.

Like an Old West showdown, the two mecha dodged, dropped, jumped, rolled, and charged, constantly firing volleys at each other, missing and blowing out deck and bulkhead plating all around them with reckless abandon. Molten sparks flew, plasma rounds skittered about, and the noise of the two mecha going at each other was deafening.

"Guns, guns, guns!" Dee continued firing. One of the alien rounds grazed the shoulder of her mecha, knocking her sideways into a spin, but her shields held. She used the added momentum of the spin to sling her a full three hundred and sixty degrees around and into a diving tackle. As she tackled the alien, it launched a tendril at her. At first the shields held it off, but then the alien fired a plasma round point blank into her torso as they scuffled on the deck. That weakened her shields enough that the tendril ripped into her cockpit and jabbed at her suit.

Dee twisted her body out of the way twice as the

tendril stabbed at her and then she managed to grab it with her left hand. But now she was flying the mecha one-handed and struggling with the alien inside and outside the ship. She squeezed at the alien tendril with her mechanized gauntlet, afraid to let it go.

You've got to let the HOTAS go, Dee. I will take the controls until you can! Bree warned her. *Let them go and deal with the attack inside the cockpit!*

Fuck, fuck, fuck!

She let go with her right, grabbing the tendril and letting go of it with the left. Quickly, she deployed the blade from her left wrist and sliced through the tendril. Glowing red and green gunk squirted about the cabin and all over her. Instantly, the Thgreeth beetle sprang to life from its pouch on Dee's suit. The legs extended as it flew from her and into the alien's opened tendril with such speed that it was a blur itself.

"Get him, Skippy!" Dee shouted, detracting her blade and grabbing the HOTAS with both hands. She stomped the right pedal to the floor hard, kicking in the attitude control thrusters and inducing a spin on her bot. With all the mecha's power she pitched it back and upright ready to blast the bastard, but then it went completely limp and fell to the floor. Skippy bore through the exterior armor of the creature's faceplate and sat there idle. Dee extended her hand and it jumped up onto her mecha and skittered about finding some hidey-hole on the backside of her mecha to wait until such time as she could bring him back inside. The mecha self-repair system was already at full swing closing and repairing the damage done by the Chiata. The cockpit was airtight once again. The power indicator to the shields flashed from yellow to green. They were back online.

"Major, are you all right?" Azazel asked as his mecha clanked down next to hers.

"No! That took too much time and we have to move!"

I have the ship plans overlaid on our position, Dee. We have thirty seconds.

Calculate a jump point. Then jump me there. Dee knew it was risky, but they were out of time. Sometimes risks paid off. Sometimes you ended up melded to a bulkhead with your atoms starting a fusion fire with the metal there. She was banking on the former.

"Azazel, I'm bouncing to the target. Try to keep up if you can." Dee braced for the possibility of QMTing into a wall, but it didn't happen. She flashed in right where she needed to be. It looked just like the other ships she'd attacked over the past eighteen months. The long dull metal gray power conduits lined across the top of the corridor and twisted toward the belly of the ship where the power systems were. Red and green luminescent circuitry lined the pipes and the occasional blue flashes from Cerenkov radiation surrounded them.

"Fox! Fox!" she continued to say as she let missiles go that tracked into the bulkheads and power conduits creating blasts and secondary and tertiary explosions that followed down the tubes through the entire megaship. Large tens of meters-long electric arcs danced about as the conduits failed. Seconds later Azazel bounced in just to her left and began targeting the remaining power tubes and blasting away at them. Plasma ruptured from the conduits throwing more and more electric arcs across the room for several tens of meters creating strong dynamic fields that caused Dee's skin to tingle even through the mecha and her suit. There was an X-ray warning popping up in her mindview, but her suit would protect her. Fires and secondary explosions continued spreading along the path of the conduit. Most of the Cerenkov radiation ceased.

"Couldn't let you have all the fun," Azazel told her between blasts from his cannon. Dee was shocked.

"You almost made a joke, Azazel. And at the right time, even." She spun about, going to bot-mode drawing her cannon and tracked the highlighted conduits in her mindview. As the targeting Xs turned from yellow to red, she went to the plasma guns. Azazel again followed suit. The two FM-14Xs' weapons were formidable and wreaked havoc on the internal power flow systems of the alien ship. There was so much chaos from the erupting systems that the Chiata in the engine power room scattered with what seemed to be random fashion and, Dee hoped, fear. Occasionally one of them would attempt to get a bead on her or Azazel and fire through the fireballs and secondary explosions, but Dee and her wingman bounced about, making difficult targets of themselves. On two separate occasions, Skippy flew from wherever his hidey-hole had been on her mecha and devoured two of the unarmored Chiata and it only took him seconds for each.

"Guns, guns, guns," Azazel pressed on. "Watch your six, Phoenix. There's one trying to get the drop on you."

"Got it!" Dee dropped and rolled backwards and up to a knee bringing the large cannon up to her shoulder to fire it. Green glowing plasma spewed across the room tracking the alien. The targeting X turned red and the plasma balls hit home. "Must have been an engineer or something. He wasn't even wearing armor. And the ones Skippy got weren't wearing any either."

19 seconds, Dee.

"Bringers Bravo Team, give me a sitrep on the control room!" Dee looked at the blue force tracker for her squadron in her mindview and could see herself, her wingman, and the other four mecha from Alpha Team near her and engaging a hornet's nest of Chiata. About a kilometer up and forward of her was Bravo Team moving in on the bridge dome.

"Phoenix, this is Molloch."

"Go, Molloch!"

"Yes, ma'am. Bravo Team has taken the bridge and are holding it. The self-destruct sequence has been triggered. You must stop the feedback in the power conduit system within a minute or the ship will explode."

"Well, we've got less time than that or DeathRay is pulling us out," she replied. "Find a target and fire the BBDs as soon as we stop the self-destruct so he knows we have the ship!"

"Roger that."

10 seconds, Dee. The builder bots have already connected the Buckley weapon from the supercarriers, her AIC added. *As soon as you take out these conduits they can fire the weapon.*

"Guns, guns, guns!" she shouted over all the inputs crowding her mind. "Come on, Azazel, we've only got seconds."

Dee spun to her right just as a red and green blur

zipped past her. She did an out-and-in and came up just beside the armored Chiata, grabbing three tendrils with one of her mechanized hands. She popped two missiles loose from her shoulder harness and grabbed them with her free hand and stabbed them through the alien's midsection. In a mad whirl, she completed an aikido-style flowing circle taking the alien mecha's energy through the circle, generating crushing centrifugal force just as she let it go.

"Detonate the missiles now, Bree!"

The mecha squirmed and spun with tendrils flailing trying to get at the missiles that had been jabbed through it and just as a tendril pulled one clear it was too late. The alien mecha exploded at the instant it impacted the backflow energy conduit creating the self-destruct build up wave. The conduit and alien and the missiles exploded simultaneously, generating a blue-white fireball and a spherical burst of electrical discharges across the deck. The shock wave rocked both her and Azazel off their feet and onto their backsides with a resounding metal to metal *kathunk*.

"Phoenix, this is Molloch. The self-destruct build up has stopped. Preparing to fire the BBDs."

"Come on, Dee!" DeathRay said anxiously as he watched her minute tick away to seconds and then to zero.

"Do I order the snap-back, Admiral?" the XO asked. The Air Boss turned to watch their exchange as well. "The Bringers of Hell are out of time."

At that moment a blue beam erupted from the target

megaship and zigged across space between two ships in front of the *Penzington*, made a port turn, and then zagged directly into the same ship the gunner had been targeting.

"Hot damn! Nothing like waiting to the last second, Dee." Jack was elated. Dee had taken the ship and that blue beam of death from Hell was her signal of triumph. "We're not tucking tails and running just yet. Get me some Buckley weapon solutions."

"Admiral, CDC."

"Go, CDC."

"Sir, there appears to be more hyperspace activity about an astronomical unit out."

"I've got them, Admiral," the STO reported. "Looks like a completely new fleet of megaships."

"Shit." DeathRay took a deep breath and cleared his mind for the brief instant it took for the *Penzington* to perform her next quantum membrane out-and-in maneuver. As reality space appeared back on the viewscreens and DTM interfaces he had an idea.

"*Penzington*, this is Phoenix, copy?" Dee's voice penetrated the million inputs in Jack's head getting his attention.

"Go Dee!"

"The Bringers have stopped the self-destruct and the ship is under our control. If the Army tankheads want to help mop up in here they could join us," Dee announced over the control net.

"Great, Dee! Ground Boss, make that happen!"

"Aye sir."

"Dee, I'm sending an attack plan to you. Get the

Buckley weapon ready to fire as soon as you see the *Penzington* let hers loose, understood?"

"Affirmative."

Candis, you see where I'm going with this. Relay it to the bridge crew DTM.

Done, Jack.

"Alright helm, next bounce is right there in the middle of those ships an astronomical unit out." Jack highlighted the area in the bridge-wide direct to mind battlescape view so everyone was clear of his plan. "We pop back in on the outermost side of them, then gunner, as soon as we hit reality space, fire the Buckley weapon."

"Aye sir. Jumping in three, two, one."

Reality space phased out about the *Penzington* and then there was the ever-familiar brilliant white flash of light and the sizzle and crackle in Jack's ears. And just like that, they had moved several hundred thousand kilometers in the blink of an eye from one hornet's nest into another. And these hornets were fresh and ready to attack.

The Chiata ships around them were almost uncountable as they popped up in the nearscape view in DeathRay's mindview of the battle. The hornets turned to swarm but little did they know that Jack had the perfect bee zapper ready and waiting.

"Fire the Buckley weapon!" Jack ordered.

"Aye, sir."

The deck plates of the ship started to hum as the immense power surge from the converted alien power generators fed through the bot built supercarrier's Buckley-Freeman point barrier shield projectors.

Full-system wide battlescape DTM Candis, Jack

thought. *Share it with the bridge. And keep a pop out window open zoomed on us unless something else happens we need to see.*

Roger that.

A direct to mind projection of the system filled the room over his head. A battlescape sphere appeared near the center, filled with a magnified display. The *U.S.S. Nancy Penzington* was exactly in the middle of it, along with a small fleet of alien megaships. The blue force tracker icons filled the projection. Jack noted that the number of red dots was significantly higher than the blue dots. He hoped that the new out-and-in capabilities on the mecha was a force multiplier that would even the numbers a bit.

The *Penzington* looked like a strange giant alligator. The snail antennae that were the tuning forks for the big blue beams stood erect upwards and out of the top just a bit forward of the middle, and the four supercarriers jutted out on each side, two in the front and two in the back, as squatty mechanical legs gave her the appearance of something built from necessity and not for beauty. But to Jack she was perfect, the most beautiful thing he'd ever seen. And at that moment the Chiata were about to see that beauty up close and personal—the awful hellaciously deadly beautiful payback.

He was giving them payback for all the death the alien bastards had caused so far. It was only a drop in the bucket as far as he was concerned. They deserved a whole lot more killing. In his mind nothing short of genocide was good enough for the Chiata for killing his wife. Jack didn't realize it but a single tear rolled down his cheek as he unconsciously wept for his lost wife—the namesake of the Hell being brought to the Chiata bastards at the present moment. His suit quickly slurped the moisture into the organogel layer and recycled it.

Emanating from the toes of the strange beast at the nose of each of the supercarriers were the blue and white flickering Buckley-Freeman barrier energy shields. At the moment they were absorbing more energy from the quantum membrane that made up the universe than they could withhold within themselves. Since the age-old law of physics that energy could neither be created nor destroyed still held true, all that energy had to go somewhere. Fortunately—for the humans, that was—the brilliant chief engineer of the *U.S.S. Sienna Madira* had figured out where to send it in a previous engagement with the Chiata.

As the shields drew power from within the alien starship's membrane extraction system, the barrier spread from the tips of each of the alligator legs and grew and then thickened and darkened and continued to spread. The four separate barriers grew until they collided with each other and then melded into a sphere about the *Penzington*. The sphere of immense impenetrable energy grew and grew. And grew.

As the Buckley weapon redistributed the energy from the quantum membranes that made up the multiverse into reality space of this universe, the barrier continued to spread and the multitude of blue beams that zigged and zagged into it had little if no effect. Likewise, any matter the barrier came into contact with was instantaneously vaporized. The ball continued to grow out to about fifty

Earth radii or so, destroying everything in its path in a matter of seconds. It took another fifty Earth radii for the barrier to dissipate to negligible energy levels, inflicting various levels of damage to ships within it along the way.

The DTM battlescape popout view above them suddenly zoomed out and back into a second blast. The second Buckley weapon effect could be seen several hundred thousand kilometers aft and starboard and more inward to the system. Dee's team had fired the weapon and the alien megaships surrounding that ship were being vaporized.

"That should put a dent in them." DeathRay breathed a sigh of relief.

"Sir, they are still popping in and out of hyperspace further out." The XO turned and pointed at the battlescape, waving her hands until it zoomed farther out. "Look here, sir, at about ten astronomical units out."

"That has to be over a hundred more ships!" Jack exclaimed. "They knew we were coming. There are more ships here by orders of magnitude than we've ever faced. This damned engagement is a trap! STO, how long 'til we can fire the weapon again?"

"Several minutes, sir. It will take the bots and the fire crews some time to replace and reroute the burned-out conduits," the STO replied.

"Understood. Alright, keep up the out-and-ins and fire the BBDs and all weapons at will," he ordered.

"Sir, if it is a trap, shouldn't we make our exit?" the XO Teena clone asked. "We have never tested the main weapon for that many multiple shots."

"Good point, Seven," Jack replied as he reconsidered

their situation. "I say we push them until it becomes too much for us and then we get the hell out of here. Maybe we can steal another megaship to take home with us."

"Understood, sir," the XO acknowledged.

The alien ships in the battlescape ball began to hyperspace jump all around the *Penzington* and Dee's newly acquired ship. It didn't appear as if there was any intent to ram the ships, but the Chiata seemed to have developed some new tactic. They were jumping in so closely that they were almost rubbing into each other. Jack knew instantly what was about to happen, because it is exactly what the Separatists Hauler Battleships would do.

"Sound the alarms and stand by!" he shouted. "They're going to try and board us! Helm, start random jumps now!"

"I'm getting no response from the jump drives or the QMT controls, Admiral," the clone at the helm replied. DeathRay wasn't certain but he thought he could detect a slight amount of concern in the Mike clone's voice.

"CHENG to Captain," the chief engineer's voice sounded over the bridge speakers.

"Go, CHENG."

"Sir, the vortex projector will need another minute or so to recover enough energy after firing the main weapon," the CHENG said. "We will not have hyperspace drive for a bit."

"What about the QMT jumps?"

"They draw power from the same system, sir."

"How long, CHENG?"

"Two minutes. And I suspect the other ship is in similar shape."

"Get me some sort of jump back online CHENG. Now!"

"Aye sir."

"I am beginning to believe this actually was a trap, sir." The XO turned to him. "Maybe they want to see how our weapon works."

"They shouldn't know about it unless we've let some aliens escape previous attacks that we were unaware of," Jack said. "This stinks of something else. Ground Boss! Have the tankheads ready to engage as the damned aliens attack. Air Boss, get every mecha you can on the hull of this ship."

"Aye, sir."

"DeathRay to Phoenix!"

"Phoenix here!"

"Dee, we're about to have two very bad minutes."

"Understood, DeathRay. I see it coming. We could scuttle and snap-back with the wrist bands."

"Last resort, Dee, but if it gets too hairy over there you all snap-back to safety, understood?"

"Affirmative."

Chapter 6

July 24, 2409 AD
Chiata Kingship
Mission Star 74
Chiata Expanse
783 light-years from the Sol System
Saturday, 11:00 A.M. Eastern Time

"Yes, my fellow Kings of the Council of Prides, the prey has indeed engaged us as the Ally has foretold," the King of the System Pride explained through the Chiata instantaneous spacetime interconnect to all of the other Kings of all of the other Chiata Prides. "The Ally is turning out to be quite useful. Until such time as we have eradicated this prey I recommend keeping this Ally alive and at our side as best as possible."

"Are these prey as formidable as warned?" one of the Chiata asked.

"So far only a small handful of prey vessels have destroyed many hundreds of Hunterships and many tens of thousands of warriors. They are surprisingly vicious and efficient at combat."

"Is their intent determinable?" one of the kings asked.

"What are they after?" another king asked as well.

"Unclear at the moment, although they do seem to be focusing on capturing one specific Huntership. They are also being led by a modified Huntership that they did not get from my Pride System. I believe they might be on a raid to collect Hunterships to create their expanding sphere of death superweapon."

"Then the warriors' tales are true?"

"They somehow can destroy hundreds of ships at once?"

"Sounds like tales to scare cubs."

"It would appear that at least some of the tales may have credence. In fact they have used the expanding sphere of death on the modified Huntership already, along with that of the Huntership they just captured only moments ago from my Pride. Somehow, the prey are able to rapidly modify our technology to create this superweapon." The System Pride's king was not afraid of these prey, but there was concern growing in the Council. After all, there had been a loss of at least twelve kings in the past two solar rotations.

"We should take this superweapon for ourselves."

"Be cautious of these prey. We must take back one of the modified ships to see how they are managing this. And we need to understand the unexplainable teleportations they are able to manifest."

"Yes, I understand. The Ally has given us the technology to trap them here in my system and he has shown me how to hide forces inside hyperspace, keeping them hidden from sensors. My Pride *will* recapture this

Huntership and we *will* rid ourselves of this prey. I have just sprung my trap."

"Very good, King. Please keep us apprised of the progress."

"Of course, your majesties. Of course."

Chapter 7

July 24, 2409 AD
Mission Star 74
Chiata Expanse
783 light-years from the Sol System
Saturday, 11:00 A.M. Eastern Time

"CHENG! Where are my goddamned jumps?" Jack shouted at the Jacob clone through the ship's commandnet. "Thirty-one, we can't wait any longer!"

"Sorry, sir. It would appear the aliens have figured out just where to hit us to slow us down. The last several hits were precisely targeted and backed us up several minutes," the clone CHENG replied. "We fix one system and the Chiata blast another. We are holding engineering for now, sir, but I fear we cannot hold it much longer. If engineering is overrun the ship will be lost, Admiral."

"Understood, CHENG. Fix my goddamn jump drive!"

"Aye sir."

"Ground Boss! Where are the tanks?"

"They are fighting their way through the blurs on

decks twenty through twenty-three, Admiral Boland, but the numbers are just too great."

"Phoenix to DeathRay!" Dee's voice popped into the bridge audio pulling Jack further into the reality that they were in a trap and it was being sprung on them. They were aggressive rats after the cheese but somebody had just dumped a shitload of cats on top of them. At some point fighting all those cats wouldn't be worth holding onto the cheese. And the cheese wasn't going to be worth it if they got killed before they could eat it.

"Shit, what now," Jack asked her rhetorically because he suspected Dee's team was in the same situation he was. He could use her and her squad on the *Penzington* now. "Go, Dee!"

"DeathRay, I don't think we can hold this ship any longer. I have an idea though," Dee responded.

"I'm all ears, Dee," DeathRay said. "I'd piss on a sparkplug if I thought it'd help."

"We QMT the ships back to base with boarding parties and all. Then we get reinforcements to mop them up." Dee paused briefly before she finished. "My engineer tells me that if we just defend the main jump energy systems that the bots can have it going in another minute or two."

"Good idea, Dee." Jack turned and looked at the battlescape ball and decided the system was a fucking loss, but if they could get out with another megaship and superweapon it wouldn't have been a completely wasted mission. He opened an all hands channel reluctantly but with purpose.

"All hands, this is Admiral Boland. I'm calling all teams to the *Penzington* or the target ship whichever you were designated. Get out of the ball and into a ship now. Once there you will stay on board your designated ship and defend the energy conduit systems being highlighted in your DTMs now. We fight the aliens back so we can repair and jump. We will jump the instant the QMTs are online whether you are with us or not so don't get left behind. Make it happen, teams! Make it happen! Boland out."

Candis, he thought to his AIC. *Keep a real-time zoomed view of the critical systems of both ships' jump systems up for the bridge crew. And give me an ETA clock for repair completion to jump. And keep track on all personnel. I know I said it, but I ain't leaving anyone behind, understood?*

Roger that, Jack.

And I want you to monitor both engineering teams constantly and let me know immediately if it looks like they are running into any hiccups.

Affirmative.

"Roger that, DeathRay," Dee replied as she switched channels back to her teams. "You heard the admiral. We get this ship ready to go and get out of here now!"

The supercarriers designed for the taking of a megaship were still supercarriers. While they could be run on auto by various AIs they still had a skeleton crew, a minimal defense team, and just about as many builder bots as could be stuffed in them. Millions of the bots would flood the Chiata megaship after it was rammed. That was the plan that had worked over a dozen times before. But this time there were so many more Chiata than ever before and they were still coming. Dee pulled up the icon for the clone CHENGs for the four supercarriers and opened a channel direct to them.

"Okay CHENGs, you heard the admiral. How long until we can QMT the fuck out of here?"

"Major Moore, we are good to go on three of the four systems presently," the ranking CHENG began. "The Chiata have concentrated their efforts on our connections between ship two here at the forward port position and the alien megaship. It is possible that we could adjust the calculations and simply encompass a larger sphere and snap back to the FOB now."

"Then do it! Do it and we'll get reinforcements there!" Dee was ready to get the hell out of that system. The flood of aliens continued to pour in on them and it didn't look like it would change anytime soon. She knew for sure that if they continued fighting the never-ending flood of alien blurs, porcupines, and megaship porcusnails they were going to die. She had too much killing to do and too much Hell to bring before she could allow that to happen.

"Yes, Major," the CHENGs replied in clone unison.

"DeathRay, this is Phoenix! Our systems are ready enough. Permission to QMT to FOB!"

"Go, Dee. If you can jump, get the Hell out of here."

"Roger that, Admiral. Don't stay behind too long."

"Don't worry about us, Dee. Get your ass home."

"Affirmative. Good luck, Admiral Boland. Phoenix out," Dee said hoping he would get his ass home safely. Dee wasn't sure her psyche could handle another major loss.

Dee looked at the blue force icons in her DTM as she

bounced around the corridor just outside of main engineering on the Chiata ship blasting away at any Chiata in her path. An alien blur zipped by her, wrapping one of the biomechanical black tendrils around her mecha, giving it a spin. Dee whirled around like a top firing her boot jets and rear thrusters doing her best to right herself. She flailed out with her left mechanized hand tearing through the bulkhead to make a handhold. Her grasp halted her spin, allowing her to stand upright and go to her guns. She burst through the bulkhead with her plasma cannons hot on the tail of the blur that had just engaged her.

The blur led her up several decks trading volleys of plasma and directed energy fire. Several times Azazel almost managed to head the alien off but he never was able to get a clean shot. Then he picked up a tail and the two of them were having a difficult time covering each other's asses.

"Azazel, I've had enough of this shit!" She looked at the blue energy lines of their two fighters overlaid on the ship's internal map and at all the red dots and lines bouncing about them. Clearly two of the lines were intertwined with theirs and were anticipating every move they were making.

"What do you propose, Major?" her wingman asked.

"Keep an eye on the QMT clock, but otherwise, I'm going to out-and-in on this mother!" She thought about her strategy for just a moment as she scrolled through the map. Then she saw the perfect spot for a killing field. "Here, Azazel. Push to this chamber and I'll be there and trigger happy. You have five seconds. Go!"

Four, three, two . . .

Now, Bree!

Dee's mecha popped out of reality space and then back in just a few hundred meters in front of Azazel and the alien blurs on their tails. Her plan had worked. When she had popped out of reality her tail had joined in the closest target, which had been her wingman. Azazel was holding his own, but couldn't last forever like that. He didn't have to.

"Major, now would be as good a time as any for you to engage," he said just as his mecha ran past her at over a hundred kilometers per hour screeching, scraping, and pounding the bulkheads and deck plating throwing sparks and plasma fire in all directions.

"Fox Three! Fox Three! Guns guns guns!" Dee locked on to the two blurs just as they burst into the room behind him. "I've got 'em!"

Dee kept on her guns until the two red dots in her mind turned black and then vanished. In reality space in front of her they weren't black dots at all. They were burning and exploding orange and white plasma fires. *Davy would have been proud.*

Dee checked the QMT clock and they still had some time so she scanned the battlescape DTM for any teams that might need some extra firepower and, for the most part, more Chiata that needed killing.

Several tankheads were holding their own against the Chiata near her and Azazel. They were presently three decks below the command bubble of the megaship doing their best to keep the aliens off the command team up there. But they'd soon be overrun if they didn't get reinforcements. Dee considered herself just that.

"Guns, guns, guns!" She squeezed the trigger on the HOTAS and then toggled from bot-mode to eagle-mode, kicking in the propellantless drive for more speed. "Listen up, everyone! No more out-and-ins until I say. We are too close now to the jump. The CHENGs are about to snap us back to the FOB."

The countdown clock was being transmitted through the blue force DTM to the entire fleet. It wound down to zero and then there was a brief flash of white and blue light and some sparkles in Dee's eyes but there was no sound of bacon frying or the prolonged flashes a standard QMT typically generated. Something was wrong with the jump.

"Engineering! What the hell is happening?" she exclaimed.

"The engines are running, but we went nowhere," the clones all answered again almost in unison.

"Why not!"

"It would appear that this solar system has a damping technology in place somewhere. I do not believe we can leave it."

"Shit! Shit! Shit! Tell DeathRay and dump all data you have to the *Penzington*!" Dee slammed her armored fist against the canopy of her mecha, with each outburst causing her personal barrier system to flicker greens and blues as she did. She screamed again several times at the top of her lungs. She had been trapped by the Chiata before and didn't want to be there again.

"Phoenix, in front of you," Azazel warned her.

Keep it frosty, Marine! Bree scolded her.

Frosty my ass.

Several red and green blurs zipped across the corridor below her and toward the aft end of the large chamber. They were getting position on her and without the out-and-ins they could target her mecha easier.

"Warning! Enemy radar targeting lock imminent! Warning . . ." Her Bitchin' Betty chimed at her warning that she was being targeted.

"Yeah, no shit," she muttered.

"They're going to lock you up, Major!" Azazel sounded frantic for the first time ever.

"All teams, the QMT out of system is nonfunctional! I repeat, we are stuck here in this system! Out-and-ins appear to be working still, so do that and stay alive. More instructions on the way!" she announced and hit the QMT jump system. Her mecha did a quick out-and-in. "At least that shit works."

Why does that work and not the bigger QMTs?

I'm asking the CHENG and STO AICs, Dee, her AIC told her.

Keep me posted!

Roger that.

"Dee, this is DeathRay. We cannot hold these ships much longer. I'm sending coordinates for ramming targets. We will scuttle your ship and pull everyone to the *Penzington*. If you can, give me one more shot with the Buckley weapon and then blow it up. Maybe we can hold out on the *Penzington* until we can figure out how to get the hell out of here!"

Chapter 8

July 24, 2409 AD
61 Ursae Majoris C
31 light-years from the Sol System
Saturday, 11:30 A.M. Sol System Eastern Time
(1:30 P.M. 61 Ursae Majoris C Capitol
Standard Time)

Copernicus stood before the shimmering control wall of
the giant QMT facility in the system's Kuiper Belt intent
with purpose and satisfied that now after thousands of
years of planning the time had come at long last. The
culmination of so many millennia of planning and work
was coming. It was finally time. His human brain was
flooded with odd sensations that as a symbiont he'd have
never felt. While he hadn't actually had a scheduled date
and time for it, events had shaped themselves into the
perfect chance for his final moves on the chessboard.
Madira was gone and so was the majority of the human
fleet. Their leading general and megaship captains would
be inaccessible to the humans, if his plans worked the way
he expected, for a long time to come if not forever.

He worked at the quantum foam that was the control wall for the giant construct. His thoughts were scattered as he considered all the years of work leading up to where he was to what was about to happen. He was letting himself be distracted from the immediate work at hand. He wondered if that distraction was a function of the human brain and body he was in or if all the years in exile had made it more difficult to stay on focus. If it was the body and brain, well, he hoped to fix that issue before too much longer.

The facility itself was the largest of any of the nearby Kuiper Belt planetoids and an absolute technological marvel beyond anything the simple humans could even imagine. Not even the most brilliant among them had any comprehension, the slightest inkling, of what the facility's main purpose was. Even Sienna Madira, as brilliant as she was and with all the enhancements to her mind that he had done over the centuries, had no way of knowing what the facility could do.

It had taken him centuries to build it. The planetoid-sized device had originally been created as a weapon to combat the Thgreeth, but then the Chiata had arrived and changed all his plans and changed its purpose. Fortunately for Copernicus, its original purpose was very malleable and thus he molded and reshaped it towards new ends that until recently hadn't included the Thgreeth any longer.

The Thgreeth had fought his race to a stalemate many millennia before and an uneasy peace had been created in the galaxy. As much as they had fought the Thgreeth and experimented on their physiology, he could not find a natural means of parasitically controlling the species.

Their independence and free will made them quite an adversary. And then there was the rise of the galactic court and commerce system whereby that unsurmountable drive for free will spread like an infectious disease across the outer arms of the galaxy. His plans within plans were almost laid to waste by the advanced alien culture once they began to align themselves with the other races of the galaxy. But then the Chiata arrived and changed all of his plans within plans within plans—some for the better where the Thgreeth were concerned, but mostly for the worse in all other regards.

The Kingdom of D'lraouth had once expanded over five thousand light-years radially from the galactic center from one side of the Perseus Arm to the other and in more than seven thousand light-years along the circumference of that arm. The arm being one out from the Orion Spur of the Sagittarius Arm where the humans were found thousands of years later and one in from the outermost arm not including the Monoceros Ring where it now appeared the Thgreeth had retreated to. Copernicus had long thought they were extinct until Madira's granddaughter recently encountered one of them. Plans had to be altered with this new knowledge.

There had been hundreds of thousands of worlds the D'lraouth had taken and implanted with infant parasites and symbiont hosts. Countless connected civilizations were created under his reign. When any of these worlds already had sentient inhabitants, they were either controlled, enslaved, or destroyed. After all, nonsubservient sentience had proven to be a nuisance to the D'lraouth in all encounters.

The war machine of the D'lraouth was simple and elegant—infect, control, conquer, move on. The species were the perfect Von Neumann probes. And then they encountered the Thgreeth who were a species that celebrated free will among sentient creatures above all things. Free will was such an opposition concept to the D'lraouth that to them it was truly evil incarnate. All creatures in the universe must be D'lraouth. D'lraouth himself knew that free will was a myth and that it only led to chaos and destruction. And so began the millennia-long conflict.

D'lraouth, now Copernicus, knew then that time would be on his side. His species could wait out almost anything and that included the eventual collapse of haphazard concepts such as free will and of civilizations such as the Thgreeth. So he waited. And he waited.

But the Thgreeth were better at governing themselves and their collective free will than any the D'lraouth had seen prior. While the war raged between them, and the galactic chess game continued, the king and queen of the D'lraouth began to note that they were losing world after world to the Thgreeth, which contradicted the simulations of their planning. With each new world taken, the Thgreeth would liberate two. If history were to continue along the same path then in a few tens of thousands of years the Thgreeth would finally overtake the D'lraouth.

The problem with the Thgreeth's liberation wasn't that the parasites were removed and sent home. Thus far, no species in the galaxy, including the Thgreeth and D'lraouth, had any technology that would enable a separation of parasite from host without killing the host. This practically led to a symbiont hunt where any creature found attached to the D'lraouth had to be exterminated. And where the Thgreeth were concerned that usually meant exterminating the parasite with the host.

The war between the Thgreeth and the D'lraouth went on and on and on. Both sides were getting bogged down in the dismal fog of the millennial war. That was when Copernicus had his eureka moment. Then the idea of the quantum membrane consciousness transfer overpowered him. If he could not control the Thgreeth parasitically, then he must find a way to do it within the laws of physics that governed the multiverse. It had become all he could focus on until it consumed his every thought. Centuries of research, testing the concepts on lesser sentient species, and finally on himself, led him to an answer. The capability could be realized that would allow him to capture Thgreeth and transfer control over them without having to make parasitic connections with the host. It was possible and only he knew how to do it.

And then the Chiata had arrived, laying waste to his plans within plans. And then the Chiata arrived and drove his enemy out of the system. It wasn't until Deanna Moore had fought the Chiata singlehandedly and taken control of an ancient Thgreeth teleportation nexus that Copernicus had learned that the Thgreeth might still exist out there in the galaxy somewhere and he still might have to deal with them. These humans continually generated unforeseen anomalies in his calculations. Madira had warned him to accept noncomputability as part of human nature and to allow for randomness and forcing functions in completely unexpected directions in any models, simulations, and particularly in his plans.

For a human with a limited knowledge base, Sienna Madira had continuously surprised him with her astute wisdom and intellect. He knew that very soon she would become too much of a risk to his plans to allow her to live. In fact, all of the descendants of herself and her son-in-law would have to be removed. He hoped that was currently taking place hundreds of light-years away.

When the Chiata came and devastated civilization after civilization on the outer arms of the Milky Way galaxy, as the humans called it, the armies of the galaxy fought the Chiata to a slow advance, extremely slow. But it was still an advance nonetheless. The galactic court system sent emissaries to the Chiata and a false truce had been established. The Chiata would face no resistance to taking unprotected and unadvanced civilizations. And that was where business and politics became weapons. Various alien cultures throughout the galaxy started purchasing futures on undeveloped systems and they filed claims of ownership and therefore the Galactic Defense Alliance had no choice but to defend them. In many cases, the Chiata either didn't recognize the claims of ownership or simply didn't care and continued to move forward with their attack wave. In some cases they were slowed, but the Galactic Defense Alliance had never stopped them.

The Chiata rolled right through the Kingdom of D'lraouth and laid waste to all of his domain. Copernicus managed to pull billions of his people back until the last of them were trapped in their original home system. The armies of the galaxy were no match for the Chiata and it was then that Copernicus pulled all of his people that still remained from their parasite minds and host bodies. He didn't have the time or ships to gather billions of his parasite brethren up and fly them away to safety. His only hope of saving his people was to save their minds. And that is what he did. He stored away as many parasite bodies as he could manage for future experiments and perhaps cloning, but more importantly he downloaded over nine billion minds, and stored them, the survivors nothing more than a quantum consciousness stored on vastly entangled and intertwined quantum membrane storage oscillators encoded in the quantum vacuum energy fluctuations of space and time.

It was then that he began jumping his facility and his people using what the humans would eventually call the "sling-forward" technology as far from the Chiata as he could manage. After years of jumps he came to where he was at the moment. He searched the nearby stars for suitable vessels until finally he found the Sol system. After all those years of searching he had finally discovered the humans. He studied them and realized that they were perfect vessels for his people. Then he devised a plan. Then he went to the Galactic Courts and he bought the futures on the human system and those surrounding it within twenty or so light-years. It was then that he studied every living human being in the system until he found just the right one. He experimented with several humans throughout time but never quite found what he was looking for. Choosing the right human took several centuries more but the D'lraouth were a patient species. Very patient.

Then he found her, a young Senator Sienna Madira. Once he had studied her intently and realized that she would be the right one, he had set his plans into motion.

The wall rippled as the quantum fabric of the universe twisted and rolled and correlated itself with the commands he input. Copernicus had almost let himself become lost in his memories and relishing of a moment he'd awaited for tens of thousands of years.

"Is there nothing more you require of us, sir?" the lead assistant and bodyguard that Sienna Madira had assigned to him asked. Copernicus looked specifically at the large Malcolm clone and realized why Sienna had assigned him as his bodyguard. It wasn't because Copernicus needed protecting, but because Sienna didn't trust him. Copernicus smiled inwardly and mumbled to himself, "And rightly so. I made you so much more than you ever would have been, Sienna."

"Sir?" the Malcolm clone asked. The other two clones standing flank, a Teena and a Sarah, stood quietly showing no particular interest or expression.

"Sorry, I was speaking to myself. Nothing just yet. I appreciate your willingness to help," he said with a smirk. Then, as Copernicus extracted one of his hands from the quantum randomness, the shimmering surface of the wall clung to him like molasses, a silvery shiny molasses with the consistency of liquid mercury. "I would like to tell the three of you that you have performed your jobs as your leader assigned you perfectly and that your lives should be commended. I thank you, my people thank you, and the Kingdom of D'lraouth thanks you for your sacrifices."

"Sir?" the Malcolm clone said with a puzzled look. Copernicus just smiled back in return.

An arc of the silvery quantum liquid leapt from the wall and engulfed the Malcolm clone's head. The other two clones reacted almost instantly and drew their weapons, but even AI-driven clones weren't fast enough. Two other glowing silvery liquid mercury like fractal shaped tendrils shot from the rippling wall and grabbed them by the tops of their heads. The liquid quickly covered their faces and penetrated their eyes, nose, mouth, and ears. The clone bodies became limp and dangled from beneath the quantum foam fractal appendages of the interface wall. Ripples of white and blue light surged back and forth along the appendages as if tremendous amounts of data were being transferred over optical interface fibers. The light ripples increased in frequency and shifted further into the blue.

Copernicus stood aside with one hand still in the control wall keeping the link between his mind and the facility functioning. He pulled up the direct-to-mind interface with the facility that he had never shown to the humans and suddenly a list of billions of alien symbols appeared before him. Copernicus searched through the symbols briefly until he found the one he was looking for.

"Hello, my dear," he said out loud as he selected the symbol and activated another command.

"Download initiated," a voice suddenly said. "I am . . . now activated."

"Very good, Yeventha. I have missed you, my friend." Copernicus smiled and continued to activate other icons. "I am D'lraouth."

"Download complete," the voice replied. "Master D'lraouth, my body and processors are not . . . not here. How can I serve you without my systems?"

"My friend, you are to engulf and facilitate this complex. It will be your new body. There is an implant in this body's brain that you are to connect to and stay connected to me at all times. Do you understand?"

"Yes master, I do. This new body is massive and quite . . . pleasing. Is there anything else?"

"There is much and we shall get to that in due time. For now, search the repository for Queen Ifgeentha, Prince Rephonja, and General Freefth."

"I have located their presences," Yeventha said. "What are your commands?"

"Place General Freefth in this vessel here, the Queen here, and Rephonja here," he said as he highlighted which clone for which mind.

"Yes, your majesty." Copernicus smiled at being called that. He hadn't heard that in a long, long time. It felt *good*.

"Yeventha, I want you to use the sensors on this vessel and search this entire system's lifeforms. You will see many like these three here with no quantum transceivers in their brains. That will make up the majority of the system population. These are clones with AI sentients loaded into them. They will require direct contact to load, like these vessels you are presently connecting with. There will be others that have quantum transceivers installed and in direct connection with their brains. These are natural-born humans with AI assistants installed. Identify all of these humans in the system."

"Yes, master, there are approximately forty-seven-thousand of these vessels presently in the system."

"Yes, Yeventha, yes! That will be enough. You are to take the top forty seven thousand of our people and load them into these vessels via the QMT connections within their assistants. And immediately teleport them here to this facility."

"Master, there are sentient presences in each of these vessels. Would you like me to store them?"

"Erase them."

"As you wish, Master."

Chapter 9

July 24, 2409 AD
U.S.S. Sienna Madira III
Thgreeth Abandoned Outpost Planet
Deep in Expanse
700 light-years from the Sol System
Saturday, 11:37 A.M. Eastern Time

"My fleet is ready and has skeleton crews of my people right now!" Sienna Madira told them. Alexander always found it interesting that she called the clones "my people". After all, Madira was born on Earth and purely human as far as he knew. The clones were manufactured by hybridizing from humanity and whatever Copernicus was. And the things were merely vessels for the artificial intelligence counterpart controlling them. Alexander wasn't sure they were truly a "people" but now wasn't the time to split hairs about the issue.

He turned to the DTM view that was being transmitted to the bridge of the hybrid bot swarm reconfigured Chiata megaship and human/clone designed supercarriers combination that was the *U.S.S. Sienna Madira III*.

"Look how many megaships the Chiata have in the system," he added.

"No matter," Madira interrupted him. "You have eleven functional megaships of your own with the Buckley superweapon and at least one already in that system— maybe two by now, knowing your daughter and Admiral Boland. I'm here in my flagship with ten fully crewed ships for support. I just delivered seventy-two more supercarriers with skeleton crews fully loaded with bots and Buckley-Freeman barrier shields and the new quantum jump FM-14Xs. The existing fleet ships here are now loaded and ready to go with the new fighters as well. We are loaded for bear on all our ships. What are we waiting for, son?"

"It's a trap, Sienna. The QMT systems will let us in but not out. And the thing that has me unsettled here is that it isn't a system blocking all QMTs. It is a cage that allows QMTs within it," Moore replied while all the time thinking to himself, *I'm not your fucking son.*

She is your mother in-law sir, his AIC added in jest.

I married Sehera not her. You were there. You know what a horrific evil bitch she was. Her present status notwithstanding, I'd still like to rip her goddamned head off and vaporize what's left of her and piss on any remaining dust just for my men that she slaughtered.

Yes sir. How would your wife feel about that?

At the time Elle Ahmi was torturing me probably the same. When she learned that the crazy bitch had killed her father, probably the same. Now? Now that she is back

*to being Sienna Madira, the savior of humanity, I, uh, I
just don't know.*

I understand, sir.

I'm not sure I do.

"A cage sir?" the XO, Sally "Firestorm" Rheims asked.
It shook him from his other distracting and troubling
thoughts. Moore turned to his longtime executive officer
and nodded.

"Firestorm, why are they letting our fleet QMT inside
the boundary of the QMT suppression field?" He asked
rhetorically because he was pretty damned sure he knew
the answer. "And on top of that, why are they letting our
ships QMT inside the bubble?"

"You've got me, sir."

"Alexander, what is it?" Sehera's avatar asked. She was
still on the planet in the Thgreeth ruins below with the
science and archaeology teams.

"They want us in there and distracted for a long
amount of time," he replied. "If they wanted us dead they
would suppress the QMTs within the trap and make us
sitting ducks. But with the QMTs we can jump around
and hold our own, maybe as long as we need to. No, this
isn't a kill box, it is a cage."

"Sir, battle sims show that the expeditionary ships
presently in the system will last no longer than an hour in
there," the science and technology officer pointed out.
"And maximum hyperspace speeds would take them
about two weeks to get out of it."

"Alexander, you do what you want," Sienna Madira
grunted at him. "I don't answer to you or your command
structure any longer. My people and your daughter are

trapped in there and I'm going to get her with or without your help."

Moore started to respond but held his tongue. He was certain that Madira chose her words carefully and emphasized it was his daughter to make the point that it was her granddaughter, but human history still had yet to uncover that bit of information or the fact that Sienna Madira had been Elle Ahmi, terrorist and mass murderer. For now, Alexander was happy with that bit of history being hidden from public view.

Besides, *his* daughter was a tough as hell by God U.S. Marine mecha jock who had come out of some of the worst combat anyone had ever heard of and could take care of almost any situation. But Alexander wasn't kidding anyone with that type of bravado. Dee was his daughter, his princess. He wanted to slap Madira dead for even considering that he was going to leave his princess in there to die. But at the same time, once they were in there, they were in there. From the images in the Thgreeth ruin's system it appeared as though the thickness of the bubble from inside radius to the outside radius of the QMT suppression boundary was nearly a light year. As the STO had just pointed out to him, that would take weeks at maximum hyperspace jaunt speeds and the Chiata hyperspace jaunts are much faster. The fleet would drop out of hyperspace right into a kill box, again. But just maybe they'd be clear of the damping field and could QMT snap back out of there with minimal losses.

"Why and how are the Chiata doing this?" The XO shrugged. "How'd they know we were coming? And who gave them the goddamned QMT damping tech?"

"Good questions all, Firestorm, but it doesn't change the fact that we have many thousands in system trapped and being attrited more and more with every second." Alexander took in a long breath and let himself relax his mind for a moment. He watched several battle simulations in his mind that Abigail ran for him. None of which had high probabilities of success. He needed a plan to get his people out and to get to the bottom of what was happening. If it were ever time for a good plan, maybe even a plan within a plan, now was the time.

"Son, sometimes, the best way to figure out who is setting a trap is to spring the trap," Madira added holding up her wrist band as if she were about to snap back to her ship. "I'm going back to my ship and preparing to jump. Are you coming or not?"

Abigail, are we battle ready? he thought to his AIC.

Yes sir. The ship is in full optimal condition according to Chief Engineer Buckley's AIC, Abigail replied.

Start working on a way get us out of there.

Of course, sir.

"Air Boss, tell the CAG that she is just going to have to get training in the new mecha while under fire," he ordered. "Helm start the calculations for a full fleet jump into the target star system."

"Aye, sir!"

"Alright, Madira, get your fleet ready. Perhaps, if we hit them in two waves from different locations we'll catch them off guard. I think we drop in at a safe distance from our people and fire half of our Buckley weapons. That should distract them enough so that we can then use the other ships to move in and support our people. I say we bounce our fighters out as soon as we get there and put them right in behind the assholes locked up on our jocks. That should mix them up a bit. I'll have battle plans sent to you all ASAP."

"Good, son. We'll be ready in five minutes." Madira flashed out.

I'm not your fucking son, he thought.

"Sehera, keep working with that Thgreeth system and see if you can figure anything out," he told his wife.

"We will. Alexander, bring her home."

"We will."

Chapter 10

July 24, 2409 AD
Mission Star 74
Chiata Expanse
783 light-years from the Sol System
Saturday, 11:51 A.M. Eastern Time

Molloch sat still in his bot-mode FM-14X and watched as the builder bots continued to keep the bridge of the Chiata megaship functioning and connected to his systems. The bots scurried about like ants and spiders and various other creepy crawlies with bizane engineering tool appendages and each with its own job welding, making structural or electrical connections, keeping the bridge controls functioning, and acting as rapid automated coders continually hacking away at the Chiata software safety mechanisms and firewalls. The giant transparent structural dome covering the oversized bridge was holding up for the time being, but Molloch could see the occasional porcupine engage and attempt to blast through it. The automated safety systems were the first things the bots had hacked and they had full control of the interdiction cannons of the alien megaship's exterior. And they were blasting away at every target of interest the systems could detect.

The rest of the Bravo Team of the Bringers of Hell were keeping Molloch's ass covered so he could manage the Chiata targeting systems DTM in order to find targets and fire the BBDs as well as to keep the superweapon functional. The actual triggering of the superweapon took some serious coordination from the Chiata megaship's bridge and the four bridges of each of the supercarriers that were connected to it. In time the builder bots and the engineers would automate and route all of the supercarrier functions to this bridge, leaving the others as backups, but for now there was still coordination between them all required. It was a lot of data to accumulate and understand, even for an AI-driven clone, so he certainly wouldn't be doing much hand-to-hand fighting in the process. But the rest of Bravo Team would do the fighting in order to give him time to focus on his job, running the new megaship.

He could see his wingman Abaddon in his mindview just outside the bulkhead and slightly beyond the platform door entrenched and entangled with several tendril wielding blurs at once. The other four Bravo Team mecha were mixing it up and bouncing to and fro like jackrabbits on amphetamines. Major Moore's Alpha Team were just beyond that doing their level best to create a first line of defense, but as fast as the Chiata were and as big as the porcusnail megaship was, that "line" was more of a roving blob. And if Molloch's calculations were correct, and they usually were to within tiny fractions, the numbers game was going to take its toll on the Bringers of Hell and the Chiata would overrun them within the next couple of minutes. He wasn't certain if they would be in position and ready to fire the superweapon with any time to spare.

For the briefest of moments Molloch let himself take in the brilliant orange and white fireball flashes of alien mecha fighters being blasted by the interdiction fire, the Big Blue Beams of Death from Hell as they zigged and zagged across space, the red and green directed energy beams from the supercarriers, and the vastness of it all. There were thousands of alien targets zipping about and so much motion and change taking place that any normal human might have an epileptic seizure just by trying to make sense of it.

The AI-driven clone realized just how impressive the human soldiers truly were to not only handle the stimulus but also the overwhelming emotions of anger and fear of dying all at the same time. But for the clones, their emotions were simply more data to account for and to manage. If they needed to, they could simply ignore the particular data streams that might cause them problems. Molloch wondered if that was how the human soldiers handled it. But he didn't wonder for more than a half of a second or so because he had a job to do.

"Phoenix, this is Molloch, copy?"

"Phoenix here, copy Molloch."

"I've identified an optimum shot for the BBDs and then we need to perform a hyperspace jump to the right location for firing the superweapon. It is online but is still charging. We need about two minutes. I'm sending the battlescape coordinates now." Molloch explained to his leader. "I am telling you this because we need to hold off on any QMT out-and-ins during the hyperspace jaunt."

"Understood, Molloch. Do that shit quickly because we can't hold this ship much longer. We'll cover your ass as long as we can, but once we've fired the superweapon our orders are to destroy this ship and snap back to the *Penzington*. Things are getting rough over there. Understood?" Dee ordered him.

"Roger that, Major. The battle sims show that if we don't fire the superweapon our casualties will be significantly higher and maybe even catastrophic."

"Understood, Molloch. You will have time to fire the weapon. I'll see to it."

"Understood, Phoenix."

The red and green blurs continued to pour in like water through a sieve and it was all the Bringers of Hell could do to keep them from breaking through their defensive swarm and rush the bridge of the megaship. The fighting was getting thicker and thicker and Dee didn't like the fact that they had just busted ass to take this ship and now they were going to have to give it up. Three buzzsaw bots spun wildly about her and Azazel's mecha chewing away as best they could at the ungodly fast aliens. One of the little metal menaces was speared clean through by an alien tendril just in front of her. Sparks flew as the bot attempted to saw its way free but the Chiata infantryman had it dead to rights. Dee wasn't going to let the menacing bot's self-sacrifice go to waste.

"Guns, guns, guns," she said and continuously fired her cannon through the alien until its shields flickered green and then out. The alien let out a guttural growl as it shot tendrils out in several directions but then its armor collapsed and the alien finally exploded from within. The armored Chiata flailed like a squid out of water on the deck plating spewing glowing fluids and screeching at audible pitches that would scare an obese female opera performer and shatter glass even quicker. It seemed to also excite Skippy as the little beetle flung itself onto the carnage and finished it off quickly. As the beetle devoured the alien it screeched and howled like a dying screech owl.

The dying alien's screams seemed to pull the attention of one of the other blurs that then seemed to put a bullseye on Dee. The creature tore through a handful of buzzsaw bots making a beeline for her all the while firing giant red and green plasma bolts at her. A couple rounds bounced off her shields, knocking her backwards, but she was fast enough on the HOTAS and the bottom right foot pedals to spin sideways and drop to a knee returning fire. Dee made a mental note that this was the first time she'd seen some sort of bonding between the aliens. She hoped with all her heart that they were best friends, or better yet, lovers. She smiled inwardly at the thought that she might have just taken one of the bastard's mates.

"I'll get this one for you too, Davy," she said through her bite block as she gnashed her teeth against it. Her inward smile almost turning into a real one. It was an insane violent crazy looking smile but real nonetheless.

She didn't smile long, though. Alien plasma balls and directed energy bounced against her mecha's shielding again and the red and a green blur rushed her flinging spearheaded tendrils at her seemingly from all directions.

She rolled her bot-mode mecha over into a backwards somersault to dodge several tendrils from the infantry Chiata. She grabbed the tendril just as it passed by her shoulder and yanked on it as she continued with the momentum of her flip twisting her body around to a kick over and then down onto a knee. She used the centrifugal force of her mecha rolling over like a combination of a karate and judo roll to sling the alien over her and into the transparent bulkhead looking out into space. Azazel landed just before her with his cannon raised in his left mechanized hand and poured volleyball-sized plasma balls into the creature's midsection. Phosphorescent red and green liquids, plasma fire, and sparking glowing white hot metal debris ripped into the window just as First Lieutenant Kali and her wingman Second Lieutenant Ifrit dropped past them back to back whirling and firing their plasma cannons and missiles like a bot-mode mecha tornado. Dee checked her blue force tracker and could see the other two members of Alpha Team, First Lieutenant Raum and his wingman Second Lieutenant Shedim were doing out-and-ins along each other's energy trajectories inside the extremely close ball of the hangar and platform elevator closing in on the only remaining Chiata mecha in that area of the ship.

The Bringers of Hell were doing what they did best, bringing Hell. Then the chamber was lit up brilliantly by a white and blue flicker as a giant blue beam of death from Hell zigged out from the megaship's spires across space into a distant porcusnail.

"Ooh-fuckin'-rah Molloch!" Deanna grunted through her mouthpiece.

The BBD hit dead on the weakest point of the alien ship causing overpressure ruptures and escaping plasma explosions. And then the white and blue flickering light was replaced as the space around them was surrounded by a whirling vortex of blue flashes of Cerenkov radiation. Molloch had sent them on a hyperspace jaunt that seemed to only slightly disorient the aliens trying to take back the ship. The microsecond it took the aliens to check their sensors or look out the window to see what was happening was just enough of an advantage that the Bringers eased off their defensive poise and pressed the attack.

Three Chiata infantrymen in armored suits bounced practically on top of her and Azazel, firing plasma rounds and slinging tendrils. Dee dodged and twisted and rolled with her mecha so fast she was a loud *clanking* blur herself that sounded like a convoy of mecha movers, a freight train, and a giant tornado hitting all at once but she and Azazel were so out of position that all they could do was evade one attack and hope they would be ready for the next.

Dee managed to swipe her blade across the torso of the Chiata closest to her but it bounced off its personal shield with no effect. As she went to go for her guns a tendril wrapped around it, throwing her off balance. It looked as though Azazel was in a similar fix.

No! I can't let them take me down this way, she thought. *QMT Bree!*

No Dee, not in hyperspace!

Don't know if we have a choice!

Just as she was about to toggle the out-and-in algorithm on the quantum membrane teleportation and take the chance of QMTing while in hyperspace Skippy appeared out of nowhere right on the alien's faceplate. The Chiata infantryman's shield didn't even flicker or faze Skippy as the little alien bot passed right through to the armor plating where he quickly ate through and was inside the alien's armored suit. The Chiata stopped instantly with its attack and started flailing wildly until it fell limp. Almost as soon as he was inside destroying the Chiata the little bot burst through the back of its head and slipped through the shields of the one backing it up and started eating it.

To Dee's surprise, she'd have sworn she saw a second Skippy bot jump from the first dead alien's body and into another attacking Chiata. But Dee didn't have time to spectate. Skippy was holding his own and giving them an extra advantage. And there were other Chiata trying to kill her at the moment.

"Keep pressing them, Bringers!" Dee encouraged the squadron. "Don't let up!"

Almost as quickly as they had gone to hyperspace they came out and the BBD fired again. And then Dee could see a countdown clock appear in her mindview.

"Phoenix, Molloch copy."

"Go, Molloch!"

"Clock is ticking. Seventy-nine seconds."

"We'll hold them off that long! You stay put until that weapon is charged and fired."

"Understood, Major."

The clock ticked slowly as more and more Chiata poured into the giant hangar-sized bay just below the equipment elevator platform that led up to the top of the porcusnail megaship's bridge dome. There was no telling how many aliens had been on the megaship before the Bringers of Hell had boarded it, but as far as Dee could tell it was a shitload of them. It looked as if every Chiata that was left on the ship was moving in to stop them as if they could see the countdown clock too. Dee knew that was preposterous, but somehow she got the feeling that the aliens knew her team was about to fire the superweapon. Maybe the aliens were still somehow tapped into engineering diagnostics and could see the energy build up. She had no way of knowing. She didn't give a shit. She just needed to keep them at bay for a minute or so more. She just needed to kill the motherfuckers.

"Just one minute more Bringers! Don't let up!" she shouted over the tacnet.

"We will not hold out against that many attackers for that long, Major," Azazel responded. "We need a better plan of attack or a miracle."

"Bringers, we are not in hyperspace any longer. Out-and-in if you need to." Dee thought for a second as she rolled from bot to fighter mode and afterburned into the center of the large chamber. "When a good Marine is outnumbered . . ."

"Phoenix, what are you doing?" She could almost hear concern in Azazel's voice. "I'm not sure that is a good idea."

"I'm buying us some time! When I come out of this, y'all better cover my ass!" Her father's Mississippi usage coming through in her voice. She kicked the HOTAS forward with her right slightly, nudged the stick back a little and then with her left dropped the throttle. Dee then took a long slow deep breath to calm herself and slapped the icon to ready the Deathblossom sequence.

Alright Bree, let's start puking! I'm going for DeathRay's record, she thought.

Understood Dee. Focus your mind and relax. I've got the controls in two, one, now! her AIC responded and Dee relinquished control of the attitude and reaction control systems and the weapons while keeping a mindview eye on her trajectory.

She closed her eyes and relaxed her breathing as best she could. She took long slow breaths in and then held it in for a count of "three Mississippi". Then she exhaled, gulped down the bile in her throat and started the process again.

The gee forces built up on her, like being hit by a hovertank at full speed while recovering from an all-nighter hangover and then getting kicked in the stomach as an added bonus. In her mindview she could read her spin rate and watched as targeting Xs filled the room in every direction. Her AIC controlled the fighter's attitude, spinning her roll, pitch, and yaw as needed and firing her weapon systems with controlled precision that from the outside looking in appeared as a maniacal whirling storm of cannon and directed energy fire. The spin rate was too great for missiles. If she fired a missile during the deathblossom the thing wouldn't likely make it out of the tube or it would get halfway out and then get stuck or worse, get kicked back in her face. Missiles were a bad idea.

Dee watched the overall vector of her spinning vehicle and adjusted the vector with the HOTAS controls only slightly if she had an intuition of a better attack posture. Sometimes the human pilot had an intuition that was better than the AIC pilot and that was another reason why they were still in the cockpit.

Nine seconds, Bree said. Dee noted the superweapon countdown clock was at fifty-one seconds. She had a long way to go. *Breathe Dee, Breathe.*

I'm good. I'm good. I'm good, Deanna chanted in her mind.

Several times the abrupt vector changes in her spin jerked at her stomach. What little fluid and food was in there still was doing all it could to get out. She choked it back and clenched her teeth down on the TMJ bite block. A fresh burst of oxygen and stims rushed against her face. The extreme accelerations of the pukin' deathblossom maneuver caused time to dramatically slow which seemed to prolong the agony to most pilots. But Dee saw it as an opportunity to get to kill more Chiata at breakneck pace and at the same time getting to savor it because of the time stretch.

The counter on the red force kills continued to tick upward as the deathblossom continued. She kept her eyes closed and watched in her DTM battlescape view from outside her fighter so her mind didn't perceive the spinning as much—a trick that DeathRay had taught her that few pilots were ever able to fully master. For all her piloting career the top dog pilot was DeathRay, a Navy aviator. That galled most Marines to no fucking end. The Navy pukes loved it. It was high time a Marine showed him up.

Seventeen seconds in, Bree said. The countdown clock

for the superweapon was at forty-three. She had a long way to go. *Hang in there, Dee!*

I'm solid, Bree! Don't stop. I'm good. I'm good. Dee felt a sharp jerk from an impact onto the spinning mecha. One of the aliens had braved a lucky shot but got its ass incinerated for its troubles. The shot didn't overwhelm the shields, but it did overwhelm her jaw muscles and her inner ear. Her stomach retched violently forcing vomit to spew through her teeth and around her mouthpiece until it forced her mouth open. Like a geyser bursting open the fluid shot from her mouth splattering with the added acceleration of the wild spinning motion.

The mantra for mecha jocks had always been that they ate their own puke for breakfast, lunch, and dinner, and then begged for more. The bravado never made it any less unbearable. Her stomach retched again beyond her control and her faceplate and helmet filled with more stomach fluids. The mad spinning forced the vomit to the walls of the inside of her helmet and into her hair and up her nostrils. Dee blew out with all her might and worked the bite block back into her mouth chomping down on the thing like a dog not wanting to give up on a bone. Stims and fresh air flooded her face again but couldn't overpower the putrid bile smell. And it smelled very bad, which didn't help with the nausea.

She kept her eyes closed but could feel the thick foul liquid splash against her eyelids and more of it forced up her nose but Dee was too much of a pro to panic. After all, the maneuver wasn't called a "pukin' Deathblossom" for nothing. She blew out again clearing her nostrils of the vomit and felt the warm feel of the antiseptic organogel reaching out to clean her face. The organic goop quickly cleaned her helmet and the air circulation system dropped the humidity to almost zero to quickly evaporate any remaining fluids. Any solids were grabbed by the organogel layer and eventually recycled for later use.

Twenty-three, twenty-four, twenty-five . . .

Dee's stomach turned again and any remaining fluids there made their way up and out. The retching was so violent that the liquid spewed from her mouth and even into her sinuses and out through her nostrils. Any sane normal human being might have choked to death at that point. In fact, many humans throughout history had done just that, drowned in their own vomit. But Dee was a mecha jock, a Marine. She had been trained how to clear her airways and not to panic under such terrible duress. She did all she could do to put her mind out of her body. The crushing gee forces still pressed her into the seat and wild jerking motions banged her brain around inside her skull almost to the level of concussion. A low dose of immunoboost was automatically injected into her system.

She tried to squeeze her legs and abdominal muscles to force blood into her brain. And she growled like a lioness fighting to protect its cubs. And she grunted guttural larynx straining profanity. But all the training in the universe simply couldn't prepare anyone for a pukin' deathblossom maneuver during combat. She forced her stomach muscles as tight as she could squeeze them, which was quite considerable due to all the push-ups and sit-ups she did daily, but squeezing her abs just forced more bile up her already burning esophagus. It was a horrible snake eating its own tail—an extremely vicious and literally nasty cycle.

She had to shut out all sources of stimulation and just disconnect from her body, which was easier said than done. There was just too much stimulation happening at the moment for her to shut out. Her sinuses were filled with burning bile and putrid vomit. Her eyes were stinging like fire ants were in them. Her inner ear control was gone. Vertigo took over her mind and everything spun so erratically and wildly even the direct-to-mind battlescape was unstable. There was nothing left for Dee to focus on that could stop the spinning. She was spent beyond use and couldn't hold onto the deathblossom any longer. But she wasn't going to let that stop her. She decided to embrace the vertigo as long as she could.

Not yet, Bree! Not yet.

Dee, your heart rate is getting too erratic and your blood pressure is through the roof.

Not yet, Bree! I can hold it longer, she thought bravely but the truth was that she was delirious from the retching, the spinning, the nausea, the overwhelming gee loads and jerks. She was spent.

"Sorry, Davy," she gasped between stomach retches and dry heaves. With tears in her eyes, perhaps from the stinging of the bile, perhaps because she had yet to feel as though she had avenged her lost loved ones. Had it not been for the pilot's couch restraints hard connected to her suit Deanna would have physically collapsed as she reached with all her remaining strength and tapped the stop icon. "I just can't hold it any longer."

Forty-seven, forty-eight, deathblossom maneuver

halted, Bree said. *Snap to, Marine! Major Deanna Moore! Snap to!*

The battlescape slowly stopped spinning and a red targeting X over the far hangar entrance was all Dee could focus on between dry heaves. A Chiata hovertank had managed to work its way into the chamber. Buzzsaw bots were rapidly making their way toward it, but they would amount to little in way of resistance to the alien armored mecha. "Fox Three!" she said weakly and between gasps for air.

A mecha-to-mecha missile rocketed from underneath her wing spiraling out across the hangar and impacted the X almost as soon as it left her fighter. An orange and white plasma ball erupted followed by a secondary explosion that was much bigger than Dee had expected, throwing shrapnel against her mecha. The high velocity debris *pinged* against her mecha's barrier shield causing little if any drain on the power system. As the debris cloud cleared the wounded hovertank pushed through, still in operation.

"Guns, guns, guns." She did all she could to get a second wind but there was nothing there. She needed a minute or more to recover and she could see the alien tank turning toward her readying itself to fire.

"Warning! Enemy radar targeting lock imminent," her Bitchin' Betty alarm rang in her cockpit.

"Fox Three," Azazel said as his mecha in eagle-mode dropped in between her and the alien tank finishing it off with a missile. "Phoenix, pull back to cover. I've got this one."

She had just enough presence of mind to note that

there were still eight seconds left on the countdown clock. She toggled to bot-mode and dropped with a two thousand kilogram *thud* to the elevator platform and then rolled behind a bulkhead just as Chiata plasma rifle rounds riddled the wall behind her, the vertigo still spinning her mind a bit with every motion.

"Shit, it never ends." She gasped to force air into her now scorched lungs. There were six seconds left.

Azazel's mecha *clanked* to a stop outside the platform entrance firing selected shots and then all of a sudden he wasn't firing his weapons. For the first second since the deathblossom Dee managed to focus on her tracker and noticed that there were no targeting Xs turning red and there were no red dots pushing into the chamber or up the elevator shaft. There were no red dots for several decks. There were five seconds on the countdown clock.

"You killed them all, Major," Azazel said, and then he quoted something that Dee had told him many times before over the last eighteen months or so that they had been flying together. It was the squadron's motto and creed and Dee had never gotten them to get the emotion and inflection right for a true battlecry. But this time, Azazel was spot on. "Out of the ashes flew the Phoenix of death and her demon valkyries. Ooh-fuckin'-rah they shouted!"

"WE are the Bringers of Hell," she replied in unison with her wingman and the rest of Alpha Team and Bravo Team as the squadron did always but this time Dee's voice was very weak as she panted through gasps of breath. Her squadron's voices strongly filled in for her. The clock on her mindview ticked down.

Three, two, one.

A surge could be felt through every deck plate and bulkhead of the alien megaship. The lights flickered and there was an extreme electric field buzz everywhere. Then the Buckley-Freeman barrier shields from the four supercarrier legs expanded over the ship and merged together. Dee and Azazel watched out the viewport just beneath the bridge dome as the impenetrable quantum barrier surrounded them completely, and then with a final blasting surge of near infinite energy from the quantum vacuum energy storage system in the alien ship, the barrier blasted outward at the speed of light, converting any matter in the blast wave's pathway to subatomic particles with scattered random uncertainty position and velocity vectors. In other words, any matter was ripped apart to subatomic particles and light. In even simpler terms, they were blown to Hell and gone.

"Bringers of Hell to *Penzington*. DeathRay, we can hold this ship."

"Phoenix, DeathRay. Not sure we can hold ours without you," DeathRay replied. "Rig that one to blow and get the Hell over here!"

Chapter 11

July 24, 2409 AD
U.S.S. Sienna Madira III
Orbit
Thgreeth Abandoned Outpost Planet
Deep in Expanse
700 light-years from the Sol System
Saturday, 11:54 A.M. Eastern Time

"Thank you for getting up here so quickly, Master Gunnery Sergeant." The general sat behind his desk in front of the large floor to ceiling window of his Ready Room. Other than the Bridge or the flight hangars it was the best view from inside the ship that she had seen. Dee had told her before that the view from the general's quarters was better, but other than being outside on top of the tuning forks of the rebuilt alien megaship, Rondi couldn't imagine a better view.

Moore sat at his desk preoccupied and only generally looking back in Rondi's direction through the million-mile-stare blank expression that most people had when doing tasks in their mindview. Rondi was pretty sure that he was more than preoccupied with all the last-minute full-scale invasion and rescue planning. Outside the viewport, the Fleet seemed still and dead. There were no fighters or transports flying about and nothing moving to or from the planet below. To most, that would seem boring, but to seasoned space combat soldiers it meant that everyone was loaded up and the hatches battened down and the fleet was about to make a jump into something nasty. There wasn't a damned thing boring about that.

Moore continued to stare blankly off into space through her as if he were ignoring her presence for more important things—his daughter, of course. She didn't blame him, though. If she had a daughter and could bring a fleet of mega-class warships to the rescue, you better damned well believe that's exactly what she'd do. Besides, Dee was her friend and she couldn't wait to get out there and help her out of a tight spot.

"Of course, General Moore. What can I do for you, sir?" Rondi stood at attention in her AEM suit with the helmet stowed over the shoulder, protocol for armored Marines. The tattoos on the side of her neck and upward to the left side of her forehead glowed red and green and she could see from the reflection of herself in the general's window that they were making her look a bit scary if not demonic. Rondi smiled inwardly. That was the entire fucking point.

"Gunny, uh, Rondi, I need you to do me a favor and sit this one out." Moore's attention turned to her fully and the expressions filed back into his face.

"Sir?"

"I know that if I take you into that system and let you and your squad loose on an alien ship you will wreak bloody Hell and havoc on the blur bastards with fearless goddamned reckless abandon that only a team of hardboiled seasoned in blood and guts by God Armored Environment Suited Marines like yourself could do."

"Ooh-fuckin'-rah, sir!"

"But I need you to hand pick a couple of AEMs and stay behind on the planet ruins with my wife." Rondi was confused. The general said that as more of a request than an order, which wasn't really like him. Was he asking her or telling her? She wasn't sure what to say next other than to take it as an order from a four-star general.

"Yes sir. Might I ask to what end, sir?" Rondi was hoping there was some secretive super plan that the general had in mind for her, but suspected that was just wishful thinking. She did her best to hide her expressions of disappointment.

"Well, you see, Gunny, you know how crazy and fearless my daughter is, right? I know the two of you are fairly close." Moore raised an eyebrow at her. Rondi still didn't understand where the conversation was going. "Hell, I don't think she'd ever gotten all those damned tattoos if she hadn't seen yours."

"All due respect, sir, your daughter blazes her own trail and follows only one other Marine that I know of and it ain't me, sir." Rondi started to apologize but wasn't certain if she was supposed to. Dee was a grownup and a Marine officer who made her own damned decisions. This wasn't like some high school fraternity clique. Rondi was almost offended. Almost. Then she instantly remembered who she was talking to.

"That wasn't meant to insinuate blame, Gunny. But Dee is reckless and tromps into situations where gods would fear to tread. Shit, I don't know that I would dare do half the shit she's done."

"Uh, yes sir. Your daughter is one crazy-assed fearless alien killin' motherfuckin' machine sir! Proud to wear the same uniform as her. Apple didn't fall far from the tree, General." Rondi smiled only thinly. She wasn't certain if he was admonishing her because of the tats or not. "And if I dare say so, she's got some pretty bitchin' ink too, uh, sir."

"Well, bitchin' ink aside Gunny, believe it or not, she gets a lot of that shit from her mother. That is why I want you on the planet with my wife. Sehera is down there with a team of eggheads and wizards and only a small security detail of Navy seamen. I am concerned that there is no telling what kind of hornet's nest she is liable to poke at down there. I have no way of knowing when we will be back and that leaves her completely exposed down there with only some E3s to watch her backside. I want you to get loaded for bear and crocodiles, bounce down there with a team, and stay with her until such time as I get back. Do what you can to keep her out of trouble. But don't look like that's the only reason you are there, because I'll never hear the end of it otherwise. Any signs of trouble you tell her to snap back to safety. Hell, insist or beg if you have to. Understood?"

"Uh, yes sir. Anything else, sir?" Rondi tried not to let her disappointment show. She was being sidelined to babysit a fossil hunt. Moore must have caught her body language because he quickly held up a hand and waved it gently and then added that smile that carried him through three terms in the oval office. Rondi had seen the man take on hundreds of buzzsaw bots singlehandedly. She had heard, read, and seen the footage of him taking on Separatist hovertanks with only a rifle and no armor. The man's reputation didn't even come close to matching the man himself. But that politician's smile was so disarming that it eased Rondi and *that* made her feel uneasy.

"Gunny, don't think of this as being benched. I need someone that she would trust, that Dee would trust, and that I would trust. Sehera has a tendency to find trouble and I don't want her finding it with just a couple of seamen with M-blasters protecting her. Besides, I could have just given you an order. Sure will make me feel better knowing a team of some of the finest of Uncle Sam's Misguided Children are there to protect her," he said.

"Sir! I am absolutely thrilled to the core of my being by your trust in me. My only hesitation, and I apologize for the unprofessional lack of control of my body language, is jealousy of the rest of you for not getting to kill more of the thrice-damned Chiata today," she said, with as big a smile as she could manage, hoping to play it back to him as he had dealt it. "Again, absolutely thrilled, sir. Thank you."

"Alright, Gunny," he laughed at her. "No admonishment from me on that. You'll get your chance soon, I'm sure. Thank you. Now get your team together and move out. You have five minutes and ticking."

"Ooh-fuckin'-rah sir. Kill some of those bastards for me." Rondi turned to clank out the door and began pulling her team roster up in her mindview. Five minutes wasn't much time to prepare for a mission with unknown ramifications, but Marines were always prepared for whatever the fuck got in their way that needed killing. And Rondi was a damned fine Marine and damned good at killing.

"And Gunny," Moore called to her as his door slid open. She turned back to him.

"Sir?"

"That is the only woman I have chosen to marry in almost two centuries of my life. You keep her safe for me. Understand me?"

"My pleasure sir. Understood." The more Rondi thought about it, it truly was her pleasure and honor. Besides, she'd get to kill Chiata soon enough she was pretty sure of it.

Chapter 12

July 24, 2409 AD
Ruins
Thgreeth Abandoned Outpost Planet
Deep in Expanse
700 light-years from the Sol System
Saturday, 12:00 P.M. Eastern Time

Sehera wasn't exactly certain how the battle was going because viewing a near solar-system wide conflict with hundreds of ships engaging the few tens of ships from the fleet was difficult. At times she considered having it shifted to mindview instead of the visual and tactile format being displayed about them but the alien system seemed to like that approach better. Sehera had been looking at mindscape battleviews for more than a century and understood them well, but being immersed in a physical holographic display was somewhat cumbersome compared to the DTM mindviews she had grown accustomed to. She thought how interesting that was considering how much more advanced the Thgreeth seemed to be in all other regards.

Sehera kept an eye on the blue force tracker so that she could note when the fleet would sling forward to the battle and to Dee's rescue, but so far none of the ships had left the Thgreeth system yet. She wasn't sure what it was that Alexander was waiting on, but she knew he was going as fast as he could. Rallying such a large invasion fleet in a few tens of minutes was a difficult task even with quantum membrane teleportation technologies. But Alexander would get there, and in time. That was the only way she could allow herself to see the situation. Besides, his little girl was everything to him and she'd seen him wade through armies of battle bots to rescue her. This would be no different.

Sehera watched and waited intently searching through the alien computer system for anything else that might help. She did her best to keep her daughter in the center of the room-sized holographic alien display system while zooming in and out of the battle to look for traps and advantages. She wasn't sure what she could do from so many light-years away but she had the idea that somehow Dee was connected to the Thgreeth system. And somehow, Sehera believed she'd be able to reach her daughter. She simply needed to discover the right set of commands. She also needed to discover the right data to send once she figured out how to send it. There was a chicken and egg paradox going on in her mind so she decided to do both at once; raise the chicken and hatch the egg. She had half of her mind chasing tactical and strategic advantages while the other half was trying to hack into this alien communications network.

"Looks like they managed to engage the Buckley

superweapon." Dr. Hughes squinted as a large section of the battlescape around Dee's location grew in brightness with a blue spherical expanding wavefront. The blue ball expanded outward to over a half-million kilometers in radius, destroying everything in its path. More than one hundred fifty of the Chiata megaships were destroyed, but hundreds more continued to pour into the system from hyperspace.

"I'm not sure it will buy them much time," CW3 Thomson Dover added. "It'll take several minutes to recharge and repair the energy conduit systems for another volley from the superweapon or even the BBDs. Their best hope will be that the QMT sling forward and snap backs are still functional and they can do out-and-ins. Hyperspace drive is probably out too."

"Too bad we can't get diagnostic information for the vessels through this system," the linguist Johan Seely added. "That way we maybe could target alien ships that have weaknesses or overtaxed systems like ours."

"How do you know we can't?" CW3 Dover asked.

"How do you mean, Chief?" Sehera asked the warrant officer. In the months she'd been working with the ruins team, she had come to realize that the warrant officers seemed to have a very keen and very pragmatic insight about things. Alexander had told her that was just how warrant officers thought about things and what their special talents were. He'd told her it wasn't their training that made warrants so special and she had come to understand what her husband was telling her.

"Well, ma'am, I mean, we don't even understand how this sensor network is functioning. How is it getting data in a real-time manner from these systems all over the galaxy separated by thousands of light-years and how does it know the blue force from the red force?" He explained with questions that weren't so much rhetorical as they were simply unanswerable. "We don't know how they are doing this, so why do we limit ourselves in our thinking of what this very advanced alien system can or can't do yet?"

"That is a very good point, Chief." Sehera thought about that while examining the battleview and the control panels about the walls of the ruins. "So, how do I ask it, I wonder?"

Pamela, any ideas? she thought to her AIC.

Perhaps I can ask the question for you. I will see. There was a brief pause from her AIC and then the battleview flickered with red numbers overlaying the red dots. *I think that did it.*

Did what, Pamela? Sehera thought.

The system is now overlaying a health status percentage on each of the red dots. Try zooming in on one and see how specific the health information is.

Okay.

"Mrs. Moore, you have done something to the battleview again, haven't you?" the ever-attentive Dr. Hughes asked almost as soon as the system view flickered.

"Damage points." The CW3 nodded and pointed. "Very useful, Mrs. Moore."

"I think so," Sehera replied. "Let's see."

She reached up to one of the red dots nearest the *U.S.S. Nancy Penzington's* icon and zoomed in on it by spreading her hands apart around it. The ship expanded, red, yellow, and green spots highlighting it. The ship appeared translucent, resembling an engineering diagram. The number attached to the ship read eighty-nine percent and all the systems inside it were either yellow or green except one in red and it was nearest the spires of the tuning fork where the blue beams of death from Hell were fired.

"The BBDs are getting weak," CW3 Dover said excitedly. "This thing is doing it! Now if we could just relay that info to the fleet somehow."

"They could pinpoint targeting and turn this battle around." Sehera finished his thought for him only to be distracted as there was suddenly a flash of white light and the sound of sizzling bacon and Sehera had to squint her eyes to adjust. The contrast of the holographic system adjusted automatically and then returned to normal. The alien system was extremely adaptive and attentive to inputs.

Three armored e-suit Marines materialized in the middle of the chamber, distracting the team's attention. The blue force tracker in Sehera's mind quickly identified the Marines as Master Gunnery Sergeant Rondi Howser, Corporal David Ibanez, and Private First Class Teri Gaines. They were in full battle gear and appeared to have extra ammo boxes slung on their backs. The first thought Sehera had was that it was Dee's friend with all the tattoos.

"Excuse us, ma'am, Chief." Howser nodded to the warrant officer and then turned to Sehera. "Mrs. Moore, we have been ordered to stay with your team to offer any *assistance* you deem necessary."

"Ha ha," Sehera laughed out loud. "*Assistance* you say,

Rondi? More like Alexander sent you down here to babysit me."

Sehera wasn't sure if she was angry at her husband or if she appreciated his overprotective nature where his family was concerned. He knew that she could take care of herself, but he still must have felt the need to send three attack dogs down to "keep her safe". She laughed again and mumbled, "Assistance indeed, Alexander."

"Sorry, ma'am, I have no training in babysitting and the general's orders were specific: to keep out of your way but be ready and willing to support you in whatever needs you and your team may have." Sehera smiled back at Rondi. She liked the Marine. She knew she was tough as nails and had been through some serious combat. Hell, the rumors among the Fleet were that Rondi was the first to ever do a pukin' Deathblossom with just her hypervelocity automatic rifle and her armored suit while her squad was stranded free floating in space and surrounded by enemy bots. She was somewhat of a legend among the AEMs and not just for her wild glowing tattoos that, according to legend, were only matched by her sexual prowess. The rumors and talk of that prowess had been quashed over the past year or so since her and CHENG Buckley had become an item, but everyone in the Expeditionary Fleet had heard them.

None of the rumors bothered Sehera or anyone else. Mainly because Rondi was an adult and could do whatever the Hell she wanted, but mostly because nobody wanted to piss her off. The master gunnery sergeant was tough and smart, but what Sehera liked most about her, tattoos and all, was that she was her daughter's friend.

Since the loss of her lover and her "big sister" Nancy Penzington, Dee needed all the friends she could get right now. Sehera suspected that Rondi not getting to go with the fleet to her friend's aid was painful for the Marine.

"Alright, Rondi. We'll leave it at that, but you and I both know his exact words were probably something like, 'keep her out of trouble' or some such nonsense. Good luck with that." Sehera nodded to the other two soldiers and motioned for them to move to the sides of the chamber. "We have an open mouth policy here on our team. Dr. Hughes is in charge here. If any of you see anything you think is interesting, strange, weird, scary, or any other out of the normal adjectives, speak up. And I mean speak up right then because you never know when we might miss something instantaneously timely and important."

"I must interject," Cinnamon Hughes added. "While on record I am officially the Principal Investigator of this research team, Mrs. Moore is clearly the senior and more experienced leader here. For God's sake, she was one of the historic resistance fighters of Mars and First Lady for twelve years. Besides that, how many people do you know who can say they actually rescued Alexander Moore? So make a note Marines to refer to her in all 'leadership' questions. I'm just a scientist."

"Yes, ma'am. Understood." Sehera watched patiently as Rondi replied to Dr. Hughes and then nodded her understanding in her direction. The AEM then turned to her detail motioning them to back off. "Out of the way and eyes peeled. Private, I want you to do a quick perimeter security sweep outside. Full sensors."

"Affirmative, Gunny," the PFC replied. "All right, Dr. Hughes, Mrs. Moore, consider us out of your way and at your service."

"Thank you, Rondi." Sehera said before turning her attention back to the chamber-wide holographic depiction of the battle happening over eighty light-years away. "Chief Dover, what were you saying about the system before?"

"Uh, well, Mrs. Moore, I was just saying that we simply don't know what we don't know about this place. We don't know the full capabilities of this system and to limit our thinking about it might keep up from using it to its full potential. I mean, ma'am, how do we know you can't communicate with Major Moore?"

"How do you mean?" Sehera was doing her best to think the scenario through.

Pamela, is it possible to communicate real time over so many light-years? she thought to her AIC.

Without a gate open it does seem unbelievable, her AIC responded.

"I mean," Chief Dover continued. "Have you tried? Did you ask the system?"

"What? Have I asked?" That snapped Sehera out of her conversation with Pamela briefly. "Why, no. No I haven't, Chief!"

Chapter 13

July 24, 2409 AD
U.S.S. Sienna Madira III
Mission Star 74
Chiata Expanse
783 light-years from the Sol System
Saturday, 12:00 P.M. Eastern Time

"I want a target as soon as the QMT ends if not sooner."
Alexander sat in the oversized armored chair that had been
built into the upper dome bridge of the alien megaship.
The builder bots had completely retooled and redesigned
the alien bridge to fit humans in armor rather than Chiata.
Moore had his visor up and was calmly delivering orders to
the bridge crew. "I don't want more than five seconds to
pass before our BBDs are firing. Understand that, Lisa?"

"Aye sir!" the Weapons Deck Gunnery Officer
Lieutenant Commander Lisa Banks replied. "BBDs are
charged and ready, sir."

"Air Boss, has the CAG got the flight teams prepped,
briefed, loaded, and ready?"

"Roger that, General!" the Air Boss replied. "Colonel

Strong says that the Maniacs, Archangels, and the Demon Dawgs all have the ball and awaiting the call, sir!"

"Good. They have full authority to sling forward into the mix as soon as the jump is complete," Moore added as he turned to the Ground Boss. "Killjoy, are the tankheads and AEMs ready?"

"The Slayers and the Juggernauts are good to go, General Moore!" Brigadier General Geri "Killjoy" Ibanez replied. "Sir, I should also add that Master Gunnery Sergeant Howser reports her team has debarked and are in place at the ruins."

"Understood, Ground Boss." Moore checked the names on the roster that Rondi took with her and noted that she had taken the Ground Boss's son.

"STO! We good to go?"

"Yes, General. Engineering is reporting all systems nominal and ready. Commander Buckley assures me that the superweapon is ready to fire at your discretion, sir," the Science and Technical Officer Commander Tori Snow said.

Moore sat back into his seat and toggled the armor restraining system to engage. The harnesses extended from the chair and locked him in. He checked in his mindview to make certain the rest of the crew was locked in as well and knew that it was time to give the order. It wasn't a particularly easy order since he wasn't so sure how they planned to escape the system. The enemy QMT damping bubble appeared thus far to be a one-way door. You could go into the system but nobody could get out. And they had no idea where the device or devices were and how they worked. He wasn't even certain they could be shut off.

"XO, you got anything to add?"

"Yes sir. Let's go kill some fucking Chiata and save our people." USMC Major General Sally "Firestorm" Rheims grunted and then added, "Ooh-fucking-rah, sir."

"Right," Alexander snarled and gave a nod to his longtime friend and executive officer. "COB? You good to go?"

"Aye sir. The boat is running like a top and so is her crew and complement," the chief of the boat replied, all the while sipping hot black coffee with a straw protruding through the raised visor of his helmet.

"All right Helmsman, let's engage the QMT."

"All right, Maniacs, we have the ball! Engage the QMT on my mark and go to evasives, out-and-ins, and attack any formations of porcupines at will. As soon as we hit the bowl we are to zoom in on the Bringers of Hell, relay their coordinates, and then we all out-and-in to them. Ooh-fuckin'-rah, Maniacs!"

"Oohrah!"

"In three, two, one, now!" USMC Colonel Delilah "Jawbone" Strong triggered her new FM-14X QMT sling forward algorithm and instantly she was out of the hangar bay and in the middle of the thickest ball she'd ever seen. Porcupine-shaped mecha blurred about firing blue beams and plasma balls in all directions. There were blue beams of death from Hell zigging and zagging across space into alien and fleet ships alike. Shrapnel and debris fields filled the ball so randomly that everything about the system was a deathtrap.

Instantaneously, targeting Xs popped up in Delilah's mindview battlescape and energy curves and targeting solutions began forming in the ball. Red curves of the enemy fighters twisted and darted about creating an entangled mesh of strands of possible flight vectors. Blue curves with discontinuities from the out-and-ins started appearing turning the mindview into an interwoven mishmash of red and blue spaghetti. Blue lines and dots filled her view from the *Penzington's* attack fleet and it was clear that they were being overwhelmed.

"Watch your six, Jaw!" her wingman warned her as he popped into cover formation on her three-nine line and fired a mecha-to-mecha missile. "Fox Three!"

"Guns, guns, guns!" Jawbone shouted as she barrel rolled clockwise all the while stomping the bottom left foot pedal and working the HOTAS side to side yawing upside down momentarily as her quantum membrane sensors locked on the nearest porcupine gomer. "Fox Three!"

Out-and-in! she thought to her AIC. *James, have you fixed a route to Major Moore yet?*

Affirmative, Colonel. Are you ready to sling forward to that position?

Hell, yes! Delilah thought as she held her abdominal muscles tight and squeezed her leg muscles to the breaking point. *Relay the coordinates to the Maniacs.*

Done.

"Maniacs, proceed to our mission objective coordinates," she ordered her squadron. Blue plasma balls bounced against her mecha's Buckley-Freeman shield just as she slung forward. There was enough momentum imparted to her fighter that she came out of the QMT with an induced spin she hadn't planned on. "Shit!"

Suddenly the inside of a large Chiata megaship chamber

closed in around her, not giving her much room to overcome her loss of attitude control and the HOTAS was buffeting against her harshly. She bounced about like a pinball against the bumpers. Reflexively, she toggled her mecha from fighter to bot-mode and as the fighter reconfigured itself the angular momentum was slowed by slinging the bot arms and legs akimbo. Almost as soon as she flipped heels over head an FM-14X in bot-mode grabbed her by the mechanized boot going full thrusters to slow down her spin. Then the other bot gently sat her down.

"Glad you could join us, Colonel!"

"We came to save you, Phoenix. But looks like things got a little flip-flopped on us." Delilah didn't need to check the blue force tracker to know the voice or the flying technique of the pilot that had come to her aid. She'd known Dee since she was about twelve years old.

"Understood, Jawbone. It's thicker than shit out there. And it ain't been much better weather up in here either," Deanna Moore replied on the tacnet. "I see the old man felt he had to come to my rescue again."

"Count your blessings, girl. There is a lot more than you know, Phoenix!" Jawbone said admonishingly. "This is a system-wide trap and there are thousands more Chiata megaships hidden in the gas giants of this system. They were going to wipe you out very quickly without reinforcements. Your attack fleet is nothing more than rats trying to run off with the cheese that is tied down to the trap."

"Then what does that make you?" Deanna asked.

"More rats. More really pissed off and violent rats," Jawbone replied as she straightened up her mecha and pulled up the battlescape of the megaship's interior.

There were no Chiata within several hundred meters of them presently, but there were red masses moving in their general direction from outside the megaship and from the aft section within. Jawbone looked around the chamber at all the dead Chiata and mangled buzzsaw bots that were repairing themselves as fast as they could go, and she realized that the Bringers must have been through one hell of a fight. And whether they wanted to hear it or not, the fight wasn't anywhere close to over. "We've got more incoming soon. We need to shut the exterior hatches to prevent further boarding and we need to secure this ship."

"Colonel, the *Penzington* is in trouble and DeathRay has ordered the Bringers to scuttle this ship and snap back to help him," Moore explained. "We were just getting started on the self-destruct systems when you dropped in on us."

"We've lost the BBDs, Admiral Boland," the XO said flatly as the *Penzington* was rocked hard by a BBD impacting the forward Buckley-Freeman barrier shields. DeathRay watched the systems all edging into the red and boarding parties had begun penetrating into the deeper bowels of his megaship. If the enemy managed to make it all the way into the main engineering decks they could really start knocking out systems. They were already on the periphery engineering decks and knocking on the door. He had to do something quickly. But what? He didn't have a clue.

The shit is getting thick, he thought.

Yes, sir. I recommend a hyperspace jaunt as soon as possible, his AIC replied.

Yeah, that sounds like a good plan. Let's do that.

"CHENG to CO."

"Go CHENG." DeathRay balled his armored fists together anticipating what was coming.

"That last BBD impact drained the power conduits so abruptly, sir, that it overloaded the power supply side of the hyperspace vortex projector," the CHENG said.

Shit again, he thought to his AIC.

Yes sir.

"You telling me we don't have hyperspace, CHENG?"

"Yes sir. We also do not have QMT momentarily," the CHENG added without hesitation.

"How momentarily, CHENG? I need some specifics." DeathRay stayed calm. One thing he learned over decades of flying mecha in combat was that losing your cool was never helpful until such time as losing your cool was the only thing that would be helpful. He hoped he wasn't there yet.

"Two minutes on the projector, approximately three minutes and seventeen seconds on the QMTs, sir. The BBDs can probably fire again in six or seven minutes. They are too damaged to give you an accurate assessment on just yet."

"Understood, CHENG! Put all the builder bots we've got to work and get our propulsion and weapons back online. Without them, we are nothing more than a big fucking bullseye waiting for a bullet."

"Aye sir!" The clone CHENG actually sounded as if there was some urgency to the inflection in his voice. Jack wasn't sure, but he thought for a brief moment he could sense some emotions being displayed. Right then, he wasn't sure if he preferred the CHENG to get emotional or if he wanted him to stay clone calm. Shit, he didn't know what he wanted other than something, anything, to go the right damned way for a change.

"Admiral, we were just rammed by another boarding party," the XO announced.

"Well, let's hope that there's enough Chiata onboard that they will quit firing the BBDs at us in fear of hurting their own people," DeathRay replied, not believing a damned word of it. "Helmsman keep moving us on evasive patterns as close to the nearest Chiata porcusnail as you can."

"Yes sir."

Another cosmic sledgehammer pounded against the shields with so much force that had they all not been wearing their helmets, the inertial change would have separated their heads from their shoulders. Klaxons sounded across the bridge and Jack could see in his mindview of the interior of the ship that Firemen details were being dispersed throughout the ship. Builder bots deployed across the bridge repairing fried circuits and putting out small electrical fires. Jack felt as though his brain had been bashed around in his skull like a penny in a tin can. He wanted that shit to stop too.

"Another hit from BBDs, sir," the science and technical officer acknowledged. "We really do not need to take another hit like that sir."

Shit! Shit! Shit! Tell me something my concussion doesn't know already, STO! he thought to himself.

Sir, the simulations suggest we will not be able to hold this ship if we do not pull the mecha squadrons all back in. And even then that is merely a stopgap method that might only slow the bleeding and not stop it. I fear this engagement is lost and so are we.

Candis, keep running sims and find us some solution. We're eventually going to bleed out if this keeps on and on like this. We need a break from damage just long enough to make some repairs.

Yes, sir.

"Helm! Get us rubbing belly buttons with that Chiata ship!" he shouted and pointed out which ship he meant by highlighting it in the bridge crew's DTM mindview.

"CHENG, CO. Get me some goddamned BBDs or FTL however you have to manage it!"

"Admiral," the Ground Boss interrupted. "Sir, the internal tank and armored ground forces report a collapse in the line at the aft hangar section and just beneath us on the bottom platform elevator nearest engineering."

Dee, where the Hell are you! he thought but was almost instantly distracted by a blue beam of death from Hell zigging just above the bridge dome and then turning into the nearest megaship that had been firing at them. The blue beams ripped into the armor plating just beneath the megaship's tuning fork spires and then standard directed energy beams followed.

"What the . . ."

"Sir, blue force tracker shows new mecha squadrons appearing in support formations throughout the engagement!" the Air Boss stated, followed closely by the Ground Boss.

"And we have a new tank division and AEMs on board, sir," the Ground Boss noted.

"It's the general!" The XO truly sounded excited or as close to excited that Jack had ever heard a clone be. "General Moore sir!"

"XO, it looks like the entire Expeditionary Fleet is with him," the Air Boss added.

No shit? Jack thought and pulled up the battlescape and toggled the blue force tracker.

I count twelve megaships, Jack. And there are also many supercarriers with clone compliments.

Get me a channel open to the Madira.

Done sir.

"Check your orders, Major. The *Madira* just dropped both the Slayers and the Juggernauts in DeathRay's lap. Sienna Madira has brought a shitload of supercarriers loaded to the gills with builder bots and clones. Plus, the general is taking up flank on the *Penzington's* position as we speak. We should hold this ship for the long fight we're about to be in," Jawbone told her. "You should go to commandnet and check in."

"Roger that, Colonel!" Dee replied. "Bringers, hold up on the self-destruct and prepare to hold this ship. Molloch, keep firing the BBDs at targets of opportunity and give me a status update on the superweapon, hyperspace vortex projector, and the QMT."

"Maniacs!" Colonel Stone called her squadron over the tacnet. "Form up with the Bringers of Hell and let's get some updated battlescape tactics here. We need to make certain we hold this ship and put it to some goddamned good use. Now move it, Marines!"

Chapter 14

July 24, 2409 AD
U.S.S. Nancy Penzington
Mission Star 74
Chiata Expanse
783 light-years from the Sol System
Saturday, 12:01 P.M. Eastern Time

"Yes, General! You are definitely a sight for sore eyes sir! Five minutes later and I don't think we would have been able to hold this ship," DeathRay told the general's avatar in the DTM mindview on the commandnet. Admiral Walker and the other megaship captains stood quietly in the background. Sienna Madira looked at DeathRay and then back at General Moore and butted in.

"Son, I see you have more red dots inside your ship than you do blue, even with the AEMs and tank squadron Alexander just dropped in for you. I can QMT in as many buzzsaw bots as you'd like," Madira offered.

"Uh, yes, ma'am, that would be gracious of you. Hold a second."

Candis bring up the battlescape interior of the Penzington, he thought to his AIC. *Give me the most urgent candidates for reinforcements.*

Roger that, Jack. It looks like the lines around engineering are leaking like a sieve. If something doesn't plug up those holes soon the simulations suggest a total loss of the engineering deck.

Understood.

"Ma'am, if you wouldn't mind I could use bot units here, here, here, and here to help push back the boarding parties attempting to get to engineering." Jack pointed at the ship diagram as he spoke. "That should distract the Chiata and help ease some of the pressure from the security details there and enable the Army and Marines to mop up. If you don't mind, could you check on Major Moore's team as well? They could probably use some more automated reinforcements as many of their bots were very recently attrited."

"Done." Madira smiled. "Alexander, I've pinpointed four megaships I think we can take. I'm setting up my supercarrier attack teams now. If you wouldn't mind giving us some BBD coverage I'd be obliged."

"Madira, we will alternate the Fleet megaships to your support four at a time. That leaves eight back including the *Penzington* and the new one just acquired by the Bringers of Hell. Use your ship as the relief for whichever ship of the four meets the most resistance. We'll exhaust the BBDs and then swap out with other fleet ships during recharging. If we can, we'll tag team these alien bastards to death. We should focus our efforts on collecting ships first and then going to the superweapons. The more alien ships we can commandeer and bring online the better." Alexander Moore told them both the battle plan. "And hopefully, between all of our collective STOs and CHENGs somebody will figure out how to turn off that damping field and we can QMT the Hell out of here."

"My STO is working full-time on it, son," Madira said. DeathRay could almost see the cringe on the general's face when she called him that.

"Admiral Walker."

"Yes, General?" DeathRay thought that even the woman's avatar was gigantic. They didn't call the Admiral "Fullback" for no reason. She'd actually played fullback in college and was as good as they came.

"Fullback," General Moore continued. "I want you to take a team of Madira's supercarriers and engage targets of your choosing. See if you can capture another megaship and bring the superweapon online."

"Admiral Boland, how long until your superweapon is operational again?" Madira asked.

Candis how long?

Engineering is reporting an issue with one of the conduit interfaces between supercarrier four and the Buckley quantum field generators. Five minutes is the current estimate, sir.

Shit.

Yes sir.

"Looks like about five minutes," he answered. "Repair crews are working as fast as possible."

"I can send you some more builder bots if you need them?" Madira added.

We are at full capacity on the builder bots, Jack,
Candis assured him.

"No thanks, ma'am. We are still at full capacity on
them."

"Alright then."

"We have a plan," Moore said, pulling the Fleet
captains meeting to a close. "My wingman and the *Madira*
will cover the *Penzington* and the new acquisition while she
is licking her wounds. Admiral Walker will take a squad of
four megaships and four supercarriers at a time to targets
of opportunity. Sienna, you will take the *Mueller* and four
megaships along with the supercarrier accompaniment to
targets of your choice. Once we've made several new
acquisitions we start firing the superweapons in sequence
until we wipe the Chiata from this system. That's the plan.
If the numbers game starts to keep us from making
acquisitions, then we will go direct to the superweapon
sequence. Until my order, we do not fire the superweapons.
Now move out."

"Aye sir!"

Jack watched the interior battlescape as the numbers
started shifting more in his favor. The tank squadron that
dropped into the aft hangar section of the megaship was
fully engaged with the Chiata boarding parties there and
was starting to put a dent in their numbers. The AEMs
were holding the line between the bridge and the giant
elevator platform that ran up through the central hangars
of the megaship all the way down to engineering. The
clones manning the lines at the interfaces between the
supercarriers and the megaship were seeing few enemy
incursions. He made a mental note that he intended to

add another tankhead squadron and some AEMs to the ship's complement in the future.

"CO, CHENG."

"Go ahead, Thirty-one." Jack toggled the avatar of his Chief Engineer Commander Jacob "Thirty-one" into his mindview. "What now?"

"Sir, the QMT systems are now operational. We managed to implement a bypass of the alien energy conduits with a Buckley junction." Jack had heard all the stories about the now very infamous "Buckley Maneuver" and wasn't too keen on his CHENG following the same procedure. Commander Buckley was known for doing some wild shit in engineering that almost always blew up or caused someone to nearly get killed in the process. But to the flagship of the Fleet CHENG's credit, the wild shit usually saved the day. Nevertheless, it still made Jack as uneasy as a long-tailed cat in a room full of rocking chairs.

"Is it safe, Thirty-one?" he asked.

"Don't worry, sir. We have implemented safety protocols. And you'll be happy to note that the hyperspace vortex projector is also back online as of this second," the clone added.

"That is good news. How long until I have the BBDs?"

"No magic we can do there, sir," the CHENG clone replied deadpan. "We just have to wait for the builder bots to finish their work."

"Understood, CHENG! Good work and stay at it. Anything else?"

"No sir."

Chapter 15

July 24, 2409 AD
U.S.S. Nancy Penzington
Mission Star 74
Chiata Expanse
783 light-years from the Sol System
Saturday, 12:07 P.M. Eastern Time

"Appreciate you Army guys dropping in on us, Colonel," Rear Admiral Lower Half Boland said to the hovertank squadron leader through the commandnet DTM interface. "We need to retake the aft hangar so we can stage our mecha for the rest of this fight. They overran our fire crews about eight minutes ago and all our mecha are off ship."

"Understood, Admiral. I'm glad we could be of help." United States of the Sol System Army Colonel Maximillian "Dragon" Slayer bounced his M3A18-TX Hovertank in bot-mode across the aft hangar bay of the *U.S.S. Nancy Penzington* all the while taking on red and green plasma cannon fire from the overwhelming numbers of Chiata infantry and what might be called mecha, but they were so damned alien it was hard to say.

"As soon as you retake that section push forward all the way to the AEMs just ahead of engineering cleaning up anything in your path," Boland told him. "The aliens are getting dangerously close to Engineering."

"Roger that, sir," he replied. "Just have your QMT tower and aft DEGs manned and ready for my signal."

"Will do, Colonel. Boland out."

"Stay sharp Slayers and be ready for my signal," he said over the tank channel of the tacnet.

Alien plasma fire continued to pound away at his tank. There were only a handful of buzzsaw bots still functioning and any surviving clone crew had already evacuated back all the way to engineering. The behemoth mecha's armor and Buckley-Freeman shield flickered with each hit but held strong. Colonel Slayer watched as the targeting Xs in his mindview flickered from yellows to reds and took some satisfaction in the fact that there were plenty of targets to choose from. At top speed in bot-mode, the tank could pound across the decking of the hangar at over a hundred kilometers per hour leaving boot-shaped dents in the floor with each bounding step.

Colonel Slayer paid the damage to his tank no thought as he knew the builder bots could pound out the dents and put a fresh coat of paint down in no time. But if the damned Chiata took the ship, the few dents didn't really matter. Dragon and his wingman Slayer Two, also known as Major Jackson Applegate, used themselves to draw the alien fire, hoping to pull the Chiata into a better targeting zone so the rest of the Slayers could then pick them off like fish in a barrel. But he had even more than that in mind. If his plan worked they should be able to trick the Chiata into a kill box and retake that part of the ship quickly.

"Guns, guns, guns!" Dragon shouted doing his best to target several incoming Chiata armored tendrils that zipped and darted at him from both sides with the heavy caliber hyper velocity automatic rifles mounted at the wrist of each mechanized hand. He dropped to one knee and braced to fire his main gun that stuck out of the bot-mode hovertank's head like a giant proboscis. The main cannon fired, filling the hangar bay with an echoing report that was only slightly louder than the myriad of battle noises already beyond ear-damaging threshold levels. The basketball-sized plasma ball raced toward the back wall of the hangar where the Chiata had penetrated the ship's hull by ramming the Penzington with some type of spear-nosed porcupine ship. One of the quills had penetrated all the way through the shields, the structural integrity fields, the armor plating, and the fire channel, then into the room from which the aliens spewed forth. And aliens still boiled from it like ants from an anthill.

Slayer's cannon fire splattered into the alien docking and boarding module and incinerated several of the magnetic barbed penetrators along the outside of the quill that held the thing in place. Several Chiata infantry were thrown in opposite directions from the concussive blast wave. He locked the targeting X onto the spraying hot metal and the erupting plasma ball at the connection point and found just the spot.

"Fox!" He ordered an active missile loose. The missile

shot forward, twisting past several Chiata anti-missile flares and then hit home, actually pinning a Chiata against the wall before it blew. At first it wasn't clear if the shot had made the impact he'd hoped for, but as soon as the plasma and white orange explosion formed the Chiata infantryman vaporized and the docking rig was knocked free from the wall into open space instantly sucking the rest of the flames through the hole into space. The explosive decompression caused debris and several Chiata to be taken out through the gash as well. The docking rig was still connected on one side by a single barbed hook but a secondary explosion from something in the debris being sucked out serendipitously knocked it the rest of the way free.

In his mindview, he could see that outside the ship the Archangels FM-14X squadron from the *Madira* pounced onto the free flying boarding porcupine-looking spacecraft and giving it more than it could take. But inside the ship there were still plenty of active targets that had managed to board before they had gotten there.

"Dragon, watch your eight o'clock!" Slayer Two warned him over the tacnet. "Fox Three!"

But Two was too late. As the decompressive airflow pulled several of the Chiata past them, one of the aliens on his aft left side skewered his armored leg with a mechanized tendril and turned itself face to face with Maximillian.

For a brief moment that seemed frozen in his mind, Max stared eye to eye with the alien creature. The strange glowing green in the eyeballs and the reds and greens glowing as they coursed through the veins across the creature's face and ridged forehead gave it an appearance of menacing evil that Slayer could have done without. The thing had an expression on its face like a lion about to eat a gazelle. It was sheer arrogance and overconfidence in its place on the food chain. Rather than putting fear into Maximillian, it instilled a resolve in him that made him even more certain that these things needed to be eradicated from the universe and he had to do whatever he must to fulfill his part in that. He sure as Hell wasn't going to roll over and die. After all, they didn't call him "Dragon Slayer" for nothing.

Colonel Slayer rolled backwards placing his left armored hand on the deck capoeira style, bringing his giant feet up and into the head of the alien, hurling them both free from the deck and rolling and tumbling with the airflow and other debris toward the gaping hole at the aft of the hangar. Slayer saw several bots and at least two clone bodies fly past him with the debris.

He continued to twist and roll his mecha as he struggled with all the might of his tank's hands to grasp the tendril piercing his leg. Head-butting the Chiata in the bridge of the forehead with the big cannon startled the alien just enough to enable Slayer to tear the mechanized tendril to shreds. Sparks and red and green viscous glowing fluids spewed out. The Chiata growled an alien guttural sound but was nowhere close to mortally wounded. As far as Maximillian could tell, he'd just pissed it off worse than it already had been. There was nothing like a pissed-off Chiata to deal with.

"Roll to your right, Dragon! Now!" Slayer Two told him. Colonel Slayer had just enough time to move his torso over as the giant armored sole of Slayer Two's left foot stomped through the alien's face shield. The shields flickered out just as Two was tossed head over boots off the two of them and into a firing solution of another alien causing him to take his own evasive maneuvers. The damned aliens just kept pouring into the chamber. The Slayers were completely outnumbered, even if all of them were presently engaging the enemy, but for now, it was only Slayers One and Two.

"Guns, guns, guns!" Dragon shouted rolling up with his knee in the creature's chest and his cannon right in its face. The giant plasma rounds continued until the alien mecha went limp and a large jagged hole glowed red hot in the deck beneath them that would take the builder bots a while to fix.

"Two, cut right!" he shouted and just then the targeting X turned red in his mindview for the alien that was still on Two like stink on shit. "Guns, guns, guns!"

Maximillian could see three plasma balls form as the armor piercing rounds hit directly against the back of the Chiata, giving Major Applegate the time he needed to break free and dive for cover. Finally, the structural integrity fields and the Buckley barrier shield closed off the damage to the megaship's hull and the hangar repressurized almost instantly. Debris fell to the deck and it became much easier to move around and fight.

"Don't let him take you down, Two!" Dragon ordered his wingman as he stood his tank up firing his weapon and at the same time twirling around looking at the overwhelming numbers of targets that were encroaching on them right into the alien's kill box—not part of the plan. Dropping backwards he toggled the tank back into hovertank mode and spun up the hoverfield. He slammed the HOTAS controls forward, pushing the propellantless drive to the redline while kicking the tank into gear at top speed in the opposite direction from the advancing Chiata. He spun the tank's big gun about, targeting the pursuing alien.

"Hoowah!" Two replied. "Fox Three! Guns, guns, guns!"

"Retreat, Two! Now!" he said. "We've got to lead them to the target point before they pick us off!"

"On your ass, Dragon!"

"Alright, Slayers get ready to spring the trap," he ordered. "Two, full power on the aft barrier shields and don't stop until we push through to the mecha QMT pad!"

The aft hangar bay of the *Penzington* was a massive cavernous room in the lower back section of the Chiata porcusnail that the builder bots had completely renovated for human use. There were mecha repair stations, catapults in case the QMT pads were down, and normally, rows of fighters and tanks from floor to ceiling, but they were all presently deployed outside in space or elsewhere on the ship.

The cooling and power conduits for the aft retrofitted directed energy weapons and several launch tubes for gluonium-tipped missiles lined the edges of the room along the walls. The room was several hundred meters front to back and left to right and more than fifty meters from deck to ceiling. There were structures, elevator platforms, and stored components on pallets scattered about. And as an obvious recent addition, there were dead and mangled alien bodies and mecha parts, destroyed buzzsaw bots, and various other after effects of combat strewn about. There were pools of coolants, lubricants, glowing alien, and some human blood mixed on the floor. The fact that there was only the occasional clone crewman body or torn-up mecha was a good sign that most of them were able to snap-back or sling-forward to safety.

The forwardmost section of the hangar bay was where the builder bots had seen fit to build the quantum membrane teleportation system for moving mecha and troops in and out of combat and at that point was where the trap would be sprung. That was, assuming that the bait, himself and Slayer Two, could make it there still alive and preferably in one piece and in fighting shape.

"Almost there, Slayers!" Colonel Slayer gritted his teeth against his TMJ bite block until he damned near chewed through it. The HOTAS slammed full forward, accelerating the tank at full hoverfield, which was more than three gees and any maneuvers added a bone rattling jerk that was many times that. The hoverfield engines whined as he redlined them and held them on the edge of their design envelope. The course he took would have been beyond the limits of any new recruit, but the Slayers were the best tank squad in the Fleet. Maximillian just gritted his teeth against the mouthpiece, forced himself to breathe, and raced over, around, and sometimes through whatever was in his way. Every little maneuver or bump in the road was damned near enough of a jerk to toss his breakfast not only out of his stomach but across the room.

He grunted through several jumps, last second swerves that carried him up sideways on the corridor walls, and as the QMT pad approached he toggled the tank over to bot-mode with a last-second leap somersaulting through the air. Major Applegate was right beside him, flipping through the air almost in synchronization with him. Both of the tank drivers fired their wrist-mounted weapons as they vaulted about with a sea of alien infantry and some mecha hot on their heels in an overwhelming flood of numbers.

"This better work, Colonel!" Applegate shouted. "Otherwise, we're gonna be in some really deep red and green blurry shit!"

"Now, Slayers!" he shouted over the tacnet ignoring Two's comment. "Hooah!"

The two of them came to a screeching and clanking judo rolling stop across the large QMT pad just as it lit up. The Chiata pursuers rushed inward at them, firing weapons and throwing spear-tipped tendrils in their direction. But Slayers One and Two bounced like Mexican jumping beans raised on a diet of caffeine, cocaine, and crack. Then there was the typical flash of brilliant white light and the sizzling sound inside his head. Slayer felt the electric buzz and the static field making his hair stand on end even inside his armored suit.

"Hoowah!" Slayers Three through Ten exclaimed as they appeared on the QMT pad all in bot-mode and formed up in an outward facing arc with their weapons drawn and at the ready. The Chiata hot on Slayer One and Two's heels flooded onto the periphery of the pad by the many tens one after the other slinging plasma balls and tendrils in every different direction. Slayers One and Two still dodging, juking, and jinking for their lives.

"Guns, guns, guns!" Colonel Slayer turned to face the onward rush of mechanized aliens and vehicles firing both of his wrist mounted guns. The muzzles flashed from the hypervelocity armor-piercing incendiary plasma rounds being used to cut away at the enemy. But there were too many for a simple face-to-face fight. Besides, Dragon had a plan. It was a good plan. It was a damned good plan.

"There are too many of them, Colonel!" Slayer Four said through guttural grunts.

"I'm not sure who's in the killbox, them or us?" Seven added.

"More targets to shoot, Seven!" Three replied.

"Keep bouncing, Slayers, but stay on this pad!" Maximillian saw Slayer Four knocked to the deck by an alien tendril but Slayer Five was there almost instantly to back him up.

"I got you, Four," Five said.

Are they in position yet? Max thought to his AIC.

A few more seconds, Colonel. We must maximize the number of Chiata on the pad for this to be effective, his AIC explained.

I know! It was my plan. Don't wait for my order to spring the trap. Just do it once they are all in place.

Yes sir.

"Keep sucking them in, Slayers! We have to hold out long enough to get as many of them as we can on the pad."

The numbers game was beginning to be too much for them as the Chiata poured in at them firing and slinging mechanized deadly tendrils at his team in every direction. While they fought fiercely, bravely, and effectively there were only ten of the tankheads and there were more than a hundred Chiata in a mix of infantry and mecha. It was clear that they had reached the point of becoming overwhelmed.

"On your backside, Three!"

"I've got 'em, Nine!"

"Guns, guns, guns!"

"Colonel, if you're gonna do something do it soon!" Seven shouted. "I've lost my right gun and my shields are overheating."

"Alright, Slayers, here we go!" As soon as it was out of his mouth there was the white flash of light again and the next thing he knew his tank squadron and a roomful of hand-to-hand-to-tendril fighting Chiata were floating in the microgravity of space directly out in front of the DEG battery of the port side aft supercarrier leg. They drifted uncontrollably in the microgravity just long enough for Maximillian to take in the severity of the combat ball. The mindview didn't do it justice. There was shrapnel and debris everywhere. Blue beams of death from Hell zig-zagged across space in every direction he could see. Mecha and alien porcupines bounced about with missiles gyrating in all directions. And in the very far distance there were hundreds, maybe thousands of lights flickering that he knew were alien megaships.

And I thought it was bad inside!

I think it is tough all over, sir.

Roger that.

"Tower, this is Slayer One. Snap us back!"

Almost as quickly as the Slayers had been teleported into space with all the attacking Chiata that were on the QMT pad, the QMT operators of the *Penzington* snapped the tank squadron back leaving the aliens floating free in the direct line of fire of the ship's aft starboard supercarrier's DEGs.

"Slayer One to *Penzington*. They're all yours, Admiral!"

"Roger that, Dragon."

The supercarrier leg of the megaship poured green beams across the battlescape at them. DEGs began lighting the aliens up just as the Slayers snapped back to the QMT pad where they'd started. There were still Chiata bouncing about but only a small fraction were left in play. Now the numbers were more than in their favor. Dragon's plan had worked better than he'd hoped. These few Chiata would be icing on the cake.

"Alright Slayers, let's mop the rest of these blur bastards up and push forward to help out the AEMs."

Chapter 16

July 24, 2409 AD
U.S.S. Nancy Penzington
Mission Star 74
Chiata Expanse
783 light-years from the Sol System
Saturday, 12:07 P.M. Eastern Time

USMC Sergeant Major Tommy Suez had never minded the sizzling bacon sound of a QMT but he always wished that there was a bacon smell to go along with it as well. He had thought that the sound without the smell was too much of a tease. But then again, he figured if it did smell like bacon he'd then complain about it making him hungry. So, he kept his mouth shut about it. Who knew? Hell, if Commander Buckley heard his comments the CHENG might actually figure out some way to add the taste and smell of bacon to the jumps.

The *Madira* slung the AEMs forward into the interior of the *Penzington* just ahead of the engineering sections nearest the lower outside hull where the Chiata had rammed and boarded the ship. They had quickly moved through the exterior hull and had pushed almost all the way to Engineering where the buzzsaw bots and the clone crew were holding the line about four decks out. Builder bots continuously built up barricades and cover for the soldiers there but the Chiata incoming fire was so hot the barricades were eroded away about as fast as the bots could build them.

As valiant an effort as the crew and bots were making, their numbers were starting to be attrited fairly quickly. The AEMs had to do something, and do it soon, or the *Penzington* could be lost to the aliens.

Colonel Francis Jones had volunteered Jones' Juggernauts to drop in behind the line and see if they couldn't trap the Chiata between a rock and a hard place. Tommy liked the colonel's plan and had every intention of doing his part to be one or both—the rock or the hard place.

But once they bounced in and their quantum membrane imagers, lidar, radar, electro-optical, and all other sensors were pegged to the right showing full up positives on the red force tracker for over seventy Chiata infantry and a mix of mecha two decks below and one in, his enthusiasm to go barrelassing in with guns a blazing waned a bit. They were only a squad of ten armored Marines and there were seven—or maybe eight if you counted the mecha—times that in alien infantry. To top it off, there would be no element of surprise either.

If the AEMs knew the Chiata were there, and it was a shitload of the blurry bastards, Tommy figured that it was most certain that the Chiata knew the AEMs were there in much smaller numbers. There was certainly going to be no element of surprise in anybody's favor and the odds were already overwhelming even for Marines. They needed something else as a force multiplier but all they had was the fact that they were all a bunch of bad-asses. Tommy wasn't so certain that alone would be enough this time.

"Colonel, the blurs are too close to Engineering and outnumber us a good seven to one here and if you add in their force multipliers, sir, well, it ain't a cakewalk, that's for goddamned certain. We have no element of surprise either. We need a clever idea or it'll be some serious meat grinding Hell in there, sir," Tommy told him. "We'll do what you need us to do, sir, but I'd sure as shit rather not feed that grinder any more than we have to."

"Top, I was just thinking the same thing. You got any ideas?" Colonel Jones asked.

"Well sir, I was just thinking, too bad they weren't on the outside deck or we could just get one of the other Fleet ships to shoot 'em with their big gun." Tommy recalled once early in his career shooting a mass driver sabot through a hole in a supercarrier to hit a Seppy Hauler on the other side. That had worked like a charm, but then the CO busted his balls for potentially putting a supercarrier at risk.

"That would be too easy, Top." Sellis almost chuckled. "And Admiral Boland would need a shitload of screen doors following something like that. I'd hate to have that repair bill garnished out of my paycheck."

"Well, other than bringing the roof down on them with ordnance it looks like a straight on barroom knife brawl sir. And the odds are way the Hell on the other side of us. And there ain't even a good pool stick or eight ball to beat 'em with." Tommy didn't like the idea of going in with such overwhelming odds from the start. The Chiata infantry were faster and stronger and harder to grab than a greased pig and the thought of jumping into a pit of the things wasn't too appealing. There just had to be a better way. There had to be a smarter way. Marines were supposed to be smart. They had to figure something out and damned fast.

"Hold on a minute, Top." Jones thought for a moment and then motioned that he was going to join mindviews with him. Then a view of the interior of the ship not much unlike what Top had already been looking at popped up in Tommy's head. "Look here, Tommy. We are here and the Chiata are two decks down and one in from us."

"Yes sir."

"Major Sellis? You listening?"

"Yes sir."

"Any thoughts?" the colonel asked his second officer.

"Well, maybe we could do a combination of what Top just said." Major Sellis, who was at the other end of the stack, then apparently reached into the virtual view and tapped bulkheads in three locations because they started lighting up. "The Chiata are only four corridors from the outside. Look here."

"See what I mean, Top?" he asked Suez.

"Yes sir."

Then the major traced a line with his armored finger, highlighting a pathway. "They are here. If we go down this one corridor here, down this conduit shaft, which, Hell, is big enough to drive a squadron of tanks and a team of elephants through at the same time, then we go through this bulkhead here and across the internal bay that as far as I can tell is mostly abandoned, and then finally blow out this wall into the exterior fire hull which leads into the starboard hangar bay we'd have a clear path from the Chiata to space."

"There are only three bulkheads sealing off the pathway from the outside, sir. We could blow them pretty easy I think, but then what? Colonel? Major?" Tommy asked.

"Well, I was just thinking, can't those blue beams of death from Hell turn corners?" Colonel Jones pondered, rhetorically as far as Tommy could tell. "Well, I wonder if they can be attenuated as well?"

"Not a bad thought, sir, but I think that is above my pay grade," Suez replied, unsure of the plausibility of the entire conversation.

"Mine too, Master Sergeant. Mine too," Colonel Jones agreed.

"The biggest problem I see, sir, would be if the ship were to move, buffet, jerk, or just damned sneeze the BBDs would rip out a Hell of new corridor or two that would keep the builder bots busy as shit. I'm sure Admiral Boland would get a little pissed too, sir," Major Sellis added.

"I agree with Major Sellis, Colonel. But there has to be a smarter way to beat these bastards." Tommy thought about it for a second and recalled blowing up his suit on Tau Ceti years before. "What if we blow them out into space, sir?"

"I'm all ears, Top."

"Well sir, I was just thinking if we timed it just right, we could pull the damned aliens into this chamber here and at the same time blow open the path to outside. The decompression will suck them in that general direction, but with so many turns we'd need a little extra oomph." Tommy reached into the mindview and tapped it. "If we set off an e-suit power core here we could blow the bastards out like flushing a toilet."

"An e-suit power core, Top?" Colonel Jones sounded as if he'd swallowed his tongue.

"Unless you've got a bigger explosive packaged away that isn't on the manifest, sir." Tommy wasn't certain, but he thought he might be onto an idea. "The e-suit power pack makes a damned nice bang. I've seen it before."

"Wait a minute, Top, Colonel, look at this." Major Sellis saw the power conduit system light up with a rerouting warning coming from the ship's CHENG. "They are about to reroute the power for the BBDs around this corridor here. I think I've seen this before."

"I know I have, sir." Tommy Suez knew exactly what was about to happen. "The CHENG is about to do a Buckley Maneuver and only two decks over from the Chiata."

"Hmmm, reckon we could get him to hold off on that for a couple of minutes, Colonel?"

"My thoughts exactly Major! The Almighty smiles down on good Marines, sir!" Tommy said.

"That would be a big fucking oohrah, Colonel!" Major Sellis added.

"Colonel Jones to CHENG *Penzington*."

✤ ✤ ✤

"Yes, Colonel, I understand what you would like for me to do, but to make that type of change to the repair plan, and likewise the battle plan, I would need approval from Admiral Boland," the clone CHENG told him.

"Understood, CHENG. Let's get him on the horn, why don't we. You want to call him or would it be better coming from me? Your call." Colonel Jones wasn't trying to be an ass to the clone officer but he was doing his best to emphasize the crucial time pressure they were under.

"Hold one, Colonel. I'm opening a channel," the clone replied and then continued. "CHENG to CO."

"Go, CHENG."

"Admiral, I've got Colonel Jones tied in. He has a very interesting concept for engaging the Chiata on the engineering decks."

"Upload it quickly, CHENG." Colonel Jones could tell the urgency in the admiral's voice and about that time the ship jerked from a heavy impact. The Chiata were firing BBDs at them again. Jones had hoped that since the enemy troops were boarding the ship, the exterior attacks would stop. But he was realizing that the Chiata were so numerous that sacrificing a few hundred or even a few thousand of their own meant little if anything to them on the grander scale. He was beginning to think of them as insects, even though there was no evidence that they had any bug heritage.

"Done, sir. But the general synopsis is to use the Buckley Junction as a weapon against the Chiata."

"Two birds with one stone?" DeathRay responded with a tone that the Colonel liked. "I like it. Any danger to the ship?"

"Only in that it will take me an extra ninety seconds or so to reroute the energy flow and to direct the builder bots in that section, sir. But no, not really."

"CHENG, do it," Admiral Boland ordered him. Colonel Jones was smiling inside his helmet.

"Aye sir. CHENG out." There was a brief pause and then he responded. "Okay, Colonel, what do you need from me?"

"Okay, Sar'nt Major, what do you need from me?" Corporal Kyle Davis stood with Privates First Class Marta Phelps and Alexia Kolmogorov on his flanks, his hypervelocity automatic rifle, HVAR, at the ready.

"Davis, I need you three to get to this deck." Sergeant Major Tommy Suez explained the plan on the interior ship's map in the DTM interface and pointed at bulkheads across the hangar bay on the other side of the Chiata line and on the opposite wall from the clone firecrews. "The Colonel and I will make a ruckus to distract the bastards, and you three get there at top speed and blow that wall. If that wall isn't taken out before the CHENG blows the junction the power will reroute across the line killing every single one of our troops on that side."

"Got it, Top. When do you want it to blow?" Corporal Davis asked.

"You have one hundred eighty seconds starting . . . now! Go." A countdown clock appeared in his DTM HUD.

"Oh shit!" Kyle gasped. "Uh, you heard the top sergeant. Move it!"

Kyle bounced his jump boots against the deck and

bounced ten meters across the deck in the wrong direction and the two privates didn't move. Kyle didn't even stop moving, hoping the privates would get the lead out of their armor. But they didn't follow him.

"What the fuck, privates? We have to move it now!" he told them. "Let's get the fucking lead out!"

"You're going in the wrong direction, Davis!" Phelps replied.

"Fucking recruits these days," he muttered under his breath and then told his AIC to highlight the pathway in the map for them. "We go that way and it is through seventy armored fucking alien blurs ready to rip your motherfucking arms out. But if we drop down one deck to the big equipment corridor we can slip past them unaware. We'll have to shoot through an extra bulkhead, but I'd much rather be shooting at a metal fucking *wall* that don't shoot fucking *back* than a wall of four meter tall monster alien motherfuckers that shoot the fuck back with big-assed fucking guns. Now MOVE YOUR ASSES!"

"Move your asses!" Major Sellis yelled at the rest of the squad as they bounced to cover firing positions on the forward side of the large equipment bay almost two hundred meters from where the fire crews were fighting in one of the harshest firefights he'd seen, and he'd seen a lot. Along the way they had managed to pick up two clone AEMs that were the only two left of their squad. One of them female and the other male and both were covered from helmet to boot in red and green glowing gunk. It was clear the two of them had been in some really serious shit.

The major had ordered them to either join ranks or flash out. Thinking they'd seen enough action he had expected them to flash out. But they didn't. The two E1 clones filed in with the Juggernauts still ready to fight. He didn't even know that the clones had Marines, but he was glad for the extra personnel. He made sure they had their ammo stocks replenished and he ordered them to take up positions on the back of the team, hoping to give them a bit of a break. Clones or not, the two were Marines and deserved some fucking respect.

Sellis picked a spot behind a mecha mover's front end crane just beneath the bucket at the pinnacle of its tower. "Pick a target and stay on that target until its shields go out and keep firing till it is dead. Do your best to open a gap for the colonel and Top. And cover their asses. If you think the colonel will be mad if we get him killed, that ain't shit compared to what Top will do to you. Fire at will!"

Several of the Chiata broke off the main attack line and turned to rush toward the seven AEMs hunkered down behind various equipment, storage racks, and conduits. A flood of buzzsaw bots appeared around them with a flash of light and suddenly swarmed into the Chiata horde like crazed carnivorous insects with oversized metal sawblades for teeth. They were merely a distraction to the Chiata, but a welcome one nonetheless. Besides, the Marines capitalized on what little diversion they could and were damned happy to do so.

"Alright, Colonel, we're in position!" Sellis said over the AEM tacnet.

✧ ✧ ✧

"Roger that, Major!" Colonel Jones popped several grenades from the launcher on the left shoulder of his suit and he could see Top following his lead and popping out a few on the other side.

"Watch their tendrils, sir!" Tommy warned him. "Those bastards are no fun."

"Understood, Top." Jones dropped and slid into an onrushing alien just as one of the strange mechanized tendrils darted to where his torso had been milliseconds before. "Shit!"

"I got 'em!" Top appeared almost out of nowhere, grabbing the tendril with his left hand and wrapping it twice over his armored thumb and elbow like a firehose reeling the alien inward all the while firing his HVAR at full auto into the head of the red and green blur bouncing about at the other end of it.

Several rounds tore through the air between leaving a faint blue glowing ion trail as the *spittap spattap spittap* of the HVAR auto fire breaking the sound barrier echoed in the colonel's ears. The rounds continued plowing the Chiata that Top had wrapped up until finally the creature's personal armor shields flickered green and went out.

"Go left, Top!" he shouted, but Suez had already anticipated both the alien's and his next move.

The alien's next move was to throw another tendril at him but Top leapt upward into a back tuck coming down on top of the tendril with both armored feet firing his rifle at point-blank range into it, cutting the appendage loose. Sparks and red and green fluids spewed out where Top had been a second before. He had already fallen backwards giving the colonel a perfect shot on the alien.

"Gotcha!" Jones depressed the trigger on his rifle and the hypervelocity rounds threw chunks of alien flesh from the front side of the creature, through its own body, and out the back side explosively. The alien screeched and fell limp to the floor in a growing puddle of the red and green liquid.

Three more aliens blurred into position where the one had fallen. The colonel rolled backwards onto his feet popping out some more grenades coming to a clanking rest against the deck in a three-point sprinter's stance. Several rounds left ion trails over his head and he could see Top spinning, bobbing, and weaving like a whirling dervish leaving Chiata body parts in his wake. The sergeant major was a powered armored killing spectacle to behold. His meter-long blade was extended from his left arm and his rifle in his right. He spun, slashed, shot, kicked, punched, and headbutted anything nonhuman in his path.

Jones sprinted into the three aliens at the full speed of the armored suit matching his speed and motion to that of the attacking blurs. To the unaided eye it would have been unclear which blur was the Marine and which was an alien. Tendrils darted in and out and around the colonel in every direction. Hypervelocity rounds tore holes in the air leaving glowing trails in every direction. The colonel fired his own weapon nonstop, tracking the blurs from one side of the room to the next.

"Alright, Top, I think we got their attention! Major Sellis, form a phalanx and attack right up the gut!"

"Ooh-fuckin'-rah, Colonel!" Sellis replied.

The blue dots behind him made a vee shape in his mindview of the battlescape and slid right across the room at over fifty kilometers per hour right in front of the colonel and just to the left of the top sergeant. As soon as they passed by him, he pinged Top in the mindview and the two of them formed up with the phalanx attack.

From the corner of his peripheral view he could see Top grabbing a buzzsaw bot by the ass end and shoving it into the gut of a nearby Chiata infantryman. He used the bot to rip the alien open from crotch to chin. Jones just shook his head in awe.

"What do good Marines do when facing an overwhelming and more powerful force?" Top shouted on the tacnet channel.

"Retreat, Hell!" the Marines responded.

"Attack!" Major Sellis shouted.

"Ray, Top and I will cover the back door. You stay on point. We've got to make a big enough splash that these bastards all want to follow us across the equipment bay," Colonel Jones told the Major.

"Affirmative, Colonel! Hope our package gets delivered on time!"

"Kolmo, is your charge set yet?" Corporal Davis made the last adjustments to his charge that was magnetically attached to what his AIC had told him was the weakest point of the bulkhead. There was a hatch about seventy meters down that had been welded shut before the fighting started and that was where Phelps had gone. Kolmogorov was about ninety meters in the other direction down a side corridor that was only big enough for about one mecha at a time to fit through. That was plenty big enough for the three AEMs and for Chiata mecha and infantry alike. He knew they'd better keep their eyeballs peeled or they might just end up shish kebabbed on a Chiata skewer.

Kyle triggered the quantum connected wireless processor on the charge and started to turn back down the larger hall just as his red force tracker alert system pinged. "Shit! We've got company. Where are you, Phelps?"

"I'm under cover, Davis, but I haven't got the charges set yet," PFC Phelps replied. "I'm pinned down."

"Shit, shit, shit!" Kyle watched as the clock ticked down to thirty seconds in his mindview.

"We don't have time for this!" Kyle looked at the ticking numbers and then at the red dots in his mindview. There were two of them between the bulkhead and Phelps. Somebody had to do something. There were more than a hundred soldiers and crew on the other side of the engineering deck and every single one of them were going to get fried if they didn't blow those bulkheads. The worst part about it was that Kyle knew that he was the ranking Marine there. So doing something in this case pretty much meant it was up to him.

"Aw Hell, fuck it!" Kyle said as he stepped out from behind the equipment rack attached to the bulkhead that had given him cover and dropped to a knee.

Targeting Xs flashed up and he pulled the trigger on his rifle at full auto. *Spittap, spittap, spittap.* The two Chiata turned and instantly fired a plasma volley at him. He bounced and rolled, never letting off of the trigger, filling the corridor with ion trails as he made it to his jump boots. He bounced about the corridor like a racquetball in a championship match.

The clock in his mindview continued counting down—sixteen, fifteen, fourteen . . .

Kyle passed by where Phelps' blue dot was dodging incoming fire. A black Chiata mechanized tendril bounced against the Buckley barrier shield on his left thigh and glanced off with a flicker of green light. The shield generator dropped to seventy percent. Another tendril hit him square in the chest, knocking him off his feet but still hadn't penetrated the barrier shield or the armor.

Shields at forty-three percent, Kyle, his AIC warned.

That fuckin' hurt, he thought. But Kyle didn't let it stop him. As soon as the tendril had knocked him down, he rolled to his left, up to one knee catching the tendril under his arm as the alien retracted it, and then he rolled himself around it pulling in until he was face-to-face with the red and green blur.

"You are one ugly motherfucker," he said. Kyle slammed the barrel of his HVAR into the alien so hard that its shield flickered long enough for the barrel to penetrate its armor. He continued to fire until the back of the alien's head blew out red and green glowing fluids against the bulkhead behind him. Just as much of the nasty shit splattered on him as well.

The clock ticked down some more—nine, eight, seven . . .

"Throw me your charge now!" he shouted to Phelps. Out of the corner of his mindview he could sense the small cubic package being hurled toward him. He grabbed it with his left hand and in one motion spun slapping the bomb against the second Chiata's back plates.

Kyle felt an intense pressure in his left side but didn't have time to think about it. He jumped backwards, falling over and kicking the alien with both feet at the wall plate, causing the alien to lose its balance. He lowered his rifle and pumped a few tens of rounds into the alien's shielding to push it closer to the wall.

"Get down!" he shouted. He triggered the explosive just as the alien regained its composure but it was too late for it.

Trigger the other two now!

Affirmative, Kyle, his AIC replied in his mindvoice.

The detonation of the first charge tossed him backwards several tens of meters and something felt as if it tore through his side. He was disoriented briefly and started to feel pain. The second and third charges blew, adding to his confusion. Then his suit started talking to him, or was it his AIC. He wasn't sure and he thought he was going to throw up or pass out. Maybe both.

Administering immunoboost and stimulants. Organogel is sealing into your wounds, his AIC explained.

Chapter 17

July 24, 2409 AD
U.S.S. *Nancy Penzington*
Mission Star 74
Chiata Expanse
783 light-years from the Sol System
Saturday, 12:12 P.M. Eastern Time

"Admiral, several tens more Chiata megaships have dropped out of hyperspace and it is clear that they see us as the easiest target, sir," the XO said, getting Jack's attention. He'd been preoccupied briefly with the fight going on in the belly of his ship.

"We really do not need to take another hit from the enemy BBDs until we get the power system back online, sir," the STO added. "The barrier shields are at five percent and the SIFs are only at seventy-one. One good solid hit and we will be breached."

"Keep us between the *Madira* and those new ships. I mean as close as we can get! Those goddamned blue beams turn pretty tight corners," DeathRay ordered. He looked at the battlescape in his mindview and plotted an energy line course for his ship. He was searching for the best way to keep himself protected from the enemy beams and the only way he could see to do that was by using the *Madira* as a shield. "Helm, calculate a course to jump right in the middle of those ships and be ready to go on my order."

"Aye, sir."

"CO *Penzington* to CO *Madira*."

"Go ahead, Jack." General Moore's avatar popped up into the mindview.

"General, as I'm sure your team has learned by now, they know I'm a wounded fish and are circling in for the kill," Jack told him.

"I suspect you are right, Jack. What do you propose we do about it?"

"Our BBDs will be online soon, sir. I say we continue to let them think we're dead. You act the part of the mama seal protecting her wounded baby from a pack of orcas. Let them circle in and then we gut them!" Jack explained his plan. "My thoughts are that I'll have Dee's team then attack from the outside as well. If we brought in twenty or more of those supercarriers we might just take us a bunch of megaships in one attack."

"I like that plan, Jack," General Moore replied. "I'll supply the cover and the supercarriers. I'll have the *Decatur* lay back with Dee."

"Yes sir. Seventy-five seconds sir, clock is ticking. DeathRay out."

"CHENG to CO."

"Go, CHENG. Please tell me my BBDs are coming

online soon! I just committed us to the general in seventy-two seconds."

"Aye sir, as long as the firecrews and the AEMs clear out by then we will be good to go. I was calling to ask you for approval of a full snap-back of the troops in the Buckley Junction danger area highlighted on the Engineering Level Three Map, sir."

"Understood, CHENG. Request is authorized. Great work. Time it with the countdown clock."

"Aye sir. Thank you, sir. CHENG out."

"Ground Boss!" Jack turned and looked to the other side of the bridge at the ground troop station. "Status on the AEMs in the engineering decks?"

"Colonel Jones is presently engaging the Chiata hand-to-hand. Looks like, as you say, sir, some 'serious shit'." DeathRay almost laughed at the clone's use of the vulgarity. "The rate of attrition from the AEMs and the firecrews is starting to go nonlinear. The Slayers are ten seconds out for support."

"Are the Chiata in position to spring the trap?" Jack asked the Ground Boss officer.

"Not quite, sir. But Colonel Jones swears they'll be ready when you are," the clone replied. "I think once the Slayers are in the mix they will be where they need to be."

"Anything else?"

"There are some minor casualties, sir, but none that can't stand a snap-back. I suggest we snap the wounded to the med bays now."

"Do it."

DeathRay to Phoenix, he thought on a private channel to her.

Go, DeathRay.

I'm sending you a battle plan. Your father is sending the U.S.S. Stephen Decatur *to your wing. As soon as you see the* Penzington *and the* Madira *going balls out on the BBDs from the center of the ball you start pounding them from the outside of it. Understand?*

Standard periphery support to a Deathblossom?

Damn right. By the way, Candis tells me you broke my record.

Did you expect that I would??

Never. Be ready. DeathRay out.

"We could use some damned reinforcements!" Major Sellis looked at the stump where his left hand had been. The suit had sealed it off and shunted the pain. Immunoboost and stims had been administered and the QMT operator had requested a snap-back to medical twice, but the major's AIC had overridden the command twice already. "We have to continue to draw them backwards as close to the smaller corridor as possible."

"Ray, you really should let them flash you out of here." Colonel Jones stood back-to-back with the major firing every weapon the suit could manage. Grenades popped from their shoulder harnesses and rounds cut through the air from the hyper velocity rifles. "We are still a good fifty meters short of the target zone and we're running out of time."

"Yes sir! That's why I ain't flashed out. Can't let you and Top have all the fun." Major Sellis stepped away from the colonel quickly as a blur tried to harpoon him with a tendril. "Missed me, you alien asshole!"

The tendril shot between the two of them, missing the target. Sellis spun quickly, karate chopping the tendril with his stump and wrapping it up with every intention of pulling the alien in for the kill. But it had been a trap. Just as he wrapped up the tendril to the point that neither of them could move quickly several Chiata blurred at him in a mad rush firing their plasma weapons. Two of the rounds hit the major square in the chest, flashing green and blue radiation over him as his barrier shields flickered out. Then a second set of tendrils darted through his back and out his stomach causing red blood to spew out of the armor briefly before the organogel seal layer stopped the bleeding. Major Sellis fired his HVAR at the thing, cutting it free but not before a third Chiata wrapped a tendril around his head, pulling him over backwards.

"Sonofabitch!" he shouted and kicked at the alien as it continued jabbing at him with one of its tendrils.

"Hang on, Ray!" Colonel Jones did a back tuck onto the Chiata, pounding the barrel of his HVAR through its face all the while firing the weapon. The alien's head exploded just as three more wrapped up the colonel overpowering him.

"Fucking Chiata!" the colonel screamed as it happened and Ray could see him extending and extracting his serrated meter-long blade in and out of any alien body or tendril close enough to be skewered. But mostly the blade ricocheted off the alien's shields or armor. Jones continued to fire his HVAR full auto into whatever was piling on and he swiped and stabbed the blade about, but he was being overwhelmed and then one of the alien tendrils pierced through Colonel Jones' right leg, then his left shoulder, then his chest.

Like a tornado, Sergeant Major Tommy Suez spun between them in some sort of butterfly spinning kick firing two rifles continuously. Major Sellis could barely tell what was going on since hanging on to consciousness was tough at the moment. But what he did manage to ascertain was that the top sergeant was saving their asses. And then he saw Top go down to all fours just as he started to tunnel out.

I guess we can snap-back now, he thought to his AIC. His last visual was of a giant metal behemoth drop kicking the shit out of one of the Chiata and then he was out.

"Are you alright, Sar'nt Major?" Colonel Slayer offered the AEM a huge mechanical hand up with his free hand. The other was squeezing the head of an alien until it popped like a water balloon.

"Yes sir. Colonel Jones and Major Sellis are both snapped back to medical and we are all beat up pretty badly, sir. None of that will matter if we don't push these bastards to that wall in the next thirty seconds!" Suez replied.

"Got it," Slayer One replied. "Alright, Slayers. We push through then push them back. We have thirty seconds. Now form up on me and start kicking some alien ass!"

Dragon pounced through the onslaught of Chiata that were on the tails of the AEMs and with a giant leap was damned near across the bay to the other side. There were several other tanks in bot-mode that followed similar paths. As soon as he hit the ground, Slayer turned and went to full auto on his wrist cannons and fired his nose big gun twice into the front of the Chiata. Rather than actually targeting them, he shot again at their feet. The tank squadron continued to march while firing at the Chiata infantry which were less suited to handle the tanks than the alien mecha had been in the aft section of the ship.

"Keep pushing them, Slayers!" He watched the clock tick down in his mindview until it reached single digits. The Chiata had moved but he wasn't sure if they had moved enough. Then there was a flash of light and the Slayers were all in a muster point near the port forward hangar bay. There were AEMs and firecrews flashing in as well. Dragon checked his blue force tracker and the wounded AEMs and seamen had been QMTed direct to medical.

Commander Jacob, "Thirty-one" as the admiral called him, traced the energy flow systems of the entire megaship and the four supercarriers attached from power generation modules in the center of the giant retrofitted alien ship all the way through every pathway and corridor and cable until it reached the exterior mounted Buckley-Freeman field generator, all the way to the directed energy guns, and all the way through the blue beam gain media and the tuning fork projectors. He knew that the systems at the beginning and end were functional. Now he just needed to complete the power flow pathway between them.

As soon as the clock ticked to zero and as soon as he

was certain all the humans—he considered the AI-driven clones to be human also whether the other humans did or not—were safe, he toggled the circuit to trigger the power transfer. The power modules collected and stored energy from the quantum vacuum at a rate based on the power needs of the ship. In order to supply the enormous energy draw required by the BBDs, conduits large enough to drive a hovertank through were required. And where the conduits had blown out, he had rerouted them through hallways, engineering access tubes, and even thermal control plenums. This had been a clever and standard technique invented by Commander Joe Buckley Jr.

While the concept worked and was clever, it also had the side effect of throwing hard X-rays off the walls of the corridors as the power was transferred. Anyone standing even within twenty meters of one of the pathways would be fried and dosed to death almost instantly. Anyone within fifty meters would be radiation dosed so hot that their insides would swell and fail within a few minutes after exposure and then they'd die. Anyone standing in direct line of sight within a hundred meters and no bulkheads between them would need almost all their organs replaced. The engineering records from the *Sienna Madira* showed that the one time Buckley had successfully done this it was on a smaller scale and across the Vortex Projector Room in Engineering only a few tens of meters. It had saved the ship, but Joe and his assistant were rushed to medical and had every organ in their bodies replaced including their testicles. The video of Commander Buckley discussing that wasn't pleasant. Thirty-one knew that the bottom line was if nonstandard conduits were used to transfer power to the big guns, staying the Hell as far away as possible was a damned good idea for everyone, and that included the Chiata.

"CHENG to CO."

"Go, CHENG."

"Sir, you have use of the main gun. As soon as you fire the BBD you will solve our Chiata infestation problem on board. Your window is very short, as the Chiata are starting to move about, according to the onboard tracking systems."

"Understood CHENG. Preparing to fire the BBDs. CO out."

DeathRay was tired of being on the receiving end of the ass whooping and damned ready to start taking the shit back to the aliens. He steadied himself in his oversized captain's chair and clenched his armored fists tight. He missed the snug fit of the pilot's couch in his mecha. He pondered briefly if they could retrofit one in place of the captain's chair. He watched as the blue force tracker showed all personnel accounted for and off the engineering deck's danger zones. Thirty-one was right. His window was open now.

"Helmsman, hyperspace jump now!" he ordered. The clone efficiently and immediately followed the order and instantly the vortex of Cerenkov radiation appeared before the ship. The whirling blue flashes formed a spinning tube around the ship and then almost as quickly they were several hundred thousand kilometers from where they had been and the Chiata saw it as a wounded animal on the run. The ships followed suit and were quickly all engaging the *Penzington*. Thirty-six porcusnails circled them like orcas moving in for the kill.

"The *Madira* just materialized ten thousand kilometers to starboard and slightly below us," the XO reported. "All DEGs and the BBDs are ready when you are, Admiral."

"Fire at will, all batteries!" DeathRay ordered and he watched his interior ship's monitors as well as the exterior ball. As soon as the ship vibrated and the two spires above the bridge dome started arcing across to each other and a circle of blue light formed in the middle of them twirling about like a maelstrom, a smile grew on his face. Then the blue beam of death from Hell shot forth putting out blinding zettawatts of power. The blue beam turned to the right then down and then back left and hit one of the megaships right at the junction between the tuning fork and the main body of the porcusnail just beneath the bridge dome. DeathRay's crew had become seriously efficient at their jobs—even deadly efficient. The BBD was spot on precisely hitting the aliens right where it hurt them most. In the *Penzington's* interior ship's map in his mindview, about seventy red dots instantly vanished from the engineering decks.

There are some more dead blur bastards for you Nancy, he thought.

"We've weakened the alien's shield considerably, Admiral," the STO said.

"Fire all weapons on that spot!" Jack ordered.

The DEG batteries of the two forward supercarrier appendages spurt forth bright reds and greens and violet beams as well as gamma rays all at the target spot. Several missiles leapt from the forward launch tubes and detonated gluonium warheads.

"Alien ship's shields still operational it appears, sir, but they certainly can't take much more of this."

"Sir, the BBDs have recharged," the gunner said.

"Fire!"

The beam zigged and zagged through the ball into the ship precisely on target again. This time the zettawatts of power in the BBD was all that was needed to knock out the alien ship's shield generators and the resulting explosions created a perfect entry for mecha.

We'll take another ship in your name, Nancy, he thought.

She would be proud of you, Jack, his AIC told him in his mind.

She was always proud of me, Candis. And I her, that isn't what this is about. Jack fought back tears. *This is more about avenging her.*

Perhaps, uh, I wish, sir, that you and Dee would both take everyone's recommendation and get some counseling on that.

Everyone, Candis, just needs to mind their own goddamned business in that regard. Dee and I are doing just what the fuck we need to and that is that. Don't start that shit right now. Jack and Candis had argued in his mind for weeks about if either he or Dee were fit for duty presently based on how they were each handling their grief. Jack had insisted that anger and a drive for vengeance was the best thing in humanity's favor right now and for her to shut the fucking Hell up about it. The problem with having an extra intelligence in your mind all the time was that sometimes they just wouldn't shut the fuck up.

Yes, Admiral Boland.

And knock that shit off too. Candis and Jack had been together for decades and he understood that her algorithms were simply concerned for him. He didn't want to completely alienate her. Hell, after all, barring having her physically—and that meant surgically—removed he had to live with her in there.

Sorry, Jack.

Forget it. Pay attention to the fight in front of us not behind us.

I thought I was.

"DeathRay to General Moore."

"Go, Jack."

"Looks like we've got one, sir! There's your entry point!" He sent the coordinates of the hole in the side of the alien ship to Moore. "Shields are down! Send in the supercarriers and the builder bots."

"Roger that! Stay at it, Admiral."

Chapter 18

July 24, 2409 AD
Bringer's Megaship
Mission Star 74
Chiata Expanse
783 light-years from the Sol System
Saturday, 12:22 P.M. Eastern Time

Major Deanna Moore had left the interior defenses in the hands of the extremely capable, and Dee had sometimes thought since the first day she had seen her as a child, "goddesslike", hands of Colonel Delilah "Jawbone" Strong. The mecha pilot had saved her life on several occasions and had been a great role model—as if she didn't have plenty of those in her life already. The woman was a rock-hard Marine pilot and still "all woman" at the same time. Dee had sometimes joked with her AIC that if she ever decided that she liked women, that Colonel Strong would be the one she'd like to start with. But Dee had too much respect for her, and perhaps even a bit of intimidation by her, that she would never disrespect her, herself, or the Marines by doing or saying anything unprofessional in Jawbone's regard. And she liked men too much at the present time to go down that path anyway.

Dee had actually sometimes thought that Colonel Strong might someday fill the sister void left when Nancy Penzington was killed by the Chiata, but they weren't that kind of close and Dee wasn't ready for that closeness with people yet. But in her mind she could fantasize all she wanted and her AIC had often told her, especially lately, that human fantasy was a good healing mechanism as long as she didn't escape completely there and never come out. None of her AIC's counseling or her parents' nurturing or her fellow and superior officers supporting her filled the void in her soul that Davy Rackman had filled. She hadn't even realized that she had that void in her until she had met the Navy SEAL. Then when she was with him she, they, were something so much bigger than either of them separately. Their relationship was a true testament to the phrase "bigger than the sum of its parts".

When Davy was killed, to Deanna, it felt as if there was a gaping rift ripped through the fabric of the universe that could never be repaired. It was an endlessly deep supermassive black hole of sadness, despair, loneliness, anger, but more than that. She didn't even have the words to express what the feeling was. A "hole" was the only way she could explain it. And it was a hole right through her very being. It was a hole through her.

Dee could only hope that she could and would someday kill enough Chiata to fill that hole up enough that she could crawl out of it, but for now the adit to her pit of despair was a tiny circle of light so far above her head that it might as well have been all the way at the other side of the universe. She wasn't sure there were enough Chiata in the galaxy to fill that void, but she was going to find out. And she was going to give her best all-out effort and then some to throw alien body after body into the pit with her. She constantly recalled DeathRay's order to her at the funeral for Davy and Nancy. He had told her that they had "too many of those alien motherfuckers to kill before dying". Deanna remembered that every moment of her life now and focused on doing just that, killing those alien motherfuckers and not dying. One day, centuries from now, Deanna wanted there to be legends in the barely surviving Chiata race about the day they met their Satan. She wanted the Chiata to tremble at the mention of her name and cower away for they would know that with her would come Hell.

She bounced off the giant equipment platform elevator with her ever-present wingman and watchdog Azazel on her flank. The two of them clanked their mecha to the oversized Chiata mecha-sized doorway and stepped through the strange alien metametal that morphed out of the way to within microns of their mecha's exterior as if they were walking through water or some quantum foam and into the giant bridge dome of the Chiata megaship. Dee had been on seven of the megaship bridges and the door must have been either experimental or a sign of newer ships because on some of the ships there were standard hatches with actual doors and on other there was the metametal.

Builder bots scurried about scraping, cutting, welding,

soldering, screwing, hammering, and every other kind of "ing" imaginable doing their best to rebuild the ship real-time and during combat. Dee took a half a second to look at the builder bots' locations throughout the ship and could see they were working diligently by the tens of thousands. With the Chiata mostly pushed off the ship and the Maniacs and the rest of the Bringers mopping up, the Fleet now had a new mega-class warship that needed a name. It also needed a captain.

"Molloch, give me a status report," she ordered her second in command. The clone was still in his mecha and linked to all the ship's system. His wingman Abbadon was standing stalwart at the translucent metamaterial morphing hatchway with his weapon at the ready.

"As you can see from the mindview battlescape, Major Moore, DeathRay and General Moore have entered a considerably overwhelming combat ball. The *U.S.S. Stephen Decatur* has formed up on our wing and we are targeting, hold one . . ." Molloch had to pause for a second and converse in his DTM interface briefly. "The supercarriers are all fully online again and are ready with the superweapon when needed. The BBDs are charged and ready to engage."

"Well, don't sit there telling me! DeathRay and the general are each in a megaship deathblossom and need exterior ball support. Fire at will!" Deanna ordered. "All weapons, all missile batteries!"

"Yes, ma'am," Molloch replied. He didn't hesitate upon her order and suddenly the snail antennae tuning fork of the porcusnail that loomed into space above the bridge dome started throwing arcs from one tine to the other and a blue whirling vortex formed in the middle followed by a blindingly brilliant blue beam of death from Hell shooting forth across the bow of the ship and out into space. The beam turned downward went around one alien megaship, missed several Fleet supercarriers and hit the aft section of the ship currently firing on the *Penzington*.

"Good shot, Molloch." Dee zoomed in closer on the ship in her mindview and realized the beam was repelled by the alien's shields. "Didn't do enough damage."

"Yes, ma'am," Molloch agreed. "Suggestions?"

"No. Just keep shooting at them."

"We'll need almost a minute to recharge the BBDs," Molloch said.

"Understood, Molloch. Don't wait on my order. Just keep firing."

Deanna, that ship has an overloading conduit at these coordinates, suddenly sounded in her head. It was her mother's mindvoice.

Mom?

But you have to fire now!

How are you . . .

Later, fire everything now!

"Molloch, focus all DEG batteries on these coordinates now!" she ordered him. "CO *Decatur*, this is Major Moore!"

"Go ahead, Major."

"Captain, please fire your BBDs at these coordinates. We have intelligence that suggest there is a weakness there!" Deanna did her best to explain and hoped the captain of the flagship's sister ship would take her word for it. Being the fleet's commanding general's daughter helped she figured.

"Understood Major. Will do."

With that a BBD fired outward from the *Decatur's* tuning fork spire and zigged around the ball until it hit home on the targeted ship with precision. The alien megaship flickered from bow to stern as the shields failed and in several locations the ship seemed to bulge at the seams until orange and white plasma erupted from it into space. The ship began to swing away and then cracked open just beneath the antenna. The large porcusnail megaship finally exploded in staggered bursts from front to back and then it was nothing but a large shrapnel field on the leading edge of a blast wave once the power system for the BBDs and the hyperdrive went. Instantly, tens of thousands of Chiata were sent to Hell.

"Oohrah!" Deanna shouted excitedly. "Take that, motherfuckers! We are the Bringers of Hell!"

"Ooh-fuckin'-rah, Major," Azazel added, with over the top and almost out of place inflections.

Deanna, target this ship here! Her mother somehow placed a DTM battlescape in her mindview and identified where to focus fire very precisely.

Keep giving me targets, mother!

Yes, here is an updated view of every ship in the system, but it is complicated and confusing. We will continue to analyze it, but I think you might understand it better than us at the moment.

How are you doing this?

The Thgreeth.

Understood.

"Molloch, new firing coordinates for the BBDs as soon as they are online!" She transferred the targeting information to him and adjusted her mecha's stance slightly to make it more stable in case they took another big hit of any sort. She didn't want to fall over while focusing on something else. Adjusting herself in the pilot's couch, she relaxed her mind and did her best to take in the mindview her mother was placing in her DTM.

The battlescape was different, more complicated, and with such detail that she suspected she could zoom in on any ship in the system down to the nuts, bolts, and rivets. Yellow and red flashing highlights appeared all over the alien megaships in multiple engagements, not just her present situation. Deanna expanded her viewpoint beyond the ball that her father and DeathRay were in and could see her grandmother's fleet and Admiral Walker's flotilla engaged in their own sub-conflicts. There were multiple balls scattered about the system that made up a larger, more complicated ball. And in each situation, it looked to Dee as if they were never targeting the alien ships at the right location, or the right alien ship at the right time. She realized how on edge the Chiata drove their ships and how they used the numbers game to overwhelm their opponents. This new intelligence showed the linchpin in their machinations of war. And it was a linchpin she intended to pull and hopefully the wheels would fly off the Chiata war machine. Somehow, this Thgreeth information was updating real-time and telling her right where to strike—in essence which linchpin to pull and when to pull it.

Had the rest of the aliens fighting the Chiata been able

to see this type of information the advancing attack waves might be slowed, stopped, and even turned back. Dee realized quickly that the megaships were running many systems redlined at once but were managing them well by playing a numbers game. They would redline a set of systems and then shuffle duties to systems in the green giving time for cooling and repairing. The intel data was so spot on that she believed she could determine exactly which ships to hit when and where throughout the entire engagement and maybe even at a larger scale.

This is bigger than just us, Bree. Can you see this? she thought to her AIC.

I'm sorry Deanna, but I cannot see what you are seeing but from the quantum interference with the standard DTM interface I can tell that you are receiving a significant amount of data. Quantum coherence between my superconducting sensors and your brain's microtubule proteins is seeing a major increase in the noise floor and bit errors, Bree explained. *Can you perhaps ask the Thgreeth if they will allow me to see the information too?*

Not sure how to do that, she thought in reply and then thought of her mother. *Mom, can you ask the Thgreeth system how I can give my AIC access to this information?*

I will.

"CO *Madira*, CO *Penzington*, copy?"

"Go, Phoenix." DeathRay's avatar popped up in her DTM mindview.

"Go, Major." Her father appeared in her mind almost as quickly.

"I'm getting amazing intelligence from mother at the

Thgreeth ruins. It is real-time and down to the nuts and bolts detail of every ship in this system," she started, but her father interrupted her.

"Cut to the chase, Major," her father said. DeathRay remained quiet if not preoccupied.

"Yes sir. I have targeting information for instantaneous weaknesses of every ship. Unfortunately, it is coming directly to my mind and I can't transfer it," she explained.

"Then Phoenix you'll have to call the ball!" DeathRay told her. "You point and we'll shoot."

"Sir," she said to her father directly. "I can see ALL ships in this engagement. I could tell every captain the optimum target at any given instant. It is a lot of targeting data but not so different from managing a deathblossom or a mecha fight in the ball."

"Stand by, Captain," her father said. That confused her, as clearly her father understood her rank structure and that he certainly hadn't just demoted her a rank. Then suddenly all the captains of the Fleet appeared in her mindview and she realized that she was on the Fleet captain's commandnet channel.

"Listen up, all," her father began. "Lieutenant Colonel Deanna Moore is now captain of the *U.S.S. Davy Rackman*. She is receiving precise targeting information from classified sources unavailable to any other Fleet personnel. If you receive a targeting coordinate information from Captain Moore that target becomes priority. Understood?"

"Aye, sir!" resounded from all the Navy captains in the Fleet.

Deanna was shocked and almost came to tears. The field promotion to lieutenant colonel was great. But she hadn't ever wanted to be a megaship's captain. She was a mecha pilot. But the tipping point, and Dee assumed that was why her father had done it, was to name the ship after Davy. Tears rolled down her cheeks. She was glad that things like that didn't get transferred into the avatar in the DTM communications nets. Quickly her suit slurped up the tears and lowered the humidity in her helmet. Then the icon on her blue dot in the tracker was updated to show her rank and new assignment. At that point she looked down at her chest and saw the rank insignia change as well. She was a ship's captain suddenly and wasn't sure what she was supposed to do.

"Well, Captain Moore, I'm ready for orders," her grandmother added.

"Captain Moore." Her father's avatar looked at her expressionlessly. "Please begin with the targeting information."

"Um, uh, yes, General." She cleared the lump in her throat and then paused for a breath. Dee pulled up the system wide DTM battlescape that all the soldiers in system could see. Then she overlaid the Thgreeth picture on top of it and they were a one to one fit. Now all she had to do was physically transfer the information to the Fleet battlescape view by verbal, thought, and touch control.

Bree, turn on all Fleet ships' name icons and broadcast my DTM view updates real-time to all the ship captains.

Roger that. That connection is live now, uh, Captain. Bree had the hint of laughter in her mindvoice. The AIC had been with Dee for so long that it knew the types of jokes that would goad her and dig into her skin.

Oh shut up. She hated the thought of not being a mecha pilot right then and there and she knew suddenly how DeathRay must feel. But the thought of using the name Davy Rackman to kill thousands, maybe tens of thousands or more, Chiata was enough to make up for it. There would always be another time to fly mecha.

"Okay, I am sending all of you my battlescape view now and will highlight your respective targets. I'll call them as they pop up in the order of maximum possible damage or impact as best I can. I can only ask that you are patient with me as this is an overwhelming amount of data to assimilate." Dee looked for the first target. There were thousands of ships in the system. It was like eating an elephant. It didn't really matter where you started but you did have to take the first bite.

Just pick a ship, Dee. They don't know what order of importance this is. They're taking your word for it. Just be close to right and it is still an advantage. Like fighting in the Ball, it doesn't matter who is killed first. Her AIC offered her some much-welcome advice, which is why the artificial intelligence counterparts were invented in the first place.

Right! It matters who isn't killed at the last. Thanks, Bree. That helps.

"*Mueller*, target this ship at these coordinates."

"Roger that, Captain Moore!" Sienna Madira replied.

"*Madira*, here, here, and here in that order!" she told her father.

"*Thatcher*, you need to hit the ship aft of you, here below the power core."

"Understood, Captain Moore," Admiral Walker replied.

"*Lincoln*! Stop firing on your present target and focus your weapons on its wingman, here!"

"*Penzington*, here, here, and here!"

"Roger that, Phoenix!"

"General Moore, we have a mass of ships hiding inside the atmosphere of this gas giant seven AUs out. Looks to be thousands. I suggest a superweapon detonation there as soon as possible. Maybe it should be followed by a second superweapon as soon as they regroup. I will keep you apprised following the first."

"Understood Captain Moore."

"General, I volunteer to hit the gas giant. Superweapon is charged and fully operational," the captain of the *U.S.S. February Ramirez* offered.

"Roger that, go *Ramirez*!" General Moore ordered.

"Supercarrier group thirty-seven, if you will soften up this ship now with your DEGs before you ram you can penetrate its shields and start taking that ship!" Deanna's mind was a flurry of information to the point that she felt as if she were in two places at once. She was momentarily distracted by the brilliant flash of blue above her head as Molloch was following her orders and firing the BBDs at his assigned targeting coordinates as soon as they were charged and ready. Dee watched briefly out the dome as the blue beams tracked across space in their strange guided zig-zag pattern until it hit home on a megaship almost one hundred thousand kilometers away. The ship flickered and then its shields failed.

"Awaiting further orders, Captain Moore," Molloch said on their mecha squad tacnet. "Might I suggest something?"

"By all means, Molloch! What'dya got?"

"Allow Azazel and myself to run the bridge of the *Rackman* as your XO and gunner and other duties as necessary so you can focus on your battle tasking," Molloch offered.

"Very good, Molloch. I thought you were doing that anyway." She turned to Azazel in her DTM tacnet view. "You heard the man. Plug in and start doing something."

"Yes, ma'am," Azazel replied.

I have a suggestion, Captain, Bree said into her mind.

Go, Bree. And seriously, knock off the 'captain' shit.

Okay, Captain, I mean, Dee. I will run a list in your mind and highlight whose turn it is to fire and will only highlight their names if their BBDs are ready to go. As I tell you who is ready, then you tell them where to fire. This way you don't have to keep up with who has been tasked and who hasn't.

Roger that, Bree. Great plan. I need all the help I can get here. Let's do that now!

Suddenly a list on a scroll menu appeared to the right of the battlescape in her mind. The *U.S.S. Joseph Strauss* was at the top of the list in bold. The other fourteen megaships were racked and stacked in order of readiness according to Dee's AIC. The ships that just fired were pushed to the bottom of the stack. The next seventeen minutes were a continuous flow of data from the Thgreeth system through Dee's brain into the Fleet connected mindview battlescape.

With each new targeting coordinate and engagement a Chiata ship was stalled, stopped, or destroyed. In a period of eighteen months prior Dee and her Bringers of

Hell mecha squadron had managed to kill maybe three hundred aliens total, and maybe once the superweapon was engaged several tens of thousands were vaporized. In those engagements it was the larger Fleet doing the killing and not by her hand, so she didn't feel as responsible and didn't feel the vengeance for Rackman and Penzington. But in this engagement, a mere seventeen minutes, she had personally directed one superweapon detonation that had killed over forty thousand Chiata, thirty-seven BBD hits, nine of which totally destroyed the vessels impacted, killing many thousands, and multiple smaller supercarrier ramming attacks. Dee felt some inner satisfaction and something a little short of satiation as she continued to fill her void with dead aliens.

While her killing of the aliens had become much more efficient in the last few tens of minutes, they were still way on the underside of the numbers game. It looked as if the Chiata had the system stacked and waiting. It was clearly an ambush from the very start. There were thousands upon thousands of alien ships in the system hiding in every nook and cranny. And they seemed to be appearing out of almost nowhere sometimes, as if they had been hiding in hyperspace or some other "unreal" place.

Dee, this will just take too long to kill them all this way, Bree warned. *There are more Chiata megaships in this system than several other engagements put together. I calculate at our present enemy attrition rate it will take us three months two weeks and four days to get ahead of the Chiata, but there are many unknown variables.*

Yes, that is a problem. I'm open for suggestions,

Deanna said in her mindvoice to her AIC. *We need a better plan but I've got nothing.*

Deanna, her mother's voice popped back into her head.

Yes, Mom? I'm here.

The Thgreeth playback holograms of your encounter says you have the weapon you need to defeat the enemy.

I think they meant the QMT capabilities needed to take that system then, she replied.

No. I don't think so.

What do you mean?

I think it is the drone you carry with you.

Skippy? Not sure how.

Me neither, but all of us here agree that it is important.

Chapter 19

July 24, 2409 AD
Chiata Kingship
Mission Star 74
Chiata Expanse
783 light-years from the Sol System
Saturday, 12:45 P.M. Eastern Time

"We are taking on heavy losses, sire." Lead Huntress of the Kingdom offered the Pride's master a detailed description of the engagement. The King and Queen both seemed apathetic to her concerns—the king more so than the queen.

"The devices given to us by the prey ally are functioning according to promise and plan, sire," one of the pride elders added. "The prey cannot leave this system with their unexplainable teleportations."

"Any further success discovering this unexplainable technology, Elder?" the Queen asked him calmly.

"Not as of yet, your majesty, but it is clear the devices delivered by the Ally are of the same design. Once this system has rid us of the prey, the elders ask to create a team with primary goal of studying them. We would also like to recapture one of our Hunterships that the prey have reconfigured with hopes of unlocking how they turn them into the expanding spheres of death."

"Yes," the queen agreed. "The rumors were not false about these prey. They are elusive, formidable, and more advanced in technology than we had been led to believe."

"Your majesties, might I suggest this ship to recapture," the Lead Huntress said displaying a three-dimensional visual of the first ship lost in the engagement. "This Huntership has already been reconfigured and has fired the unexplainable expanding sphere of death. They have taken countless others and appear to be in the process of reconfiguring them as well. It is only a matter of time before they are using them as superweapons too. There are likely still pockets of resistance hidden on these Hunterships and interestingly enough it appears as though the prey are protecting that first Huntership in particular more than the others. It is of high suspicion that the prey our ally warned us of is on that ship."

"The Elders agree as well, your majesties. There has been a significant increase in Warrior losses since that Huntership became offensive for the prey. Battle analysis would suggest that, while it is unclear why and how, the prey seem to be targeting our vessels at the optimal times for most infliction of damage. We do not suggest toying with this prey much longer, sires."

"The Hunters and Warriors agree, sires," the Lead Huntress added. "We should not continue to play with our food as it might slip away before we are able to eat it."

The queen stood straight from her dais and in a red and green blur of light had traversed the ten meters between them and her talons were around the neck of the Lead Huntress. Black and grey tendrils wriggled outward from the queen's backplates and entangled themselves around the subservient alien. The tendrils tightened to the point that the Lead Huntress' eyes glowed red and she gasped for air.

"Do not pretend to tell your masters what we should or should not do! I should separate your body and soul for such insubordinate behavior!" the queen said into the creature's ear hole with a booming screeching voice. "Remember your place, Huntress."

"Forgiveness, your majesty. No disrespect was intended." The Lead Huntress stood firm against the queen's grasp. "So far we have very few survivors to learn from following engagements with these human prey. They are fearless and fierce and use tactics that are unexpected and unnerving at times. I simply wish to stall their attack and deliver the rewards of their war machine to the pride."

"Enough, my Queen." The King waved a hand at them. "I do not believe the Lead Huntress is guilty of anything more than a poor choice of phrase."

"Yes, my King." The Queen nodded and released the alien huntress. She snarled at the alien over her shoulder as she returned to her throne.

"And, I do believe you are correct, Lead Huntress," the king continued. "We as a species were only successful in thwarting their first invasion of one of our brother Prides. The Council of Prides has decreed that we will do what is necessary to capture the tools to defeat them and stop their advance."

"Yes, my King."

"Furthermore, this system is my Pride. It is our pride. We will not let some single-system backwater species take it from us. We have them trapped here. We will kill them and enjoy the rewards of their technological secrets and the taste of their flesh." The King snarled out a growl that echoed across the chamber as it reverberated off the dais like it had been amplified through a speaker.

"Orders, my King?"

"Kill them all, but capture that ship intact. Release all the forces our ally showed us how to hide in hyperspace."

"Yes, your majesty."

Chapter 20

July 24, 2409 AD
U.S.S. Sienna Madira III
Mission Star 74
Chiata Expanse
783 light-years from the Sol System
Saturday, 12:45 A.M. Eastern Time

General Alexander Moore sat in the oversized retrofitted captain's chair on the dome bridge of the *U.S.S. Sienna Madira III* overseeing the battlescape of the entire star system and paying little attention to the actual view of the battle outside the dome. He just couldn't get enough of a strategic planning vantage point from within the fight. There had been several smaller sub-battles scattered about the system earlier on, but with the new guidance from his daughter on the *Rackman*, the battlescape had morphed into a larger, more orchestrated campaign. The new tactic was working well. However his wife and daughter were managing the intelligence from the ancient Thgreeth ruins, he hoped it continued as long as they needed it. In the past forty minutes or so they had managed to double the number of megaships under their control and they were all coming online. The mindview showed the Fleet at twenty-seven megaships with active superweapons. There was still some fighting going on inside those ships, but he hoped that would soon be taken care of. His other battle simulations also suggested that they were reaching the maximum number of megaships they could clear internally of Chiata and continue to hold with the personnel they currently had. It was time to come up with a new attack plan and to start figuring out how to get the hell out of this system.

"General! We just had about a thousand hyperspace vortex tubes open up on the circumference of the engagement," the XO shouted.

"STO?"

"Aye sir, they are all megaships sir. We are severely outnumbered," the STO replied. Alexander could hear the defeat in his voice.

Abigail, give me a rundown.

Yes sir. The engagement ball is approximately eight astronomical units in radius. There are—as of this moment—eleven hundred thirty-eight Chiata megaships in the system. The majority of them are spread out in a circle, mostly in the system's ecliptic plane in standard Keplerian type solar orbits. They are all within the nine or so AU radius where the QMT damping field begins. They could easily target and fire on all of us at once with multiple ships, sir.

"All ships, all ships, this is General Moore!" He opened the commandnet vocal and DTM channels. "Stop what you are doing and immediately go to random QMT jumps out of the ecliptic plane. Put as much distance between yourselves and those ships as possible and do it quickly. Rotate between QMT and hyperspace jaunts to help keep from overtaxing the systems. Use minimal time between jumps so as not to allow for targeting solutions. Seventeen seconds at best, people. We will all hold fire and put all engineering efforts into maintaining the jump systems and performing repairs until further notice. Move!"

"Sir, we can't do out-and-ins forever," the XO said. "Any ideas what to do next?"

"I do have an idea, but I need to game it first," Alexander replied. He didn't really have a plan, and not so much of an idea as the spark of an idea. He had to do some sanity checking on it first.

"Helm, you heard the CO, get us the Hell out of here. Nav, find us a good spot to land," Firestorm ordered the Navigation Officer.

Alexander pulled up the DTM battlescape in his mind and put it on simulation mode. He looked at the big picture for a moment and wasn't exactly sure what he wanted to do next. The flash and sizzle of the jump only slightly distracted him.

Alright, Abigail, randomly distribute all the ships out of the ecliptic and calculate how much time that gives us before they can jaunt to within range, target, and then fire their BBDs.

Yes sir, running now, his AI counterpart responded.

We know that once in range, they only need seventeen seconds to target and then speed of light travel time for the beams. Extrapolating their hyperspace speeds from previous engagements they can traverse to our maximum separation distance, which looks like about nine AUs or seventy-two light minutes give or take, in roughly one minute. At best we'll have one minute and seventeen seconds between jumps assuming they chase.

That's a start. One minute can go a long way.

Yes sir, but not long enough.

I know, so I have something in mind. Alexander paused briefly to focus his mind and his spark of an idea was becoming more of an idea and maybe even a plan. *Abby, run a sim for me if we spread out in the system and do twenty-seven superweapons at once.*

I see sir. I will run a Monte Carlo simulation and show you the average results.

Good. Maybe even run staggered attacks where we trigger the weapons at various intervals.

Understood sir.

After a brief moment the optimized average simulation ran before him. The Fleet ships all QMTed out to random spread out positions and started firing the weapons. It was much more disappointing than Alexander had hoped for. Space was big and these Chiata were smart enough to know not to bunch up in standard attack groups as the aliens had done in previous engagements. Instead they had spread themselves out homogeneously across the system and therefore minimized the effectiveness of the superweapons.

Damnit.

Yes sir.

Alexander thought on the attack further, but he wasn't coming up with any particularly brilliant ideas. His century of fighting and planning battles both on the battlefield and in politics had done nothing to prepare him for such overwhelming odds. Or had it? He thought about all the battles he'd ever fought in all the way back to the Mars Desert Campaigns where he and his men were so outnumbered that they were all either captured or slaughtered. The fortunate ones had been killed on the battlefield. The others were tortured and experimented on by Elle Ahmi for months and even years in some cases. With the knowledge he had now about how Sienna Madira had developed the clone technologies with the alien Copernicus, he suspected that some of the survivors might have been tortured for years, but couldn't be sure of it. He had no idea what the Chiata would do to them if captured. He wasn't even certain they took prisoners.

But the Martian conflict gave him a thought. He had rescued his men by going in headfirst and killing every Separatist bastard he could get to until he had attrited enough of them to put fear in their minds. At that point they were shooting at random noises and shadows. And then it was just him and Sehera against about eighty Separatist regulars. The odds there were about the same here around forty to one.

Abby, how many hits does it take from the BBDs to not only disable a megaship but to destroy it?

At least seven, sir. I'd say nine if the ship is operating optimally, but perhaps with Deanna's precise targeting intelligence we could do better.

Damn, we don't have enough ships.

No sir. We are outnumbered roughly forty-two to one, sir.

Yeah, I've already done that number in my head. Thanks. Even with the Buckley weapons there just isn't a good solution.

No sir. As the simulations showed the trick would be to get the ships close enough together that the superweapon will be effective. The Chiata appear to have learned their lesson in that regard.

Okay, then, for now, until we come up with a better plan, we send attack groups of seven, seven, seven, and six each focused on a single target in equidistant points from one another. Have Dee tell the ships which ones and where to attack and we just might start chipping away at these numbers. While we're doing that we pull all mecha into the ships we have and secure them from bow to stern port to starboard. And have everybody working fire and repair crews.

Yes sir, I'm sending the attack plan now. There was a brief pause and then she added more. *Sir, if we managed to destroy a ship each time and there are no unforeseen events it would take us almost five hours to destroy every ship in this system.*

Keep thinking Abby. We need a better plan than this! It is a pipe dream to think that we won't lose some ships, or at least some weapons, shields, engines, or something. War is hard to predict. And do we know if this is all the ships they aliens have? Who knows.

Yes, sir. We need a better plan.

"We've formed up with the *Decatur*, the *Rackman*, *Penzington*, *Mueller*, and the *Lincoln*, sir. We're taking on the short straw I see?" Firestorm asked rhetorically. "Who wants a fair fight anyway!"

"My sentiments exactly, XO," the COB added.

"CDC to CO!"

"Go CDC," Alexander said reluctantly, afraid of what might be coming next.

"Sir, we have another one thousand contacts just entered from hyperspace about zero point three AUs from the star in standard Keplerian orbits."

"STO confirm that!"

"I've got them, General. They are Chiata megaships."

"Fuck me," the XO said.

"My sentiments exactly, Firestorm. My sentiments exactly." Alexander did his best not to let his frustration show.

Chapter 21

July 24, 2409 AD
Thgreeth Abandoned Outpost Planet
Deep in Expanse
700 light-years from the Sol System
Saturday, 2:51 P.M. Eastern Time

"Well, they've been at it for almost three hours and are only putting a small dent in the Chiata fleet. The aliens are a lot more responsive to the attacks than I would have thought, even with the Thgreeth intelligence we are feeding them." Chief Warrant Officer Three Thomson Dover shook his head back and forth and shrugged the shoulders of his armored suit with palms up. "Mrs. Moore, they need something else. As good as our people are, if you push a starship like this for long periods of time systems will overheat and fail. They need something better."

"I know, Chief. They can't keep this up forever," Sehera replied. She paused and took a long slow breath as she looked about the millennia-old ruined temple around them. She for whatever reason thought of ruins as a temple, but this place was nothing of the sort. It had been a strategic headquarters for a final defense posture and cover for the evacuation of an entire species from the galaxy. The place was far from the definition of the word "temple".

"Mrs. Moore, I suggest we need to decipher what the Thgreeth meant when they told your daughter she had the key to defeating the Chiata," Cinnamon Hughes said. Sehera agreed one thousand percent with the cosmologist but had no brilliant answers in that regard. In fact, she'd been playing it over and over in her mind since the first time she heard it and had yet to make anything useful of it. After her last communication with her daughter, she wasn't sure Dee had thought much of the Thgreeth comment, but she wasn't certain.

"Ma'am, mind if I interject here?" Master Gunnery Sergeant Howser asked from her position at the entranceway to the ruins.

"Rondi, I already told you to speak up whenever," Sehera said to the Marine, perhaps a little too harshly. "We need all the help we can get."

"Well, ma'am, I've watched those videos now as you have several times, but all you are getting at is words and phrases with unclear meanings. Perhaps we should be looking at different data rather than the same thing over and over," the Marine told them.

"What do you mean, Rondi? I'm not sure I follow you. What 'different data'?" Sehera wasn't sure where she was going with this line of thinking, but it was a different path they hadn't considered yet. Sehera was ready to traipse off down any pathway or even trailblaze on her own, but she had no good idea of which direction to go.

"Well, you all seem to think that it is Dee's pet that is the key, right?" Rondi asked.

"I believe it is, Ms. Howser," Dr. Hughes agreed.

"Well, then, why aren't you looking at footage of those things? I mean, Hell, there are mounds and mounds of them just outside. They've been lying dormant in those mounds for thousands of years and even while under Chiata occupation the blur bastards wouldn't come up here because they were afraid of the beetle bots. They seem to stay dormant unless you throw a Chiata carcass on them. There was video from Dee's suit where she fought them and rolled the aliens on top of their mounds and they would boil out and eat the aliens. And Dee has had that thing with her on every engagement she's been on since she got it. Why not watch her combat footage and see what the thing has done so far in combat? I know for a fact that on her last mission it did something to the alien ship's engine that was important. I know this because my AEM squad and the tankheads were right there with the Bringers, ma'am."

"I see." Sehera nodded. "How do we get that footage here and watch it?"

"No problem, ma'am," the CW3 told her. "I'll take care of it."

"Thank you, Chief." Sehera waited as the CW3 carried on DTM conversations with someone. Then Sehera could see through his visor that the expressions filled back into his face and he nodded toward her.

"Okay, I've got the authorizations, where do you want to start?" he said.

"How about with the engagement Rondi mentioned where the bot did something to the ship?" Sehera said.

"Okay, here you go. I'm handing over control to your AIC, ma'am," Chief Dover told her.

"Thank you, Chief."

Then the DTM mindview changed from the blue force tracker view they had been overlaying on the Thgreeth holographic display to the interior of a Chiata megaship's engine room. The room was enormous and cavernous and very alien looking. Sehera had only been inside one after the builder bots had rebuilt it and didn't realize how different and eerie the things were.

The replay of the battle was an amalgam of all the sensors on all the friendly mecha's and troop's individual sensors so there were multiple sensors in multiple locations taking advantage of multiple physical phenomena. The final product the simulation system had for display was a full-ball view of the battlescape and from pretty much any point of view one would like. The tool was exceedingly useful in perfecting tactics, training, and post engagement analyses. In order to get any vantage point one wanted to see, all they needed to do was move it around in the mindview just like any other mindview image or scape.

Instantly the battlescape started moving about her as she took up a stationary position in the center of the engagement. Sehera watched as the combat inside the megaship became so fast-paced and filled with movement that she could no longer keep up with what was happening. A central ball view was like standing at one spot on the crossing of multiple interstates and trying to explain what the driver in a vehicle that passed by five minutes ago was seeing now. She wasn't really sure how the mecha pilots did it.

I can't make heads or tails of this, Pamela, she thought.

Might I suggest you choose one pilot and follow his or her path? Perhaps Dee or her wingman? Pamela offered.

Okay, let's do that.

Then the view changed, and it was as though they were looking out of Deanna's cockpit. There was so much happening that it was a serious mindboggling blur. When the blurs of the Chiata engaged her daughter's mecha the background seemed to spin about in wild random directions and Sehera was beginning to realize the craziness that it was just to be a mecha pilot and how doing so was damned near superhuman.

The alien spearheaded tendrils fired all around her and somehow Deanna was managing to anticipate their direction and avoid them. She would spin, duck, jump, flip, bounce, roll, and a myriad of movements that Sehera had no words to describe and all of this at the same time she was manning the controls and understanding sensor data and commanding the squadron of pilots. Sehera was proud of her daughter, but at the same time had tears forming in the corners of her eyes, a lump in her throat, and a burning sensation in her gut as she realized how horribly dangerous her daughter's everyday life was.

"Anybody getting anything useful?" she asked. "I'm still spin-dizzy just from watching this."

"Not yet. Perhaps we could fast-forward to when the little drone shows up? And, if you don't mind, maybe slow it down just a little. I'm afraid I'm going to be sick," Seely said through what Sehera took as clenched teeth. Sehera agreed with the linguist though. It was so crazy a pace that it had to be slowed down, and watching anything more than where the drone was concerned was wasting time.

Pamela, move forward until we see the drone. In fact, only show us parts with the drone. And slow the speed to about three quarters normal.

Understood, ma'am.

"Okay, here we go." Sehera watched and the little drone appeared seemingly out of nowhere. "There it is. Keep your eyes on it."

Pamela, follow the drone.

Yes, ma'am.

The view changed to a vantage point behind the drone and the thing moved fast, even faster than Dee's mecha view. But immediately, the little beetle like bot flew into an alien mecha and nothing slowed it down until it was inside the suit and not to be seen until it fired out from within the alien and into the one closest to Deanna's line of fire. It was clear that it was protecting her. The first Chiata writhed and flopped like a fish out of water and then fell limp to the floor. Then the second alien did exactly the same.

"Wait a minute," Chief Dover said. "I thought you said there was one bot your daughter carried with her."

"That's right Chief. There is just the one," Sehera said.

"Yeah, Chief, I've seen the little thing. Just one of them," Rondi added. "It crawls around on her like a pet spider and she keeps it in a pouch or an equipment box on her suit. Damned thing is sort of creepy. Oh, uh, sorry Mrs. Moore."

"No apologies, Rondi, it creeps me out too."

"Then why are there two of them here?" The chief did his best to keep them on topic.

"What? Two? No, Chief, I'm telling you she only has one of them."

"Back it up and replay it in slow motion from the point that the bot passes through the shields of the alien mecha like they aren't even there. That alone should have everybody all excited," he added. "That could be a serious force multiplier right there."

Play it back like the chief said, Pamela.

Yes ma'am.

"See it, right there. It passes right through the shields and armor like it isn't even there." The chief pointed out by putting a highlighted circle around the area of the playback he wanted them to see. Sehera almost gasped. There were two of them.

"It is almost as if it is quantum teleporting through the barrier," Dr. Hughes pondered. "That is a technology we do not have."

"Lieutenant Colonel Moore does," Rondi added. "She just doesn't know it."

Then a blur, even in slow motion, flashed across the screen and into the armored Chiata mecha nearest by. Sehera didn't see it at first, but after backing it up and playing it at an even slower speed, there it was. Just as the bot passed through the Chiata's barrier shield and armor, it split into two bots and the second one attacked the other Chiata. There was a ripple that formed on the Chiata's armor and there was a hole left where the second bot formed.

"There are certainly two of them." Sehera was

startled by the fact and wasn't even sure that her daughter knew this. "Where did it come from and where did it go?"

"Let's keep watching and see what they do," Dr. Hughes suggested.

"Right," Sehera agreed.

After watching the battle for several minutes, they saw several more splits and in each case the bots passed right into the Chiata and proceeded to devour the aliens until there was nothing left but most of the alien's armor. Finally, after several playbacks, they only ever saw evidence of one bot returning to Dee. They had no idea if it was the original bot or one of the copies. Where the other bots vanished to went completely undetected by all the sensors in the battle. Somehow the bot was unaffected by Chiata armor and shielding and somehow it had the power to self-replicate. The little bot was somewhat of a technological miracle or at the very least, yet another demonstration of how much more advanced the Thgreeth were than humanity. It bothered Sehera that the Thgreeth had given up on the fight against the Chiata and evacuated the galaxy, as advanced as they were. That thought was frightening to her.

"I'm pretty sure the bot is using the armor material to build its replicas from," Dr. Hughes said. "These things are like replicator bots using whatever is available to replicate with. Perhaps they are programmed to only use Chiata armor or flesh?"

"That would make sense from a weapon strategy," the Chief replied. "I mean you'd want your weapon to only destroy the bad guys and their stuff."

"This is important, but I'm not exactly certain how," Sehera pondered out loud.

"Just imagine if that bot could tell us how to neutralize the alien shields and armor the way it does." Rondi sounded excited. "It would be one shot, one kill every single time!"

"Good call, Gunny," the chief warrant said. "We need to transfer that idea to Lieutenant Colonel Moore and see if she can figure out anything further to do with it."

"I'm on it." Sehera immediately opened the mind to mind link she had with Dee through the Thgreeth system.

Chapter 22

July 24, 2409 AD
U.S.S. Davy Rackman
Mission Star 74
Chiata Expanse
783 light-years from the Sol System
Saturday, 3:08 P.M. Eastern Time

Lieutenant Colonel Moore was a mecha jock at heart. In fact, she'd never wanted to be anything but a mecha pilot. It was what she did best. Being a pilot was what made her feel invulnerable in an otherwise dangerous as Hell universe. It was the one thing that had kept her going once she had lost Davy Rackman. She'd certainly never even considered becoming a megaship captain for the Fleet, but here she was. Not only was she captain of one of the newest megaships in the Fleet, but she was also directing the entirety of the Fleet in their attacks. She'd only been captain for a few hours but it already seemed like years and she was longing to be just a mecha squadron leader again.

"Phoenix, the Maniacs have swept and mopped from bow to stern and this ship is clean," Colonel Delilah Strong told Dee through the tacnet. "Red force trackers show no other hits. She's all yours, Captain! And congratulations, Lieutenant Colonel Moore."

"Uh, thank you, Jawbone," Dee replied. "But until such time as we are either safely in control of this system or safely out of this system, I'd say that congratulations are premature."

"Spoken like a true ship's captain," Strong replied. "Any orders, ma'am?"

"At last look, Jawbone, full birds still outrank a silver leaf," Dee told her.

"Yes, ma'am, but you are the ship's captain. You need to tell us what you need from us, Dee." Delilah mentored her a bit. "For example, we could refuel, repair, and replenish our mecha in case we need it sooner than later."

"Yes, that is good. Do that, if you don't mind." Dee thought through processes and things that needed to be done for a moment. "Colonel, if you don't mind, I'd like it if you took charge of the Air Group until such time that you are recalled to the *Madira*."

"Very good, Captain, it would be my absolute pleasure to CAG for you. I will see to it." Dee could hear the chuckle in Colonel Strong's voice.

"Forty-one seconds until our next QMT, Captain," Molloch, her acting XO, told her.

"Great Molloch, how are the engines holding up?"

"So far we are managing to flip back and forth between the hyperspace projector and the QMT system without any signs of immediate fatigue. The BBDs on the other hand, are getting a workout," he said.

"Azazel, tell me about the BBDs."

"Yes, Captain." Azazel flashed up an image of the BBD coolant conduits in her mindview. "The primary coolant line to the spires has ruptured on this deck here as you can see. I've temporarily rerouted it and dispatched builder bots, but that is a big pipe, ma'am. It would be great if we could replace it. I've identified several conduits about the ship that are not in use that we could put there."

"You have? Azazel, you sound like an engineer all of a sudden. Maybe being gunner is the wrong job for you." Dee laughed at her wingman, but the clone either didn't get or care for the humor.

"How long a section do you need?"

"Ten meters."

"Understood. Get the builder bots there and ready." Dee opened the tacnet channel. "CO to CAG."

"Strong here, Captain."

"Jawbone, I'm DTMing you a spare conduit's location. I need you to get a couple of mecha over there and pull it off the wall and then take it to this location here. Builder bots will be waiting for it when it gets there," Dee ordered her.

"Aye, Captain."

"Be ready for Azazel. Anything else?"

"No, ma'am. Well, I would add that I am not a CHENG and perhaps one of the supercarrier CHENGs should be brought here to main engineering to help us out."

"Should have already thought of that," Dee scolded

herself. "Molloch, pick the CHENG from the four supercarriers with the best record and scores and have him or her pick an engineering team and report to duty here ASAP."

"Yes, ma'am."

Deanna? I need to speak with you.

Mother?

Yes. I have information that you need to know.

Okay, what?

Your drone is unaffected by Chiata shields or armor. It passes right through them. We've played back all of your combat video and have seen it. Also, it replicates into multiple bots when engaging the aliens.

I knew about the replication part, but didn't know how it was getting through the shields.

Do you know what happens to the bot's copies after combat?

Never found one. I just assumed they dissolved or joined back with him somehow. How is he passing through the shields and armor?

We don't know how it is doing that. We just know it is. You need to ask it if it can transfer that power to you somehow to use against the Chiata on a larger scale.

Makes sense. I will. Thank you, mom.

Deanna?

Yes?

Stay safe.

Yes, mother.

"Hmm, not sure what that means." Deanna tapped at a few controls and popped open the cockpit to her mecha. After releasing the restraints she bounced down from the bot-mode mecha with a *kathunk* onto the bridge deckplates. "Skippy, come here."

"Captain, is everything okay?" Azazel turned to her with what Dee thought was an expression of concern. He must have been surprised she was leaving the safety of her mecha.

"It's all good, Azazel. Can't sit in that mecha forever. I need a captain's chair built in here. Or maybe, I will just keep the mecha, but, not like that."

Bree, toggle the mecha to eagle-mode and center it in the bridge.

Yes, Dee.

"Molloch, you need to move over to your left some," she warned him. "And as soon as we have some builder bots available, let's get them in here to build us a human bridge."

"I will tell your new CHENG, ma'am," Molloch agreed as he stomped his mecha over to the port side of the bridge. Her mecha transfigured to eagle-mode and floated quietly to a more central spot and settled. Her cockpit opened allowing her access to her pilot's couch.

"Hi there, Skippy. Been a busy day, huh?" Dee held out her hand and the little bot skittered up onto her wrist and then up onto her forearm as if it were awaiting her commands the way a falcon might. "I need you to help me out with something."

The little bot just sat there staring in her general direction with its small glossy black eye sensors. Deanna wasn't sure if talking to it was doing any good or not, but somehow in the past the bot had always just done what it was she needed it to do.

"I need you to help me beat the Chiata's shields like you do when you fight them. Do you understand me?" Dee almost felt silly as she talked to the bot. But almost as soon as she felt that way the beetle bot jumped from her arm to the deck and started skittering toward the door. Then it paused and turned back at her moving back and forth as if it wanted her to follow.

Skippy waited for her to step in behind it before it continued to walk and then it started skittering to one of the Chiata control consoles on the other side of the large bridge dome. The bot jumped up onto the console and dug all of its appendages into the surface. Suddenly, a holographic projection opened up above the console and parts of the ship started flashing by rapidly.

"Ten seconds to our next QMT, Phoenix," Molloch warned.

"Molloch, take control for a couple of minutes. If you need me I'm here, but otherwise, you know what to do." She turned her attention back to Skippy. "What are you showing me, Skippy?"

Then finally the holographic display stopped flipping through systems and came to a stop at one. There was a large box about the size of a hovertank with multiple conduits protruding from it and running off in multiple directions. The largest of them led to the Chiata's quantum vacuum energy collection grid.

"I recognize that," Dee said out loud. "Azazel, look at this. Isn't this the power transfer box to the BBD spires?"

Azazel's mecha turned about and his canopy popped up. He sprang from the bot-mode mecha to the deck beside her and then looked intently at the hologram for a few moments.

"Yes, ma'am, that is exactly what it is. It is about three decks below us and a bit to the starboard side of the ship."

"What do we do with this, Skippy?" Dee shrugged her armored shoulders at the little drone. Then the box became transparent in the display and the inner workings of it became visible.

"Three, two, one . . ." Molloch counted down and then there was a hyperspace tube forming in front of them and seconds later they were formed up with their attack group engaging their next target.

Dee pulled up the Thgreeth attack data in her mindview and quickly told the other five megaships in her attack group where to engage. Then she showed Molloch the final spot to target and the big blue beams of death from Hell sparked out from the antennae overhead and across space into the target. The shields failed, but all six ships in their group had exhausted their BBDs for at least another thirty to forty seconds.

"Jump us out, Molloch," she ordered and then turned back to Skippy. "We've got another minute or so to figure this out."

There were several components inside the energy transfer box that Skippy highlighted in red. Then the view jumped all the way to the forward supercarriers and highlighted the Buckley superweapon generators. He zoomed in on one of them all the way to the power conduit input tube. The view backtracked down the tube almost all the way to the interior of the Chiata part of the megaship to where the builder bots had connected the supercarrier conduits to the Chiata ship's conduits. There was a wye junction there where the conduits were highlighted again and a section about ten meters long was removed and then left open.

"Wait, you want us to disconnect the forward Buckley shield generators?" Dee was beginning to think she needed to call the *Madira* and get Commander Buckley over there. Then the view zoomed back to the forward generator and at the output projector a conduit was added shunting off where the shields and the superweapon field were projected from.

The tube was then led down the same path to the junction where the tube split into the wye. In one direction was the input from the supercarrier's internal power source and in the other direction was toward the Chiata ship's power tube. Now Dee realized that the section that Skippy had removed before was the one bringing power to the shields from the Chiata ship. Skippy showed a conduit being placed all the way from the output of the shield generator back to the input of the Chiata ship.

"Okay, hold on. That's like one hundred meters or more of conduit. We need a CHENG or a STO up here." Dee pulled up the assignments roster and looked to see who Molloch had assigned as her new CHENG. It was a Deedee clone. She wondered if Molloch had chosen her as some sort of joke, but knew that her XO didn't have a sense of humor. The clone was the only Deedee that Dee had on the roster so she figured she could just use her name and rank.

"CO to Lieutenant Commander Deedee."

"Deedee here, ma'am."

"CHENG, flash up to my position immediately, please."

"Yes, ma'am."

"Captain our next QMT is in fifty-three seconds," Molloch told her. Then there was a flash of light and a sizzle of bacon sound.

"Captain." The CHENG stood at attention.

"At ease, Deedee. I want you to see something here."

Chapter 23

July 24, 2409 AD
Chiata Kingship
Mission Star 74
Chiata Expanse
783 light-years from the Sol System
Saturday, 3:20 P.M. Eastern Time

"The new spatially distributed attack posture has minimized the impact of their expanding spheres of death, sire," Lead Huntress of the kingdom told the pride's master through the Chiata version of a tactical communications network. The king and queen both paid close attention to her combat situation report. The Queen still appeared angry with the Huntress, but the king merely shrugged it off as territorial behavior and that she hadn't liked being challenged by her previously.

"The devices given to us by the prey ally are still functioning according to promise and plan and with our full attack force engaging the prey it is only a matter of time before we can capture one of their reconfigured megaships," one of the Pride Elders added. "And . . ."

"Do not be so hasty in your analysis, Elder," the Lead Huntress interrupted him. "While the prey has stopped attacking us with their main weapons, they have engaged a new tactic that is almost as equally elusive."

"Please explain this new tactic," the queen ordered.

"Your majesties, might I suggest that this engagement is, in fact, not moving in our favor," the Lead Huntress said, displaying a three-dimensional visual of the first ship lost in the engagement.

"What?" the Elder interjected. "Impossible. They are beyond outnumbered and clearly do not possess enough energy and firepower to take on almost three thousand Hunterships of the Pride with the mere twenty-seven reconfigured Hunterships they have? This is preposterous, your majesties."

"Elder, let the Lead Huntress have her say," the King held up his hand.

"Thank you, sire." The Lead Huntress bowed her head slightly. "The prey have divided into teams of three groups of seven and one of six. They seem to have surmised that seven hits in the right sequence and targeting locations from the Huntership's primary weapons are enough to disable a single targeted Huntership. This tactic appears to be successful thirty-two percent of the time."

"I see, please go on, Lead Huntress," the king said as he paid very close attention to the battle replays and simulations. He watched and could clearly see the tactic his lead soldier had pointed out. These prey were clever. His concern was growing as to how effectively clever they were. The creatures could seemingly adapt from one situation to the next with very little need of time to retool their war machine or to retrain their warriors. It was almost unbelievable. It was if each and every one of these prey were all trained in all Hunter and Warrior jobs and perhaps even more.

"These prey then use either a standard faster-than-light propulsion system, which is considerably less advanced than our own, or their unexplainable teleportation technology to then move to equidistant points from our ships. This gives them anywhere from one to ten minutes' rest before they must make some movement again, because that is how long it takes us to locate them and then travel to them to engage. Also, notice sire, that we believe these prey have the technology to instantly locate targets upon reentering reality from any FTL jumps, which is a technology we do not possess."

"How many have we damaged since this new tactic was initiated by them?" the queen asked. The king smiled at his mate. She had been a good choice. Their cubs were strong as well and would someday enable him to transition the lineage to an equally fit king heir.

"We have not destroyed a single one, sires," the Lead Huntress added. "We have likely inflicted damage, but they seem proficient at repairing their systems quickly as must be clear from their abilities to quickly capture and retool our ships for their purposes."

"Yes, of course." The king nodded and snarled. The royal mark on his forehead ridgeplates glowed red and green with his growing impatience in these prey.

"The prey are slippery and cunning, sire. They attack and run, attack and run. They have been doing this for hours and in the process have been successful in destroying eleven Hunterships and damaging many more."

"Yet we have destroyed none of their ships?" This unnerved the king more deeply than any other conflict he had been exposed to in centuries. While a loss of a few ships, even a few hundred ships most times meant nothing to the Chiata, losing ships while inflicting no damage on the prey was unheard of. "This is something that we must stop now, Lead Huntress. We must stop this prey."

"I agree, my King." The queen nodded and snarled a growl of distaste for the prey and the red glowing veins about her shoulder plates suggested a bit of anger towards the Lead Huntress as well.

"I have a suggestion, sire," the Lead Huntress replied. "A different tactic might be in order."

"Yes?"

"I suggest we use the same tactic on the humans as they are using on us."

"Go on," the king said.

"I believe we should target a single ship with overwhelming force," she said. "And focus our efforts thusly."

"No, sire. The Elder Council does not agree with this tactic. The prey could initiate their superweapon and become even more effective. We have analyzed this situation and show that the bog of war and time will finally overwhelm these prey. We are on the positive side of the numbers and probability here. These prey simply cannot maintain this tactic and this engagement for the time needed for them to defeat us here."

"I agree, my King," the queen practically harrumphed

in support of the elder's approach as she gave a look at the Lead Huntress that was unmistakably full of disdain for her.

"That is my alternate tactical suggestion, sire. Of course, I will perform whatever such tactics you prefer as best I am capable. Orders, my King?" The Lead Huntress stood unmoving looking back at him and not allowing herself to glance to any of the others.

"We will do both," the king replied. "Lead Huntress, you will lead a hunting party of one hundred Hunterships on our previously determined target. Chase that target to the ends of the system until you wear it down and take it for the Pride. We must capture one of these reconfigured ships. Once you capture it leave this system immediately with it."

"Yes, your majesty. And what of the rest of the prey?"

"I will lead the hunt myself."

Chapter 24

July 24, 2409 AD
U.S.S. Davy Rackman
Mission Star 74
Chiata Expanse
783 light-years from the Sol System
Saturday, 3:38 P.M. Eastern Time

"Commander Buckley is right about one thing here, Dee," her father was saying as he stood about four meters away from her holding up the other end of a very long piece of energy transfer conduit. The two of them had pitched in to do anything and everything to help, and Marines in e-suits were better than forklifts.

"What's that, sir?" she asked her father as her armored suit strained against the section of pipe the two of them carried. It had to weigh several tons, but to the person in the suit it might as well have been made of paper maché.

"Well, let me see if I can get this word for word." Her father paused to think on the words briefly and then even added some of Buckley's vocal inflections. "Begging your pardon sir, but, uh, um, only a ship commanded by a Moore, and no doubt that apple fell right beneath the tree, uh, sir, would take weapon design plans of unknown purpose from an unknown alien robot, remove their forward shields, reroute the most powerful weapon known to man backwards into the input to the second most powerful weapon known to man, and then traipse into battle with it on her back ready to pull the trigger at a moment's notice all the while having absolutely no idea what thing was about to do. Uh, um, sir," Alexander said, quoting the CHENG's attempt at a humorous compliment.

"I think you should bust his balls for such insubordination," Dee laughed. "And to use that apple reference is so cliché even for Joe."

"Maybe I will. Bust his balls, I mean. But I'll wait until he and your CHENG finish building this contraption of yours."

"It's not my contraption. It is the Thgreeth's," she corrected him.

"Well, princess, I hope you're right about this," her father said, a little more sincerely and discreetely. Dee could tell he was looking about to make certain nobody overheard him call her by his pet name for her.

Dee didn't mind, as she loved her father with all her heart and when he called her "princess" it made her feel twelve again and briefly forget all the woes and other troubling shit that made her what she was presently. She so much just wanted to hug her father and call him "Daddy" and to think that he would take care of everything. But Dee was her own adult self now and those days were long in the past. While she had hoped that a certain Navy SEAL was going to be able to take on that role of holding her and making things better but that hadn't happened either because of the fucking Chiata. The. Fucking. Chiata!

"This is going to work." The mood sensors in her eye implants detected the change and started glowing fire red.

"Well, I hope your little pet knows what it is doing."

"Skippy's never let me down so far. And I keep telling everyone that it is not a pet. It is a Chiata killing machine."

Just like you, Captain, her AIC poked at her.

Knock that shit off, Bree.

Yes Captain Moore.

Damnit Bree.

"Alright princess, let's hope you're right about that." Her father almost laughed at her response, but Dee could tell it wasn't an admonishing or a making fun of type laugh. It was more in his 'that's my girl' laugh.

"Dad, don't call me 'princess' where the clones can hear," she said more or less to poke back at him and then thought it would be more effective if she quickly added, "Uh, General, sir."

"General's prerogative, Lieutenant Colonel Moore. They should've chosen that for your callsign. Maybe I could make that happen. Lieutenant Colonel Deanna 'Princess' Moore. Has a nice ring to it."

"Don't you dare!" Dee looked about and while there were troops and bots bustling about everywhere on the Engineering Deck there was nobody in hearing distance.

All of the Bringers of Hell, Maniacs, the AEMs, all the engineering teams from the *Rackman's* supercarrier legs, an army of builder bots, and several teams from other Fleet ships that could be spared were flurrying about and grunting through pure physical hard work. The goal was to implement the ship modifications needed on the *Rackman* in order to test the new weapon concept the Thgreeth bot had shown them. After Dee had shown her chief engineer the concept the AI-driven clone admitted selflessly and with zero hint of embarrassment that she was not the expert on the subject at hand and that Commander Joe Buckley Jr. from the *Madira* was the closest thing to an expert available to them. A few conversations later and a visit from her father, Joe and a handpicked team of engineers along with her clone engineers were scurrying about the *Rackman* like worker ants.

They had quickly realized that the modifications to be made were even more difficult than the connections of the supercarriers to the power grid of the BBDs that enabled the Buckley superweapon. The builder bots could make those modifications in about twenty minutes by themselves mostly, but these mods would require all hands and bots and then some going at balls out for a half hour or so.

"Excuse me, sir." Commander Buckley bounced next to them.

It was the first time Dee had seen Joe in a very long time. Perhaps even since the funeral. Her nonstop volunteering for missions since that time had not allowed for much personal time. Dee hadn't wanted it much anyway.

"Congratulations, Lieutenant Colonel Moore," he said

to Dee, taking a second accidental stare at her glowing eyes and tattoos on her face.

"Hello Joe, thank you. I wish there was time for small talk but there isn't. So, where do you need this thing?" Dee asked informally, knowing full well where the tube went as her mindview of the plans for it were lit up showing her exactly what to do with it.

He didn't salute or anything, and Dee wouldn't have expected it even if her hands weren't full. Joe was never a stickler about rank much anyway and now they were at the same rank. They had been friends and drinking buddies long before that. Dee was close to his girlfriend Gunny Howser. She wondered how she was as well. She made a mental note to go drinking with them sometime soon as long as they promised not to talk about Davy.

"We'll need that conduit you're both carrying right over there. Lieutenant Commander Deedee is ready to test the power standing wave ratio at the junction as soon as I get it mated into place."

"Joe, you've gone over all this?" Alexander asked his CHENG again for the thousandth time. "We're not just going to destroy the ship here, are we?"

"Yes sir, I have gone over it as best time has allowed me to. And no, I don't think it will destroy the ship. I think I know what is supposed to happen, but I can't be one hundred percent certain without further testing, which of course we don't have time for," Buckley said. "The feedback from the shield generators will set up a quantum uncertainty field that interferes with the blue beams as they transmit. Somehow that field uncertainty will be superimposed onto the BBD in such a way as to make it 'unreal' to the alien's ship and it will therefore pass through the alien's shields and maybe even exterior armor plating. Again, that is if I'm understanding the Thgreeth bot's design information, in theory at least what I think is going to happen. I'm assuming, again, according to the blueprints the bot is showing us of the control distribution box, that the bot is going to insert itself there somehow and manipulate the beam oscillator on a quantum scale. I think it will be the control system from then on, but how all that will work is physics that I don't think even exists yet, sir. At least it doesn't for humanity."

"Will it, uh, hurt him?" Dee asked Buckley. She'd had Skippy for a long time now and didn't want to lose him. In a way he was like a friend, at least a crutch, to her.

"Uh, I never thought about that. Does it feel pain? Sorry, I just don't know even how to guess an answer for that." The *Madira's* CHENG shrugged and kept at his work having them align the pipes with the junction. "A little to the left, a little more . . ."

"Lieutenant Commander Deedee to Captain."

"Go ahead, CHENG," Dee replied as she and her father stood holding the conduit in place for Joe. All the while, builder bots modified the material edges into a flange and then welded it into place. Joe had looked up when she had said the word 'CHENG' but he quickly realized there was more than one CHENG on board and she wasn't talking to him.

"Ma'am, we are putting the final touches on the connections here and following the power standing wave ratio test we will be ready for your bot," Deedee explained. "That is assuming the tests are satisfactory."

"Roger that, CHENG. As soon as we're done here, Skippy and I will flash down." Dee patted the little bot's compartment on her suit affectionately. "How much longer until we can use the weapon?"

"Thirty minutes, maybe less."

"Make it less, CHENG."

"Aye, Captain Moore, I'll do my best."

"All hands, all hands, this is the XO. Next QMT jump will be in ten seconds."

"General, are you staying here for this one?"

"Firestorm can handle the *Madira* for now, Dee. I want to help you see this through." Her father sounded a little more sheepish than usual. "If this works, it will only be fitting that it will come from your ship."

"We should fix the *Penzington* next."

"If it works, and there is a way, we will fix them all if we can."

Chapter 25

July 24, 2409 AD
U.S.S. Scotty P. Mueller
Mission Star 74
Chiata Expanse
783 light-years from the Sol System
Saturday, 3:50 P.M. Eastern Time

Sienna Madira looked at the battlescape in her mindview and noted that two of the other attack groups had just completed their latest run against the Chiata. The *Mueller* and the rest of her attack group were still twenty seconds out from the end of theirs. She had been attacking and jumping, attacking and jumping, and repeating the process for the better part of the day, and was getting tired of it. The one saving grace they had discovered was that the Chiata's sensors were still speed of light limited and after the Fleet ships engaged and then flashed out of that engagement to some "safe" spot they were always at least an astronomical unit from another Chiata ship, giving them eight to ten minutes before they were detected, and then almost instantly the Chiata could FTL jump to them to engage. But there were times that they managed to get more than an astronomical unit away. The speed-of-light sensor lag the Chiata technology suffered from gave the attack groups a much-needed break from combat to fight fires and make hurried repairs. The unfortunate side of it was that they had only eight to ten minutes to fight fires and make repairs before the Chiata engaged them again. The constant deliberation was whether or not to attack or run again to allow for more repair time. She was beginning to lean toward the latter more often than not.

Because of the QMT damping bubble they were trapped in there was little they could do about their constant hit and run schedule. Sienna knew before going into this trap that the Chiata didn't have QMT technology of any type and the only QMT damping she'd ever seen was either the Thgreeth's technology or technology that she herself through Copernicus' help had implemented. Even the other aliens they had met while they had QMT communications and teleportations did not have the QMT damping capability. The key here was that Copernicus had taught her how to create it. And she certainly didn't know all of the ins and outs of his plans within plans within plans, but she was getting more and more suspicious as to their end game. And her current suspicions were pissing her off.

Madira knew the history of the origins of quantum membrane technologies as far as humanity was concerned, and what she knew certainly narrowed down the list of benefactors from whom the Chiata might have gotten the technology. She was pretty certain the Thgreeth wouldn't have done anything to lessen their advantage in any future confrontation with the Chiata and given the capability to an enemy they seemed sworn to fight. She knew as a matter of certainty that she had not now, nor ever would give away mankind's only advantage against the alien attackers.

Defending humanity against the oncoming invasion was all she'd thought about for almost a century and a half. She was a bit concerned with what her daughter and son-in-law might believe based on her checkered past, however. What Sienna did know with absolute certainty was that there was only one other living entity that could have sold out humanity and she wished with all her being that she'd killed that sorry alien sack of shit after having sex with him earlier that morning. She personally wanted to take care of that problem herself.

The biggest problem Sienna had at the moment, along with the rest of the Expeditionary Fleet, was that they were too busy fighting for their lives to figure out how to escape from the trap they were in. General Alexander Moore had stated in several instances on the commandnet that once they had "cleared the AO" they would then start investigating the way out. But according to Sienna's math it might take them days or more to "clear the AO" if everything went exactly according to plan. So far, only about half of everything was going according to plan. They were able to engage the enemy porcusnails and to attack them with seven BBDs at once. With the intelligence Dee was giving them all, they were more effective than normal, but were still taking down the alien ships only about once every three engagements or so and sometimes not even that often. The math just wasn't working out, as far as she could tell.

And as history had shown, Sienna Madira was more than just good at math. She was beyond brilliant at complex simulations of systems of seemingly chaotic dynamic dependent and independent variables. Her understanding of coupled systems of differential equations, tensors, continuum mechanics, quantum analysis, and ergodic theory was pretty much beyond compare. She wasn't a superwoman of math by birth, she had just worked amazingly hard at it for nearly two centuries and had an alien mathematician tutoring and amping her brain up with quantum membrane technology and artificial intelligence quantum computing along the way. Until recently she hadn't realized that said alien had been altering her mind, but she'd finally evolved her mental capacity to the point that the calculations came to no other solution to explain her abilities.

In fact, it was mostly her many mathematical analyses that had driven the last two centuries of mankind's development and journey out into the stars. And the math that she had run over and over in her mindview of this particular engagement against the Chiata while trapped in their killbox led her down the same solution path every single time. Eventually, the red force was going to overcome the blue force if they didn't get out of that damned trap. They had to find the QMT damping devices and shut them down and get the Hell out of there. Then they could QMT out far enough to give them all the time they needed to rest, repair, prepare, and attack that they would need. They could return to ordinary tactics and bounce in and out and out and in until they attrited the alien force to zero. Without the QMTs the battlescape was leveled or even tilted in the Chiata's favor. No, somebody had to find those damping devices and give the Fleet an escape from the trap. Sienna was beginning to decide it was up to her to do it. Everybody else was too focused on the gunfight in front of them, and rightfully so. But Sienna's brain didn't work that way, at least not anymore.

"Ma'am, we just received the targeting coordinates from Lieutenant Colonel Moore's AIC," her clone XO told her. "There is a limited weakness on the forward shield generators."

"Don't waste time telling me about it!" Sienna ordered him. "Fire the BBDs and then get us to some random safe spot."

"Aye, ma'am."

Seconds later the big blue beams zigged and zagged across the battlescape and hit the Chiata porcusnail that her seven-ship attack group was engaging. The *Mueller* was the last ship to fire. The beam hit the targeted location on the ship but its shields held and then the alien porcusnail counterpunched with its own BBDs. One of her attack group's megaships took a full hit just as they QMTed out.

"Shit! Get us out of here, helm!"

"Roger that, ma'am."

The bridge flashed and Sienna eased back into her captain's chair a bit as the sizzling sound filled her ears. Her team was starting to feel the toll of the continuous fighting and she hoped that the ship that got hit had manageable shields. As they dropped out of the QMT instantly she pulled the status of the megaship up onto her mindview and could see systems failing all over it. The shields were down and so were the BBDs. They desperately needed time to work on their systems.

"Scotty," she called her right hand clone and personal assistant. "I don't know about you, but I'm tired of all this hit and run. Why haven't we figured out where this damping system is yet?"

"Mainly because we haven't been focusing on it," the clone replied. "I have been running all sensors full-time since we arrived in this system. There are some trends analyses being performed but it is a lot of data, ma'am."

"Okay then, send me the link. I'm going to run some of my own algorithms on it."

"Yes, ma'am."

"XO, take the bridge. Keep us out of the fight until all of our group is back up to at least eighty-five percent operational status."

"Yes, Captain Madira," the clone XO replied.

Chapter 26

July 24, 2409 AD
Thgreeth Abandoned Outpost Planet
Deep in Expanse
700 light-years from the Sol System
Saturday, 3:54 P.M. Eastern Time

Sehera was tired of watching the battle and her brain was exhausted from studying the details of the Thgreeth records. Since Deanna had contacted her and told her that her bot had given them designs for some sort of new superweapon, they were all sitting anxiously awaiting some good news and for the red force dots in the system to start vanishing, but so far there was nothing. Sehera decided it was time for a break, maybe have a snack, and get some air even if it was high in carbon dioxide.

She sat outside the ruins on a large sand-colored stone knee wall that lined the path into the river. The path descended right off into the water like a boat launching ramp. She wondered to what purpose all of the ramps like that had been used by the Thgreeth. Sehera imagined that the alien culture used hovercraft that would make use of the river for cargo and transport and the ramps were used as exits from the main river route. Of course, she truly had no idea, but it was an interesting thought to ponder to give her mind a break from the constant struggle of the day. She noticed several of the meter-or-so-high red clay beetle mounds along the river bank and outlining the walking paths that had been there for thousands of years.

"Ma'am, are you doing alright?" Gunny Howser had followed her out being the good watchdog. It reminded her of the days of being First Lady and how her bodyguards were always present back then. One of them had died guarding Dee as a teenager and the other was still with the family and ran security at their Mississippi estate.

"I'm fine, I just wanted to take a break." Sehera popped open her visor as she fumbled about her suit's chest compartments for a meal bar. She took a bite of it and savored it for a long slow moment. The sweet and savory flavors hit her tastebuds at the same time making her mouth salivate anticipating the next bite. For rations, the meal bar was pretty darn good. The serenity of something as simple as chewing was interrupted by her suit warning her that there was too much carbon dioxide in the air and that she would need to close the visor in less than eight minutes.

"Don't worry about the air. Your head will start hurting long before you pass out," Rondi told her through her open visor. Sehera looked a little closer at the Marine's tattooed face. She and Deanna had very similar tattoos, she thought. She wondered if they had gotten them at the same place. "And you can also have the helmet continue to flood you with pure O2 about every minute or so. That will allow you to keep the visor up three or four times longer than normal. Can't waste it as the scrubbers just pull in air from the planet and clean it up."

"Thanks, Rondi. But you know I'm a Martian, right?" Sehera didn't have to explain what that meant. Every human knew that the inhabitants of Mars had lived with high carbon dioxide levels in the atmosphere for centuries. Before the wars had started, she and her mother had lived near one of the terraforming ice farms where giant lasers in space were beaming down at the ice caps and melting the water and dry ices into the atmosphere. She recalled the brilliantly beautiful red, blue, and green beams interplaying with the steam and throwing rainbows in different directions.

"Oh, yes, ma'am. I didn't mean to imply you were an idiot. That is just the NCO in me. I'm the one that gets her ass busted if I let my troops fuck up and die by forgetting to do something so basic. Oh, uh, sorry ma'am, about the language I mean. And, uh, implying that . . ."

"Ha ha, relax, Rondi. If language bothered me, I'd never have been able to stay with Alexander." Sehera laughed a bit and felt an urge to see her husband and their daughter. "And, well, Dee didn't fall too far away from that tree either. It was very difficult explaining to her third grade teacher why Dee knew how to appropriately use the phrase 'go fuck yourself' and why Alexander didn't seem too concerned about it."

"Ha ha." Rondi almost guffawed at Sehera's anecdote

about Dee and the general. "Yes ma'am, the mecha ace is even better at stringing together expletives and superlatives than she is at flying fighter planes."

"I like this." Sehera waved her hand back and forth between them indicating their chat. "It is personal and human. There is so much down to business and planning and fighting this war these days that we never get this. Dee needs this."

"Yes ma'am, I agree on all of it."

"And, for me anyway, it's good to just talk a little instead of all that DTM and comms." Sehera took another bite of the meal bar and then bit on her water tube in her helmet. The cool water rejuvenated her spirits a bit. "I get tired of that after a while. I have never been comfortable with all the mindvoices and AICs. Growing up, I saw it go, well, very badly in some cases. I only recently had mine implanted."

"Yes ma'am. I understand," Rondi replied, but Sehera knew that nobody could really understand how afflicted she had been as a child watching her mother turn from her brilliant loving self to the megalomaniacal mass-murdering terrorist all due to the implant in her head.

"Not to change the subject, but, you were here during the battle, weren't you?" Sehera could use a little small talk at the moment if for any other reason than to let her mind rest and subconsciously process all the data she'd absorbed during the day. Somewhere in all that information was an answer, she just knew it. But she wasn't exactly sure if it was an answer that would be enough. The Chiata swarmed the galaxy and devoured everything in their path. All the other aliens, including the Thgreeth, had yet to stop them.

And now, they were putting their hopes in a race that decided to leave rather than stay and fight.

"Yes, ma'am. All this region was pretty thick with Chiata. In fact, if you will look right over there." Rondi pointed her mechanized gauntlet a bit to the south and downstream of the river. "You see that larger structure jutting up just above the river canyon wall there."

"Um, yes I do."

"We were trapped there by the superior numbers of Chiata, but they wouldn't enter the canyon. At the time we had no idea why, but it must've been because all this Thgreeth technology and the drone beetles everywhere. Then Dee showed up out of nowhere after fighting hand to hand with the Chiata all day. What she did then saved all our butts, maybe even humanity."

"Where was Dee at the time before she showed up doing the fighting?" Sehera had heard stories and seen some of the video data but she didn't quite have the geography down yet.

"Oh, she was way north of here, like several hundred kilometers or more. There should be a historical marker there someday for what she did there. I'm not sure that anybody has ever singlehandedly taken on that many Chiata practically barehanded and come out of it alive but her. Dee took them on and killed them one after another even as they broke her body she just kept moving forward. The fighting was beyond anything anyone has ever done, ever."

"I've never heard that description of what she did before." Sehera finished her meal just in time. Her mind was starting to fog up and her head was beginning to hurt a bit at the temples. She closed her visor for a few seconds and took in some proper air. Her mind started to clear up after a few breaths. "What I do know is that she barely made it out alive. Had it not been for the Thgreeth saving her . . ."

"Begging your pardon, but no, ma'am. Major, uh, Moore fought her way to that help. It was her cunning, strength, and iron fortitude that persevered and got her to the goal line. The aliens were just the extra point." Sehera understood the football reference but only vaguely. She had never been interested in it until she had married Alexander, who had played in college. She still was only politely interested.

"Mrs. Moore! Mrs. Moore! We need you back in here!"

Both Rondi and Sehera were startled by the sudden excitement. Rondi jumped to attention drawing her rifle and her visor popped down in place instantly. Sehera was certain that the Marine was pulling up tactical data and sensor information expecting an attack.

"Mrs. Moore, you need to see this!" Dr. Hughes was calling for her as if she'd stepped on a snake or something.

"It never ends," Sehera muttered as she pulled herself up.

"No, ma'am. It doesn't," Rondi agreed. Sehera noticed how the soldier's head bobbed about taking in every angle and direction about them. Her head was on a swivel, as the infantry said.

"So the system view just shut off and changed or what?" Sehera wasn't sure she understood what had happened, but the holographic display was no longer showing the battlescape of the target system the Expeditionary Fleet were trapped in.

"This is a different system and why does it have this dark red hue to it?" Sehera asked her team but none of them seemed to have a good answer.

Pamela, ask the system to go back to the target system.

Yes, ma'am.

The display changed briefly back to the target system engagement and then quickly slipped away at tremendous speeds and stopped back where it had been on this red highlighted system. The deeper darker red hue flashed on and off like an alarm.

"What in the world?" She cocked her head slightly to the left trying to get a closer look. The system continued to flash in alert. "Where is that?"

"You would need to zoom out to a galactic spur view perhaps to give us reference," Dr. Hughes suggested. "Maybe add some known reference points."

"Oh, okay." Sehera reached up and waved her hands about zooming out on the view.

Pamela, show me when I zoom out far enough to see Sol.

Oh, then stop, you have already gone way beyond that.

Label Sol.

Done.

Wait, can you label the stars, too?

Certainly.

Then star names covered the field around the system in the center and over the star in question. The system was only about twelve or so light-years from Sol.

"It's Tau Ceti!" CW3 Dover sounded excited. "Is it being attacked?"

"Perhaps we should overlay the force tracker data over the map, Mrs. Moore," Johan Seely suggested.

"Good idea," she agreed.

Pamela?

Yes ma'am, I've got it.

"Look at that!" one of the other technicians shouted as the system's blue dots were vanishing rapidly and the purple dots meaning civilians were rapidly changing to the dark red color. After a couple of minutes there was no blue or purple remaining.

"Are the Chiata invading?"

"I don't think so, ma'am," Rondi said.

"Why is that?"

"Because it is a different color red and there is not any Chiata green mixed in either. This is something different," the Master Gunnery Sergeant replied. "Look how quickly the defense forces and the civilians are being changed."

"Yeah Gunny, you're right," CW3 Dover agreed. "They aren't being attrited. They're being converted."

"Converted?" Sehera was confused. "Converted to what? And how could so many be 'converted' so rapidly?"

"I have no idea, Mrs. Moore, as to 'what' they are being converted to," the chief warrant officer replied. "But they are being converted to the red force 'whatever' it is. This is a system-wide invasion and it would appear that the Tau Ceti colony, all nine billion or so of them, have fallen."

"Jesus," Johan Seely gasped.

"I'd say it is more likely the devil," Rondi replied. "This is different. This is not something we've seen before."

"Chief, find me a weapon." Sehera ordered him.

"Uh, yes ma'am." The CW3 didn't hesitate and turned to the seamen in the back of the room. "You two, M-blasters, HVARs, and ammo boxes. Now."

"Mrs. Moore, I'd sure like to know what you are thinking." Rondi stepped in a little closer to her as if she might try and stop her. Sehera quickly shifted her weight and looked at the Marine intensely. Sehera wasn't sure she could take the Marine, but kind of hoped she wouldn't have to.

"Something is happening there. Something bad. The Thgreeth are trying to warn us. Someone has to go to figure this out." Sehera reached out to take the weapons from the chief but he pulled two of them back.

"Sorry, ma'am, but these two are yours. I'll be needin' some weapons myself," Dover told her, attaching the weapons onto his suit. "Gunny, I suppose you'll want to bring your other two AEMs along too."

"Indeed, Chief." Rondi turned to Sehera and slipped her visor up. Sehera could tell she wanted to talk face to face. She personally preferred that. "Mrs. Moore, I can't let you run headfirst into an invasion without some support. We're going with you."

"No, Rondi, you and the Chief can go. But leave the other AEMs here to protect this location. We don't know what is going on here," Sehera said.

"I'm sorry, ma'am, but my orders were to . . ."

"To what, Gunny? Huh? To keep me out of trouble?" Sehera knew why Alexander had sent them, but this was going to take finesse and too many involved might just be a disadvantage, especially if they had to do a lot of sneaking around.

"Mrs. Moore, I have to agree with the master gunnery sergeant here. You really should allow her to bring the rest of the AEMs with us." Dover opened his visor and told her directly. "This looks very dangerous, ma'am. We don't even know what this is."

"Somebody needs to see about this. This is a full-scale invasion only twelve light-years from home. That is a stone's throw from our front door." Sehera attached the blasters to her suit as she had done it a million times. She could see the raised-eyebrow looks from Rondi and the chief. "You two look surprised. I'm not sure what they teach in history class anymore. I've been fighting far longer than either of you have been alive."

"What about the intel to the Expeditionary Fleet?" Dr. Hughes asked. "Don't you have to be here, ma'am?"

"Dee is directly connected into that now. I'm just a middlewoman there anyway."

"Ma'am, do you have a target location in mind?" Rondi asked her.

"Well, if you were going to invade a system, where is the first place you'd hit?" Sehera didn't have to think about it. "We're going to the Presidential estate."

Chapter 27

July 24, 2409 AD
Presidential Estate
Tau Ceti Planet Four, Moon Alpha, a.k.a. Ares
New Tharsis
12 Light-years from the Sol System
Saturday, 3:59 P.M. Eastern Time

Since the last battle of the Separatist War on Ross 128 and a few final skirmishes at Tau Ceti over fifteen years prior, the Presidential Estate had been completely rebuilt and an even bigger city had risen up around the capital of the first truly independent offworld government about a star other than humanity's own. Oh, there had been colonies that were territories of the United States of the Sol System, but it was Tau Ceti, planet Ares, at the city of New Tharsis that was the first independent government from Sol—even if it was only a separate government for a few years.

The terrorist Elle Ahmi had led the people of the colony to secede and to plan the Martian Exodus as well as Ross 128's secession. All of that had been a century-long plan within a plan within a plan that Sehera's mother had led. Back then even Sehera didn't realize that her mother was the former President Sienna Madira and her father the former U.S. Supreme Court justice Scotty P. Mueller. The two of them had managed to keep their identities shrouded very well.

As a child, she had never been to Tau Ceti with her mother, and by the time she was a teenager her mother had conscripted her into the revolution, which kept her busy. At that point, however, her mother had shown her the magic quantum membrane teleporter pads that enabled travel across the stars instantaneously. She always wanted to travel with her mother to the stars but her mother had told her that her place was on Mars, keeping things straight there.

Sehera had always looked up to her mother and father and would have fought with them to the end. But then she started to see her mother acting strangely and manically and that scared her. But she stayed true to her right up until she had discovered Major Alexander Moore and his unit of armored environment-suit Marines being tortured to death, brought back, and tortured again, and again, and again. Some of the soldiers were being experimented on for reasons uncertain at the time, but now she knew that her mother and Copernicus were perfecting the cloning process and maybe even AI-to-mind transfers. What she did know back then was that the torture and treatment of the prisoners was wrong. Her stomach turned and her eyes were opened to how seriously, to put it the way Alexander did, "batshit nuts" her mother truly was.

She then went on to betray her mother and join the Americans. She had gotten older, more educated, and much wiser to her parents' plots and neither of them could hide their past from her any longer, either. Sehera had seen her mother grow into the most hated woman alive and had even fought against her with her husband Alexander Moore. And once she discovered that her mother had murdered her father she had taken it upon herself to stop her mother at all costs. Her final showdown with her had ended the war and, they all thought, her mother's life. Sehera had actually taken to impersonating her mother's Elle Ahmi persona in order to have the Separatist troops across the systems to stand down.

In the end, the actions that she, Alexander, and a few trusted others like DeathRay and his lost wife had ended the war. But that war's end was just the beginning of something worse. It had been another one of her plans within plans, and the likeness of her mother they had killed wasn't her at all, in fact, it had only been a clone driven by an AIC. Sienna Madira had planned it so carefully down to a mock-up of the first generation AIC they had pulled from the clone's head. They were all fooled. But as part of the plans her mother left Sehera and Alexander a trail of breadcrumbs to follow that led them to her and the knowledge that the Chiata were coming to wipe out humanity soon. The entire thing, the Mars Desert Wars, the Martian Exodus, the colonies seceding from the union, her death, all of it was nothing more than part of the plan to make humanity more ready for the even bigger war that was coming.

And now humanity was doing what it could do, with

her mother's help, to fight that alien attack wave off before it ever arrived in Sol space, but it was a seriously difficult and uphill battle. Oddly enough, while Elle Ahmi had vanished from existence fifteen years prior, her mother, who was again going by Sienna Madira, had reconciled with humanity and her daughter and was fighting alongside them as though history had been forgotten. Sehera often wondered how scarred humanity would become if they ever learned of the awful truth about her mother's shaping of humanity's past two centuries. Most certainly she and Alexander were scarred from it. She was certain that once all was done with the Chiata that her husband intended to make her mother pay for her sins. Sehera wasn't sure she could stop him or even that she wanted to. Her mother needed to pay for the murder of her father, at the very least.

At the close of the war, Sehera had visited New Tharsis many times as the First Lady. She had seen the war-torn public change from being Separatists that hated all things American to another colony of mankind and its government. That had taken years. The new president of the colony was elected and had been good for the planet's economy, making use of the QMT technology to create fast moving markets in commodities that could only be found near a Jovian planet. The tourism trade was fairly large as well. People came from all the colonies to see the beautiful views from Ares. The moon of the gas giant was perfectly placed in its orbit to view the purple and blue and reds of the rings looming over the mountains, valleys, and beaches of Ares. The planet was one of the most beautiful humanity had yet to find. Nearly fifteen years ago, Sehera had forced Alexander and Deanna to meet there just after the war had ceased, for a vacation, but they hadn't returned in years. Neither Alexander nor Deanna were the vacationing type.

Nothing looked as Sehera remembered it from those trips. While the Presidential Palace was still on top of the mountain looking down over the valley, it seemed bigger than she remembered and more, well, ornate and decorative like a place for fairy tale royalty rather than the house of a democratic leader. And the city around and up the valley to the base of the palace seemed to have grown chaotically in every direction with little city planning. Fortunately for Sehera and her team, the city was a large tourism draw and therefore detailed information of the city was available on the net. They would have to make use of that data to move about. Sehera had already had them perform several line-of-sight sling-forward QMT jumps.

As the sizzling bacon sound subsided from their latest jump, Sehera stood in the middle with Rondi to her right and the chief to her left. Instantly, their suits updated the cloaking mode to match the local scenery. Sehera hadn't done any sneaking about for almost a decade or more since the end of the war, but knowing how to keep quiet and out of sight quickly came back to her. As the three of them moved about, their suits blended in with their environment to the point that someone would actually have to bump into them to find them. That was, as long as nobody overheard their boots clanking against the sidewalk.

"How do you want to play this, ma'am?" Chief Dover asked.

"I'd recommend against just charging in all guns a blazing, ma'am. We need to do some serious recon here," Rondi added.

"Let's take a high road for a better view and just watch and listen for a while. Keep all your suit's sensors on passive and see what we can pick up." Sehera didn't have a plan in so much as she didn't even know what was going on. Gathering intelligence was the most important thing at the moment that she could think of to do.

"Sounds good, ma'am," Chief Dover replied. "That skyscraper just a few blocks out from the Presidential Palace there might be close enough that the audio snoopers and QMTs can pick up some intelligence there."

"Yes, good." Sehera looked at the building and considered methods for getting up there and decided the best approach would be another sling forward jump.

Pamela, calculate a position a couple meters above the roof of that skyscraper and sling us up there, she thought to her AIC.

Yes, ma'am.

"Hang on. Here we go," she told Rondi and the Chief.

Then with a flash of light and the sound of sizzling bacon her stomach jumped into her throat as she was freefalling. But it was a short fall to the top of the hi-rise building. The three of them dropped as softly as they could. Sehera went down to one knee as she landed with a *kathunk* and then a *crunch* against the pale green Ares gravel that covered the rooftop.

"Alright, take vantage points and let's sit quietly for a bit," Sehera ordered her team.

"Ma'am, you know what is just bugging the living Hell

out of me on this trip?" Rondi asked her through an open visor.

"What's that, Rondi?"

"Well, the red force tracker is showing nobody anywhere. And, this is the busiest city on this planet and I haven't seen a soul. Where the Hell are they?"

"You're right, Rondi." Sehera almost gasped at the thought. The master gunnery sergeant had a point that she hadn't even noticed yet.

She had been so caught up in the emotions the place brought to the forefront of her mind that she hadn't focused on what was truly happening around her. They had bounced about for about three or four minutes and stopped at several spots to do QMTs. While they were doing their best to stay in shadows, alleyways, and rooftops, they had yet to come across a single person anywhere.

"Where the Hell *is* everybody?" CW3 Dover asked. "They were all here before we jumped from the ruins."

"We need to find them," Sehera said. "There's only one way I know of to move nine billion people that quickly."

"A QMT," Rondi said almost under her breath.

"Shit," Chief Dover added.

Pamela, do a full system-wide sensor spread and see what happened to all of them, Sehera thought to her AIC.

Yes ma'am. You'll need to open your battlescape mindview.

Do it and share it.

"I'm sharing my battlescape," she said out loud through her open visor. "Maybe we can find them that way."

As soon as it popped up into her mindview she could see the others looking about at it as well. There were no people anywhere on the planet. Then the view slid outward and beyond the last planets into the Kuiper belt of the system. And there was a single blob of over nine million red dots.

"There!" Sehera pointed. "There they are."

"What are they doing way out there in the Kuiper belt region?" Rondi sounded as perplexed as she was.

"And what is that big structure they're on?" the chief added. "It's as big as a small moon."

"We need a closer look." Sehera reached up into the mindview and zoomed in and what she saw shocked her. "Jesus."

"Is that what I think it is?" Rondi asked.

"It is the QMT projector facility that Copernicus built, but I thought it was at 61 Ursae Majoris." Chief Dover turned to her and popped his helmet off. It folded itself into a compartment on his right shoulder. "Nobody's here, so I'm taking a break from that damned thing. Ma'am, I think that alien 'ally' of ours has pulled a fast one on us."

"This was all a setup." Rondi jammed her fist into her hand as her helmet retracted. "The sonofabitch handed the fleet over to the Chiata so he could take us out himself?"

"We need to get to that facility and have a look around." Sehera was postulating what was going on and nothing short of full-scale invasion would come to mind. "We need our people back from that Chiata trap."

"Yes ma'am, but we're here, and I agree with you that we need to look around. I'm sure that thing is plenty big

Chapter 28

July 24, 2409 AD
Tau Ceti Planet Four, Moon Alpha, a.k.a. Ares
Kuiper Belt
12 light-years from the Sol System
Saturday, 4:09 P.M. Eastern Time

"Stay alert, ma'am, we don't know what we're looking for here." Rondi was moving her hypervelocity rifle about methodically and her head was on a swivel doing her best to cover the general's wife. The HUD in her mindview was showing a live feed from every sensor sweep the suit had looking for threats. Rondi wasn't scared for herself, but she was nervous for Mrs. Moore's safety. She had promised the general that she'd keep her out of trouble and as far as Rondi could tell they were in it about ass deep and maybe even deeper than that.

She hated everything about their current situation. She was on a forward recon mission deeply inside an unknown enemy environment with only a Navy warrant and a civilian. All the backup they could hope to ever get was trapped in a star system about seven hundred light years away and most likely couldn't come to their aid any time soon. They were literally on their own as far as she could figure. Rondi hoped all the stories Dee had told her about her mother were true. Otherwise, the general was going to kick her ass, assuming they survived their current situation.

"There are nine billion people here," Mrs. Moore said in disbelief. "It looks like all of them are down a couple floors and inward in this interior section here. I can't imagine the difficulty in performing that many QMT jumps so quickly. Before now, I'd argue it couldn't be done."

A section of the map in her mindview lit up and zoomed in as Mrs. Moore talked and bounced. Rondi couldn't believe the number of people that had been teleported so quickly either. The details of the logistics of that alone were mindboggling. She couldn't even fathom what the engineering complexity must have been and figured it was a problem that Joe Buckley would love to tear into. She hoped to get back to him alive so she could spring it on him. One thing Rondi figured was that even the best of human minds couldn't have pulled something like that off so quickly. And it was that thought that had her skin crawling and all of her other senses maxed out.

Fucking aliens, she thought.

I agree, her AIC replied in her mindvoice.

"Hold up a minute, ma'am, and let's get our bearings a bit." Rondi studied the map until she decided on a workable path. The red force tracker was showing no red dots between them and the spot on the map. In fact, there

were no red dots anywhere else but in the belly of the
facility a couple of klicks inward.

"My suit's sensors are picking up a massive
electromagnetic disturbance in that direction," CW3
Dover said, nodding his head in the direction down the
passageway. "Something big is happening up there ahead
of us."

"Let's get there quickly and find out, then." Mrs.
Moore didn't stop and kept pressing forward. They
covered the ground quickly at top suit speeds. It was a
little too quickly for Rondi's taste. She wanted them to
slow down and make sure they were covering the corners
and high ground. She wanted them to operate more like
a well-oiled forward recon team of Marines.

But Sehera and the chief were doing a pretty good job
of soldiering. For a second there, Rondi felt more as if she
was on the move with Sehera's husband or her daughter,
but she quickly reeled those thoughts in. Rondi had
accepted from the start of this babysitting gig that the
former First Lady, the general's wife, was the boss, but
what she didn't want to do was let herself think the woman
was a trained and seasoned soldier no matter what history
classes might or might not have taught.

"We need to dogleg slightly here, down this stairwell,
and then across this large open room to the central ring
corridor." Sehera highlighted in the mindview map for
them to see. "And we need to do it quickly before they
figure out we're here."

"Yes, ma'am. We should stay in a cover formation
though, leapfrogging each other from back to front.
Understand what I mean?" Rondi hadn't gotten the words

out before Sehera had bounced twice to the point position about thirty meters ahead of them, dropped to a knee with her rifle at the ready, and was giving them hand signals to come on. "I guess she does understand."

"Looks like it, Gunny." Dover laughed and then bounced to a point ahead of Sehera.

"Shit." Rondi bounced until she reached the head of the stack and then took position waiting for her turn again. Sehera, then the chief bounced by. It was her turn again. Bounce, point, Sehera, the chief, then it was back to her.

As she bounced she took in as much of the surrounding battlescape as possible, hoping to gather any information that might help them understand just what the fuck was going on. Everything about the alien-built QMT facility was gigantic and didn't necessarily make sense from a military, logistics, or even a human dwelling point of view. The ceilings of the corridors were more than ten meters high. The walls were made of girders and grid plated metal and looked surprisingly new to be thousands of years old, according to the intel briefings on the place. How the facility was kept looking so new and in working order was beyond her. As far as she could tell they never passed a broken station, repair in progress, an upgrade of any sort, or any bots scurrying about fixing things. Then, finally, as they dropped down a ladder to the next deck and then across the big open room, they passed several floor to ceiling windows that overlooked an interior chamber. The chamber must have been hundreds, maybe thousands of meters across and seemed bottomless.

Her AIC had calculated that for nine billion people to fit in there the room must be about two kilometers by two kilometers by two kilometers. Rondi had her sensor sweep fill in the map with more detail and realized that her AIC was dead on with the calculations. According to her QMT sensors that was exactly how big the cavern was, barring a bit of extra volume in the center of it about the size of a hovertank drop tube and four long walkways leading out to it from the periphery one at each quadrant leading north, south, east, and west. If Rondi had to guess, she'd say that room was designed just for the purpose of housing nine billion people. But why nine billion people? That was a conundrum that she couldn't figure out. Had the bastard alien, Copernicus, known all along that he was going to abduct the Tau Ceti colony? And had he actually known what the population was going to be? As far as she knew the facility was hundreds maybe thousands of years old, so how could he have designed it with abducting the Tau Ceti colony in mind?

As they approached the entry level to the chamber just above the passageway to the central structure, the red force tracker enabled them to separate the threat forces a little better. There were four dots standing on the platform in the center of the room and the rest were lined up, stacked up, and in row after row surrounding them.

"Look at that." Sehera stopped cold in her tracks at one of the large floor to ceiling windows that gave them a full view of the chamber. The look on her face made Rondi very uneasy. "Oh my God."

In the distance about a kilometer away where the central platform sat, a glowing silvery shimmering ball that looked like a teleportation gate when it was open fluctuated in brightness and size slightly. Long plasma filaments shot outwards from the quantum foam ball in every direction. Those filaments bifurcated over and over again as they stretched across the room.

Closest to them several filaments ended in the heads of people who were suspended midair floating about. Row after row and column after column of people with glowing white plasma filaments protruding from their heads just behind the ear where their AICs were implanted. This was the scene leading back to the center of the room as far as they could see and it was eerie and startling and confusing all at once. Rondi wasn't sure what was going on but she knew it couldn't be good.

"What the . . ."

"Well, we found them," Chief Dover said.

"I don't know what he's doing to them, but we need to stop it." Sehera started looking about as if she were about to burst into the room through the window.

"I might remind you, Mrs. Moore, that the Thgreeth system has already painted them red when they were blue before. For whatever reason the Thgreeth think they've already been turned into enemies," Chief Dover recalled.

"Maybe we can reverse it," Sehera replied. "Let's go."

"Wait, ma'am! What are you planning?"

"Have you ever fought with Admiral Boland, Master Gunnery Sergeant?" Sehera asked her.

"Um, yes, ma'am."

"Well, he has an attack plan that I think would be appropriate right now." Sehera said. The Chief looked bewildered as he clearly didn't know the admiral. "You see those four dots in the middle have to be the bad guys. I suspect Copernicus is the one in the middle."

"Yes, ma'am. I'd have to agree. And, I think that I do know of the attack plan you speak of." Rondi smiled. Everyone who served with DeathRay in any form of combat was well aware of his damned near legendary extremely simple, but effective, battle planning. He had been the CAG for the *Madira* for so long and General Moore's go-to man for all things of special tactical nature since her and Dee were in grade school. Rondi knew his approach to combat fairly well. Hell, everyone on the *Madira* most certainly knew it, even the noncombat crew.

"Pardon me, ma'am, Gunny. I'm not familiar with this plan as I came on board the *Madira* after Admiral Boland had been commissioned to the *Penzington*. What is this plan?" CW3 Dover asked with a bit of concern in his voice.

"Go ahead, Rondi, you tell him." Sehera smiled as she brought the rifle up and pointed it at the window. "And get ready."

"Well, Chief, DeathRay is famous in combat circles for his battle plan because he only uses one plan ever." Rondi smiled, trying not to laugh. She stood with one foot slightly back behind her like a sprinter about to start a race.

"And it always works for him?"

"In three . . ." Sehera started counting down slowly.

"Sort of. But I've often heard other pilots say it is due to talent and skill as opposed to tactical or strategic brilliance. I couldn't say which, but they don't call him DeathRay for nothing." Rondi laughed this time and then she took in a long deep breath like the race was about to start. She was showing the chief that it was time to get serious. Serious in that she knew they were about to go headfirst into some shit.

". . . Two . . ."

"So the plan is?"

"Well, chief, as DeathRay would say, and I quote, 'we go in there and we kill those motherfuckers!'" Rondi said.

". . . One!"

Rondi raised her rifle as Sehera fired into the window. *Spittap, spittap, spittap* sounded and that was the starting pistol. She raced at the full speed run of the suit then hit her jump boots and bounced through the glass with a *crash* and fell the twenty or so meters to the walkway beneath them that led to the central platform. "Ooh-fuckin'-rah," she said to herself as she landed against the deck making a loud metal-to-metal *thud*.

"Move quickly, Rondi!" Sehera said over the suit's local tacnet.

"Roger that! We bounce fast before they can react."

"Unless they're in suits, we should have them well outgunned," the chief said. Rondi thought for an experienced warrant he was not experienced at fighting aliens. You never knew what the fuck to expect with the bastards. Even something like buzzsaw bots became severely menacing when they had the numbers game on you.

"Don't count on it, Chief. Keep your guard up. Buckley-Freeman switches on!" Rondi's shields flashed on around her suit. "At max speed we can cover this kilometer path in about a minute. Keep leapfrogging the stack. Keep your eyes peeled. Weapons up!"

"Look at that!" Sehera pointed to their right and up a couple of floors. "Are those Marines?"

Rondi used her visor sensors to zoom in on the section

and there were more than fifty Armored Environment-suit Marines in suits. Their helmets were removed and the white filaments of plasma protruding their heads just like the rest of the people there. But the bad part was that several of the suits were being turned upright and Rondi could see the system boot-up lights kicking on.

"I think they are waking up. If they are on his side, we are outnumbered and have very little cover here." Rondi looked about not quite in panic mode, but certainly in her better-think-of-something-quick-or-get-her-ass-shot-off mode. "They know we're here!"

Battlescape view, combat mode! she thought to her AIC.

Combat mode on.

The battlescape filled her mindview and started seeking out potential targets. Green and yellow targeting Xs appeared all around her. Red force tracker dots completely encompassed them. They were in a sea of enemy targets. She just hoped all of them weren't brought to life at once.

"Shit. I'm beginning to think this was a bad idea."

Chapter 29

July 24, 2409 AD
U.S.S. Scotty P. Mueller
Mission Star 74
Chiata Expanse
783 light-years from the Sol System
Saturday, 4:17 P.M. Eastern Time

"Shit. Scotty, I'm beginning to think this whole thing was a bad idea." Sienna Madira held on to the arms of her captain's chair so tightly that she bent the metal into the shape of her gauntlet fingers even more so than it already had been. As the ship rocked backwards from the impacting blue beam of death from Hell, she bit down hard on her mouthpiece and prayed the shields held up. A system mounted to the wall of the dome burst into sparking flames as a crack formed across the panel control station. Repair bots moved about quickly, making repairs as best they could in real time. One of the bots scurried up to her chair and started to repair the armrests where she had gripped it, but Sienna shooed it away and told her AIC to have it sent somewhere else.

"Yes, ma'am. Shields are still holding on all the ships, but barely," her right-hand clone replied. "I wouldn't suggest we continue to press our luck much longer, ma'am."

The sensors did indeed detect a fluctuation on the previous engagement Sienna, her AIC told her. *You were right. On each engagement, firing on certain ships has caused this and firing on others has not.*

That means some of these ships are connected to the damping field and some aren't, Sienna thought. *Makes sense. They wouldn't all have to be part of it. I think they'd need just enough of them to connect the field generators into one cloud.*

Yes, I agree.

That would also suggest that there must be ships scattered about the thickness of it.

Yes, it would.

Find them.

Yes, Sienna.

"That ship there. The big one in the front of the phalanx. Hit it!" she shouted.

"That isn't the ship Lieutenant Colonel Moore has targeted for us, ma'am," the clone manning the gunner's station replied.

"I didn't ask, gunner. I ordered you to hit the lead ship in the phalanx."

"Yes, ma'am. Sorry, ma'am." Sienna thought about how in her past as Elle Ahmi she might have gotten up just then and killed the gunner, but that was then.

The blue beams zigzagged across the bow of the *Mueller*, around one of her other attack group ships, and then into the bow of the lead megaship she had in mind. The shields of the alien porcusnail flickered from bow to stern but didn't fail. Sienna wasn't expecting them to. But what did happen was exactly what she had been hoping for. She watched her system-wide mindview of the sensor data as the blue beams impacted the lead ship and there was a very brief spike in the quantum vacuum energy fluctuations at the event horizon of the QMT damping field.

Clearly, this ship is part of the damping network.

Yes it is.

"STO! Track that ship and do not let it out of your sight! Gunner, hit it again!"

"Twenty seconds until we can fire again, ma'am."

"The attack group has taken several hits, Captain. Shields are down to half power across the board," the XO told her. "We need to start thinking about jumping, Captain."

"Understood, keep maneuvering us about and one of these ships fire at that damned target!"

A blue beam from the *Mueller's* wingship fired and tracked into the same porcusnail. The QMT damping field spiked again at the same location. This was the data that Madira had been looking for and hoping she could find and it was repeatable. The biggest ship they could find in each of the Chiata fleet attack groups was likely the command ship of that subgroup and somehow it was connected to the damping fields. Every single time according to her review of the records that the lead and largest megaships were hit the damping field generated some random quantum energy fluctuations spread over the hard X-ray band of the electromagnetic spectrum. The quantum fluctuations were then actually manifested into reality as real measurable tangible photons.

Following the thermodynamics of event horizons the entropy was directly proportional to Hawking's constant and the surface area of the horizon. If there was real energy lost at the surface of the horizon then, again according to cosmology developed centuries prior, whatever was inside the horizon was oscillating or there was some sort of interaction between the quantum vacuum and tangible matter and energy. That meant that something, a device of some sort, was losing energy somewhere and could be found and hopefully destroyed.

"Ma'am, we have to leave now," the XO stated matter-of-factly. "Two of our attack group megaships are suffering from shield failure and are jumping out now. Our shields are down to thirty percent."

"Very well, get us out of here." She leaned back and breathed a sigh of relief as the flash of light and the sizzling began. "Maybe, just maybe, we can soon find a back door to this place."

"Yes ma'am, QMT in five seconds."

There are indeed Chiata megaships positioned throughout the thickness of the damping field. Using data from all the Fleet vessels' sensors I believe I can give you a detailed map of at least fifty percent of them. The damping field is creating some uncertainty in the effectiveness of the QMT sensors.

Damned good.

❖   ❖   ❖

"Alexander, how soon until this new weapon is available?" Sienna asked over the commandnet. "I might just have a target list for it."

"We are minutes from the first test firing, Sienna. What type of target might you have?" Moore replied. Sienna could always sense the distaste in the man's voice every time he spoke with her. She understood it. She had tortured him for months to the brink of death. She had actually killed him a couple of times but had the medics bring him back. What she'd done to him was atrocious, horrible, and most certainly scarred them both, and maybe even her daughter who witnessed it, for life. She wouldn't be surprised if he was the one who doled out a death sentence to her someday. She'd expected it for decades.

"I've been doing an analysis of the fields in this system and each time certain megaships, the biggest ones, we should really start creating classes of them by the way, get hit by a BBD there are energy fluctuations at the event horizon of the QMT damping fields." Sienna could see Moore's eyebrows raise. "I thought you'd like that, son."

"Can you identify these ships, Sienna?"

"Yes. Yes I can, but it takes a hit from the BBDs to be certain."

"That can be arranged." Moore paused a bit and seemed to be speaking to someone in the real world for an instant before returning to the conversation. "Okay, Sienna, stand by. Avoid engagement until we are ready to make an attack to find your target."

"Good plan, son. We're standing by until you are ready for us. We've got some wounds to lick anyway."

"Understood. Moore out."

Chapter 30

July 24, 2409 AD
U.S.S. Davy Rackman
Mission Star 74
Chiata Expanse
783 light-years from the Sol System
Saturday, 4:19 P.M. Eastern Time

"They just popped out of hyperspace, Captain. One hundred megaships." Azazel almost sounded flustered but since Deanna was still in Engineering, she couldn't say for certain. The ship being slammed by an enemy BBD was enough to fluster her, especially since the forward shields were nonfunctional.

"Holy Hell!" Dee shouted as she pulled herself up from the deck. "Keep the aft end of the ship pointed at them. The forward shield generators have been rerouted into the BBDs! We need some cover quick or we need to get out of here."

"Sorry, Captain," Molloch joined the conversation. "The QMTs are down now and the hyperspace projector is still charging. We need forty-seven seconds before we can make an FTL jump. They knew right where to hit us and with the forward shields down, it did some serious damage."

"Dad!" Deanna turned to her father who was regaining his balance a few meters to her right. He had been in some DTM conversation and seemed distracted just as the BBD hit. "Are you okay?"

"I'm fine Dee. Just lost my balance." That was so uncharacteristic of her father. She wasn't sure she'd ever seen him fall in her life, but then again, she'd never seen him being slammed by an alien blue beam of death while having a DTM conversation either. After all, the beam impact had knocked her all the way to the floor.

"Dad, we're outnumbered bad and need some cover fire here!"

"Yes. Abby has shown me the battlescape. I'm snapping back to the *Madira* and will cover you as best we can. I'm calling in all the attack groups here to protect this ship. Get that weapon firing!"

"Thanks . . ." he was gone in a flash before she could finish saying, ". . . Dad."

"All hands, all hands, prepare for an incoming message from the general."

"This is General Moore. The *U.S.S. Davy Rackman* has a possible asset on board that can destroy the Chiata. We are preparing to fire that system in the next three minutes, but the ship is defenseless and stranded in place until that time. All Fleet ships, I repeat, *all* Fleet ships are to converge on the *Rackman*, giving it cover until such time as it can fire this weapon."

✧ ✧ ✧

"The *Penzington* just dropped out of QMT right on our bow," Molloch alerted Dee through the tacnet. She looked at the ball in her mindview and could see several of the megaships converging on her.

"Good. We need all the help we can get right now."

She was doing her level best to push the CHENG and Commander Buckley to finish up the weapon. As fast as they were moving, with builder bots scurrying about the ship so fast they looked like little mechanical blurs, it still was going to take some time because the ship was just so big. There were more than ten kilometers worth of power conduits and couplings coursing through the ship. The conduits started at the shield generators on the two front supercarrier legs, traveled down each of the respective three kilometers long supercarrier's interiors, into the alien porcusnail, and then made a long slow curved turn aftward and down to the Engineering deck where they met and joined in a much larger Y shaped conduit big enough to drive a hovertank through.

"Talk to me Deedee," she said to the clone chief engineer. "How much longer?"

"Ma'am, it is still three minutes until we can fire the weapon." Dee wasn't sure but she thought she heard a bit of annoyance in the clone's voice.

"What about the hyperspace projector?" Dee wanted to get to a safer location as fast as they could. That weapon would do them no good if they were dead before it was finished.

"Captain Moore." Commander Buckley stepped in between her and the Deedee clone and made a subtle nodding gesture at the clone CHENG. "Might I have a quick hand here, please?"

"Sure Joe, what can I do to help?" Deanna followed Joe as he led her about ten meters to the other side of the Main Engineering Room and through a hatch. A few meters further down he led her up a ladder to the junction box where Skippy was going to have to control whatever it was the little Thgreeth drone bot was going to control.

"Well, Captain, I thought you might have your little pet walk about here and see if it will do anything." Commander Buckley gestured with his hands toward the panel they had removed that showed the main controller computer boards. They didn't really look much like the computer boards that Dee was used to seeing. There were no quantum processor chips, no self-healing organogel circuit packs, no memory QMT buffers, nothing resembling anything on standard supercarriers. Instead, there were many centimeters-long odd shaped flowing crystals of reds and greens with protruding long glowing hair thin filaments jutting out like cotton candy in every direction. Each filament glowed and pulsed either red or green or some combination of the two. There were panels that slid in and out and had multiple crystals of the exact same dodecahedron shape held in place in premolded slots. The filaments fed into the edge of these "boards" of crystals in as adventitious of a way possible. Joe, Deedee, and more importantly, Skippy seemed to understand it enough to manipulate it and that was what mattered. Dee didn't have a clue. It didn't look anything like the inside of her cockpit and it only vaguely resembled the guts of a dead Chiata.

"Okay." Dee tapped her chest compartment and it unfastened itself and opened. "Skippy, come on out and get ready to fire the main weapon."

The little bot crawled out of its pouch like a baby marsupial and dropped to the deck. It crawled around a bit and then suddenly it flew in a blur to the controller box. The legs of the beetle-looking bot dug into the cotton candy circuitry and then seemed to melt into the circuit and its legs started glowing yellow and white as if the metal were very hot. Red and green optical flashes began to wash over him. Dee was concerned it might be harming him.

"What do you think it's doing, Joe?"

"You got me. But I hope it is running startup routines and diagnostics."

The ship was hit so hard that both of them were thrown to the deck. Dee was getting tired of being tossed about like a rag doll. Had they not been wearing their suits with the helmets up they'd have likely both just been killed. Dee's ears were ringing so loud that she was pretty sure she might have a concussion. Just in case, she had her suit administer a small dose of immunoboost that stopped the ringing in her ears almost instantly.

Casualty reports coming in across the ship, Dee, her AIC told her. *A lot of concussions and some neck injuries.*

Where's my cover! she thought.

DeathRay is fighting back and it would appear that Admiral Walker's group has dropped into our sub-ball as well. Your father just fired the BBDs of the Madira. *Would you like me to open the energy scenarios in your battlescape view?*

No. I can't focus on that right now. We have to make this weapon work first.

It will not do any good if we are destroyed first.

Good point, Bree.

"Joe, we're getting slammed, we have got to fight back or get the Hell out of here," she told Buckley. "You two super CHENGs have got to give me something. Now."

"We're doing what we can. We've got this here, Captain. You should get to the bridge and do what you do best." Buckley turned to her. "No offense, Dee, but you are kind of in the way down here. Up there, you rule. There's hardly any other tactical fighter alive as good as you. We need you doing that, not doing this. Go do what you do."

"I, uh, . . ." Dee wasn't sure what to say at first, but she realized that Joe was right. She wasn't trained as an engineer or even an engineer's mate. She was a trained fighter, a trained Chiata killing machine. Her eyes started to glow red again. "You're right. I get it. I get it."

"Sign of a great captain, ma'am." Joe smiled at her. "Go do what you do, we've got this."

"You take care of Skippy," she told Joe and then turned and patted the back of the little beetle bot. "Skippy, don't destroy yourself. I'd miss you if you did."

The bot didn't move but just before Dee could turn away a blur shot from it to her shoulder. She and Joe were both slightly startled by the fact that Skippy was suddenly perched on her shoulder, but Dee less so. Dee turned and looked back at the computer panel and there was Skippy still embedded in the control box. Dee had never really bothered to ask herself if it was exact replicas or still him or what when he did that. But she'd seen it on several occasions while fighting Chiata.

"He just copied himself. Did you see that?" Joe asked her in bewilderment.

"He does that," Dee said nonchalantly as the bot crawled down in his compartment on her suit.

"Really? I mean, out of what materials? Is it exact? Who's controlling it?" Joe seemed surprised but more than that, he suddenly had a million questions. Dee could see the CHENG wheels starting to turn in his head. He was getting some sort of crazy assed Buckley idea she was sure of it. "Is it a copy or is it still him like a quantum pair or image or matter hologram?"

"I've never bothered to ask him. That's how he eats the shit out of Chiata."

"What, you mean he eats them and replicates?"

"Yeah. I've seen it on a much bigger scale. Don't make a big thing of it." Dee flashed out and then was standing on the bridge beside her empty mecha in the middle of the giant transparent dome that encompassed the bridge. Her FM-14X was in eagle-mode with the canopy up and nose pointed down almost touching the deck. She gave herself a short pause to admire the sleek lines of the wings and the twin tails with the fiery demon logos. She read to herself but slightly out loud, "We are the Bringers of Hell."

Okay Bree, full up battlescape and also I want the ship's diagnostics view. I need to see what systems are in trouble when. And pull the attack list back up into my view so I can call shots for the Fleet if I need to. Maybe the Thgreeth data will help us here some more.

Aye, Captain Moore.
Aww shit, don't start that again.
Sorry, but you ARE the Captain, Dee.

Chapter 31

July 24, 2409 AD
U.S.S. Davy Rackman
Mission Star 74
Chiata Expanse
783 light-years from the Sol System
Saturday, 4:20 P.M. Eastern Time

The battlescape was suddenly a flood of overwhelming numbers in the very near combat ball about the ship. There were Chiata porcusnails every direction she looked. Dee suddenly wished she could do a puking Deathblossom with her megaship, but that wasn't happening anytime soon—although she was going to put it on the list of things to talk to the CHENG about for future engagements.

There was a three-dimensional phalanx of more than twenty alien megaships in a close cone formation pushing through directly toward the bow of her ship just in front of the BBD spires like a spear, a very pointy spear. Dee couldn't actually see them because both the *Penzington* and the *Madira* were sitting on top of her so closely that Dee was pretty sure she could feel their hull gravity fields pulling at her. The *Thatcher* had taken up a position on her aft section and the *Decatur* was underneath her.

All of the Fleet megaships protecting her were firing their BBDs, DEGs, missile batteries, and anti-aircraft fire in a continuous concert of blues and reds and violet ion contrails that were filling the ball like a light show at a rock concert. And to add to the visual cacophony the Chiata were firing their own blue beams of death from Hell in every zig-zagging pattern imaginable with apparent designs on the *Rackman* for whatever reason.

The other Fleet ships were doing their level best to keep between the alien BBDs and her. So far, they had managed it, but who knew how long that would last? The alien beams could turn on a dime and make change. Dee had seen the Chiata porcusnails practically thread a needle with the beams in previous engagements, so, she wasn't sure if close formation protection would work all that well.

"Captain, CHENG Deedee."

"Go, Deedee."

"Ma'am, that last hit knocked another conduit out in the hyperdrive projector power unit. We are tens of minutes away from hyperdrive being functional and that is if I pulled crews and bots from the weapon build," CHENG Deedee said. "And there was some minor damage to the weapon power grid but we are rerouting that now with hopefully very little delay. What do you prefer, ma'am? Do we call off resources for the drive or stick to the weapon?"

"No, keep all personnel and bots working on the weapon. We need that weapon now!" Dee was even more concerned that the aliens seemed to be after her and they were practically defenseless and dead in space.

"Aye Captain."

"Incoming enemy mecha, Phoenix." Molloch's canopy started cycling downward as he called her on the tacnet. The interdiction cannons on the outside hull near the periphery of the dome started firing nonstop at the new porcupine targets flooding the space above the dome with orange and white hot tracer rounds. "Definitely porcupines, ma'am, and something more. We just took an impact on the hull several hundred meters starboard. Perhaps for safety, ma'am, you should mount up. Look."

"What?" Dee turned and looked out in the direction Molloch was pointing. She could see Azazel hopping up into his mecha as well. There was a dropship boring itself into the hull plating of the *Rackman*. Dee was certain it was filled with at least twenty or thirty mechanized Chiata and possibly that many infantrymen. Then several more drop ships slammed into the hull and penetrated it across the surface each time with a bone rattling *thud*.

"Shit! We need some support out there!" Dee thought for a second. She needed to be out there fighting them, not stuck in here in a captain's seat. But at the same time, somebody had to captain this ship and fire that megaweapon.

Bree, give me an open channel to all hands.

Done.

"All hands, this is the captain. We are being boarded by Chiata mecha now. All mecha and infantry report to the assigned decks and protect the Engineering teams. Note that Colonel Strong will continue to serve as CAG of the flight wings and Colonel Slayer will lead the Ground troops until further notice. Good luck!"

She then opened the commandnet channel and pinged all the ship captains of the Expeditionary Fleet.

"This is Captain Deanna Moore. The *Rackman* is being boarded by multiple Chiata drop ships capable of carrying many mecha and infantrymen. I believe for whatever reason the Chiata have singled us out for recapture or destruction. We could sure use some help over here."

"Understood, Dee," DeathRay replied. "I just detailed two mecha squadrons to you. Help is on the way."

"Hold tight, Captain Moore. I'm sending as many buzzsaw bots as I can manage," her grandmother replied.

"The Demon Dawgs and the Gods of War mecha units are on their way. AEMs are on the way. And so am I, Captain," her father said.

"Thank you, Captains!" Dee could feel the ship continue to shake against the boarding ships ramming and boring into the hull plating. The stern of her ship looked like a porcupine to begin with due to all of the alien antenna farms, sensors, directed-energy systems, and just sheer damned alien architecture. But now, with all of the drop tubes sticking out of the hull plating, the madness to the design appeared even more, well, mad.

There were more drop ships dug or digging into her ship than she cared to count.

"Firestorm!" General Moore shouted at his XO. His longtime friend and second in command could handle the *Madira* in a fight just as good if not better than he and at the moment his daughter needed him.

"General, go, I can handle this," Sally told him with a nod. Alexander returned the nod and then saluted her.

"The *Madira* is yours Captain Rheims," he told her.

"Aye sir. She'll be waiting for you when you get back." She returned the salute. "Give those alien bastards Hell, sir."

"You too, Firestorm."

Alexander hit his wristband and flashed out from the *U.S.S. Sienna Madira* and reappeared on the bridge of the *U.S.S. Davy Rackman*. He looked about the bridge and realized just how much of a skeleton crew Dee had been functioning with. There were only herself and two of her clone mecha pilots commanding the ship.

"Alexander Moore reporting for duty, Captain! Where do you need me, ma'am." He looked up at his daughter who was locking herself into her fighter's cockpit. The canopy started cycling downward.

"Dad, somebody needs to run this ship, and at the same time, somebody has to fight these damned boarding parties," Dee told him over the tacnet. "I can do more damage with my mecha than you can in your suit."

"While that's debatable, I won't argue it for now. Understood, Dee. Not what I had in mind, but understood." Alexander turned and looked for a captain's chair but none had been built yet. There was something like a chair in the middle raised console station but it was designed for a Chiata and likely wouldn't be worth sitting in. He jumped up on it anyway and settled himself onto the alien dais. "I can take the bridge. Abigail can log in and run whatever systems I need to get at from here."

Right, Abby?

Of course, sir.

Good girl.

"The rest of Molloch's team are just outside by the big elevator protecting this entrance. They are four badass motherfucking Marines, clones or not. They've got your back. If they fall that means you're in some serious shit."

"Understood."

"Thanks, Daddy, uh, General, the *Rackman* is yours. Please take good care of him."

"Done. Be careful out there lieutenant colonel and watch your six." His daughter's eyes started glowing demonically and the tattoos on her face surged red and green. Alexander figured the prefight adrenaline was surging through his little princess like acid through her veins. She looked nothing short of fierce. He turned and pointed at Molloch and Azazel. "You two, watch her six!"

"Roger that, General," both of the clones replied and saluted him.

Abby pull up the respective team leads and tie into the CHENG AICs.

Yes, sir.

Give me the ship's diagnostics page and the battlescape in my mindview.

Yes, sir.

And send DeathRay a private message that his second could probably handle that ship because Dee could sure use a hand. Tell him we have plenty of admirals here, but what we need is a good DeathRay!

Done, sir. Setting up the chessboard sir?

It is time to stop taking this beating and start giving

it. Now let's get to work. Find something we can use against them.

Yes, sir.

"All Fleet ships, all Fleet captains, this is General Moore," he said on the commandnet. "I want all ships to focus on the ball combat space around the *U.S.S. Davy Rackman*. I want you jumping in, taking your shots, and jumping out. I want all of the ships focusing on targets in this part of the system. Keep fighting and good luck. Moore out."

What have you got for me, Abby? Tell me you've found something we can exploit.

I would like to point out that I'm using the Chiata comm system network built into this ship and I'm picking up signals emanating from the drop tube ships, sir.

Yeah? What does that mean, Abby?

I think they are control signals or command signals.

Alexander looked at his red force tracker and could see that the drop tubes still had a handful of Chiata in them. He knew exactly what was going on as soon as he saw that.

Abby, those are command centers, tactical operations centers. If we take those out the infantry will be without leadership.

I think you are right, sir.

Open me a channel to Dee!

Done sir.

"Dee!" he said.

"Go, General!"

"The tubes aren't emptying all the way. There is a TOC in each one. You need to take those out and it will confuse the infantry being commanded from them."

"Understood, General! Thanks!" He'd kind of wished she'd have called him "Dad", but he understood.

Alexander allowed himself a few seconds more to watch his daughter in her true element. She wore her fighter plane like a second skin and it looked like if fit her perfectly. He kind of wished he hadn't thrust the captain's chair on her the way he had because it clearly wasn't where she was happy. And to top that off, she still had a whole lot of avenging to do for Davy Rackman's and Nancy Penzington's deaths. He could see it every single time he looked at her that she was all torn up inside and for the time being, flying and killing Chiata were the only things that seemed to make her happy. While he'd been worried about her only hanging around clones, the two she had been with seemed to genuinely have her back. They appeared to be good Marines, clones or not.

The power plants of the FM-14Xs started spinning up and reverberating against the deck plates to the point that made Alexander's bones and teeth rattle. He watched them as they sprang to life and then slung forward with a flashing brilliant white light that rippled through the quantum membrane fabrics of the universe. They vanished briefly from his blue force tracker and then reappeared just outside the dome. He caught the return flash a few hundred meters out instantaneously as the mecha reappeared in reality space. The vehicles were already transforming into fighter mode and the one on point was already firing cannon rounds and engaging an enemy fighter.

"That's my girl."

Chapter 32

July 24, 2409 AD
Mission Star 74
Chiata Expanse
783 light years from the Sol System
Saturday, 4:23 P.M. Eastern Time

The Lead Huntress sat at the dais of her Huntership leading the hunting party of one hundred of her best hunters after the forsaken and elusive prey. She held a holoprojector in her clutches before her watching the projection of the human prey she was after. The ally had given the Pride full video holographic images of this human and they were indeed shocking. The Lead Huntress had watched the video projection over and over many times and could not believe that any mere prey could bare handedly kill so many of her warriors and hunters. But there was something awful and nerve shaking about this particular prey. She had a drive and a bloodlust of her brethren that was unmatched by any prey she'd ever encountered. One of the most unnerving visuals of her was the imagery the ally had sent of her out of her armor. The prey had visibly and permanently marked or scarred itself for each Chiata kill and wore the marks proudly. Unlike the other prey, her scars surged red and green like Chiata blood and her eyes glowed like fire. She was truly a demon. She was truly a killer.

As one of the warriors pierced her body with its tendrils the creature's eyes glowed even brighter and fiery red with anger and she continued to fight even harder rather than running, rather than succumbing, rather than dying. This alien not only didn't run, but pulled the warrior closer to her so she could look into his soul as she ripped it apart with her blade from groin to throat. Then she held it in place as it writhed in death in her grasp, staring into the warrior's eyes until the glow left her brethren and the prey herself was bathed from head to claw in Chiata blood and entrails. And then there was a flash of the prey's teeth showing pure enjoyment in the Chiata's death. This wasn't hunting for survival. The Lead Huntress recognized this as killing for pleasure.

This creature, this "Phoenix", this "Deanna Moore", scared the Lead Huntress beyond anything that had ever scared her before. She had in all her centuries never seen a prey formidable enough to call an 'adversary.' The Pride had never lost a fight since she had been alive and now they had lost several and each time this demon was there. This prey was the embodiment of any devil the Chiata might have. While the Lead Huntress never had believed in such primitive concepts as demons and devils, she felt it quite possible that she was looking at its likeness before her.

"Lead Huntress, we are ready to deploy the warrior dropships on the targeted Huntership as well as the support fighters," her second hunter told her.

She raised up her gaze from the holoprojection and looked out the dome at the prey's formation. Several of their repurposed Hunterships were taking up a shielding formation around the prize. That seemed cowardice to her or perhaps there was some other reason they were protecting that particular ship. This prey had proven to be unpredictable in the past and every engagement seemed to travel down a different path and lead to an unusual outcome. Unbeknownst to the majority of the Chiata Kingdom of Prides was how severely these prey had defeated them over the past couple of years. The Lead Huntress understood the King's desire to finish this prey off quickly and why he would even deal with the ally he'd made agreements with. The ally had promised to deliver this demon and the entirety of her pride.

"She is there, I'm certain of it," she said nervously to herself. "Deploy the warrior dropships."

"Yes, ma'am."

The Lead Huntress sat the projector on the dais and let out a guttural cry. The rest of the bridge crew followed suit and growled and howled and screeched the Chiata hunting party cry. She then rose from the dais and turned to her second hunter.

"Second Hunter, have my predator ship readied for me. And have my squadron readied for battle. I'm going on this hunt," she ordered. "You are now Lead Huntress until I return."

"Yes, Huntress," the second replied.

✧ ✧ ✧

The warrior ships had dropped and most of them had made it to the surface of the prize ship as planned. Some of them had jumped out of hyperspace too quickly and were destroyed by impacting the other human ships. The Lead Huntress would have to punish the commander of the hunt for poor planning. Otherwise, the battle seemed to be going according to plan but with these prey it was always unclear as to how a hunting party's plan might play out. These human prey were so quickly changing their tactics and fighting posture that they were harder to ensnare than rodents in an open field. And these rodents had a propensity for biting back.

She stepped under her warrior ship and raised her arms. She could feel the hunt energy flowing through her as the surging light flashed red and green through her veins and skin and eyes. She tilted her head back and the ship dropped down over her body and attached itself as the amorphous armor became one with her mind and body. She flexed the warrior ship's tendrils testing them and liked the way they felt on her body. It had been too long since she had been on a good challenging hunt. She growled softly and then opened up her tactical communications systems.

"Okay, hunting party, let us move out!"

Chapter 33

July 24, 2409 AD
Mission Star 74
Chiata Expanse
783 light-years from the Sol System
Saturday, 4:23 P.M. Eastern Time

"Guns, guns, guns!" Dee grunted through a barrel roll and pitch reversal as she tracked a porcupine cutting backwards and toward the dome. She had to add counterclockwise yaw in order to keep the targeting X in her mindview red. The maneuver was gut wrenching but she muscled through it with pure grit.

Just to the left and beneath her Azazel dropped to the hull and switched over into bot-mode onto one knee as he tracked the same fighter as well and Dee was pretty sure they were going to take the bastard out. But the alien's wingman had other plans and zoomed just over Azazel's head right into Dee's three-nine line.

"Bank left, Phoenix!" Azazel sounded genuinely excited. "You got one sneaking in at three o'clock with intersecting energy lines."

"Got it!" Dee slammed the HOTAS forward and stomped hard left outer pedal tossing her into a rapid nose over tail spin that moved her just out of the way at the last second. The maneuver put bone-crushing gees pressing against her in every direction and made her feel as though her internal organs were being squeezed in a vise and her bones were being stomped on by a giant. She grunted and breathed through the extreme stress on her body and kept her mind focused on the energy lines in her mindview. She had to make certain not to collide with the Chiata's mecha as it approached at mind-blurring speed that took quantum membrane sensors to track. The alien passed so close to her that their barrier fields interacted with each other causing both vehicles to flicker with multispectral shimmering light as they rocked against each other like tanks colliding.

"Where the Hell are you Molloch?" she growled.

"Fox Three." Molloch's voice rang over the tacnet as music to her ears. His blue dot showed up in her mindview in just the right place at just the right moment. Their three-man formation had been enough to throw off the two-on-two game the Chiata were used to.

Molloch had done an out-and-in and popped back in just behind the mecha crossing her midline but in the relative above position. The vanishing and reappearing act had managed to confuse the alien pilot enough so that it appeared uncertain as to which one was its target and it also, apparently, didn't have time to react to Molloch's mecha-to-mecha missile.

Dee stomped right pedal and pulled back on the stick stabilizing her attitude just in time to catch the missile's impact against the alien mecha. The impact created a glorious and beautiful orange plasma ball against the green flickering barrier fields surrounding the mecha. The shields failed from the high explosive impact and both she and Molloch went to guns.

"Guns, guns, guns!" they shouted as the large plasma rounds ripped chunks of armor plating away from the mecha until it shattered into pieces. Shards of glowing reds and greens filled the debris field as the alien's blood boiled off into space.

"Could use a little help here, Phoenix." Azazel was getting swarmed by multiple porcupines that were bouncing on the hull of the ship and doing their best to maximize damage to the hull in the typical Chiata red and green blur fashion. It also appeared as if they were trying to push him toward the bridge dome. "I've got several targets with your name on them over here, Phoenix. But you need to hurry, ma'am."

"Hang on, Azazel! Out and in!" Dee checked the mindview for a good vector solution but the damned alien mecha was zipping about on every vector. Any, and she really believed ANY, direction had a viable targeting solution vector.

"Fox Three." Azazel released a missile into the alien mecha closest to him. The amorphous tendrils and quills wriggled and writhed out of the way and the missile missed the Chiata and passed by Molloch so closely that he had to jink and juke to keep it from colliding with him but the blue force tracker would have made the warhead inert even if it had impacted. Just when it looked like the mecha had Azazel dead to rights, he flashed out of reality space and then popped back in several hundred meters away and to the starboard of the onrushing alien craft.

"Great, I've got him. Fox Three!" Molloch locked up on the porcupine and quickly took it out with a missile followed by plasma rounds from his cannon. "That's two for me if you're counting Phoenix, ma'am. Do you think I should get a tattoo, ma'am?"

"Jokes now, Molloch? Really?" She'd been trying to get the clone to lighten up for months and was surprised by his proper use of humor and improper timing.

"Sorry, ma'am," he replied. Dee thought briefly that a human wouldn't have apologized, but everybody was different, and who could be sure?

"We've got to make progress and we're not going to do that by just mixing it up in the ball. I think that is what they are hoping we'll do. We can't win that numbers game without help." Dee looked at the mindview and quickly charted some energy curves through the drop tubes embedded in the hull of her ship. She shared the optimal path with Azazel and Molloch DTM and then explained her plan. "We drop low, and go fast. Our objective is to take out as many of those drop tubes as we can. Understood?"

"Yes, ma'am."

"Out of the ashes flew the Phoenix of death and her demon Valkyries. Fox Three!" Dee started the battle cry as she weaved in and about the first drop tube. The missile hit the base of the boarding vessel and knocked the barbs partially free. Sparks and glowing hot red metal were thrown about the hull radiating infrared heat out into space.

"Guns, guns, guns." Azazel followed her tearing the alien tube the rest of the way loose.

"Fox Three." Molloch was first to hit the second tube just as he did an out-and-in.

"Ooh-fuckin'-rah they shouted!" Dee continued the battle cry. "Fox Three!"

"Guns, guns, guns." Molloch popped back into reality space just as Azazel popped in and out by the third tube with guns a blazing.

"Fox Three!" Dee followed him to it.

"WE are the Bringers of Hell!" Azazel and Molloch said in unison with appropriate emotion, fervor, and inflection.

"Goddamned right we are," Dee whispered to herself. "Guns, guns, guns!"

Too many smaller drop ships to count appeared out of hyperspace all around the megaships. Several of them must have miscalculated and slammed into the *Penzington* and the *Madira* underbellies and vaporized against their shields because they were moving too fast on reentry into reality space. As soon as the ships dropped from hyperspace they opened and alien porcupine mecha started filling the sky. Dee's red force tracker suddenly was going nuts and targeting Xs appeared in every direction, at every angle. She had thought the ball was target-rich moments prior, but now it was more than target-rich. The ball was overfilled and stuffed with enemy mecha.

"Holy shit! We've got to move fast, Bringers! Watch for energy lines crossing from multiple angles at once and go with the out-and-ins as often as possible." She grunted and then opened a commandnet direct to mind channel. It was easier to talk in her mindvoice and fly than to talk verbally with all the multitasking she was already doing in the overfilled combat ball.

Colonel Strong this is Phoenix, copy?

Roger, Dee.

I need more mecha support on the surface of the ship.

Sorry, Phoenix, we are overwhelmed on the inside keeping them off of the Engineering Deck. I have nobody here to send to you. All of the mecha from the nearby Fleet squadrons are on the Rackman, *fighting.*

Damnit. What about the rest of the Bringers?

Stay calm, Phoenix. No, the Bringers are covering the AEMs and are barely holding ground. You are on your own for now. Good luck.

You too, Jawbone.

"Shit."

"Phoenix watch your six!"

"Warning! Enemy targeting lock is imminent! Warning! Enemy targeting lock is imminent!" Her Bitchin' Betty alert started. Then it changed. "Warning multiple enemy targeting locks are imminent! Take immediate evasive action!"

"Yeah—no shit!" she grunted as she had her mecha full reverse and fire upwards like a rocket at liftoff.

Dee slapped the out-and-in toggle and broke the enemy lock from several of the Chiata with a quantum membrane jump only to jump back into lockups from other enemy mecha once she had rematerialized in reality space. It appeared to be all that Azazel and Molloch could do to stay alive were wild moves followed by out-and-ins.

The numbers game had just gone bad in a hurry. Even with the force multiplier of the QMT capable FM-14Xs at some point numbers of enemy troops outmatched technology. Hell, just flying through the ball without hitting something was difficult enough and all of those somethings were trying to shoot them. Hundreds of them were trying to shoot the three of them.

Dee knew she had to stop the incoming flood of mecha or Colonels Strong and Slayer would never be able to stop them from ripping the ship apart from the inside. And they needed to keep that ship together long enough to fire the new Thgreeth weapon. She needed to find a better tactic and needed to focus on stopping the drop ships instead of just fighting the mecha.

"Fuck!" She let out a scream as she was suddenly spinning out of control. Several rounds slammed against her right wing so hard that it tossed her mecha into a wild uncontrollable spin in all three axes. The rapid spin rate was overpowering the attitude control system and the thrusters were having a hard time trying to compensate.

Breathe, Dee! Breathe, her AIC told her in her head.

I've got it. I've got it. She bit down on her TMJ bite block and a burst of fresh air and stimulants washed over her face with a cool refreshing smell. *Cut some of the energy lines and give me the most probable target solutions.*

Very good. But first we need to take care of this spin.

I said I'm on it damnit!

Dee fought against the HOTAS at first but then her years of training kicked in and she let off the pedals with both feet and pushed the stick all the way forward and pulled the throttle to the middle.

Activate the auto recovery attitude thrusters.

Auto-recovery system is on, Bree informed her. *But, Dee, we are picking up too much speed relative to the* Rackman's *hull for the automatic system to complete the maneuvers.*

That's what I'm counting on.

"Warning—enemy targeting lock imminent! Warning—enemy targeting lock imminent! Take evasive action immediately!"

A porcupine had picked up on the fact that she was out of control and started zeroing in on her. Plasma ball tracer rounds whizzed past her so closely that her visor dimmed to protect her eyes. But Dee had seen the alien's energy curve and had expected it to take the bait. Now the trick was just not getting her ass killed.

The wild spin quickly subsided into a steep dive straight at the *Rackman's* hull. That was better than a wild uncontrollable spin, but not by much. The ship's hull was filling her canopy view and growing so quickly she was beginning to think she wouldn't have time to stop herself. The Chiata kept on coming.

"Pull out of the dive, Phoenix! Pull up!" Azazel shouted at her.

Dee yanked back on the HOTAS and put the throttle in full reverse but realized that wouldn't be enough to stop her from splattering against the hull like a bug on a windshield of a hovertank at full speed. Instead of trying to slow down she kicked the topside aft thrusters and the nose bottomside thrusters on, turning the others off. Then, she sped up. She worked the stick back slowly as she increased the throttle, trying her best to ride out the dive and flare up. More enemy plasma balls fired all around her from her six o'clock.

At the last second she realized that her fighter was going to hammer into the deck too hard so she hit the bot-mode toggle. The fighter mecha rolled forward into a flipping transformation hitting the deck hands above her head like a sloppy somersault. The force was too great for her to brake completely so she tucked the mecha into a ball as best she could and started judo rolling across the hull of the *Rackman*. The alien mecha appeared to realize what it had done and fired its propulsion systems in full reverse with every tendril shooting plasma out their tips. But Dee's gambit had paid off. The alien slammed so hard into the deck that it exploded on impact while Dee herself continued to bleed off speed in her rolling bot-mode mecha until she rolled to an arms and legs out *thud* against the bridge dome. The dome rang like a bell and she could see her father standing atop the Chiata captain's dais about to soil his suit. His visor was up and Dee's cockpit was slammed directly against the transparent metal dome. She could see her father staring into her eyes and mouthing something at her.

"Get up!" Her tacnet opened to his voice. His AIC must've patched him in briefly. "Get up, Marine!"

That was all he said as he watched her next moves. Systems on her mecha rang with warnings but the barrier shields held and there was no specific damage. Her brain sloshed around hard enough inside her skull to give her a mild concussion, but that was nothing that some immunoboost couldn't fix in a few seconds. It was nothing she hadn't had many times before.

"Administering immunoboost," her suit told her.

"Warning—enemy targeting lock imminent!"

"Shit! It never stops!" She took in three hard breaths and squeezed her abdominal muscles and quadriceps, forcing blood into her brain. Just as she started to make her move, tracer rounds slapped across the hull and into the dome just beside her. interdiction fire from the *Rackman's* cannons lit up the ball all around her and she hoped some of it was at this latest bastard trying to lock her up. Dee managed to push herself up off the dome structure, shook her head clear, and then one hand somersaulted to the right, drawing the mecha cannon up with her left about to go to guns.

"Fox Three!" a familiar voice said. "I thought I'd taught you better than getting yourself into an overpowered dive to the deck with no escape route, Phoenix! Now get off your ass and get up here. We've got work to do."

"DeathRay!" Dee was surprised and excited to hear his voice over the tacnet. "Glad you decided to quit goldbricking in a command chair and join the real fighting."

"Guns, guns, guns!" DeathRay followed up his missile into the six of the alien mecha until the thing burst into glowing fragments. "What do ya say Dee, wanta puke on these bastards?"

"I was just about to decide it was our only chance," she replied and with a big leap from the hull of the megaship she toggled back into fighter mode and kicked in a full thrust acceleration to DeathRay's wing. "Either that or getting the Hell out of here. I'd prefer killing a bunch of them first."

"What's the plan here?" DeathRay asked her.

"We have to take out as many of the drop ships as we can. The general told me that every one of them on the ship are tactical operations centers for ground troops. We hit those and we remove the leader and command center of each of the attack teams that deployed from it. Hopefully, it will disorient the bastards and give our guys inside the ship a bit of advantage. I'd love to target some of the ones that are still offloading troops," Dee explained to her former wingman.

"Alright then. We do it in tandems." DeathRay immediately was in charge. "Molloch and Azazel will hit the targets while we puke to give them cover. We all then out-and-in to the top side hangar of the *Penzington*. It is a safe haven and the mecha pad coordinates are built in to the QMT snap-back algorithm. We get our breath and re-eat our cookies and then it will be our turn to hit the targets while Azazel and Molloch puke."

"Sounds like a plan, Jack! A real puke and go tactic!" Dee took several deep breaths and then closed her eyes. "It's a bit overly complicated for your typical tactics!"

"No one likes a smartass, Lieutenant Colonel." Jack did his best to give her shit while at the same time doing his best not to get his ass shot off.

"Yes admiral." Dee gave the shit right back. "You ready, DeathRay? I say we go in there and we kill those motherfuckers!"

"I like that plan. Ready when you are, Phoenix."

"Azazel, Molloch, start your attack runs now!" Dee ordered them.

"Oohrah, Phoenix," Azazel replied.

Okay, Bree, let's start puking.
I hope this isn't a bad idea, Bree added.
Shit, me too.

Chapter 34

July 24, 2409 AD
Tau Ceti
Kuiper Belt
12 light-years from the Sol System
Saturday, 4:23 P.M. Eastern Time

"I'm beginning to think this wasn't a very good idea," Sehera said doing her best to remember to breathe as she fought. She rolled to the left just barely far enough out of the way and in time to miss the blade extended from the left hand of the AEM's suit her attacker was wearing. She struggled against the possessed Marine as the blade *clanked* against the walkway with each repeated stabbing attempt. She continued to twist and roll from side to side doing all that she could to get out from under the attacker.

Then a blade extruded through the chest plate and back out and the AEM slumped onto his right side with his shoulders pinning her to the floor. Rondi stood behind him with the bloody blade still extended ready for another target. The master gunnery sergeant turned firing her rifle into the side of another AEM's helmet until his personal shields went out and the rounds came out the other side.

"Fuck you!" Rondi shouted, kicking her jump boots against the deck, throwing her upwards and over into a back tuck to the other side of Sehera, landing on another one of the attacking possessed, or whatever they were, AEMs. The two of them traded kicks and punches so fast you could barely see them moving. The blocks and impacts sounded like a freight train crashing each time.

You need to get up ma'am! her AIC exclaimed into her mind. *Mrs. Moore, get up!*

Right. Sehera pulled the dead possessed AEM off of her and picked her weapon up and leveled it just in time to shoot another one of the AEMs in the back reaching to grasp Rondi by the nape of the neck.

"Chief, you still with us?" Sehera called him but there was no answer. She didn't have time to pull up the blue force tracker and check his vitals as another AEM grabbed at her from behind. She dropped to a knee tossing him over her then extended her own blade through the soldier's faceplate. "They're everywhere, Rondi!"

"The chief is dead. Just keep fighting," Rondi told her.

They had managed to make it about halfway down the walkway in the large chamber and were still a good five hundred meters from where Copernicus was at the central island platform. It was at that midpoint in the walkway when more than twenty AEMs had come to life and started dropping to the walkway attacking them.

"Maybe we should flash out of here!" Sehera told her. "We're outnumbered here about nine billion to two."

"Good idea." Rondi nodded to her and then slapped

her wristband snap-back algorithm. Sehera did the same.

"Nothing happened," Sehera said. "We're still here."

"Shit fuck!" the master gunnery sergeant replied. "Shit! Fuck! Shit!"

"We've got to get off this walkway, Rondi." Sehera did a backbend to miss a blade being swung at her and then lost her balance as the blade glimmered in the dim plasma filament lighting only millimeters above her faceplate as it swung past. She fell to the deck flat on her back. This time she pulled the M-blaster from her left thigh and fired two pulses into the midsection of the AEM. "Enough of this."

Sehera rose to her feet with the blaster in her left hand and the rifle in her right, both on full auto fire. She spun, ducked, jumped, dropped, and sidestepped all the while firing nonstop. Rondi fired her rifle and slashed with her blade, but there were too many of them. There was no way to take that platform. Sehera knew that if they stayed there they were dead.

"Let's go, Rondi!" Sehera bounced her boots against the floor and leaped out into the chasm of floating bodies doing her best to miss the plasma tendrils connected to their heads. She landed mid-torso of one of the floating bodies and the body gave way as if she had landed on a tree branch that couldn't hold her weight. The unexpected freefall made her stomach jump into her throat, but she managed to choke it back down and regain her composure.

Rondi hit a body three or four rows over and Sehera could see her falling as well. The two of them spread out like skydivers using the bodies to break their falls. With their armored suits on they fell like rocks. They continued downward through one body after another after another for what seemed like an eternity, each one giving way like a dead tree branch. Finally, they came to a hard stop after about a full thousand meter drop. More than a hundred bodies had piled up underneath them breaking their fall in a bloody squishy mess. The two of them scrambled as hard as they could to free themselves from the bodies until they reached the edge of the mound of flesh and could roll to the surface. The gore of it reminded Sehera of the Martian Desert Campaigns and the torture camps she had seen so many years ago. That was where she had found the U.S. Marine Major Alexander Moore. She had seen a lot of gruesomeness over her lifetime, including triage in the supercarriers after the last few years of battle, but Sehera still felt sick from the sight of it all.

"Oh God, what a mess." She choked back bile and had her suit hit her with some stimulants and fresh air.

"Well, we're even further from the central island now than when we started," Rondi pointed out. "But at least the crazed AEMs aren't after us."

"No wonder the chief didn't snap back when he got into trouble," Sehera said. "He must've tried and couldn't."

"No, ma'am. I saw him go down. He went fighting to the end and I couldn't get to him to help. Those AEMs were amped up on something," Rondi told her and Sehera could tell by the tone of her voice that the AEM wasn't happy with how all this had gone down. "Whatever that filament of light is doing to them, I think it is making them stronger as well."

"I'm sorry to have gotten us into this. We should have

waited for Alexander to get back," Sehera said. "Maybe an entire squad or some mecha should've come."

"No ma'am. Had we waited we might have lost them. Who knows what plans this guy has and where he plans to go next?"

"Right. I mean, you're right. He might be planning to go somewhere else." Sehera had to think for a second. "Sol System, maybe? One of the other colonies?"

"You know what bugs me about all this?"

"What's that, Rondi?"

"These people here were all real people, not clones. He'd been living on 61 Ursae Majoris all this time. Why didn't he just take them? Or why didn't he just get Madira to crank out clones for him?"

"I think you're on to something there. What is different between clones and regular humans?" Sehera wasn't sure yet but there was something nagging at her.

"Well, none of them have AICs because they are AICs aren't they?"

"Oh, my God!" Sehera realized what was happening as soon as Rondi had made the comment. AIC implants were the key to this. "Those filaments. Come on. Let's take a closer look at one."

Sehera and Rondi worked their way around the pile of bodies inward towards the island to the closest body with the plasma filament attached to its head. The filament wrapped around the head of the person and appeared to enter just behind the ear where the implant would be located.

"I think he's using the implants as some kind of transceiver." Sehera studied the body closer.

"Yeah, but what is he transmitting there?" Rondi shrugged. "And why can't the people or the AICs keep him from doing it?"

"Let's go ask him, why don't we?" Sehera turned to get her bearings and stopped as Rondi placed her armored gauntlet on her shoulder.

"Wait a minute, ma'am," she said. "I just had a thought. We could QMT into this place but couldn't QMT out of this place, right?"

"Yes, so it would appear. What's your point, Rondi?" Sehera was not sure where the Marine was going with this but she thought of what Alexander would so eloquently often say.

I'd piss on a sparkplug if I thought it would help, she thought in her mindvoice.

Yes, ma'am, her AIC replied.

"Well, this seems an awful lot like the trap the Expeditionary Fleet is in doesn't it?" Rondi waved her hand about as she talked. "I think this place is a trap just like that star system. And while they can't QMT out, they can within it. I've seen something like this before too."

"Of course you have. This is just like where Jack and Nancy found the first abandoned supercarrier fleet that Madira had hidden. You were with them, weren't you? I can't believe I didn't see that." Sehera turned and looked at the central control island in the distance. "I'll bet you anything the QMTs work in here."

"My thoughts exactly," Rondi agreed.

"What do you think, about ten meters above them?"

"Sounds good to me."

The two of them used the sensors in their visors to

pinpoint the spot above the platform and transfer the coordinates to the sling-forward algorithm. They nodded to each other as they prepared for the jump. Rondi extended her blade and wielded her rifle in her right hand. Sehera had the blaster in her left and her rifle in her right. She checked the ammo counter on her HVAR and only had three hundred and nine rounds left.

Her blaster would stay charged as long as there was a quantum vacuum in the universe. Fortunately for her, the quantum vacuum energy should exist for billions of years to come. Unfortunately for both of them, the M-blasters worked great against bots and unarmored people, but they only slowed armored people down. It took multiple hits from a blaster to bring down an AEM with barrier shields. Sehera frowned a bit at her rifle's ammo count. On full auto three hundred and nine rounds would go quickly.

"What's your ammo status, ma'am?" Rondi was checking her own and as far as Sehera could tell she wasn't frowning as much as her.

"Three oh nine," Sehera told her, trying to hide her frustration. "It will have to do."

"Are you using your targeting Xs or just freehanding it?"

"Freehand," Sehera replied sheepishly.

"Go to the targeting system and only fire when the Xs are red. That way is much more efficient and will help preserve your ammo. You can even have your AIC pull the trigger for you but you are out of the decision loop there."

"I knew that. It's been a while since I was actually in a firefight. Should've been doing that from the start. But not my AIC in control."

"Ma'am, you're fighting like a pro. Nothing to apologize for. I say when people are trying to kill you the only thing you can do is whatever you know how to do to kill them back."

"Thank you, Rondi." Sehera meant it. She hated having to be "protected" or "looked after" or whatever it was that Alexander had told her do. But at the same time she appreciated what the Marine, and the now dead Chief Warrant, had done to keep her safe.

"Are you good to go?" the Marine asked.

"When you are." Sehera slapped the HVAR activator and reset the targeting system for her blaster.

"Alright, let's keep moving."

"Okay, in three, two, one, go!" Sehera tapped the wristband and there was the usual flash of light and sizzling sound. The next thing they knew they were free falling from ten meters above the island and there were four humans beneath them. The large white quantum foam plasma ball was just to their right off the edge of the platform with maybe billions of filaments extending out from it randomly.

Rondi made quick work of two of them and Sehera shot the woman through the midsection with her blaster, putting her down. She then followed the targeting Xs in her mindview and fired two rounds from the rifle into Copernicus' legs, taking him down. She didn't want to kill him just yet. They needed to find out what the Hell was going on.

"No! Ifgeentha!" Copernicus shouted at the woman Sehera had shot and crawled to her, pulling her body to him. "Ifgeentha speak! Your king demands it! Ifgeentha . . ."

"What is all this?" Sehera put the tip of her rifle in his face pushing him back from the woman's body.

"What have you done? What have you done? You've killed my queen!" Copernicus tried to rise but his legs were nearly cut in two and Rondi stepped in and kicked him back down with her armored boot. His head made a hard thump against the deck plating.

"I'd suggest you answer the lady," Rondi said, not letting up the pressure on his chest.

"What is all this, Copernicus? And what have you done to the Tau Cetians?" Sehera poked at him with her barrel. "You need to start talking now!"

"Ha, ha, ha," he started laughing uncontrollably, hollowly, as if it were forced laughter, and it was very unnerving.

"What are you laughing about?" Sehera prodded his forehead with the muzzle of the rifle.

"You better start answering questions now!" Rondi dug her boot into his wounded right leg a bit. The alien mind controlled clone didn't even flinch from pain. Instead he continued to laugh madly.

"You, the daughter of the great Sienna Madira, have just killed my general, my brother, and my queen." His voice started rising in volume. He continued to laugh wildly and uncontrollably. Sehera thought it extremely eerie and maniacal. She also flinched a bit when he let the cat out of the bag as to who her mother was in front of Rondi. History showed that Sehera Moore was an orphan of the Martian wars. "Or should I say, daughter of Elle Ahmi?"

"Answer me, Copernicus. What have you done to the

Tau Cetians?" She only side glanced at Rondi who was still holding her weapon on him. She wasn't sure if what he was saying registered with the Marine or not.

"You have always been just like your mother." He laughed some more. "A total unpredictable anomaly, or to borrow her expression, a pain in the ass."

"Mrs. Moore, he's stalling. Those AEMs could be here any second."

"Correction, Marine, they are here now." Copernicus made a strange expression on his face that didn't seem to match any particular mood or behavior either of them understood. Sehera had seen the alien do that many times growing up. He had never quite gotten the hang of human facial control and expression. She turned and saw AEMs and other humans in Army Armored Infantry suits and even some police officers pounded down the walkways that led toward them from each direction north, south, east, and west. They were clearly outnumbered.

Mindvoice connection to Rondi now.

Done.

Rondi, we need to flash out of here now. Perhaps our entry point?

Meet you there then we'll need to jump again quickly.

Do it!

They both tapped their wristbands and nothing happened. Copernicus continued to laugh.

Chapter 35

July 24, 2409 AD
U.S.S. Davy Rackman
Mission Star 74
Chiata Expanse
783 light-years from the Sol System
Saturday, 4:24 P.M. Eastern Time

"So what are you telling me, Joe?" General Moore asked him to explain in greater detail, but Joe wasn't sure he could or had time to do so. There was so much to get done and he just didn't have time to spend explaining it to the senior officer.

"General, just, uh, think of it as there are three simultaneous things that have to happen in order for this weapon to go. You have to man the control panel on the bridge and target the beam and press the fire sequence. Somebody has to get this conduit here on the forward starboard deck put in place and then throw the breakers or crowbar them at the junction box about twenty or thirty meters down from there. And then we have to dump the superweapon shield generator energy through the BBD projectors via the control circuits in Engineering. At that point we hope that Skippy will do his thing. But those events must happen before we can fire the weapon."

"Okay Joe, fine. Give me the coordinates for this conduit and I'll send a team. Do you need to send an engineer to do it?"

"Sir, I'm going to do it myself. CHENG Deedee can handle things here in Engineering. After all, it is her ship, not mine," Joe explained as he forwarded the coordinates where the bypass conduit had to go.

"Shit Joe, that is right in the middle of the fighting," Moore told him. "You'll need help."

"Yes, sir. Mecha preferably. And AEMs, if we have them to spare."

"Get your gear together and start moving. I'll have Colonel Strong and her squadron escort you personally. And I'll have the Juggernauts meet you there. They are only a few decks over from the fighting in that part of the ship."

"Yes, sir. CHENG out."

Joe turned and grabbed his tool bag and looked at the clone CHENG, who was moving about the Engineering Room like a worker bee that never tired.

"Deedee!"

"Yes, Commander Buckley," the clone replied. Joe noted that her voice was very melodic and soothing. He also noted that she wasn't hard to look at. Though Rondi would kick his ass if she caught him staring at another woman.

"CHENG, I'm going to fix that forward conduit and

reset the breakers. I'll just jumper them if I have to," he told her. "I'm assuming you've got everything under control here and don't need my help?"

"Taking the forward conduit problem will be of great help to me here, Commander Buckley. Thank you," Deedee said. "Commander, please be careful."

"Yes, right," Joe muttered. "I plan on it. Just be ready to go once I get that thing set."

"Understood. Good luck." She had it under control here and there wasn't anything else he could here to help. Deedee and her crew were so efficient that he would just be a fifth wheel if he stayed. And Joe hated nothing worse than a fifth wheel.

Then he looked at Skippy and figured the alien bot had gotten them this far, so he didn't need to worry about it. He knew that come Hell or high water that General Moore would come through on the bridge as well. The weakest link in his plan was himself. He was going to have to go into a combat situation and do an engineering job while getting shot at. He really wasn't very excited about the detailed aspects of that.

"Well shit, Joe," he said to himself and sort of half-laughed. "Time to pay the bills."

"Alright, Madira," Alexander Moore spoke frankly to his mother-in-law over a private channel. "It's time for you to pay the bills."

"Ready when you are, son. What do you need from me?" Madira replied in her typical arrogant wise-elder demeanor. And Alexander still couldn't help but cringe every time she called him "son".

I'm so not your fucking son, lady, he thought. *Abby, give me the full system battlescape.*

Yes, sir, Abigail replied.

"I will need your flotilla to find the right ships to target and then I need you to feed that to me as rapidly as possible. At that point I will use the new weapon to engage them." It sounded simple enough. Alexander hoped it was simple enough.

"Understood. What is your desired ETA for that data?" Madira asked him.

"Five minutes."

"Very well. Five minutes we start taking this fight to them again."

"My thoughts exactly. Moore out."

Alexander looked at the battlescape in his mind and began deciphering how to translate positions in the mindview to targeting positions for the Chiata BBDs without the command chair that he was used to back on the *Sienna Madira*. It took him and his AIC a couple moments or so to figure it out and then he started locking on to various targets without firing the system just for practice.

"Moore to Buckley."

"Buckley here, sir!"

"You have four minutes and eleven seconds to get that conduit in place."

"Understood, sir. It's pretty thick up here."

"Four minutes two seconds, Joe. Moore out."

"You heard the CHENG, Maniacs! We have to push this piece of pipe from here to the other side of that chasm and hold it in place while the bots weld it. We have three minutes!" Colonel Strong kept the CHENG shielded from the incoming fire as best she could knowing that he was their best hope of stopping the Chiata bastards and getting the Hell out of that system. Several plasma rounds sprayed off her shields, throwing bolts of energy into the bulkhead around them in a shower of sparks. Her barrier system flickered green and white across the surface of her mecha.

"Shit!" she heard Joe say. Delilah wanted to tell him that was her thoughts exactly, but she had work to do.

Her red force tracker was lit up like a Christmas tree and they were right in the middle of Chiata central. There were alien infantry and mecha blurring about them like angry red and green hornets and now they had to fight and build at the same time. The AEM squad Jones' Juggernauts had formed a line of cover behind several partial bulkheads and some makeshift barricades. They were bouncing in to attack and then snapping back to cover in shifts. Several swarms of buzzsaw bots were mixed in with the AEMs adding to the attack. The number of red dots versus blue ones in her tracker mindview, on the other hand, was very disproportionate and not in their favor.

Delilah looked across the chasm. Large catwalks on each side led to the forward starboard shield generators. There was a section of the catwalk missing and a Chiata drop tube protruding through the hull. Several Chiata infantry were held up on either side of the opening of the tube using the giant metal barbs holding it in the hull as cover and taking sniper shots from their high perch. On each side of the tube were the jagged and bent ends of a power conduit.

"Let me guess, Joe," she started. "That drop tube is where the conduit was knocked out?"

"That's right, Colonel. Shit, I didn't realize the thing would be protruding inward like that. We don't have enough conduit to bypass it as long as that tube is in the way," Buckley told her. She knew what that meant they had to do.

"Colonel Jones!" She called for the AEM leader. He was still moving slowly from injuries he'd already suffered earlier in the day. She had heard that more than half of his team were still in medical bays.

"What can I do for you, Jawbone?" He looked up at the mecha cockpit at her. "You are going to have to cover the CHENG for a bit. Keep him safe and watch our material too. The Maniacs are going to knock out that tube. Feel free to give us whatever cover you can."

"Understood, Jaw. Will do." Colonel Jones tapped Buckley's armored shoulder with his gauntlet. "CHENG, you should probably just get over here and hunker down. I'd prefer you not shoot back unless you have to, so you don't draw any attention to yourself. Understood?"

"Got it, Colonel," Buckley replied and Delilah figured he was in good hands for the moment, and she had work to do.

"Great. Top! I've got something for you," the AEM leader shouted over the tacnet.

"You good, Joe?" Delilah asked once more.

"Go, Colonel. Go!" Buckley told her.

The CHENG was in good hands, and she had to get

her team to work. Delilah turned and kicked in her boot thrusters while locking her sensors in on the drop tube that was about two hundred meters above them. She thought for a brief moment that most people just had no idea how truly gigantic these alien megaships were. She couldn't see the end of the chasm without the aid of her sensors when looking along the bow to stern line.

"Cover me, Maniacs!" she said as she burned upward with her targeting Xs locking onto the drop tube. "Fox!"

She let a free triggering missile loose and it tracked outward across the chasm but a porcupine blurred across the room in front of her entangling the missile in its tendrils and then slingshotting it around and back at them. The propellantless drive of the munition left the air ionized and glowing in the dimly lit chamber. As the Chiata and AEMs fired their weapons, the room flashed like a nightclub on college night in New Tharsis. Tracer rounds, ion trails, and plasma balls filled the air.

"Shit, guns, guns, guns!" She rolled sideways firing her guns at the missile knocking it down and leaving it in fragments. The porcupine started locking her up as it bounced about the room.

"Warning—enemy targeting lock . . ."

"Oh no, you don't!"

Delilah spun upright and cut her thrusters, letting the ship's artificial gravity pull her down in a freefall. The Chiata plasma rounds tracked through the air she had just fell from. Then her wingman was covering her with guns going full auto.

"You better watch your six Jawbone!"

"That's why you're here." She dropped over backwards

and got a full radar lock on the drop tube position and squeezed the trigger. "Fox One!"

The missile zipped across the room and a Chiata infantry blur jumped in front of it at the last minute, sacrificing itself to keep the drop tube in place. Jawbone wondered if it was a selfless act or if the alien was being commanded or compelled to make the sacrifice.

"Shit. Looks like we are doing this the hard way," she said. "Maniacs, keep that cover fire up. I'm going to do this one by hand."

"Yes, ma'am!"

Delilah streaked her bot-mode mecha all the way across the cavernous expanse between the outer hull and the inner hull of the alien megaship and made it almost all the way to the catwalk before a porcupine sprang forward from within the tube firing at her. She juked and jinked and managed to dodge the alien's tendrils as the dark spears shot towards her. And then a missile hit it square on the side, knocking it into her.

Jawbone used the momentum of the missile exploding against the alien mecha's shields and grabbed the nearest tendril with both of her mechanized hands and stomped her right pedal giving her full speed yaw. She spun like a ballerina doing pirouettes, tossing the alien mecha hard against the mouth of the drop tube. As she let it go, a second missile streaked by her, exploding against the mecha. The force from the explosion threw her backwards but she managed to control her attitude. Bringing her cannon up and targeting the explosion she went full auto on her plasma rounds.

"Guns, guns, guns!" she shouted and continued

pouring plasma round after plasma round into the alien mecha until it exploded in the mouth of the drop tube, throwing orange and white plasma and red-hot metal fragments in most directions. Several fragments pinged off her barrier shields, causing them to flicker. The explosion knocked the tube partially loose from the hull, so she kept on chipping away at the mouth of it with her cannon. "Guns, guns, guns!"

Finally, the barbs that held the tube in place on the right side tore free and the drop tube partially gave way. She could see a crack between the hull and the tube a meter wide, but the barb on the left was still holding it in place. Air from the chamber was pushing out of the gaping hole and debris was being sucked along with it. One of the dead alien infantrymen's bodies was sucked up to the hole and stopped the air outflow for a moment.

She rolled and then pitched over forward, kicking in her boot thrusters at full speed. Just before she reached the tube she pitched backwards slamming her feet first into the remaining barb. The multiton mecha hit into the tube so hard that the entire chamber rang like a bell. The barb was pounded almost back through the hull but there were millimeters of metal hull still holding it in place.

"Come on damnit!" She kicked at it again but had to duck as Chiata plasma rounds caught her in the back and then hit beside her. She turned and jetted upwards and sideways, firing her cannon back at the target, but just as she went to fire an infantryman wrapped her barrel up with several tendrils.

"Shit!" Delilah cursed while yanking the alien towards her. She spun both of them around and then slammed her mechanized knee through the creature's chest. The infantryman was little competition for the new FM-14X's armor and Jawbone could feel the alien's body crunch against her fighter. She slammed the alien's body into the jagged metal wall at the droptube's barb and managed to force her cannon to the alien's face.

"Guns, guns, guns!"

The alien was partially vaporized and partially splattered into the hull and back onto her mecha, but the final shot melted the last bit of metal hull plating holding the barb in place the rest of the way through. The droptube was blown free by the overpressure in the hull and Jawbone was almost sucked out herself.

There was suddenly a gaping hole leading out into space large enough to fly three mecha in fighter mode through, even if they were flying side-by-side. Several Chiata infantrymen were sucked out into space and Delilah wished them good riddance. She turned with her thrusters and pulled herself back from the hole a few tens of meters.

"Alright, CHENG, let's get that tube in place!" she said. "Maniacs keep covering us."

She dropped to the deck and picked up the conduit with both mechanized hands. The piece of pipe must have been at least thirty meters long, four or five meters wide, and weighed at least twenty tons and it was awkward to balance by herself but she managed it because she didn't want to pull in other mecha from fighting the Chiata.

"You need a lift, CHENG?"

"No, Colonel. I'll meet you there," Buckley told her. Then she saw him flash out and reappear across the chamber at the breached hull. He must have magnetized his boots, as he stuck sideways to the wall and started walking about there. She carefully fired her boots and pushed herself across the room doing her best to ignore any cannon fire or missiles that might happen to zip by.

"I need that end here, Colonel. Hold it as still as you can until the builder bots pin it down and tack weld it in place," Buckley told her.

"Okay, but where are the bots?" As soon as she said it there was another QMT flash and hundreds of little bots appeared all around them. "Never mind."

"Commander, I'm still not seeing the flow loop. There is no current making it to Engineering," the clone CHENG told him. Joe knew why, too.

"Deedee, I've flipped the breakers and reset the junction box, but I can see a main feedback conduit is knocked out. There's a good three or four meters of it missing." Joe was hugging the floor and the AEM's top sergeant was standing on his back firing his HVAR in damned near every direction.

"You'll have to complete that loop or the circuit will never know how to shut itself off," Deedee told him. "Are there any tubes nearby you can take?"

"I'm looking, but who knows what these damned things do. We don't know half of what these Chiata parts are for." Joe was a bit frustrated. There had to be something he could use.

"Top! Look out!" Colonel Jones shouted at the AEM. Joe watched in horror as a Chiata mecha porcupine dropped in a blur on top of him and Sergeant Major

Tommy Suez. The tendrils of the mecha engulfed them like the arms of a squid.

Joe could see the AEM's blade flashing about and figured that anything he could do might help so he extended his suit's blade and started squeezing the trigger on his rifle. He couldn't move otherwise, but the rifle seemed to make the alien mecha flinch. Then Suez's blade swiped very close to Joe and tore through a tentacle arm and Joe fell to the deck wrapped up in about four meters of alien tendril. He squirmed like mad kicking himself free of the thing as it spewed red and green viscous fluids at him.

"Oh God! Shit! Get the fuck off me!" He pulled free of it just as Colonel Jones landed on top of him.

"Stay down, Commander!"

"But Suez needs help?" Joe pushed back at the AEM and reached for his rifle. As soon as he raised it the colonel pushed it down with his armored hand.

"No. You might hit him." Colonel Jones stopped him. "Besides . . . Look!"

The AEM was destroying the alien mecha from the inside out. The porcupine fell to the deck in jerks and fits spewing reds and greens in viscous burning liquids in every direction. All Joe could discern was the sound of rifle fire and the flashing of a metametal blade until the mecha stopped moving. The creature made one last surge, or so Joe thought, but it was the Top Sergeant blasting an opening for him to crawl out of.

"Commander Buckley, there is still no feedback connection," Deedee coaxed him over the engineering net.

"I know. I have no idea what to . . ." He looked down at the mechanized alien tendril at his feet. The damned things were some sort of self-healing metamaterial that took a metametal blade to cut . . . "Give me a second. I've got this."

Chapter 36

"Didn't . . . beat . . . my . . . record," Dee panted like a dog recruit in basic that had just run a marathon with another dog recruit on her back. She choked back the bile and took a drink from her tube and was thankful that the aft hangar of the *Penzington* was completely uneventful and calm, almost serene. Then she thought to add, ". . . Old Man!"

"That's . . . Admiral . . . Old Man . . . to you," DeathRay replied as equally spent. Dee could hear him vomiting again on the tacnet just as he cut it off. The sound was almost enough to push her back over the edge and she fought against the urge as hard as she could. The tickle in her throat and the retching of her gut were difficult to overcome but she bit down hard and clamped her abdominal muscles so tight that nothing could escape back up her esophagus.

"Azazel, Molloch," she had to stop mid-sentence to bite down on the mouthpiece to keep from heaving. She managed to keep from getting sick again as the spins and vertigo lessened only enough that she could open her eyes without throwing up. She hit the stimulants and some fresh air and gulped big to regain her composure. The puking deathblossom maneuver was tough on the best of pilots, and the two best pilots in the Fleet had just pushed the limits on it and each other. "Situation report."

"Roger that, Phoenix. We managed to hit seven of the tubes. At least five of them let go from the ship and the other two were mostly free but not destroyed," Azazel replied.

"We will be ready to go when you are ma'am," Molloch said.

"DeathRay, how you doing?" She was beginning to regain her composure and the stimulants were starting to do their job. "I could use another sixty seconds."

"Me too, Dee. Good work. Starting a countdown clock now for the next run. Fifty nine and counting. Azazel, Molloch, it's your turn to puke," DeathRay told them.

"Tag—you're it Bringers," Dee added and closed her eyes again. She went through some mental exercises that focused her mind and calmed her body as best she could. Sixty seconds wasn't a lot of time for a body to recover from an extreme event like a deathblossom but in combat it was an eternity so they couldn't goldbrick for too long or more people would die. Every second those control centers in the alien drop tubes were embedded on the hull of the ship was a second that soldiers were fighting against enemy infantry and mecha, and dying.

They sat quietly for the remainder of the time as the clock ticked down. Dee continued to focus herself on what she was about to have to do and knew that following that would likely be time for another deathblossom. This had already been a shit of a day and the shit was just getting thicker and it seemed like it would never end. She looked at the mindview battlescape and could see DeathRay was mapping out the next ten or so tubes to hit. He had the battle plan covered. Azazel and Molloch knew what to do. She gave herself a brief second to pull up diagnostics on the *Rackman* and see how it was coming along. She hoped her father would get that superweapon up and firing before they had to do too many more deathblossoms.

Forty seconds, Dee.

She popped open her visor for some fresh air and brought up a mindview image of Davy Rackman to take her mind from the fight and at the same time remind her what she was fighting for. He was in his Navy t-shirt and workout shorts. He was holding a long fork in one hand cooking hot dogs on the thermal grate in their hidey hole back on the *Madira*. She used to love those moments with him more than anything in the universe. They would cook out, drink beers, and make love. The food was shit, the beers were okay, but the love was nothing short of universe bending to her. The memory of his arms around her and her melding and giving to him with all her heart and soul was so powerful that she didn't feel that she could ever let go of it. To Dee it wasn't first love crush.

To Dee it was true love and she was crushed by that soul deep love being ripped from her so abruptly.

She couldn't ever let go of him. The image unfolded as Davy continued to cook and then there she was eating a dog from his hand and then taking his beer to wash it down. There she was, her former naïve self, almost two years younger with her long flowing black hair and clean pale Martian complexion sans tattoos. She was Ms. Clean the Marine. She was Apple1. She was so in love. She hoped that she would soon be Mrs. Davy Rackman even if he was Navy.

Dee looked through the mindview image and could see her reflection in the canopy. Her eyes glowed bright red and the tattoos across her face threw odd shadows and glimmers of reds and greens like alien's blood. Her nose was scrunched and her eyes squinted in anger. The shaved sides of her head and disarray of her hair was twisted and disheveled and wild. She looked angry. She was not that little girl, that lovestruck fool. She was a Phoenix that had torturously risen from her true love's ashes. She was Lieutenant Colonel Moore that you don't want to fuck with!

A tear streaked down her face but it didn't make it far before her suit's organogel layer slurped it up. Dee looked at what she'd become in her reflection. It angered her because it wasn't what she'd become, it was what the Chiata had made her. She was pure anger, hatred, and death. She cried.

Fifteen seconds.

Dee locked her visor back down and took a long sniffling breath inwards. She bit down on her bite block mouthpiece giving her more stimulants. She growled fiercely inside her head until it came out vocally and gutturally. If she could have gone to guns without hurting someone else at the moment she would have just to hear the report of the cannons to match her anger.

"I miss you, Davy. I miss you," she whispered. And then she screamed at the top of her lungs and beat the inside of the canopy with her gauntlets. She slapped her helmet several times. And screamed again, continuing to hit her helmet with loud *thuds* each time her gauntlets made contact with her helmet.

The screams turned into a growing fierce growl like a lioness ripping a prey apart. She beat the sides of her helmet so hard she could feel the organogel flatten against her skull. She just needed to feel something other than the pain she could hardly bear any longer. Anger would have to do so she forced it to grow within her. Anger was a better feeling than the pain she constantly felt from Davy's death, so she replaced the sorrow with anger. The mood sensors in her eyes and tattoos triggered them to maximum brightness and the QMT sling-forward algorithm started counting from five. Dee grunted, growled, and continued to scream.

Four, three, two, one!

Chapter 37

July 24, 2409 AD
Mission Star 74
Chiata Expanse
783 light-years from the Sol System
Saturday, 4:28 P.M. Eastern Time

The warriorship deployers had done their jobs beautifully.
The Lead Huntress started her drop to the surface of the
target ship just as her alert system activated. Four prey
mecha magically appeared almost right on top of her
hunting party. Two of the prey started the mad spinning
death that the warriors of the pride had encountered and
reported throughout the day. The prey flyers were crazed
and attacked ferociously and she could honestly tell the
king that she had never seen anything like the way these
prey fought. Warriors were being hit all around her
forcing her to keep moving at top speed and maximum
gee loads. Even for her, the Lead Huntress of the pride,
the maneuvers were extremely taxing. She couldn't
imagine such frail creatures as this prey surviving them.

She turned her mecha downward toward the droptubes on the ship, hoping to use them for cover, when she noticed two of the prey breaking off and attacking the tubes. They were using the mad spinning prey as cover fire. It was a very sound tactic, she thought. But it wouldn't be enough to stop her.

The Lead Huntress moved her mecha from tube to tube at top speed trying to predict a trajectory to intercept the prey so that she could pounce on them and protect her warrior brethren in the tubes. The two prey fighters magically appeared in and out of space before her and then one of the prey dropped into her lap almost by fate. The fighter was running at the nearest adjacent upright tube and wasn't paying close enough attention to its midsection lines. It fired missiles into the tube and then banked away and towards the next one on the list.

The Lead Huntress dropped the warriorship right on top of the prey firing her plasma disruptors at the enemy mecha. The mecha was caught by surprise, it seemed, and one of the rounds hit it square on the empennage. The prey had barrier shields and was lucky.

"She's going to lock you up, DeathRay!" Dee dropped in on her wingman's nine o'clock going to guns hoping to disrupt the Chiata's targeting radar. "Guns, guns, guns!"

"I'm popping out, Phoenix! Take this bastard out!" DeathRay's mecha vanished and reappeared four hundred meters to Dee's starboard.

"I've got you, motherfucker!" Dee grunted and pitched upside down relative to the mecha as it passed by so closely that she could see the alien sitting in the middle of it underneath the canopy that looked more like a single eyeball of an octopus rather than a cockpit.

Dee yanked back on the HOTAS and then stomped the left pedals yawing her about so she could track the alien. She slammed the throttle forward and bit down hard on her mouthpiece to keep from losing her stomach which had just been thrown into her throat. Her tracers followed it but the Chiata porcupine managed to drop behind one of the tubes for cover and reverse its energy line.

"Shit."

"It is you!" The Lead Huntress was both excited and frightened at the same time. She could see the pilot of the prey mecha and through the visor were glowing red eyes. The Huntress was certain it was the demon the ally had warned them of. She suddenly was nervous, like a cub on its first hunt. "I will rid the pride of you now."

She jumped out from behind the tube at full throttle and firing continuously at the alien mecha. The Lead Huntress had been flying mecha and she had been hunting and killing prey for centuries. This prey would be no different. This was her opportunity to stop these human prey once and for all. She was certain that if she took out this demon, the prey would lose their drive to fight.

But the prey was being very elusive. In fact, every time the Lead Huntress made a movement the alien prey, the demon, had a counter that brought it closer to a firing solution on her. The Lead Huntress was getting frustrated and pushed her warriorship even harder.

"You will not get away from me."

❖ ❖ ❖

"What the fuck!" Dee barrel-rolled and reversed her pitch so that she was flying backwards with a velocity vector relative to the alien porcupine. It seemed glued to her and was doing its best to lock her up. At first she thought of doing a Fokker's Feint but there were just too many other porcupines in the mix and she might get this one but then be a sitting duck.

"DeathRay, can you get a solution on this motherfucker?" Dee rocked the HOTAS left then right trying to find a path that would shake the porcupine. "Can't get this asshole off me."

"That thing is on you hard, Phoenix, like it has a serious hard-on for you," DeathRay told her. "I don't like it! You need to out-and-in."

"Right." Dee started to cycle the QMT sequence but the alien closed the gap quicker than she was expecting. "Shit."

She had to bank left and drop to miss an impact but as the alien zoomed past it fully reversed thrust and must have taken twelve or more negative gees doing so. Then several tendrils slammed into her mecha straining against her shields. The porcupine wrapped her up like a kraken taking down a pirate ship. Dee hit the toggle for bot-mode and the mecha strained and groaned against the alien's grip but managed to make the transformation, throwing a few of the alien tendrils loose. She kicked in her thrusters and spun about the pitch axis but wasn't able to pull loose.

"Get the fuck off me!" Dee pushed her boot thrusters on full throttle driving her back into the alien mecha and pushing the two of them backwards against the hull of the *Rackman*. The impact was great enough that the porcupine momentarily lost its grip on her. At the same time Dee was stunned and had to shake stars from her eyes. It was a hard hit.

"Dee, quit screwing around and flash out!" DeathRay shouted. "That's an order, Marine!"

"You will not escape me!" The Lead Huntress forced herself through the pain of the impact, shook the blood from her nose and the stars from her eyes, and rose back up to her mechanized tendrils. She threw several of them back around the alien prey's feet and arms and then managed to force one through the barrier shield of the mecha's leg. "I have you now!"

The Lead Huntress could feel the victory coming. She could taste the alien prey's flesh on her lips. She was going to have this demon's head and show the pride that these humans were nothing to fear and that their ally was exaggerating their abilities. She forced another tendril through the shoulder of the mecha on the left side and out its back.

"Yes!" she growled!

"Warning, structural breaches in multiple locations." The Bitchin' Betty was the epitome of obvious and redundant. Dee took in a deep breath and stood her mecha upwards straining against the alien's grasp on her. The power plants of the FM-14X were redlining against the strain but they managed to generate enough force to overpower the tendril's downward pull.

"QMT now, Dee!" DeathRay continued to order her over the tacnet. "I mean it! Get out of there!"

"Out of the ashes flew the Phoenix of death and her demon Valkyries!" Dee grunted and then raised her right elbow up and brought it down against the alien tendril in her mecha's leg with all the force of the mecha torso and arm. She grabbed the tendril as it snapped free and then wrapped it around her giant armored right wrist. "Ooh-fuckin'-rah, they shouted!"

"Dee! Azazel and Molloch are done. They have snapped back. We have no more cover!" DeathRay continued to shout at her over the tacnet. "Phoenix! Snap back!"

Dee could see through the canopy the Chiata pilot inside who appeared to be in disbelief that she was able to fight her back at this point. The creature's eyes widened and the veins and skin glowed bright like her tattoos. Not only was Lieutenant Colonel Deanna "Phoenix" Moore than you want to fuck with going to fight back, she was going to kill that fucking thing with style and reckless abandon. She was going to make it pay for killing the people she loved. She was going to make it feel fear of death. She was so going to kill that alien motherfucker dead! Dead! Dead! Fucking dead!

She jerked hard at the tendril pulling the alien even closer to her. She squeezed the tendril so hard that the mechanical telescoping metametal crushed in her mecha's strained grip. Dee pulled it even closer, as close as her canopy could get to the alien's canopy, because she wanted to stare it in the eyes as it died. She then cycled her elbow backwards as far as the mechanisms would allow it until it strained the gears and joints against the pull of the alien tendril so much that her mindview dashboard diagnostics lit up like a Christmas tree warning her of looming system failures.

"WE are the Bringers of Hell!" Dee smiled a menacing toothy smile that was bordering on insane as tears flowed down the glowing tattoos on her cheeks.

"I am the Bringer of fucking Hell!" she shouted as loudly as her strained vocal chords would allow and she let go her hold on the arm and the alien tendrils pulled it forward like an arrow on the string of a bow. She guided the fist through the cockpit, into the alien pilot, and almost all the way out the other side. The cockpit crunched and creaked and shattered away and shards of reds and greens of boiling and freezing viscous Chiata blood spilled into space.

Dee retracted her arm and hit the cockpit again. This time she grabbed the alien and ripped it out of the mecha and tossed it across the *Rackman's* hull. The alien's body was crushed but still trying to scramble away on the exterior hull of the ship as its life faded away. Dee took three mecha steps and loomed over the alien that was staring back up at her in fear, visibly shaking. Dee's eyes were never more red than at that moment. Dee's anger was never more volatile than at that moment. Dee had never been so close to the edge than at that moment.

"Here's a tattoo for you, Davy!" She stomped the creature several times until there was nothing left but a red and green stain on the metal armor plating. She ground everything into red and green goo until there was literally nothing left of the alien's body but stains in the metal hull when she was done. This was more than war. This was murderous payback. This was her needing to kill the Chiata bastards.

"Phoenix! Snap back now or I'm calling a vehicle override protocol and snapping you back myself." DeathRay ordered her.

"Roger that, um, roger, DeathRay." She suddenly realized how vulnerable she was standing tall with no cover on the hull of the ship and Chiata porcupines blurring about everywhere.

What am I doing? she thought.

My thoughts exactly, Bree replied. Dee felt a bit sheepish. Then she shook her head and hit the QMT.

Chapter 38

July 24, 2409 AD
Mission Star 74
Chiata Expanse
783 light-years from the Sol System
Saturday, 4:29 P.M. Eastern Time

"Your majesty, the Lead Huntress has fallen in the hunt," his second male told him. The king showed his teeth in anger and rose from the dais.

"I warned you about her, my king. I knew she was not up for the task. Send me," the queen said proudly. The king shot her a look of disapproval.

"Now is not the time for such boldness nor pettiness, my queen." He stepped down to the bridge deck plating and looked out the dome at the fighting way in the distance. "Very well. Close the gap. We are no longer trying to recapture the prey ship. We will destroy them all!"

"Sire, would you have me order the entirety of the pride to attack?"

"Attack."

✧ ✧ ✧

July 24, 2409 AD
Mission Star 74
Chiata Expanse
783 light-years from the Sol System
Saturday, 4:29 P.M. Eastern Time

"Commander, please tell me—you are ready?" Alexander listened to the engineering net and could tell that Joe was having some difficulty getting the equipment working properly under extreme duress in the forward section of the ship.

"Try the feedback loop now, Deedee!" Buckley shouted.

"Yes, Commander. That is it. We have a good signal coming through here. I suggest you and your team clear out of there now." Alexander thought he could actually hear the concern in the clone's vocal inflections. The more he worked around them, the more he was getting attuned to their nuances.

"Do you need me there, CHENG?" Buckley asked her.

"No, it would probably be good for you to go to the bridge in case there are problems there."

"Understood. Buckley out."

Suddenly there was a flash of light on the bridge, and Buckley appeared about a meter off the surface and fell, not so gracefully. Alexander watched his long-time CHENG pull himself up off the deck and noticed that he was covered in Chiata blood.

"Are you all right, Joe? I mean, son, you look like Hell."

"Sir, aye sir." Joe caught his breath and Alexander

could tell he was discussing something DTM with his AIC. "We are ready to go, sir!"

"About time," Alexander cheered.

Abby, get me an open channel with Sienna Madira.

Done, sir.

"Moore to Madira."

"Go ahead, son." Alexander was beginning to think that maybe she just called everybody son. He still didn't like it. Then he realized that he'd just called Buckley "son".

Shit, he thought.

Yes, sir.

"Time to pay those bills we talked about."

"Understood. I already have five targets for you. Your AIC has them now," Madira replied.

Here they are, sir.

Got it. Transfer them to the targeting system.

"Okay, Joe, you sure you are ready?" he asked.

"Yes, sir."

"Moore to CHENG, Deedee."

"Go ahead, General."

"Are we good to go on the weapon?"

"We are good to go General."

"Thank you CHENG. Moore out." Alexander grasped the strange control grip with his right hand and sat his left trigger finger over the membrane panel. "Targeting Xs locked. Firing!"

At first it looked like nothing was happening, but then the lights throughout the ship flickered a time or two and a vortex started forming between the tuning fork spires above the dome. The ship started vibrating and humming from bow to stern and suddenly a super bright, even brighter than normal, blue beam of death appeared in the sky as if it had already traveled and made many turns to targets. It simply appeared fully fired and propagated all at once. The beam entered in one side of the ship targeted by the system in Alexander's mindview, but kept going in a line that zigzagged through the alien ship adjacent to it. It turned upwards and penetrated two ships above it and then turned again passing through another ship.

The beam wasn't there one second and then it was there from spires all the way to the last target. It seemed for a second like time was frozen and the targeted ships in reality had to allow for the universe to catch up with what was happening to them. They appeared as alien megaships, porcusnails, on a zigzagging blue skewer. Then each of the ships started to bulge at their seams and they exploded. The beam appeared to stay in place for almost a full two seconds and then it was gone.

"Holy shit!" Joe shouted! "Yes! The beam went straight through the shields to the power plants! Damn Skippy, perfectly targeted!"

"Madira! I need the next targets!"

"That will take a moment, Alexander. I didn't expect such success!" Sienna Madira replied.

"Me either." Alexander looked into the mindview for more targets as suddenly a mass of hundreds of ships dropped out of hyperspace near them. He didn't have time to react and he didn't target or press the button, but another beam appeared from the spires.

The blue beam passed straight through the group's leading ship as it emerged from hyperspace and continued through it zigging and zagging through a dozen more.

Each of those ships instantly exploded, throwing debris into the ships nearest them and causing what Alexander assumed to be the Chiata's version of disarray.

"Great shot, sir!" Joe cheered him on.

"I didn't do that one, Joe. It fired itself."

"No shit?" Joe stammered and quickly added, "Uh, no shit, sir?"

"No shit, Joe."

"Skippy must be doing it." No sooner than the words had left Buckley's mouth than another beam appeared from the spires. And then another. And then another.

The beams continued for several minutes decimating the Chiata fleet and giving them no time for evasive action or to attack. With each firing of the weapon, Skippy must have been getting more efficient at targeting because he managed to hit a larger number of ships with each successive firing. The latest firing had torn through more than thirty Chiata ships. And then the panel Alexander had been manning burst into flames and went dark.

"Shit! Joe!" Alexander waved for the CHENG to check it out as he stepped back out of the way.

"I've got it, sir." Alexander stepped back and watched as the CHENG went to work. He pulled a fire extinguisher from his tool kit and sprayed the panel. Then he crawled up underneath it. "Yeah, there's a power transfer relay here that is nothing but charcoal. It will take me a minute to replace it. For now the superweapon will be down. But only a minute or so. If you'll excuse me sir, I need to flash down to engineering for some parts."

"Do what you've got to do, Joe. Quickly."

"Yes, sir."

✧ ✧ ✧

July 24, 2409 AD
Mission Star 74
Chiata Expanse
783 light years from the Sol System
Saturday, 4:35 P.M. Eastern Time

"Dee, do I need to be asking you about what the fuck just happened back there?" As soon as they had landed in the *Penzington's* aft hangar bay, DeathRay had gotten out of his mecha and bounced up to the cockpit steps on her bot-mode mecha. Azazel and Molloch were still in their cockpits recovering from the deathblossoms. The clones had done well, but still weren't even close to Phoenix's and DeathRay's times. Jack looked over in at her and retracted his helmet to his shoulder compartment and stared her down. Dee could tell he was pissed at her.

"I, uh, no, Admiral. You do not. I'm frosty. Just got caught up in the moment and adrenaline, sir," she replied as her canopy opened up the rest of the way and she slid her helmet off. She didn't bother to retract and store it, she just took it off and set it aside. She looked DeathRay in the eyes and couldn't tell what he was going to do next.

"I am not asking you as Admiral Boland, Dee." Jack looked at her. She could see the big brother look in his eyes. He was genuinely worried about her. "I'm asking you as your friend who has been there for you since you were twelve. Are you okay? I mean, that shit was intense and looked more like, well, like murder more than it did war. You forgot everything around you and weren't acting as a seasoned combat veteran. I am absolutely for killing every damned one of the Chiata in the universe for taking my wife from me, but you didn't just kill it and move on. What was that stomping and grinding it into the hull all about?"

"War is murder, Jack." She couldn't stop the tears from flowing and she wasn't wearing her helmet to catch them. "It is nothing but one big murder after another. It is horrible, and nasty, and it takes everything you love away from you. It took him away from me and I want him back! If I can't have him back I will kill every last Chiata there is!"

"Dee, I, uh, I know." That was all that he said. Dee had expected more. Some big brother lecture or some senior officer wisdom that would assure her that everything was going to be okay and that the hurt would stop, but there was nothing. That was all Jack said to her. But what he did made all the difference in the world. He placed his armored hand over hers and patted it as gently as an armored suit would allow. He stayed there like that for a few tens of seconds just looking at her. "It will be okay. I promise you Dee. It will get better."

"I know it will. I'm going to make it okay." Dee told him.

"How?"

"By killing so many of them that they will never bother us again!"

"At what cost, Dee?" Jack shook his head. "No. What you did was put yourself in deeper danger and at further risk of harm or death than you needed to. That alien had you locked up and tied up and you should have flashed out. What happens the next time when you can't overpower it and it hurts you bad or kills you or your wingman? How would your mother and father feel? It would destroy them to lose you. How do you think I would feel? You are like my little sister, Dee. I can't let you go in and get killed because you were being stupid and angry."

"It didn't happen, did it?" Dee was growing tired of the lecture and perhaps allowed a bit too much defiance to show through her voice and facial expression. After all, Jack was her superior officer by a good number of promotions. "I killed it good."

"Yeah, you did. And you were lucky one of its compatriots didn't kill you. This is going nowhere, I see that now." Then he dropped to the floor. Dee wasn't sure if he was angry at her or what. She knew he had a look of concern or disappointment on his face as he turned away from her. She had always seen DeathRay as a god, as her big brother, as the pilot everyone wanted to be. She didn't want to let him down. But at the moment, she just couldn't be a different person. She had to do what she had to do.

"I'm okay, Jack. I'm okay." She almost pleaded with him. The tears had mostly subsided from flowing and the squint to her eyes and snarl on her nose and cheeks replaced them again. The sorrow was still there but it was so overpowered by the anger within her. Her eyes and tattoos began to glow brighter.

"Lieutenant Colonel Moore, you are grounded from flight duty until such time as you have received a full psychological evaluation from medical and been cleared for combat duty," he said as he walked away from her.

"Sorry, Admiral Boland, but I and the Bringers of Hell are no longer under your command. We were recently all transferred, in case you have forgotten." Dee spat the words at him. "I am captain of the *U.S.S. Davy Rackman* of the Expeditionary Fleet and the Bringers are under my command. I answer to the commanding general of the Fleet now, sir."

"Go on then. I will not fly with you as long as you are like this. You're just too dangerous to everyone around you," Jack told her. "Don't think I won't have words with the general on this matter, Lieutenant Colonel."

"I would expect nothing less from you, Admiral. Thank you for your concerns, sir." Dee leaned back in her seat and considered cycling the cockpit and ordering Azazel and Molloch back to the *Rackman*. She hated to leave things like this with Jack, but for now she didn't know what else to do.

Deanna! I need help now!

Mother?

I've been captured by Copernicus. He has killed the entire Tau Ceti colony. Rondi and I are here now and we need help!

Hang on mother. I'm coming!

"Jack! Wait!" she shouted at him. "Mom is in trouble! She says that Copernicus has killed the entire Tau Ceti colony!"

"We couldn't even get to her to help her." He turned and looked at her and Dee could see the look on his face meant he wasn't sure he believed her. And, there was still some seriously bad blood between them that was going to have to be dealt with some day. Nancy could have fixed it for them if she were still alive. Fucking Chiata.

"I'm still connected with her through the Thgreeth system. Copernicus has captured her and Master Gunnery Sergeant Howser," Dee said frantically. "She's afraid he's going to kill them. We have to see my father now!"

Dee started cycling the mecha canopy down as she placed her helmet back on it sealed itself to her suit and the hardpoints reached out and attached her to the mecha. She looked at DeathRay to see if he was going to say anything.

"Alright Dee. Shit, let's go."

Dee didn't wait for Jack to bounce into his mecha before she flashed out and back to the bridge of the *Rackman*. Her father and Commander Buckley were there working on the firing systems for the BBDs. She looked out the dome and in her mindview and from the looks of it the Chiata were finally getting pushed back and the superweapon Skippy had given them was doing the job.

"Dad! Mom has been captured by Copernicus and is in trouble. She says he's killed all of the Tau Ceti colony. We have to get to her now!"

✧ ✧ ✧

July 24, 2409 AD
Mission Star 74
Chiata Expanse
783 light years from the Sol System
Saturday, 4:37 P.M. Eastern Time

"Sire, the prey have some new weapon that is destroying the Pride. This is even more effective than their expanding spheres of death. Our shields and armor of no use against it," one of the Elders said in a panicked voice. "We must escape, your majesty, to tell the Council of Prides."

"We could beat them through the damping field, sire," the second male told him. "Our standard faster-than-light is faster than theirs. We can simply outrun them."

The king had never had to "outrun" any prey since he had been alive. This was new territory for him. He had never called a retreat, ever. He was beginning to realize that perhaps this prey was not a prey at all but something else. What else they might be was unclear, but the only other knowledge of such events had happened millennia before he was born by an ancient race. The stories he'd heard were that that race had finally given up fighting with the Chiata and had left the galaxy. One of the prides in charge of studying their ruins had been destroyed by these humans. Perhaps there was some connection between them and the ancient stories.

"Very well. The pride is lost." The king looked more than frustrated. These prey had defeated his best attempts even with information and secret weapons given to them from an ally who had betrayed these prey for his own self-serving and unclear reasons. The Council of Prides would likely remove him upon hearing of this, but the Chiata Pride in total needed to know of what these prey could do. Therefore, he must return with data about them rather than stay and fight to the last soul, which is what he would truly prefer to facing the council in defeat. His fate was sealed. The council would likely feast on him following the debriefing. He had to ready himself for that outcome.

"Do we order a retreat, sire?"

"Yes. There is no longer any need for further loss of our warriors and hunters." He sat back down on his dais and placed a hand on his queen's shoulder. "Retreat."

"What of the warriors and hunters on the prey ships?"

"Recall the tubes. Save as many as we can."

"I am sorry, my King." The queen looked at him soulfully. He was certain she understood what retreat meant for them both.

"Me too, my Queen."

Chapter 39

July 24, 2409 AD
Mission Star 74
Chiata Expanse
783 light-years from the Sol System
Saturday, 4:40 P.M. Eastern Time

"Well, son, if we just keep moving in one path through the damping fields we might could fire the new superbeam in there and create a QMT path?" Madira suggested through the command net. Alexander had all the captains, CHENGS, and senior officers in the conversation hoping somebody would have an idea. Over the last several minutes the Chiata had apparently sounded a full retreat and they were leaving the system as fast as they could manage. The Expeditionary Fleet's concerns were no longer fighting to stay alive within the system. Instead, they were trying to figure out how to get out of the system, to get to Tau Ceti, and to save Sehera Moore and Rondi Howser.

"That might take days, Sienna." Alexander told her.

"Sehera, Gunny Howser, and Tau Ceti are in trouble now."

"I understand that, son!" Madira seemed to be losing her temper and Alexander understood why. He was doing his best to fight down the urge to do anything. It was her daughter in trouble, but it was the love of his life that was in trouble.

"Wait a minute," DeathRay interjected. "Gunny Howser is there. That reminds me. Captain Madira, the planet where we first found your ships a few years back. Nancy Penzington found a backdoor out of there. You had some sort of damping field up but she found a way out."

"Yes son, but that was in software, not actually a physical damping system. I have no idea how that physics works," Madira replied. "I don't think any human being does."

"That wasn't my point, Captain," DeathRay continued. "You've worked closely with Copernicus for years. Would he put a backdoor in a system like this?"

"Hmm, I don't know. Maybe. I have no idea how to find it."

"What about your beetle bot, Captain Moore?" Admiral Walker asked. "It was your bot that allowed you to transfer QMT capabilities on the Thgreeth planet. And I have a suspicion that the Thgreeth are more advanced than whatever Copernicus is."

"He's a D'lraouth," Madira said. "Used to be parasites on bears or something similar. It sounds nasty."

"What about it, Dee?" Alexander turned to his daughter. "Have you asked it?"

"I hadn't even thought of it," Deanna replied, and

then tapped the compartment that Skippy stayed in. "Skippy."

The compartment on her armored suit opened and the beetle jumped to her shoulder in a blur. Dee reached up with her left hand and patted it like a pet. Alexander watched and wasn't sure how comfortable all that made him. Actually, he knew it made him uncomfortable as Hell.

"Skippy, I need to go to Mom. Can you get me there?"

Suddenly, Dee's mecha QMT drive activated and Skippy jumped from her shoulder to the control panel near the HOTAS. Then the mecha flashed and there was a sizzling bacon sound on the Bridge and Dee was gone. Mecha and all.

Chapter 40

July 24, 2409 AD
Tau Ceti
Kuiper Belt
12 light-years from the Sol System
Saturday, 4:40 P.M. Eastern Time

The QMT flashes stopped and Dee and her mecha were suddenly nearly seven hundred light-years from where she'd been, inside a strange dark room filled with bright white plasma filaments bifurcating like lightning in every direction. She was also freefalling above a big white plasma ball that the lightning seemed to originate from, and there was a platform with people just below her.

"Shit!" Dee reacted to the freefall and kicked in her drive system to arrest the fall. Instantly, the blue force tracker kicked on in her mindview and she saw two blue dots. One of them was her mother and the other was Gunny Howser. They were right below her, being held by several AEMs. Copernicus was on a hoverchair near them, surrounded by other AEMs.

"Stop that mecha!" Copernicus shouted and pointed in her general direction.

Mother! I'm here!

Get us out of here Dee!

Will do.

Dee dropped to the platform. Suddenly a mix of AEMs, Army Armored Infantry, and civil forces dressed people rushed her from every direction but with no rifles they were little match for an FM-14X. Dee wasn't sure what to do, as they were human.

Dee! They are no longer human! They've been taken over by something alien.

Understood, mother!

With a swipe of her left hand she cleared the path to her mother and Rondi. The distraction gave Rondi and her mother all they needed to spring to action. The two of them started fighting their way free of the AEMs holding them in place. Several of the AEMs jumped up on her mecha slicing away at her with their blades. The blades had no effect on the barrier shields. She crushed one of them against her like swatting at a mosquito, and then she tossed several of them out through the strangely lit chasm.

Dee! Let's go!

Hang on!

Dee toggled her bot to eagle-mode and then grabbed her mother with her right hand and Rondi with her left. She jumped with the eagle-mode's talons off the platform and into the chasm and thought about leaving behind a very explosive gift for Copernicus, but still was unclear about what was going on there. She didn't know if the humans could be saved or not, so she didn't want to kill them if there was a chance to save them.

"Skippy, can we snap back to the *Rackman*?"

The QMT system flickered on and the usual white flash and sizzle of bacon sounded in her ears. Suddenly, Dee's mecha was on the bridge of the *Rackman,* right where she'd started. She clanked to the deck and lowered the nose of her fighter until it touched. Then she cycled the hands open letting her passengers free.

"Is everybody all right?" she asked and then she raised her visor and her canopy. The hardpoints let go of her suit and she sprang out of her pilot's couch and slid down the nose of her fighter to the deck. Her mother and Rondi were gathering their respective composures but it didn't slow down her father, who had already bounced beside Sehera.

"Are you hurt?" her father asked her mother. "Are you shot? There's blood on your armor."

"Honestly, Alexander, it is not my blood. I'm fine." Her mother seemed a bit annoyed.

"Gunny." He held out a hand to shake hers. "Are you okay?"

"Fine, sir," she replied.

"Thanks for watching over her."

"General, something odd is going on at Tau Ceti." Dee decided they needed to focus. There was no telling what was going on there and how time was going to play into it.

"Sehera, what is going on?" Alexander asked her. "You are tied in to the commandnet so everyone can hear you."

"I see." Sehera paused for a second to collect her

thoughts. "Well, Copernicus has taken his facility from 61 UM all the way to Tau Ceti. He has transported all of the nine billion or so population of the Tau Ceti colony onto his vessel and has transferred some sort of alien mind control over them. All of them."

"That rat bastard, son of a bitch," Sienna Madira cursed out loud over the net. "I knew I should have killed that asshole this morning."

"Sienna?" both her mother and father said at the same time.

"He isn't controlling them. He has been after me to make him nine billion clones for years but we just hadn't been able to do that yet," she said.

"Why, Sienna?" Alexander said. "What does he want with them for?"

"I think it has been his plan all along to create vessels or hosts for his people," Sienna Madira continued. "Those people aren't being mind-controlled. He has wiped them completely. They are dead. He is replacing their minds with the minds of his people."

"I don't understand." Sehera stopped her. "I thought his people were dead?"

"No, not dead. They were in storage in that facility. That's what that facility is for. That's the number one purpose of that thing. The only way his people escaped the Chiata advance thousands of years ago was for him to download all of the remaining survivors of his people at the last moment into that facility. There were no longer any viable hosts for the parasites, so he figured out a way to save their minds." Madira's tale seemed almost unbelievable and fantastic, but from the years she had known her grandmother, Dee had never known her to spin yarns.

"Are you telling us that Copernicus has just killed nine billion humans?" Admiral Walker asked. Dee noticed that the jaw muscles of the Admiral's avatar were clinching.

Nine billion people, Dee thought.

Staggeringly awful, Bree replied in her mind.

Yes. Jesus.

"Is there any way to reverse it, Captain Madira?" the clone captain of the *U.S.S. William Bainbridge* asked.

"Not that I know of," Madira replied. "Knowing Copernicus, he had little regard for human life other than it being a means to whatever ends he had in mind."

"He has an army of nine billion people, then. He is only about a dozen light-years from Sol," DeathRay added to the conversation. "Is he going to attack one of the other colonies or Sol itself? We need to get back there and stop him."

"Madira, what do you think he is planning?" her father asked.

"I don't know, son. He had only ever asked for nine billion bodies. I find it mathematically intriguing that Tau Ceti was the exact size he needed, as if he'd been planning it all along. Sneaky asshole." Sienna Madira was shaking her head back and forth. "I should have killed him when I had the chance. Sehera, did he hint to you what his plans were?"

"No."

"We need to get there and check it out." Her father then turned to her and looked at Skippy. The little bot was resting on her shoulder as always. "Dee, do you think that thing could flash the fleet out of here?"

"I'll ask." Dee pulled the little beetle from her shoulder and held it in her hand. "Skippy, is there any way we can take the entire fleet to Tau Ceti like you just took me?"

At first it seemed that the bot didn't do anything, and then suddenly the direct-to-mind battlescape of the system popped up. There were nineteen Chiata ships that popped up along a highlighted pathway through the length of the damping field. Dee wasn't sure what that meant at first and pondered it almost to the point where her father and the rest of the command teams were getting impatient.

"Dee?" Her mother tapped her shoulder. "Anything?"

"Um, I'm not sure but he is showing me a specific path and nineteen specific Chiata ships in the damping field," she told them. She was still unclear what that meant and then a simulation of the *Rackman* QMTing through to each of the ships and destroying them played out. "Wait, I think he wants me to destroy them."

"Those are probably the ships with the damping devices." Madira explained.

"I see. So once those are destroyed then all of the QMTs will work?" Dee asked.

"That is most likely yes," her grandmother told her.

"If the *Rackman* can QMT there. Why can't the rest of us?" Admiral Walker asked.

"I can probably answer that one," Commander Buckley chimed in. "Lieutenant Colonel Moore's bot duplicated itself and is controlling the power distribution, propulsion, and weapons systems of this ship presently."

"Then if it can do that why doesn't it duplicate itself and move to each ship?" DeathRay asked.

Then almost as soon as he had said that two clocks appeared in her mindview. One of the clocks had a line attached to it and a callout window pane was showing the original simulation of the path through the damping field. That clock showed four minutes and thirty-seven seconds. The other clock showed six hours and change.

"Skippy tells me it would take six hours or more to retrofit the other fleet ships and it would only take a few minutes for the *Rackman* to cut a path through the field."

"Makes sense," Joe added. "It took us about thirty minutes or more to retrofit the one ship with nearly every bot in the fleet working on it. Granted we were also building the super-BBD weapon but I suspect a lot of the same conduits would have to be altered, retrofitted, and replaced. There are fourteen megaships in various states of repair. I'd be surprised if we could pull it off in six hours."

"I concur with Commander Buckley on that," CHENG Deedee agreed with him. "It took a Herculean effort to alter the Chiata and supercarrier systems for the bots designs to function."

"Very well, then." Her father turned to her. "Captain Moore. I'm turning your ship back over to you and we will follow your trail."

"Understood sir." Dee noticed a surprised look from her mother and Rondi. She couldn't bring herself to look at DeathRay. "As soon as you and the rest of your crew can get off my ship, I will get us underway, sir. Please give my best thanks to Colonels Strong, Slayer, and Jones, sir."

"Very good, Captain. Don't wait on us." Her father turned from her and focused his avatar on the rest of the

Fleet commanders. "Alright, Fleet, we have our plan. Get ready to move out. We need to keep a watch for the Chiata. Just because they retreated doesn't mean they won't return. We will form up on the *Rackman* and jump as soon as our QMTs allow it each time. Moore out."

The commandnet shut off and only Dee, her mother and father, Rondi, and Buckley were standing in the bridge. Buckley looked across at Rondi and then back at the general as if he wasn't sure what to do.

"Go Joe," Dee told him. "Dad."

"At your leisure Commander." Then her father grabbed her mother around the armored waist.

Both of their helmets retracted and he kissed her and held her to him awkwardly in the armored suits. It was cumbersome and beautiful at the same time. Dee couldn't watch. Then Joe and Rondi bounced together and that was even more awkward.

Dee retracted her helmet and wiped the tears from her eyes. The glow of her tattoos reflected off the transparent metal dome as she walked closer to it. She touched the glass with her armored hand and then decided to retract the gauntlet. She felt the cool dome surface with her fingers and then she pressed her forehead to it.

"You and me, Davy Rackman," she whispered through her sobs. She rested there for a moment or two and then took a deep breath. She was startled by her father's hand on her shoulder. She looked up and could see both her mother's and father's reflections in the dome.

"Thank you, Princess," her father said.

"For what?" She didn't move. She hadn't done

anything more than usual. At least, not as long as you didn't count the conversation that DeathRay would have with them sooner or later.

"For rescuing me," Sehera said. "And Rondi."

"No, for all of it, sweetheart." Her father turned her to him. "You have sacrificed so much for us and humanity. You have done so much more than your duty, Princess. I am so proud of you. You took this day. You are taking us home. You and the *Davy Rackman*. Maybe this is where you belong for now. Here with Davy." He touched her armor on the chest plate just above her nametag pointing at her heart.

She just couldn't take it any longer. She had held back the emotions for so long. She had turned her grief to sorrow for so long. Oh, the Chiata were still going to pay, die, be fucking destroyed. But she needed to grieve and she'd never allowed herself to do so. Dee fell against her father's armor crying uncontrollably. Her mother wrapped her arms around her.

It took several moments for Dee to collect herself and for the sobs to stop, but finally, she managed to straighten herself up.

"There's another thing we have to deal with, Alexander," her mother said, nodding at Joe and Rondi behind them. Dee looked up and wiped her cheeks. "Copernicus told her."

"Ma'am." Rondi looked up from Joe's embrace and cleared her throat. "It doesn't matter to me who anybody's parents are. I never knew mine. If you are keeping that a secret for whatever reason that is your business and not my place to discuss it with anybody else."

"Thank you, Gunny." Her father nodded at her. "When there is time, Dee can explain it all too you."

"Sir, I will say that really good friends are sometimes hard to come by," Rondi said. Joe looked confused about what was going on. "I mean the type of friend that will help you hide a body, as the joke goes. I am and always will be that friend to your daughter and therefore by default, unless you became assholes to her for some reason, I am that type of friend to you and Mrs. Moore too."

"Ooh-fuckin'-rah, Marine!" Dee grunted and held out a fist toward her friend.

"Hell, yeah," Rondi replied, bumping her armored fist to Dee's. "Lieutenant Colonel? Captain? Dayumn giirrll! You've got a lot to fill me in on."

"Soon."

Dee tapped the helmet deploy control and both her helmet and her gauntlet were in place in a second flat. Her visor came down and lit up. The fire in her eyes started to grow.

"Phoenix to Azazel and Molloch." She opened the tacnet. "Get your asses back on the *Rackman* and get the Bringers in full battle rattle."

"Roger that, Phoenix. In the hangar now," Azazel replied. "Orders, Captain Moore?"

"We're going to bring some Hell."

"Understood, Captain."

"Sir, if you don't mind, I want to get the Hell out of this fucking system," she told her father.

"Aye aye, Captain Moore. God speed." Her father saluted her and he and her mother flashed out. Joe and Rondi were right behind them.

Dee did a backflip into her cockpit and sat back in her pilot's couch. She brought up the battlescape that Skippy had given her in her mindview. The little bot crawled up on her shoulder and sat quietly as usual.

Bree, give me the ship's diagnostics page and tie in to the bridge controls through my mecha and mindview.

Got it, Captain Moore.

Captain Moore. Not a bad ring to it.

Not at all.

Just me, you, Skippy, and Davy Rackman *taking on the universe.* She laughed a bit.

And a crew of clones, and the Bringers of Hell.

No Bree, you are confused.

How so, ma'am.

The Bringers of Hell is the name of the flight squadron, true. But we, humanity I mean, WE are the Bringers of Hell!

Yes, ma'am. I see, the metaphor.

Not a metaphor, Bree. A fucking universal truth. Now let's go kill some Chiata and get the fuck out of here.

Yes, ma'am.

Epilogue

July 24, 2409 AD
Presidential Estate
Tau Ceti Planet Four, Moon Alpha, a.k.a. Ares
New Tharsis
12 light-years from the Sol System
Saturday, 5:05 P.M. Eastern Time

"Eerily quiet." Sienna Madira stood at the steps of the Presidential Palace looking down the mountain at what was once her home a long time ago during the Separatist War. She had always been awestruck by the rings of the gas giant that filled most of the sky. Tau Ceti sat in the distance and was about to drop below the horizon casting long rays of light across the sky rippling in the turbulent atmosphere over the cityscape. The beautiful mauves, reds, maroons, and some of the purples blended into planet-sized megastorms in the gas giant's atmosphere creating one of the most amazing panoramas anyone could imagine. The various moons of the giant were scattered about the zodiac along with Ares appearing as moons of sizes ranging from large rocks to planetary equivalents of Ares itself.

"Everyone is gone. Everyone," Dee said. She was fiddling with sensors from her pack. Sienna was glad to see her granddaughter finally out of that suit. She was glad to finally be out of that suit for a while. Dee was clearly in a DTM conversation with either her AIC or from the *Rackman* which was hovering in a non-Keplerian orbit overhead. A formation of nine FM-14Xs passed overhead patrolling the sky. They were Dee's squadron. "Azazel says they're getting nothing on blue, red, or purple trackers."

"And you had no idea this was what he was planning, mother?" Sehera asked her. "After all those years the two of you were together. Nothing?"

"How could I? No. No way would I let him destroy nine billion lives. I wouldn't let him do it to the clones at 61 UM and he had asked me about that just this morning. I threatened to kill him if he did anything to them. I should have killed him when I had the chance. I most certainly wouldn't have sat still for the killing of natural-born humans either."

"The Fleet has swept this system from star to Oort and there is no sign of the facility or any survivors. Any idea where he would have gone?" Alexander asked. He was clearly in constant communications DTM with other ships in the Fleet that were patrolling the system as well as conversing with his AIC. "Any clue would be nice."

"Away," Madira replied. "He was at his core a coward. A sorry, good for nothing, stab-you-in-the-back coward if I ever saw one. He simply wanted to run away from the

Chiata with his people. Maybe there was vengeance in his plans somehow, but mostly he wanted other people to do the fighting for him. He manipulated us into fighting for him. I believe we never really had a choice in the matter."

"Jesus, nine billion, just like that. How did he do it?" Dee asked. "He must have had them stacked in that facility like cordwood."

"Somehow he was using AIC implants to change them," Sehera said. "And you weren't there long enough, Dee, but they were stacked up inside there as far as you could see them. All of them had some kind of plasma filament connected to the side of their heads that their AICs were implanted."

"I was afraid of that." Sienna Madira let out a sigh. She had always seen the AIC implants as an improvement to mankind's efficiency and as a perfect companion to everyone. She hadn't let herself consider the fact that they just might very well be a Trojan horse. "Your phobia of implants all those years might have been well founded, Sehera. I think he helped humanity develop and perfect them to become the perfect transceiver for his device to quickly download his people into the human mind. He's been planning this for centuries and I didn't see it. We will have to think on ways to protect ourselves and our AICs in the future. Some sort of physical barriers for them perhaps. Maybe that chief engineer of yours, Alexander, might come up with something. He seems to have a very unique perspective on all of this alien quantum membrane technology."

"He might at that." Alexander nodded. "Buckley is, um, unique."

"I just can't get over how duped we all were by him," Sehera said. "Copernicus used us from the beginning and planned all this out over thousands of years and we never saw it coming."

"He used us and tricked us and betrayed us. History might not ever get it all right. I'm not even certain I understand what of our history was us and what was him," Sienna told her daughter. Seeing all the emptiness of what was once a buzzing major metropolis and civilization was mind-numbing, almost nauseating. Sienna just couldn't believe how used and betrayed she felt. She was angry as well. "I had thought Mars was a heavy burden to bear, but this . . ."

"He used us all at a heavy price, Sienna. Perhaps you more than any," Alexander agreed with her, which was unusual for him. Maybe he was starting to forgive her, she thought. But she knew better.

"Son, it was a heavy price, but I have to look what we gained from it or else I will go even more off the deep end than I already am." Madira had to see the silver lining in the storm clouds. Something had to justify the centuries of mass bloodshed. Something had to justify all the blood on her hands. If something didn't justify it all then she truly was one of the most bloodthirsty evil bitches of all of human history. She didn't want to be that person at all. "There was a pending invasion of overwhelming force and because of humanity's interaction with Copernicus, humanity just might now not only survive, but thrive. I wish there'd been another way. Hell, there might have been another way I didn't think of, but history is history. We took on severely heavy losses, but we as a species have survived thus far and I think we will keep on going. We just need to figure out what to do next."

"I wish we could find a means to stop this war other than just the constant engagements in system after system. I don't see how that approach will ever win the war for us. Too little impact, like spitting in the ocean," Dee said solemnly. Madira was so proud of her granddaughter and felt so sad for her at the same time. But the young soldier was absolutely right. They needed to impact the galaxy on a bigger scale. Humanity had to make a much larger splash on the galactic scale if they intended to survive a long term war with the Chiata.

"I've been thinking on that, Deanna." She rested her hand on her granddaughter's shoulder and gave her a heartwarming half smile. "Copernicus talked several times about this galactic court system where he originally bought the futures rights on Sol and its surrounding systems to keep the Chiata from overrunning us thousands of years ago. He said that by purchasing those futures the galactic fleets had to protect us until the time limit ran out on them. They were getting close to the end and the Chiata attack wave was pending. While the galactic fleet apparently could never stop the Chiata, they could slow them down some and cause them pain. In turn, the galactic fleet, or whatever they were, caused the Chiata enough heartache that the glowing bastards adhered to the court's rulings until their populations reached such levels that they needed another system. Copernicus talked about this court a lot. We need to go there."

"Do you know where it is, mother?" Sehera asked

excitedly. "I mean, we should get an audience with them as soon as we can."

"No, I really don't. But I think we need to go in there with the entire Fleet, armored up, gnashing our teeth, blasting some macho sounding death metal punk the kids listen to, and put our little demon here right out there in the front and let her tell them that it is time they back the fuck off or the wrath of humanity will be coming. I'm thinking we should make as big a show of it as possible. Big guns, mecha, rows and rows of mecha and of AEMs." Madira was certain she had that look of making plans within plans on her face but she didn't care anymore. She was making plans for a good fight. "Some good old-fashioned diplomacy is just what we need right now."

"Sounds good," Alexander agreed with her again. That was more than once in one day which was infinitely more than ever before and all times put together. Maybe, just maybe, they were beginning to bridge the pain and the gap between them. She wasn't getting her hopes up on that. After all, she had tortured a man to death on several occasions. "But we have no idea where to go."

"Oh, I bet Dee can tell us," Madira said reassuringly as she made eye contact with her granddaughter. She raised her left eyebrow as she nodded her head up and down. "Can't you, dear?"

"What? I don't know? This is the first I've heard of any galactic court. I have no idea where it is," Dee protested.

"Mother, seriously?" Sehera asked her. She glanced at Alexander but the man remained stoic. His poker face was about the best she'd ever encountered.

"I didn't say you knew, dear. I said you could tell us.

There is a significant difference in the two statements."
Sienna laughed.

"That makes no sense, grandma." Dee wrinkled her
brow and shook her head at her. Sienna liked it when she
called her grandma. It made her feel somehow closer to
them all as if they were actually a family and not some
band of crazies that had been fighting aliens, whether they
knew or not, for the better part of their lives. "How could
I do that? I've never heard of this galactic court. I have
no idea how I can 'tell you' where it is."

Sienna paused and rested her hands on her hips. Her
family was smart and brave and bold and beyond honorable,
but when it came to thinking through the back doors and
more conniving parts of life, history, or plans within plans
they still needed some work. She looked at Alexander who
was still standing expressionless and listening only and she
wondered how he had made it as a politician through three
terms as President of the United States.

"Well, mother?" Sehera asked.

"Don't all of you suppose that the Thgreeth would
have known about this galactic court?" Madira grinned as
she spoke. She had been thinking along this path for quite
some time now but wasn't sure when to bring it up. Now
seemed like the perfect time. "Hell, I bet they started it.
I'm sure Skippy, that is what you call him right? Skippy?"

"Uh, yes, Skippy."

"I'm sure Skippy can tell us where we need to be. If
he can't I'm sure it is in those ruins in that ancient
database somewhere. You and your mother can find it."

"Of course!" Sehera was clearly getting the epiphany.
"Dee, I'm sure it is in there somewhere. It might take us

a few weeks to sort through it all and figure it out, but it has to be there."

"In the meantime, Alexander, Dee," Madira continued. "We need to get Skippy there to fix up all of our Fleet with the superbeam weapon and the Thgreeth QMT capabilities. We will certainly want to show up at this galactic court making as much noise as we can."

"Perhaps, Madira, you're right about this." Alexander looked at her and met her gaze, for the first time in a century not looking as if he were about to rip her head off. It was a start. "Perhaps, we've already made enough noise that when we show up they will already know who we are."

"They know who we are all right. Don't they, Deanna?" Sienna looked in her granddaughter's glowing eyes with so much pride. Even with all of the crazy tattoos and fire eyes she was beautiful. She looked just like her mother and had her father's spunk. Dee and all the other granddaughters and grandsons out there were the only thing that made all the centuries of her horrific life worth it she thought. They will get to live on.

"And who is that, Princess? Who do they think we are?"

"Alexander you can be a brick wall sometimes," Madira laughed. "They don't 'think' we are son, they, 'know' we are. Tell him who we are Deanna."

"Dad, it is quite simple and true and I hope it is ringing in rumors throughout the corridors of every Chiata megaship across the galaxy." Deanna snarled and squinted and looked back at all of them, her tattoos and eyes all ablaze giving her the appearance of a fiery demon. "WE are the Bringers of Hell!"

Epilogue 2: The Blockade

January 4, 2414 AD
U.S.S. Davy Rackman
Uncharted System with Thgreeth Ruins
1200 light-years from the Sol System
Saturday, 5:05 P.M. Eastern Time

"And what if they make a run on the blockade, Captain?" Chief of the Boat Command Master Chief Cameron Simms said over his Navy coffee mug. He was much older than she was and may have had more experience in the Navy, but nobody had more experience fighting the alien horde than her, except maybe her father and her mentor and "big brother" Captain Jack "DeathRay" Boland. But both of them were over four thousand light-years away in different directions fighting other battles.

Deanna simply turned to the COB, one of her few birthed-human crewmembers, and snarled. The clone crewmembers hardly ever asked questions. She liked the clones. They were much easier to deal with. They didn't ask a bunch of questions with obvious answers.

While the clones were still human, in body for certain, their minds were filled with quantum computer-generated artificial intelligences, so they reacted and thought differently than standard humans. They were certainly alive, and Dee had for a long time realized that they were just as "human" as anyone else. They were just a little different, smarter in some ways but not in others. Physically, they were the same but seemed to be able to turn their minds off to pain a little better and could therefore push themselves closer to the human body's physical breaking point. That made them great pilots and soldiers. Conversationalists they were not. Even the clones' facial expressions were few and far between and hardly ever appropriate to the situation. She sometimes envied them and sometimes thought they were funny, but she all the time thought of them as her crew.

Dee was all human. She had been raised by two of the most influential human beings of the last century. Her father was one of the first armored environment-suit Marines sent to Mars to stop the revolt there. They had been extremely outnumbered, mostly slaughtered, then captured and tortured. He had managed to survive by the help of the head resistance terrorists' daughter. The two of them then managed to wipe out over a hundred resistance troops and then escape. Her father had later become a senator from Mississippi and then a three-term president. After all that they had learned of the coming alien invasion and he had become the commanding general of all the human Expeditionary Fleet.

And her grandmother was probably the most influential human over the last two centuries. It was likely because of her that humanity had been prepared for the Chiata invasion before it came. Between her parents and her grandmother and a lot of help from hundreds of thousands of soldiers and clones and an ancient alien race called the Thgreeth humanity had become the only superpower force in the outer rim of the galaxy holding off the Chiata and actually pushing them back. Dee had been there from the day she was born.

Clearly, her family had shaped history for well over two hundred and fifty years. It was her turn to drive for a while. She had become a natural-born human turned alien-killing demon through that history. When she entered an alien system all the aliens knew who she was and feared her. Her very "demonic" appearance struck fear into the Chiata Pride kings and queens. While over the past five or so years since she had lost her true love at the battle of the Thgreeth Homeworld System her demeanor had calmed somewhat, her bloodlust for the aliens that had taken him from her had never waned. Dee was absolutely driven to kill the Chiata—all of them.

The tattoos on her face and body marked her most memorable kills and glowed green and red like the blood flowing through the alien Chiata's skin and tendrils that she had destroyed. The brilliant red-orange implants in her eyes made them look like the fire that still burned inside her.

The blockade had been a standoff for two days. The Chiata and their allies had decided to take out an ancient Thgreeth planet that was ripe with ruins and potential technology before humanity could make use of any of it. Her father had sent her and a small flotilla of megaships to hold the planet until the archaeologists and scientists sent there recovered what they needed. With each new Thgreeth outpost uncovered, some new technological advantage was added to the Fleet. The Chiata were beginning to figure that out and were attacking those systems as soon as they could identify them.

"We are truly outnumbered right, Captain Moore?" the COB asked.

The Chiata had sent ships to destroy the planet's surface. Dee's flotilla was outnumbered by them three to one. So what? She didn't mind the odds. She'd fought in situations with much more overwhelming numbers during the first Chiata Horde engagements. The Chiata didn't annoy her. She liked killing them. But questions from new COBs, well, questions on the other hand . . .

"I mean, we have ten ships blocking insertion orbits but they have thirty sitting right out there likely having a dang similar conversation, ma'am," the new COB continued.

"I have a suspicion that you're right COB," United States Marine Corp Colonel Deanna Moore, Captain of the *U.S.S. Davy Rackman*, replied calmly. Deanna took in a deep breath and looked at the full battlescape in her mindview. "They haven't moved in two days. Perhaps our warning to them when we got here slowed them down. And besides, we've put down many more than thirty Chiata ships before. I don't think they expected us to be here."

"The longer we wait, Captain, the more likely they are to be reinforced." The COB stated the obvious. The clones knew her better and didn't waste their time telling her things she already knew. Her clone executive officer turned to her with an expressionless face and attempted to smirk. Dee almost chuckled. The Samantha clone was fit and attractive and had no idea how to smirk. At least she was getting better at when to do it.

There were twenty Chiata ships out there and ten of their skinny tall alien allies. It hadn't been until the last couple of months that humanity even realized that the Chiata had allies. These new aliens were almost three meters tall with multiple appendages and they looked more like a praying mantis than the insect itself did. That is, if the insect itself were three meters tall. The Fleet had started referring to them as "preying mantises" because if they ever brought you down and managed to take out your armor they fed on you instantly. As far as anyone could tell, even the aliens from the Galactic Court Alliance, the preying mantises were subservient to the Chiata, who lived in hierarchical prides a lot like lions although they didn't look anything like a cat.

The direct to mind visuals of the battlescape showed her that the twenty Chiata ships had taken up positions in the rear and the ten preying mantis ships were forming a phalanx formation in real-time as she watched. That suggested to Dee that they were getting ready to make that run into the line. It was about time. Dee was getting tired of all the waiting around anyway.

"Captain to CHENG." She opened a channel to her clone Chief Engineer.

"CHENG here Captain Moore," the clone responded in her usual deadpan voice.

"Looks like we're about to get started, Deedee. Keep

my shields, jump drives, and superbeams up and running." She didn't want to suddenly have a failure of one of her critical systems right as the fighting started.

"We are, as you like to say, Captain, purring like a kitten." The CHENG was beginning to learn her sense of humor or was getting one of her own. Dee suspected it was from spending so much time working on technical system with her father's CHENG U.S. Navy Captain Joe Buckley Junior. Joe was probably the most full of crap, and decorated, CHENG in the Fleet. Dee was happy he was rubbing off on hers.

"Keep it that way, Deedee. CO out."

"Gunner!"

"Aye, Captain."

"I want you to target that lead preying mantis ship with the superbeams and fire on my command."

"Aye, Captain."

"Alright, everyone, armor on and shields up," Dee ordered as she thought her armor up. "XO, Buckley-Freeman barrier shields up!"

"Aye, Captain," the Samantha clone replied.

Dee used the direct mind link to the suit and triggered it to deploy from the belt at her waist. The molecule-thick alien metal alloy instantly covered her body like a second dull gray camouflage flexible metallic skin. The armor around her head and face was transparent and somehow managed to not fog up as she breathed and spoke and would allow her to eat and drink normally whenever she so desired. She'd never tried it but she believed she could have sex in the thing if she wanted to.

The new armored suits were nothing if not fantastic

when compared to the clunky metal ones she had worn in the first engagements years prior. With those suits, you were literally in a high technology suit of armor that was also a spacesuit. The new suits were more like a second skin. The new suits had even required changes in the uniforms as they were designed to be skintight. So the modern Fleet uniforms, the Universal Combat Uniform, had been made even tighter and was only microns thick. The UCU covered the body from toes to neck with built-in toe boots, gloves, pockets, insignia and rank patches, and smart seams for removal and body functions. Various parts of the UCU could be deployed or retracted as desired or needed.

The UCUs themselves would stop most fragments and projectiles and would function as bandages, splints, or compression in the event of a soldier being wounded. The built-in AI circuitry and software managed the suit and anticipated the wearer's needs. It could perform first aid, administer meds and stims, and maintain a soldier's life functions even after the most horrific injuries. The armor once deployed had personal quantum displacement shields that would stop a direct hit from an alien plasma blaster. Not only were the uniforms and armored suits highly functional, they made the wearers look damn good. Any weapons or packs or gear simply melded to the suit as needed. The suit would then manage the balance of the load to make it as distributed and optimal for mobility as possible. When combined with the quantum membrane teleportation technologies the modern soldier was an unstoppable war machine that was almost impossible to target. But the Chiata could and often did.

"It looks like the fun is about to begin."

"Captain, ma'am, your idea of fun and mine are somewhat different I think," her new COB added.

"You'll get used to it, COB." Dee flashed him a smile with her white teeth shining in contrast with the red and green glowing tattoos and the blazing eyes. "Air Boss, are the Bringers of Hell ready to deploy?"

"The mecha squadron is on the transport pad, ready to bounce into the fight whenever you need them, ma'am," her clone Commander of the Air Wing and third in command replied.

"Very good. Hold until we need them. XO, maybe a few shots over the bow of these jerks will back them down. I think we could light them up with the forward directed energy guns without really hurting them too badly."

"Yes, ma'am," the executive officer clone second in command replied. "Gunner, prepare the forward DEG batteries."

"Aye, ma'am." The gunner sat at the ready. "DEGs are charged and ready to fire at your command."

"Captain?" the XO asked.

"Fire." Dee nodded and then she watched in her mindview the outcome. She zoomed in and could see the green beams splash across the bow of the lead alien ship. There was little to no impact discernable to the ship.

"Direct hit, Captain!"

"Give me an assessment STO!" Dee turned to the science and technical officer.

"As we would expect, ma'am. The DEGs did not penetrate the Chiata shield technology," the STO said stoically.

"Right, as we would expect. That wasn't the point, yet."

"Yes, ma'am," the Jonathan clone replied.

"This could be easier. Maybe our love tap there will give them some pause before escalating this any further." Deanna continued to watch the aliens' progress in the battlescape playing out in her mindview. "I wish the general would have authorized us to just to take them out instead of sitting here on our thumbs and posturing."

"Yes, ma'am," the XO agreed.

Deanna? the artificial intelligence counterpart or AIC that was implanted in her head just behind her right ear thought to her.

Yes, Bree, Dee replied in her mindvoice.

It is unlike the Chiata Horde to enter a system with so few ships.

Yes, I know. That's why my father won't let us just engage them outright. He wants us to find out why they are here. And at the same time give the archeology team on the planet below long enough to extract all the artifacts and snap back to Fleet space to safety.

Yes, so, the team below is giving an estimated time to completion of another hour, the AIC said in her mindvoice.

Okay, now that is a long time to hold off the Chiata and the preying mantises if they attack. Bree, I want you to start running battle sims on this engagement and find me an optimal attack plan.

Yes Dee, running them now. The AIC was certainly efficient and in the blink of an eye could run thousands of battle simulations. This gave Dee the advantage of always knowing the statistics. *With the numbers as low as they are a straight on attack is the simplest plan. However, maybe they will not attack.*

Fat chance. They're here for something. What? Now that is the question.

I agree. I will stay on it.

Good.

"Captain, it looks like they are slowing," the clone at the helmsman's station said.

"And they are getting dangerously close," the XO added.

"Hold tight, everyone. Gunner keep the superbeams locked on the leader, but hold your fire for now. Helm, be ready to give me a quantum teleportation sling-forward or snap-back on my command. Go ahead and calculate spots for each."

"Aye, ma'am."

"What are you up to?" Dee tapped her armored fingers against the armrest of her oversized captain's chair. She rose to her feet and looked out the giant transparent dome that covered the bridge. The *Rackman* was slightly larger than the alien ships only because it was based on a captured Chiata megaship that was about seven kilometers long and it had four three-kilometer-long human supercarriers attached to it in leg positions that made the megaship look like a giant alien porcupine alligator mix with giant snail antennae on the upper forward third. There were shorter spires scattered across the central megaship structure, looking like the quills of a porcupine. Many of the "quills" bifurcated at the tops into two and three points looking more like the ends of tridents than quills. The simplest way to describe the alien megaships was that they looked like giant porcupines crossed with sea snails. The Fleet had referred to them since day one as "porcusnails" or megaships.

The ships fired extremely destructive and powerful blue beams from the snail antennae. The beams could turn corners and track targets using spacetime gravity modulation technology. With the help of a small robot that looked like a beetle that the Thgreeth had given Dee, humanity was able to turn the alien blue beams of death from Hell, as they were referred to, into quantum uncertainty beams of death from Hell. The human-Thgreeth upgrade to the beams made them appear instantly from antenna to target as if they'd always been there and there were no alien shields or metametals that stopped them. The Chiata had learned to throw sacrifice ships at the human Fleet ships to occupy the superbeam weapons while they attacked with other nontargeted ships. That meant that the Chiata always attacked with large numbers of ships—many more than thirty.

"The phalanx ships have reached a relative full-stop, Captain," the helmsman said.

"I see that, helm."

"Aye, ma'am."

Bree? You got any ideas on this? she thought to her AIC.

No, Dee. I'm not certain what is going on either. Perhaps they want to talk?

I doubt that. The Chiata never talk.

At least they haven't yet.

The Chiata never talk. All they do is destroy and kill and devour whatever is in their path.

"Captain Moore, I'm reading a buildup of electromagnetic interference and virtual particle pair production. It's a hyperspace projector," the science and technical officer, a Jonathan clone, said from the STO's station. "Several of them are going to jump, ma'am."

"Where!?" Deanna pulled up the mindview of the battlescape and then reflexively flinched as there was a brilliant flash of blue light and a large explosion on the planet's surface.

"They jumped into the planet!" the COB almost shouted. "Oh my God!"

Dee zoomed in her mindview and could see the entire planet being consumed with a blast wave and an expanding spherical cloud that looked like it had come from an asteroid the size of a small moon impacting the planet at extremely high velocity. If a spaceship moving at over seventy-five times the speed of light hit a planet, the energy imparted would be devastating, and that is exactly what the Chiata had just done.

"Jesus!" Dee said as she checked the blue force tracker to see if any of the team below had made it back to the ship in time. It looked like nine out of the two hundred had managed to teleport using the snap-back algorithm to the relative safety of the *Rackman*. "They jumped a megaship into the planet just to keep us from getting whatever was there. Helm! Evasive maneuvers. Gunner! Fire!"

The ship bounced hard, throwing Dee back into her chair as alien megaship blue beams of death from Hell impacted the barrier shields. The quantum barrier bubble surrounding the ship flashed from bow to stern and port to starboard with a blue-green wave of fluorescent light as the beams were absorbed and redirected into uncertainty. The BBDs from the other alien ships continued to pound into the shields. Ship systems warnings started going off in her mindview showing that various systems were being taxed by the attack from bow to stern. But the *Rackman* was tough, just like her namesake had been, and she could take it.

The safety restraints of Deanna's chair did some software handshaking with her suit and then they reached out and tugged her safely into place. She squirmed against the restraints to get herself situated and then she pounded the armrest with her armored fist. She had let the stalemate of the blockade and the last two days make her slow-witted. She'd let them run the blockade and destroy a planet's surface and whatever it was down there that humanity could probably have made good use of.

"I should've seen that coming! XO I'm pulling flotilla command positioning control to my mindview. I want you to take the bridge while I focus on that. Do not deploy any mecha. We're going to do this megaship to megaship."

"Aye, ma'am."

Dee focused her mind on the full three-dimensional mindview battlescape in her head. She looked at the other nine megaships in her flotilla and watched as ten of the Chiata ally ships and nineteen Chiata megaships engaged them at random. The aliens were too smart to group up and fly formations because if they did that any of her ships could fire the Buckley-Freeman weapon which was an expanding sphere of blue directed energy and quantum uncertainty that would destroy any matter within a radius of five hundred thousand kilometers that wasn't shielded appropriately and only the Fleet ships were shielded appropriately. Anytime they fired that weapon, the ship that did so was stuck dead in space for several minutes making repairs from overloaded power conduits and energy breakers being blown out. In essence, firing the weapon had the result of killing a lot of aliens but at the same time made you a big mega sitting duck in return. So, unless using that weapon removed all the threat when fired it wasn't really a great idea to fire the thing. The superbeams, on the other hand . . .

Dee reached out in front of her face and began moving the ships' icons about like men on a chessboard until she found a position that she liked. She compared her planning with the simulations that her AIC had run and found the optimum approach. At least she hoped it was optimal in impact on the Chiata and minimal on impact to her group.

She locked in the plan and transmitted it to the flotilla. Almost instantly her minifleet started moving. Several of the ships carried out hyperspace jumps to the position she had chosen. Within seconds she had the team lined up the way she wanted them. All the flotilla ships showed green on the superbeam systems and could fire on command.

"Okay, now, everyone fire the superbeams!" she ordered to all the ship captains over the mindlink commandnet. "Now, now, now!"

Instantly the sky was filled with blue beams that zigged and zagged in every direction. The beams didn't travel from a barrel, or antenna in this case, instead just appearing in place. Each of the beams penetrated several alien ships along its path and there wasn't a single enemy vessel in the local space that hadn't been hit. After about a second, the reality of the beams being inside and through the alien ships manifested and then the ships started exploding and outgassing violently. The giant porcusnails burst at the seams with orange and white plasma balls that quickly dissipated into space creating shrapnel and debris fields. More than five of the alien megaships cracked at the base of the spires and blew apart into two giant drifting pieces.

"Great shot, Captain!" The COB whistled and turned to look at Dee in amazement. "Quite the fireworks show ma'am."

"Glad you liked it, COB." Dee watched as the secondary and tertiary explosions rocked through the alien vessels until there were only three of them still even functional but at a diminished capacity. It was likely that all hands on the other vessels would be lost within the next sixty seconds or less as the ships continued to spiral to catastrophic failure. "Comm, open a channel and send them our standard surrender message."

"Aye, ma'am."

"This was too easy and yet, we lost the planet below." Dee shook her head in disappointment in herself. "I should've seen that coming. Next time, orders or not, we should disable their jump drives if we can."

"Not a bad strategy, Captain," the XO agreed.

"Hindsight. Did this planet and the away team no good." Dee scolded herself for letting that happen. She hadn't expected the Chiata would sacrifice a full-up megaship with tens of thousands of soldiers on it just to stop the humans from looking at some old ruins. "Clearly, there must have been something on that planet the Chiata feared."

"We still have two Chiata ships in-system ma'am. What do we do with them?" the XO noted.

"Well, we might as well get something out of this mission. Deploy the Air Wing and the Ground Regiment. Let's take those ships for our own. Maybe we can find some intel about this system in their computers." Deanna sighed. She hated how she'd let this turn out. Stalemates and standoffs weren't her forte. Fighting was.

"Yes, ma'am," the XO said. "Air Boss, Ground Boss, you heard the captain. Standard megaship capture protocols. Prepare to deploy."

"XO." Dee released her harness from her chair. She'd had enough captaining for the day. She needed to do some killing. "You have the bridge. I think I'll give the Bringers a hand."

"Understood, ma'am." The XO turned to her. "I wouldn't be a good XO if I didn't point out that you should stay on board where it is safe, ma'am."

"And you are a good XO, Samantha." Dee grinned at her.

"Uh, ma'am, where are you going?" the new COB asked as Dee touched the wrist panel on her suit and vanished with a flash of light.

Dee reappeared in the hangar bay beside her Marine FM-15X space fighter transfigurable mecha with quantum uncertainty engines. She smiled at the fire-eyed blue beam firing trident wielding demon emblem on the twin tailfins as she rubbed an armored finger under the thirty-seven Chiata skulls on the empennage just under the words "Colonel Deanna 'Phoenix' Moore". She thought to her cockpit to open as she leaped upwards into a backwards tuck coming to a rest onto the pilot's seat. Deanna watched as pilots and mecha drivers in the hangar rushed back and forth getting ready to deploy. The sight was far more exciting than the one on the bridge, at least in her opinion. She wiggled her way into the seat as the auto-harnesses snugged her in and snapped in place.

"Bringers of Hell, this is Phoenix copy?" she said over the pilot's tactical network as the canopy cycled down. She wrapped her hands around the throttle and stick and rolled her neck left then right. She did a couple of breathing exercises and started getting excited.

Yeah, this is a chair more to my liking. she thought.

Dee hadn't asked to be put in command of a starship at all. That had been from necessity and her father's idea. He probably had thought it would help keep her out of the thickest stuff and less likely to be killed on the bridge than out in a furball of mecha combat. But it had never stopped him and, well, like father like daughter.

Home again home again, Bree replied. *Standard energy curve analysis and red force tracking algorithms, Dee?*

Same as always until it quits working. If it ain't broke let's don't fix it. Start the out and in quantum uncertainty sequences as soon as we hit the combat ball.

Roger that.

"Go, Phoenix," nine voices replied and their names ranks and mecha stats popped up in her blue force tracker mindview under a screen labelled "Bringers of Hell".

"Let's snap over to one of those megaships and start bringing some Hell to the Chiata that stayed behind. What'd y'all say?"

"Oorah, Phoenix," her wingman, Azazel, replied. "Ready to bounce when you are, ma'am."

"Follow my jump." Dee patted at a small compartment on the belt of her armor that opened to her touch. A little robotic beetle crawled out so fast it appeared as a blur to the unaided eye. It stopped and rested on her shoulder. "You ready to take down some Chiata, Skippy?"

The little Thgreeth bot shook back and forth as if it were getting fired up for a fight. Dee patted it on the back and laughed. Nobody but her and the Thgreeth that had saved her back at the Battle of the Thgreeth Homeworld System would truly understand what Skippy was, but what they did understand was that the little bot was a Chiata killing machine of extremely advanced alien design and it did whatever Dee wanted it to do. Those were two powerful combinations.

It pained her that she had lost a team of scientists, a habitable planet, and potential advanced alien technology. Dee hated failing and she hated losing. She knew that those scientists had families, children, mothers, fathers, lovers. She was still devastated by the loss of her one love to the Chiata. She told herself the same thing she continued to tell herself every single day since she had lost people she had cared about. She planned to have some very private and heated words with her father for putting them in that situation to start with. Her father's blockade idea hadn't been a good one. Either that or she hadn't been briefed fully on what it had been he was up to. He often did things like that. Those things pissed her off as well, but at least she understood the need for them better.

"They didn't die in vain. This is only a minor setback. The Chiata will be stopped from ever taking loved ones again. I will see to it," she muttered to herself. She did that often.

A tear rolled down her cheek throwing glints of reds and greens about the cockpit as it rolled over the tattoos. The sadness was so overwhelming an emotion that the only thing that helped temper it and keep her functioning was the anger and hatred she was filled with. And she had plenty of that to spare. "Davy Rackman, I miss you. I'm going to kill some more of the aliens for you today. I love you."

Dee deployed the flight helmet into place and pulled the mouthpiece in biting down on it to trigger the oxygen flow. She let up off the bite guard and cycled the visor down. She gripped the hands-on-throttle-and-stick controls and toggled the control marked bot. Her fighter plane flipped up and rolled over as it transformed into a standing battle mecha in bot-mode. She pulled the main plasma cannon up into her giant left armored hand and toggled all the weapons systems online. Targeting Xs appeared in her battlescape mindview but they were a very long way off, but not for long. Quickly she scrolled through her weapons inventory and made certain she was loaded for a long furry mess. She was. There was about to be a serious knife fight over there on those Chiata ships and she was bringing a very big gun.

"Bringers of Hell, this is the tower. You have the ball at your discretion."

"Roger that, tower." Deanna smiled almost maniacally. The tattoos on her face glowed fiercely with her excited mood and her eyes blazed like the fires of the underworld. "Alright Bringers, let's go kick some alien . . ."